PRAISE FOR RACHEL D. RUSSELL

## THEN CAME YOU

Warren and Russell's latest novel exudes all the comforts of coming home as we return to the beloved town of Deep Haven. With a relatable theme of embracing the lives we've been given rather than the lives others expect of us, *Then Came You* is a whirlwind of sweet, fun moments between serious Boone and playful Vivien fending off their instant attraction while discovering what's truly meant to be. Fans of Nicholas Sparks' *Safe Haven* will love this story of true beauty, protective heroes, and hope undaunted.

— JANINE ROSCHE, BESTSELLING AUTHOR OF
THE MADISON RIVER ROMANCE SERIES

Fans of Deep Haven and the PJ Sugar series will be delighted to see familiar faces in this sweet romance— plus a few new ones! If you love hunky detectives, sassy actresses and small town shenanigans, this is the book for you!

— JESSICA KATE, AUTHOR OF *LOVE AND OTHER
MISTAKES*

# STILL THE ONE

Fans of Susan May Warren's Christiansen family novels will fall head over heels for Rachel D. Russell's charming debut. With its likable romantic duo and cast of familiar supporting characters, *Still the One* is a worthy addition to Warren's beloved Deep Haven collection.

— CARLA LAUREANO, RITA® AWARD-WINNING
AUTHOR OF *FIVE DAYS IN SKYE* AND *THE
SATURDAY NIGHT SUPPER CLUB*

A new story set in Deep Haven? Yes, please! *Still the One* captured my attention from its opening pages. I adored wounded Cole right off the bat (heart eyes for days!) and found myself relating to heroine Megan. Weaving together heart-tugging romance and small-town charm, debut author Rachel D. Russell is sure to win readers with this hope-filled story.

— MELISSA TAGG, CHRISTY AWARD-WINNING
AUTHOR OF THE MAPLE VALLEY AND WALKER
FAMILY SERIES

A debut author to watch, Rachel D. Russell has crafted a story packed with genuine emotion, irresistible characters, sizzling chemistry, and well-deserved second chances. The path to love is not easy for long-separated childhood friends Cole and Megan, but the hope and healing they each offer and find along the way will fill the reader's heart to overflowing.

— BETHANY TURNER, AWARD-WINNING AUTHOR
OF *HADLEY BECKETT'S NEXT DISH*

# THEN CAME YOU

SUSAN MAY WARREN
RACHEL D. RUSSELL

sunrise
PUBLISHING

# A NOTE FROM SUSIE MAY

"Can Boone go to Deep Haven?"

When Rachel Russell came to me with this idea, my heart just exploded. How I love Boone. Broken-hearted, misunderstood, tough but sweet Boone from my PJ Sugar series. Yes, he was from Kellogg, MN, but why couldn't he take a vacation in Deep Haven?

And maybe it could change his life.

As my readers know, I LOVE to cross series and pluck a character from one book and settle him/her into another—even a different world. I've been able to cross my Russian books with my SAR books, my Montana Books with my Alaska books, and my Deep Haven books into all of them...but the PJ Sugar series was feeling a little left out.

"Yes! Please!" I said.

Admittedly, I was a little worried about Boone and how he'd fare in Deep Haven.

But Rachel nailed it.

First, she loves Boone as much as I do, so she did him justice. Then, she created a character in Vivien who is the perfect match for our dear Boone (if he can just open his eyes and get over PJ enough to see it!).

In fact, Rachel might have written a better version of Boone than I did! Sexy, strong, wise, but still getting over PJ—Boone is right where he's supposed to be in Deep Haven, and I'm so thrilled with his story.

And then there's Vivien—you met her in the previous Deep Haven books, and in the Christiansen series, but she was waiting for the right man. Her humor and spunk are exactly what Boone needs...but is HE what SHE needs?

Rachel's voice in this story is excellent. Funny, poignant, sweet—you'll love the blend of North Shore/theater romance with a hint of mystery/suspense. The perfect summer read— enjoy as you read by the lake.

I know PJ would.

Thank you for reading the next book in the Deep Haven Collection!

Warmly,

Susie May

*For my husband and sons—*
*Thank you for all the laughter you bring into my life.*

# CHAPTER 1

*V*ivien Calhoun needed a man within the next five minutes.

Her gaze swept across the Deep Haven Coast Guard station parking lot. Unfortunately, the Sunday Fish Pic crowd brimmed with either the townees who knew her or tourists who'd come with their families in tow.

But she'd do anything to avoid a mortifying face-to-face with her evil half sister. Sabrina Calhoun stood on the sidewalk, her blonde hair loose, in a teal mini and white tank. She might look innocent enough to the casual observer, but Vivien knew the truth.

Sabrina knew how to draw blood and the fact that she was here in Deep Haven, on the North Shore of Lake Superior, couldn't bode well for Vivie. What on earth was she—the ruthless mean girl—doing in Vivien's hometown?

Vivie didn't care—she just knew that she couldn't be seen as the loser in the unspoken war between them. She glanced at her reflection in the side mirror of the 1954 Chevy Bel-Air next to her. Excellent. The August heat hadn't unseated her false lashes. She tossed her long sable locks over her shoulder and promptly whittled down her extensive eligible-bachelor criteria to three stellar qualities in a man.

Single, attractive, and present.

She scanned the crowd of the Fish Pic car show again, hoping Sabrina hadn't yet spotted her. Maybe she could buy a few more minutes to execute her plan.

There, standing near a red Mustang. Tall, blond, and *wow*. Definitely not a local. Pale blue eyes took in the festival-like atmosphere and a brush of whiskers darkened his jawline. Short-cropped hair. His tan said he spent a lot of time outdoors and he had muscles to boot. Oh, she'd cast him as a hero any day.

The newcomer couldn't possibly be single—she jockeyed into position to view his left hand. No ring. No indentation. Not even the faintest hint of a telltale pale line.

No. Way. Today might be her lucky day.

Mr. Hottie was her man.

She pressed her lips together, ensuring full coverage of her hour-old lipstick, smoothed her vintage sundress over her hips, and wove through the crowd, keeping her eyes on the stranger. He wore a faded green T-shirt over his tan cargo shorts. Definitely ready for an adventure. His blue eyes landed on her with the kind of arresting gaze that caused a woman to surrender.

"Vivie!" Her roommate snagged her arm, drawing her attention away from the target. "Did you already announce the Labor Day weekend play?"

"No, Ree, and you have terrible timing." She pulled Ree Zimmerman behind a green 1970 Chevelle parked on the scruffy grass at the edge of the lot. "Get down," she hissed.

"Have you lost your mind?" Ree squatted beside her and tucked a wave of her long blonde bob behind her ear. "Why are we hiding?" She adjusted the cuff of her denim shorts and straightened her Mad Moose Motel T-shirt.

"Because for some reason, Sabrina is here." Ree was one of

the few people who knew the truth about Sabrina. Vivien flicked grass blades from her sundress before pulling Ree's back away from the sleek car. "Hey—be careful. Don't scratch the paint."

"Sorry." Ree scooched away from the car. "Why would she be here?"

"I don't know." Because, really, seeing Sabrina was more than enough reminder of everything that had gone wrong in Vivien's life.

Ree popped her head over the Chevelle. "I think I see her. If she's the blonde in the teal skirt that seems to be missing a few inches of fabric at the hem, she just went around the corner toward the music stage." She slid back down next to Vivien. "I wonder what she's doing here."

Vivien blew out a breath. "No doubt trying to make my life even more miserable than it already is."

"Well, I'm still trying to finish up the news story on the community theater event. I need a few quotes from you to polish it up."

"Right now? I'm a little busy." She gestured toward the car they hid behind.

"Now's a perfect time. I tried to do it last night, but you came in too late and I have to get the article to press this afternoon." Ree shuffled through her purse and withdrew a piece of note paper and pen. "Okay, sorry, reading through my notes here— so, you're opening up the community theater. How will that support your return to Broadway?"

Vivien's stomach turned. "I don't—um, I think I'm done with that." She smiled and declared, "For a while."

"What? That's always been your dream. Why aren't you going back?"

"I didn't say I wasn't *ever* going back." Vivien shook off the waves of nausea and straightened her back. "You know what? I just want to focus on being behind the scenes this summer. Give myself time to decide what I want to do."

"Are you kidding me? You were born for the stage."

Maybe born for it, but a stalker, a two-timer, and an on-stage disaster had pretty much destroyed those plans. "I'm ready to be a director." She gave Ree another assuring smile. "For now. I mean, I'll go back, of course." Someday. Maybe.

Ree's jaw dropped open. "Of course? Please. I have been your best friend since second grade. I know your tells. What's the deal?"

The problem with dear friends is they didn't always know when to let something go. "The best directors have been on the stage, Ree. I think it's great to do both. Diversify. I mean, look at Robert Redford. Angelina Jolie. Jodie Foster. So many." She waved her hand in the air, dismissing the discussion.

"Viv—"

She patted Ree's shoulder. "I'll show you I've still got it. See Mr. Hottie by the red Mustang?"

Ree took a look. "I take it you don't mean Nathan Decker."

"Obviously not. No, Mr. Hottie, the guy talking to Nathan." Vivien leaned forward and took a quick peek to make sure Sabrina hadn't come back through. "He's going to be my plus-one for a little while so I can rob Sabrina of her smug, self-serving victory." She winked. "He just doesn't know it yet."

Ree's mouth fell open, her eyes wide. "I thought you said you were done with relationships. I'm pretty sure you used the word *indefinitely*."

"I am. I simply need a plus-one for today. A stand-in."

Ree tugged on her arm. "Viv, you can't do that. You don't even know that guy."

"Oh, watch me." She fluffed her dark waves. "It's not like I'm preying on a defenseless man, stealing his fortune. I just need him for the next few minutes and it really doesn't look like he has anything else going on." Besides, it was just another role for her to play in life.

"I can't talk you out of this, can I?"

"Nope."

"Well, then I should warn you Sabrina's still on the prowl." Ree pointed with her pen toward the judges' booth where the prima donna was engaging locals in conversation, her laughter less than genuine.

"Then, take notes, my dear. This is how it's done."

Vivien stood and made her way around the Chevelle to the red Mustang as Nathan departed. The man turned, his eyes meeting hers across the hood of the car. He stilled. Stared.

"Nice ride." Vivien smiled, looked down, and ran her hand across the pale interior of the convertible. "Is this the 225 or the 271 V-8?" She raised her eyes back to his.

He tilted his head, smiled. "You know your cars. The V-8."

Oh, yeah, she knew the beautiful car had the V-8 under the hood. "This must be your first time in the car show. I'd definitely remember this car." And its driver, who managed to look even better close up. She stepped closer and a faint hint of cologne, a blend of citrus and sandalwood, reached her. A woodsy, masculine scent that made her want to lean into it.

"Thanks. It's actually not in the car show. She's just my baby."

Definitely not married.

"Oh?" She held out a hand to him. "Vivien Calhoun. And you're...?"

"Late." He said it with a twinkle in his eyes and pulled his car keys from his pocket.

She laughed. "Okay, Late. Hey—I need your help with a little something, and you look like the kind of guy who'd help out a girl in trouble."

He frowned. "What kind of trouble?"

Sabrina had started wandering through the cars.

Vivien placed a hand on his arm, gave it a little squeeze. He stopped in his tracks and looked down at her, a little blaze in his eyes. "Here's the deal. All I need is for you to take a walk with me—you know, like we're...together...so Ms. Venom-for-Blood leaves me alone." She tilted her head toward the blonde interloper who'd started toward them.

He gave Sabrina a casual glance and turned back to Vivien. "Ouch." He smiled, something slow and teasing. "What if I told you she's my date?"

"Oh, hon, if she's your date, then you really do need me to save you."

A rich, warm laugh broke free. The kind that thrummed through her like a favorite show tune. "I thought I was saving you."

"We can save each other."

He laughed again. "I'm sure she can't be that bad."

"Trust me. If you consider the totality of her transgressions, she is exactly that kind of terrible, no-good, very-bad person."

Several drivers started up their engines, the rumble so deep she could feel it in her chest.

"I'm really sorry, but I need to get going." He stepped away.

"Ten minutes into town and of course, I run into you." Sabrina sauntered over, ensuring she was loud enough to draw stares. Sabrina was beautiful, with her long legs, perfect white teeth, and deep blue eyes.

But Vivien had acting chops. She wouldn't have landed the role of Belle in *Beauty and the Beast* in New York if she didn't. Vivien turned. Flashed her megawatt smile. "Oh, Sabrina. What a...surprise." She seriously doubted it was the fishing contest or smoked walleye that had brought Sabrina to the remote location.

"What are you doing here?" Sabrina waved her hand in the air. "Oh, that's right. All those things that happened in New York City caused you to turn tail and practically run out of—"

She covered her mouth, her snotty smirk still visible. "Oh, there I go. Sorry. Well, I know that was probably so humiliating. I can't even imagine how mortified you must have been."

And a little piece of Vivien broke away. Because Sabrina was right. Flames of embarrassment heated Vivie's face, burning hotter than the summer sun. And, just like in New York City, she stood alone. All eyes on her.

"Hey, Viv—you ready to go?" The voice, rich and deep and solid, reached right through the chaos of emotions, grabbed her, and held on.

She blinked, felt a solid hand slip around hers, and turned to see her hero nod toward his car. "The parade is about to start."

Sabrina's eyes painted Mr. Hottie in slow motion, up and down, landing on his hand joined to Vivien's.

Yeah. Hottie for the win.

Vivien swallowed, nodded, tossed her goodbye to Sabrina. "See you around." Or not. Handsome held open the passenger side door and she slid in. The daggers in her back from Sabrina didn't even hurt as they pulled away.

"That. Was. Awesome." Vivien turned, blinked away the moisture in her eyes. "Did you see her face?"

Her rescuer nodded, his face tight.

Oh. "Hey—I'm sorry. I didn't mean to make you even later."

"It's okay." He tilted his head toward Sabrina's indignant figure behind them. "I have little use for people like that."

"Well, thank you."

He nodded. "Clearly a friend of yours." He looked over at her and winked.

And that made her smile. "Right. You can drop me off at the end of the parking lot and I'll catch a ride with my roommate." She could find some other way to avoid Sabrina the rest of the afternoon.

He stopped the car. "Oh no."

"What?" Vivien followed his gaze. "Oh no," she echoed. Cars

had pulled out in front of the Mustang and behind. The car show entrants. "Um, looks like you're going to be in the parade after all."

"I was kidding."

She started singing. "You've got to... Live a little... Laugh a little..."

"I don't think you understand. I—" He made a face. "This is bad."

"So, what's your name? I mean, if you're going to be my plus-one for the parade, I should at least know your name."

"Plus-one?" He shook his head. "Boone Buckam. And I can't believe you got me into this."

"Well, Boone Buckam, you're about to find out exactly how much fun Fish Pic can actually be. Think of it like it's a happy accident."

He gave her a look and she shrugged her shoulders, kicked off her heels, and began waving to the crowd that lined the streets—their hands filled with everything from cotton candy to fish burgers, the spoils of a day spent at the community celebration.

"What are you doing?"

"Have you never been in a parade before? You've got to wave to your adoring fans. Like this." Vivien took off her seatbelt and stood, letting the breeze lift her hair. "See—those are the Christiansens." She pointed to John and Ingrid, who stood with their son Darek, his wife Ivy, and their own children, Joy and Tiger. Ingrid stood with her husband's arm around her, her short bob haircut still stylish as ever. "Well, that's some of them. They own a resort on Evergreen Lake. John's the family patriarch." She looked to see if he was paying attention. "Big family."

"I see." He put on his sunglasses. They made him look very James Dean, thank you, Classic Movies channel. "For someone trying to make a great escape, you seem pretty comfortable in front of a crowd."

She turned back to Boone. "I'm an actress. Well, I was. I'm focusing on directing next. A community theater summer program."

"I see."

"Oh—and that's Cole Barrett and his wife, Megan. He's part of some new Crisis Response thing they've started up here. Also a deputy sheriff."

She cast a look at Ree on the sidewalk, whose wide-eyed laughter was drowned out by the raucous cheers of the crowd on either side of her.

Well, Ree knew better than anyone how easily Vivien could put on a show. How much easier it was for her to be someone else.

And her newfound chauffeur-slash-fake boyfriend certainly wasn't slowing her down. He drove through the parade, his mouth in a tight half smile, as if he might be enjoying himself.

The parade wound its way back to the Coast Guard station's lot, the crowd gathering for the judges' awards. They parked in the lot, watching the rest of the cars pull in and letting the breeze lift the heat of the day off them. The station stood at the end of the peninsula, the harbor on one side and the open waters of Lake Superior on the other. The two-story white building stood like a sentinel over the ever-changing waters.

She scanned the crowd. No sign of Sabrina.

"Are you sore?" Boone leaned in.

There it was again. Faint cologne mixed with heat, a little earthy and intoxicating.

"From what?"

"All that waving." He lifted his hand, gave her a perfect royal wave, his hand rotating side to side on his wrist.

"You know, you're actually pretty funny for such a serious guy."

The microphone let out a squeal before the emcee, Ed Draper, began the drone of naming award winners from the stage at the end of the lot. Funny, the dog sled guy was manning the car show. Ed had always reminded Vivien of a younger Paul Newman. His graying hair had never diminished the classic handsome features and his clear, bright blue eyes. Edith must have exercised epic powers of persuasion to convince her son to participate in Fish Pic this year.

One by one, various participants made their way to the stage to collect their trophies.

Vivien turned back to her driver. "Thank you. I owe you one."

Boone slid his sunglasses back on his head and held her in his dangerous blue eyes. "You're welcome."

"I'm sorry I made you super late for whatever your thing was."

"It's okay." He lifted a book from the center console, shoved it under his seat before she could read the title. "I'd planned to lay low. Relax."

"Hey—that's you." Ree had appeared next to the Mustang.

"What's who?" Vivien asked.

"You guys won." Ree was pointing toward the stage.

The crowd had turned, applauding, eyes on the 1965 Mustang.

Ed held a trophy, staring at the paper in front of him, his voice booming over the mic. "I don't see an entry number or name here." He looked up, pointed to the Mustang again. "Vivien, would you and your...uh...friend come claim your award?" The crowd began to clap again.

"You've got to be kidding me." Boone shook his head.

"You shouldn't be so surprised that your baby won."

"We're not even entered."

"Go, you guys, go." Ree waved her hands to usher them out of the car. Boone stood, rooted to the ground.

"Oh, come on," Vivien slipped on her shoes and grabbed

Boone by the hand. They made their way to the stage to stand next to Ed.

Ed tried to hand the trophy to Boone, who didn't take it.

Oh, please. They'd won an award for Pete's sake. Who turned down an award?

Vivien took a bow to the applause and accepted the heavy glass award, hoisting it over her head, bringing it down to cradle in her arms.

"Can I have the mic?" Vivien held out her hand to Ed.

"Um, sure." He gave it to her and stepped back.

"Hi, everyone. I'd like to thank you for coming out to the Fish Pic car show today. Let's give a shout-out to Ed Draper, who helped organize the event with the local booster club. I'm super glad I could share this afternoon with my dear friend Boone."

Friend might be a stretch, but, oh, well. If Sabrina was still stalking the grounds, Vivien wasn't going to give up on the charade. "And, wow—the People's Choice award? Thank you. I'd like to announce we'll be holding auditions for a summer community theater event on Wednesday evening at the Arrowood Auditorium in the high school. While the last show had a youth cast, this time all you adults get to give it a go. I'll have a short synopsis and character list at the library community events table. We'll be performing *Then Came You*, and I can't wait to see you all Wednesday at the playhouse." Murmurs rippled across the crowd.

"Thank you again." Vivie held up the trophy. She imagined for a moment that she held an Oscar and smiled for her adoring audience. Well, a girl could dream, right? The crowd cheered one more time.

She stepped away from the mic and followed Boone off stage while Ed announced the end to the car show portion of the activities. The crowd dispersed and Vivien found herself facing Boone across the open convertible.

"People's Choice. Not a bad way to end the ride." And, shoot, she wasn't sure why, but she didn't really want it to be over. She swished the skirt of her sundress side to side. "What about my ice cream?"

"What ice cream?"

"Oh, come on. Every convertible ride ends with ice cream."

He rubbed his hand across his face, a curve at the corner of his lips.

"Is that a smile?" She squinted at him.

He shook his head. "Get in. I'll take you home."

"Ice cream first?"

"Fine."

She pointed the way while he drove three blocks to the Licks and Stuff ice cream shop. They stood in line among the rest of the Sunday afternoon crowd, and Boone leaned in, his voice low. "What do you recommend?"

The close tenor of his voice did annoying things to her pulse. Like, sent it into the staccato of a marching drum. Clearly, she hadn't been around any eligible men recently. And he was hardly anything less than cover-model material, so she could let her heart beat a little. It did a girl good.

"You have to try the Moose Mocha Madness in the home-made waffle cone." In answer to the question on his face, she added, "Espresso ice cream, chocolate chunks. A little hunk of paradise in a confectionary masterpiece."

"When you put it that way..." He turned to the server, a cheery high school girl with a nose piercing and several purple streaks in her dark hair. "We'll have two of the Moose Mocha Mad—"

"Just one—" Vivien interrupted.

"What?" He raised his brows.

Vivien looked over the ice cream display. "One double-scoop Moose Mocha Madness in a waffle cone and one..." She perused the colorful vats. "One Ravishing Rainbow sherbet in a sugar cone."

"I hope the Moose Mocha Madness is for me, because I think I'd lose my man card if I ate the Ravishing Rainbow sherbet," Boone said as he paid for the cones.

She laughed. Um, no worry there.

He handed the sherbet cone to her and held the door for her on their way out. He slid under the window awning into the shade.

"We're not eating these in the car."

She pressed her hand against her chest. "I would never."

He started toward a bench along the sidewalk, weaving through the Fish Pic stragglers who smelled like sunscreen and smoked walleye, the din of children's chatter competing with music from the stage. "I thought you said the Mad Moose Mocha was the best." He looked from his oversized frozen treat to her bright sherbet.

"Moose Mocha Madness." She licked the melting top off her scoop, the sweet-tart raspberry melding with the orange sherbet on the roof of her mouth. "And, it is, but I don't know. Today felt like a rainbow sherbet kind of day for me."

"I didn't realize that was a thing."

"Oh, yes. There are days for chocolate chunk, days for mocha madness, days for sherbet." She considered her cone for a moment. "I suppose there are even days for vanilla."

"You don't strike me as the vanilla type."

"Well, I haven't had a vanilla day, but I'm leaving open the option that there could be a vanilla day."

"Hmm. I see." He took another bite of ice cream. "This is really good, by the way."

"I told you so. I know my ice cream flavors." The band had started playing in the park and the smells of cheese curds and smoked fish floated on the breeze. Families still crowded the downtown streets, squeezing the last hours out of Fish Pic.

They watched a metallic blue Impala drive by. "Oh, that's a nice sixty-four," she said.

"You seem to know a lot about classic cars."

She turned from the car, her eyes settling on him. "I've always had an eye for fine things." Oh, sometimes she wished she could filter what came out of her mouth better. But he was standing there, tall and strong and utterly adorable with his double-scoop waffle cone. "I'm actually car-less right now. I moved back here a few months ago from New York City." She lifted a shoulder. "Didn't need one there."

"I see. But, you're in the market for one?" He took another bite of ice cream.

Well, hmm. "Not yet. I'm not sure when I'll be heading back to the City." She took a bite, savoring the tang. "You're not half-bad at this acting stuff. You're not, like, some soap star from Hollywood, are you?"

He cut her a look over his cone and sat on one of the benches along the sidewalk. So, that was a hard no.

"What do you do then? What brings you to the village of Deep Haven?" She sat down next to him.

"Village?"

"Well, we are quaint. I think it sounds so much more picturesque than 'town.'"

He looked like he was running an inventory of exactly what to say, finally settling on, "I'm a detective. Taking a vacation."

Oh boy. "A detective? As in a police officer?" Vivien's heart rate ratcheted up a few notches. "And I asked you to impersonate someone else? Good grief, why didn't you say something?"

And there was that warm rumble of laughter again. "Well, technically, I didn't impersonate anyone else. I just pretended to be something I'm not."

Oh, like every day of her life. She shot him a smile. "Aha. So, we'll consider it an undercover operation."

He seemed to be considering her, as if she intrigued him. Maybe the detective in him. "Why don't you tell me about this theater thing? You said you're an actress?"

"I'm not currently acting. I'll be directing the show I announced."

"Well, Garbo." He tossed his napkin into the trash and stood. "I'll give you that ride home now, if you'd like."

Garbo? This guy was trouble of the most scrumptious kind. "Just so we're clear, I wouldn't normally accept a ride home with a strange man. Which probably sounds funny since I rode in the parade with you, but that's different. I may be—I may come across as—dramatic, but I'm really just a small-town girl." She refrained from breaking out into "Don't Stop Believin'."

"A villager."

And this time, she laughed. "Yeah. I'm just a villager with big dreams. Hoping to shine." Vivien followed him back to the car. "But, if you're really a cop—and maybe you need to show me some credentials—then, yes, I'll let you drop me off."

He pulled his wallet from his cargo pocket and flipped it open.

Oh, Handsome really was a cop. "Thank goodness." She tugged off her heels and slid into the seat. "I did not want to have to walk home in these. They look super cute, but let me just say, they are painful."

"I'll take your word for it." He closed the door and slid into the driver's seat. "You know, the solution would be to wear something more practical."

"Practical?" Hardly. She wasn't the kind of person who could get away with practical. "Oh, you can't imagine. A girl's got to keep up appearances. The world is a stage, after all."

"Indeed."

"Head up the hill, past the gas station," she said, pointing the way. "After that cute yellow house—we call it the Butter House —go down the street past those big dogwood trees."

He followed her directions. "Here?"

She urged him to keep driving. "Go past Edith's house—it's the one with the pink gnome in the front yard. Stop at the blue bungalow on the corner."

"Oh, you mean the one with the giant walleye and salmon eyeballing the neighborhood?"

"It's a walleye and a trout." She grinned. The gentle breeze swung the two 4-foot-long papier-mâché fish from the porch rafters. "That's the one. Well, mine and Ree's. Until she gets married and moves into her fiancé's gigantic log house. She's my best friend and the town journalist." Why was she babbling?

He pulled up to the curb.

She glanced at him. "Thank you again. You nailed the role."

"You're welcome."

"Will I—will I see you around?" Oh, shoot, and now she sounded needy. She shot him a smile, picked up her high heels, and stepped into the grass. "I mean, how long are you here for?" Lovely. That made it sound like a prison sentence. She shot him a smile, a little big, like she might be on the local tourist council.

"Five weeks." He picked up his book and waved it. "I foresee a ridiculous amount of reading by the lake." His tone held something of sadness. Or regret?

And she dearly wanted to ask, but before she could, her eyes fell on the foreign objects lying across her porch floorboards.

She stilled, her breath caught.

No. That wasn't...no, this could not be happening again.

"What's wrong?" Boone asked.

She turned back to the car, stepping over to block his view of the porch. "Oh, nothing." She waved him off. "Just a neighborhood prank from the boys next door. I'll see ya."

He paused, as if he had something else to say, and she gave him another flash of smile until he pulled away.

She had the sinking sense that Sabrina wasn't the only

person who'd found her in Deep Haven. Those roses looked exactly like the last ones she'd received from her stalker.

So much for a relaxing start to his five-week decompression.

Boone sank into the deck chair of his rental cabin. All he'd wanted was to slip into Deep Haven with the tourists. Sit by the lake. Read the stupid book his boss had given him.

Be in a place where he could be a man without anything to prove, didn't have his history dogging him every single day.

And maybe figure out how to get his life back.

Problem was...well, he wasn't exactly sure Vivien was a problem.

But she might be. He had to admit that Vivien probably wasn't the prescription for tranquility.

But he also had to admit he'd enjoyed his impromptu tour around Deep Haven very much.

The parade, the ice cream cone, even the song she'd sung.

If only he could get his mind to forget the look on her face when she'd seen the black roses on her doorstep.

*Burned* roses. Scattered across her porch beneath the garish walleye and trout.

No way did he buy her words when she said they were probably a prank by the boys next door. That it was no big deal.

Like he should just let it go.

Right.

The thing was, letting go wasn't really in his blood.

*Relax.*

He leaned back on the deck chair and took a long drink of his iced tea. The sun had sunk low in the sky, painting the few clouds deep orange, pink, and purple. Lake Superior stretched out in front of him, the waters reflecting the brilliant hues, setting the world ablaze in color. Condensation dripped off his glass and he let the evening sunshine soak into him. At least he was finally settled into his home-away-from-home after his crazy morning at Deep Haven's annual Fisherman's Picnic.

It had been just his luck that the key was missing from the lockbox at the cabin, forcing him to drive into town earlier in the day to meet Nathan Decker, the man who managed the rental. Too bad he hadn't thought better than to park his Mustang in the middle of the car show when he went looking for Nathan in the crowd, but, well, he loved a good car show. And he loved showing off his own classic car restoration.

He probably should have just asked Nathan to meet him by the main entrance, grabbed the key, and left. Instead, he'd lingered. Enjoyed a fish burger. Let the wind off Lake Superior carry the scents of tangy cheese curds and sweet kettle corn to him.

Then he'd spotted the dark-haired woman wearing her retro dress with yellow sunflowers on it. The halter-style top hugging her curves and slender waist made her hard to miss in the crowd of T-shirts and shorts. Like she'd just stepped out of 1950s' Hollywood. False lashes, manicured nails, polished makeup.

*You look like the kind of guy who'd help out a girl in trouble.*

Yeah, well, he should have known she was trouble, especially when he saw her grab her friend and duck behind the Chevelle. Who did that?

But she'd impressed him with her car knowledge when she'd walked over. Promptly followed by the shock when she'd asked him to pretend to be her boyfriend. Yeah. Who did *that*?

*Have you never been in a parade before? You've got to wave to your adoring fans. Like this.*

In her panic, she still made him laugh though, and there was something entirely alluring about her. Not just her deep blue eyes and sable waves, nor the hint of jasmine that had embraced him when they'd sat down for ice cream. Like, maybe behind all the glitz and glamour, there was something…more.

He'd had no intention of going along with the farce until he'd seen the other woman approach in her fancy shoes and designer skirt. And then the woman had started to drag out the dirty laundry in front of everyone like her sole purpose was to cause pain.

He knew what it felt like to be on the receiving end of public shaming.

So, what else could he do but step in? Extract his new "girl-friend" from the degrading fangs of Venom-for-Blood.

*We can save each other.*

He hadn't held someone's hand since…he didn't even know when. A long time. Her skin had been soft in his, as she'd curled her fingers around his. And she'd looked up at him like he might actually be the good guy.

The one others believed him to be up until three weeks ago.

She'd been on the verge of tears and then, just like that, she'd smiled and buried whatever pain Ms. Venom had drawn out.

He'd spent too many years as a detective in Kellogg to miss those details.

If only it hadn't landed him in the middle of the small-town car parade where she'd transformed into a superstar before his eyes. Just kicked off her high heels and soaked in the limelight. She'd sung a few lines, her voice soft, sultry like the summer heat and quiet enough to make it seem like her words were only for him.

*Live a little. Laugh a little.* Right. So much for laying low. Well, even he knew the next line had something to do with letting your heart break—and he'd had enough of that to last a lifetime.

Tires crunched on the gravel drive and Boone set down his tea and walked to the back corner of the wrap-around deck. A silver Dodge Ram parked outside the cabin and he caught the smile of the driver through the windshield. Caleb Knight, his one friend in town, and the man who had told him that Deep Haven was "the perfect place to hide."

Apparently, Caleb hadn't accounted for Miss Garbo.

Well, at least no one else knew him in town and, by tomorrow, he could go back to being just another summer tourist on the lakeshore. Invisible. Unknown.

He met Caleb on the driveway with a handshake before pulling him into a man-hug, sizing up the former medic. "It's good to see you. It's been too long—you look good."

The man wore a faded Huskies T-shirt with athletic pants, his prosthetic invisible. Even the thick burn scars on his neck, ears, and hands didn't conceal the light in Caleb's eyes. "I'm still staying in shape." He patted his hip. "It got a lot easier once I came to terms with this." He adjusted his ball cap on his head. "I couldn't believe it when you said you were looking for a place up here. How's the cabin?"

"Well, now that I've been able to get into it, pretty good." He gestured for Caleb to follow him up to the deck. "Have a seat—I'll grab you a drink. Tea or Coke?"

"Coke. Thanks."

When Boone returned, Caleb leaned forward in his chair and made an adjustment to his prosthesis. "I just got refitted," he said to Boone by way of explanation. "Takes a little getting used to."

"Are you sore?"

Caleb gave a noncommittal shrug.

"So, that's a yes."

The corner of Caleb's lips curved in a crooked smile. "I'll be fine. Just all the walking at Fish Pic."

Boone nodded. "It seems like our Army days were so long ago. I guess, in many ways, they were."

"Yeah. We were just kids." Caleb took a drink of his Coke.

"How's Issy? It's been ages since we met up in Minneapolis." While Boone had only met his friend's wife,

Isadora, a few times, they'd spoken on the phone often. She'd always been eager to share Caleb's latest football coaching stats when she'd been expecting him to walk in the door any minute.

"She's doing really well. Thinking about writing a book about her experiences as a radio show host and the most memorable stories." He grinned. "Ours, of course, being tops."

"Of course." Boone still couldn't believe Caleb had fallen in love with, quite literally, the girl next door—who'd also been a radio love-talk-show host at the time.

"How are your parents doing?"

"Good. My mom's still volunteering with several sobriety support groups. Attending Bible study weekly."

"She's really turned her life around."

And, yeah, that caused a little bit of pride to swell in Boone's chest. "She has. It hasn't been easy for her. It took a long time for the fog in her brain to clear. She still has some memory issues."

"And your dad's doing well?"

Dad. Somehow, that still left a nebulous cloud of questions that he'd never figured out how to resolve. "Yeah." Boone took a drink. "He's good. Same old Roger Buckam."

If Caleb had read between the lines, he didn't ask. Let the stories Boone had shared about his dad sit idly in the past. If only Boone could.

"So, do you want to tell me how you got banished to the North Shore, five hours from home?"

"My boss says I have some anger issues." Boone let out a humorless laugh. "I'm just here to check off the boxes so I can get back to work."

"Oh, wow. You didn't tell me that on the phone."

"It isn't something I'm proud of." Boone rubbed his hands over his face and released a breath. He let his gaze rest on a sailboat in the distance, its sails aglow with the setting sun. He still couldn't believe he'd been encouraged to leave his gun and badge at home.

"Something happened?"

Not ready to go there. "There was a case I was working and...things didn't go well." He stopped. Swallowed. Pressed down the frustration starting to boil inside him at the injustice of it all.

"You can't save everyone, no matter how hard you try."

"Yeah, well, I didn't. And then I got slapped with a brutality lawsuit."

"Oh, sheesh." Caleb shook his head. "That's terrible."

"Yeah. It was just an incident that got out of hand. The suit was dropped by the suspect, but Landry—my police chief—says I need to find someone to..." Boone looked out over the lake, not sure he could really talk about any of it because it still made him want to put his fist through something.

"Find someone to talk to?" Caleb knew the code phrase.

"Yes. His sister. She's a therapist up here—Rachelle Newman."

"Oh, I know Rachelle. She's excellent. Issy saw her. She'll be the first to tell you how good Rachelle is."

"I'm not looking forward to it." Boone took a drink. "It just burns me up. I try to save lives and I get put on leave. What am I supposed to do with myself up here? How am I supposed to relax?" He picked up his book. "He suggested I get into better shape. Find some hobbies. Read this book."

"You still look pretty fit."

Boone laughed. "He's just worried about my health. My blood pressure's too high and there are some other things my doctor's looking into." He set his drink down. "It should be a good thing that he cares, but it doesn't feel like it." Nope. Penance and punishment.

"Well, it could be worse." Caleb gestured toward the blue

expanse of Lake Superior. "I mean, you can't beat a view like this."

"Maybe. I'll give you that." He smiled at Caleb's optimism. Such a coach.

"See? I knew you'd come around." Caleb lifted his Coke and took a drink.

"I'd hardly call that coming around." Boone shook his head. Stared out across the shimmering water as the orange hues darkened to magenta. "Seriously, though. I need to get back to Kellogg." His gaze shifted to a squirrel scampering through the branches of a birch tree. "I need my job back, Caleb." Boone turned, looked his friend in the eyes. "Being here—as nice as it is—I feel lost. I've got *nothing* to do. This isn't where I'm supposed to be, you know?"

Caleb took a drink, set down his glass, and wiped the condensation off on his pants. "We can't live by what's 'supposed' to be."

The words, spoken gently, still pummeled Boone. Bounced off the shielded places in his heart. "There are...oh, you know —expectations."

Caleb stood and walked over to the rail to stand next to him. "I've learned you have to embrace the life you have, not the one you expected you'd have—or the one others expect you to have." Caleb clapped him on the shoulder. "And that's when I finally found where I belong." He pointed to the book, abandoned on the table. "I'm sure you'll find something to do here—besides reading."

Boone gaped at Caleb. "Like what? Fishing? Do you know how much I hate sitting around, waiting for something to bite? Stakeouts are more exciting than that."

Caleb laughed. "Okay, in between your reading sessions, you could help me coach football."

Yes. *Now* he was getting somewhere. Except— "I have to stay calm. This whole fiasco could turn into something worse if I don't jump through Landry's hoops."

"Nothing much happens here. I'm pretty sure you'll find what you're searching for." Caleb looked out over the water.

"It might be good to be on the field again, even if not as a player." Maybe help a new generation chase the dream a broken ankle had robbed him of. "I could probably swing by and watch a practice. See where I might be able to help if it's going to be low-key." He finished the last of his tea. "After everything that happened with PJ, the last thing I need is drama."

Caleb nodded. "How is she?"

"You know, she's good. She's with a guy named Jeremy." He and Caleb had spent enough time on deployments talking about PJ Sugar, the girl who'd gotten away. It'd been a way to pass time for Boone. That was back when he still thought there was some sort of future for them.

"So, it wasn't meant to be."

"No. Definitely not. She's moved on. I've moved on." The ache had subsided years ago, a few hard lessons learned. "It just feels like I've never been able to shake free of it all. It's hard, you know, living in the same town you grew up in. Having your past chase you around." Feeling like he was always missing the mark. Second best. "I don't know. Maybe there'll be some silver lining to five weeks in this town. Only knowing you."

"Well, *Vivien* and me. I didn't realize the two of you were friends."

Oh. "I don't know her, actually." Boone shook his head and pressed his fingers against his brow, trying to press away the tension. "That just sort of happened." He looked up at Caleb. "You saw that?"

"*Everyone* saw that."

"Everyone?"

"Um, hello, parade through town in your convertible. The

coveted People's Choice award?" Caleb quirked a brow at him. "That did not look like you didn't know her."

"Seriously. We'd just met—she was in a bit of a jam." Vivien had seemed to know the entire population of her little...village. He'd lost count of the names she'd called out as she'd waved like a red-carpet VIP.

"I'll bet she was. Well, Vivien has a way of knowing everyone." Caleb took another drink, looked out at the lake before glancing back at Boone, his eyebrows raised and a hint of a smile on his lips. "You're supposed to stay calm, right?"

"Right."

"Hmm." Caleb gave him a look. "Interesting."

The way Caleb said it gave Boone the feeling that he'd just invited a little bit of trouble into his life.

And he didn't exactly hate it.

# CHAPTER 2

*V*ivien deserved an Oscar for her Fish Pic performance. Granted, playing opposite Mr. Hottie hadn't hurt. Oh, no. That hadn't hurt at all and she wasn't going to let Sabrina's surprise visit or those stupid flowers on the porch ruin her day. Nope. No matter how much they'd rattled her, she'd shake it off just like everything else.

She slipped into a T-shirt and running shorts before grabbing the trash can and returning to the front porch.

Vivien squatted and went back to work, cleaning up the mess. She'd bag up every last charred petal and stem that littered the porch to destroy all vestiges of those ridiculous roses before Ree got home. The last thing she needed was an inquisition.

She ignored the darkness tunneling through her as she snatched up each flower, the acrid smoky scent stinging her nostrils. The scorched petals disintegrated between her fingers. How dare Sabrina come to town, try to ruin her day. Well, she who laughs last, laughs best, right?

And it sure felt like she'd bested Sabrina—for once—when

her new friend had rescued her. So what if it wasn't real? Real, it seemed, was highly overrated.

She took deep breaths and stilled the wavering of her hands. There was no way Vivien would have been found by Freaky Fan Guy, right?

Her phone buzzed in her pocket and she pulled it out to look at the name. Joslyn Vanderburg. Joslyn, the role- and boyfriend-stealing mean girl in New York City. She could just imagine the smug look on the woman's face. She swiped the notification away. Nope. Not going to deal with a second mean girl in one day. She shoved the last ashy pieces into the can and moved it back into the kitchen. Her hands were smudged with black and she turned to the sink to wash them.

"Dinner!" The front door swung open.

Vivien dried her hands and stepped in front of the trash can that stood like a pillar of deception in the middle of the green-and-white checkered kitchen floor, the black roses still jutting out at all kinds of odd angles like Pick-Up Sticks.

Ree carried in a few bags of groceries, nudged the door shut behind her, and let her purse slide from her shoulder onto the coffee table on her way through the living room and into their kitchen. She plopped the groceries on the counter.

"A little help?"

"Sure." Vivien calculated it would take exactly three-point-two seconds to tuck the trash into the cupboard beneath the sink. She smiled, waited for Ree to turn away.

Ree froze and looked at Vivien. "Is everything okay?"

"Um, yeah. I mean, as well as it can be when Sabrina shows up out of nowhere and seems to—" She stopped. How did Sabrina know about what had happened in New York City? Vivien hadn't even been able to tell Ree. "Why?"

"I don't know. You seem...off."

Vivien smiled. "Just a long day."

"Tell me about it. And remind me—why did I want to be a writer?"

Vivien dried her hands on her T-shirt. As soon as Ree turned back to her bags, Vivien pivoted, snagged the can, and tucked it out of sight beneath the sink.

"I think you said, 'Change the world through the written word,' or something whimsical and fancy like that." She closed the cabinet door and stood to face Ree, who was still rummaging through the grocery bags.

"I don't know what I was thinking. Deadlines. I loathe deadlines." She wrinkled her nose. "Would you believe I still need to sit down and write up my articles on Fish Pic and your community theater event before I can crash? I'm never going to get to bed tonight."

Vivien handed her a cold Coke from the refrigerator and took the yogurt from her.

"Thanks." Ree took a long drink and drew her finger through the condensation. "You may have outdone yourself today, Viv. Even Seth thought so."

"How's that?" Vivien began unloading the groceries and putting them into the refrigerator.

"Riding in the parade with that guy? Wow. That was gutsy." Ree tucked a lock of blonde hair behind her ear.

"It was an accident that we ended up in the parade."

"That didn't look like an accident. And then, winning the People's Choice award?"

Vivien smiled. "Well, the car deserved it."

"And the driver?" Ree waggled a brow. "Who's he?"

"Some guy passing through. A detective from Kellogg."

"Ohhh. A detective? Sounds like someone's gotten herself into a little trouble with the law."

"Stop." Vivien held up a palm toward Ree. "He's only here for five weeks. And, as you know, I'm done with dating—maybe forever."

"Oh, there's some irony there, Viv. Come on."

"How is *that* irony?" She held up a tub of baby greens and a carton of fried chicken from Ree's purchases. "I like how you balance your nutrition. *This* is irony."

"It's exactly irony. A straitlaced detective with our reckless Vivie?"

"I'm not reckless." She frowned. "Not anymore."

Ree reached out and touched Vivien's hand. "I'm sorry. I shouldn't tease you about that."

It was true, though. Vivien had been just a little too wild in her younger days. A little loud. A little rowdy. And a detective wouldn't be her kind of guy, even if she were still looking.

Except she wasn't. Because she'd come to one solid conclusion after Ravil and his tryst with Joslyn—relationships were overrated.

"I heard the announcement you gave. So, if you're doing another community play, are you really not going back to New York City? Were you serious? You haven't said anything about it." She grabbed a chicken leg from the carton and took a bite.

Vivien paused. "Yes. Like I told you earlier—I'm ready to direct. I just…needed a little time to finish the last show before I finalized it in my head. Yesterday's final curtain call was the push I needed. *West Side Toy Story* was a success. This is what I want to do. I want to work with the youth. Work with the community."

"Why not go back to New York?" Ree leveled a look at Vivien over her drumstick. "And don't feed me the line about great-actors-make-great-directors. You've always wanted to be *on* the stage."

Vivien swallowed. Because how could she admit that twice she'd failed? The gasps, the finger-pointing. The muffled words uttered in low tones behind the hands that covered their faces.

"Sometimes our dreams change." She grabbed a Coke for

herself and opened the can. Okay, so the dream was still there. She just didn't know how she'd ever follow through.

"What are *these*?" Ree was standing over the kitchen trash can, an empty chicken bone in one hand and several black roses in the other.

Oh. Whoops. "Nothing."

"Black roses in the trash aren't 'nothing.'"

Vivien feigned a noncommittal shoulder shrug. "They were on the porch."

Ree sucked in a breath. "With our Fish Pic decorations?"

"Yeah."

"Why would anyone put these garish things out with our papier-mâché walleye and trout? They don't exactly go together."

Vivien raised her brows. "Does anything *actually* go with giant papier-mâché fish?"

Ree narrowed her eyes. "I think my selection of rods, reels, and nets do quite nicely. Who knew I'd find such treasures at the antique store?"

"But the fish, Ree. They're four feet long and hang from the rafters. I think you scared off the neighbors for all time."

Vivien's phone buzzed again and she picked it up. This time a text from Joslyn.

I THINK YOU'RE IN DANGER.

What?

A second message arrived after she'd cleared her notifications.

RAVIL FIRED ME TOO. SOMETHING'S GOING ON.

Ree laughed. "Just wait until you see what I'm planning for Halloween."

Vivien took the flowers from Ree and shoved them back into the can. Several fell to the floor and she bent down to scoop them up.

"Your hands are shaking, Viv. Hey, what's going on?"

"Nothing."

"Something's going on." Ree stood back, her arms crossed over her chest.

Vivien shoved those last few into the can too. "Really. Nothing."

"You can't lie to me. What are those black roses from?"

Vivien sighed. Considered Ree's demand. "I don't know. There's just..." She could see Sabrina sauntering around the car show.

"What?"

"It was probably Sabrina. Just trying to get to me." And, truly, the black roses did pretty much sum up her stage life. Something that was supposed to be beautiful—*amazing*, even—that had instead turned dark and ugly. She snatched the last remnants off the floor and the petals shattered. She brushed her hands together over the trash can, letting the final crumbled rose petals fall in.

*You're in danger.*

"Why was she here this time?"

"I didn't stick around to ask. Probably staying at one of the lodges for the weekend. She's always prided herself on making my life miserable—showing up in town to surprise me." Vivien walked over to the table and retrieved her drink. "I've never understood it. I'm the one who lost everything." Shoot. She wasn't ready for that conversation. She paused. Then, "You know we've never been on good terms. It was probably her. I'm sure she'll crawl back to Minneapolis by tomorrow. We're too small-town for her."

"Wait a minute. *Probably her?*"

"Yeah."

Ree came up to the table. "What aren't you telling me? Who else could it be?"

Vivien rubbed her hand across her brow. "You're going to give me frown lines and I am really not into Botox."

"Tell that to your false eyelashes. I want the truth, Viv. Who else could it have been?" Ree crossed her arms again and leaned against the countertop.

"Could have been her. Don't you have a story to write?" She looked up, smiled like she was in a toothpaste commercial.

Ree was staring at her with the I-can-do-this-all-day look.

Fine. "There was this guy—a fan, I suppose. He started showing up all the time. Everywhere I went. Like he was... stalking me or something."

Ree's brows raised. "You had a *stalker*? Why didn't you say something?"

"Yes. No. I don't know—it's like, I couldn't nail him down on anything exactly against the law." And she'd never told the police.

"Vivien, that's creepy. Stalking is a crime."

She'd thought so too. But no one at the theater had believed her. Her director, Ravil Kozlovsky, and her understudy, Joslyn Vanderburg, had both laughed in her face. *Who would want to stalk you?* As if that was how those kinds of crimes worked. They'd told her she was overreacting.

Maybe she was. "He always had a good excuse. He showed up at the gym and said he was a member there—had started a new job and changed his workout time. Or the coffee shop. He'd just appear there, like he was passing by. So many coincidences."

And yet, everyone told her he was harmless.

Of course, then there was the memory of Joslyn and Ravil in their intimate embrace outside the ritzy Harry Cipriani. It made her cringe.

"Viv, that's serious. I can't believe you didn't tell me."

"I felt like a fool." All the doubts they'd fed her seemed to rise up, as if to swallow her whole. "He always made it seem...plausible." Made her look like she was crazy. Too dramatic. A prima donna. "He'd leave black roses."

Ree reached out and touched Vivien's arm. "Do you think he'd come here?"

"I'm sure it's nothing. Sabrina, trying to twist the knife a little deeper." Vivien laughed, probably a little too boldly to convince Ree. "Well, I got her, didn't I?"

Ree was still staring at her. "Could he find you here?"

Vivien looked at the trash can. "I don't know how he'd find me here." Except, well, she hadn't exactly thought to make her life secret. She'd posted updates on her Facebook page of the play, and even before that, pictures of her at the Java Cup, or standing on the shore. Selfies meant to show the world that she was fine.

Just. Fine.

Even a first grader could have found her.

"Viv?"

"I'm so stupid. All my social media. Our playbill even had biographical sketches about each cast member. I put it right out there, in black and white. So, yeah. He would know where I live. Really, Sabrina probably left them just to spite me."

"It still seems a bit...sinister, doesn't it? Charred black roses?"

"I told you she isn't very nice. But, really—I'm sure it's nothing." Everyone was probably right. She was too dramatic. Over-reacting. She swallowed. Maybe she didn't even believe herself anymore.

She swept the trash can back under the cabinet and shut the door. Put on her red-carpet smile. The show must go on.

But the flowers felt like an omen. She shuddered, slipped into their wallpapered bathroom, and leaned close to the mirror.

She flicked the base of her false lashes with her fingernail, willing the rubbery glue to relinquish her lids back to their natural state for the night. She managed to loosen an edge and peeled the long strip off, setting it onto the plastic mold. She pried the second one off, snapped the plastic case closed, and washed her face.

The bathroom countertop of the Fifth Avenue West bungalow was a postage stamp compared to the wall-length one in her old dressing room. While the thirteen square inches might satisfy Ree, Vivien found it desperately lacking.

She scooped up her collection of powders, creams, lipsticks, and brushes from the countertop and tucked them back into the tacklebox-style organizer, adding her false lashes before latching it.

Failure hounded her. Had chased her back to Deep Haven twice. And if she didn't find a way to make the community theater a success, well, then she was everything the critics who'd seen her epic fail had said.

Naive. Unseasoned. Not suited for theater—or anything else, to hear them tell it.

Regrettable and forgettable. A poor imitation.

Because without a role, without her name on the marquee, she was just a silly girl with a dream. Like thousands of others.

Vacation should include more sleep. Unfortunately, Boone's night had been spent tossing and turning, his investigative drive dissecting the curious find on Vivien's porch. The one she didn't want to talk about that had his wheels spinning. He'd finally rolled out of bed before sunrise and slipped on his running gear. Let his feet carry him down the trails through the brisk morning.

The cold air burned his lungs as he sucked in gasps at the end of his run. Okay, so maybe he hadn't kept up his cardio fitness as well as he should have. He pressed his hand against his chest and clambered up the cabin steps to watch the sunrise paint the sky fiery orange and red. Tried to slow his breathing with deep breaths.

Nope, nothing like an early morning run to remind himself of the doctor's words.

*You have a heart murmur.*

He still couldn't believe the doctor had told him he needed to ease back into exercising. Manage his stress. And wait for the readings of his echocardiogram.

Information he was eager to keep private, especially from his boss, whose name popped up on Boone's CallerID as he reviewed his pace time on his cell phone app. He should have known his boss would check up on him before he'd even spent twenty-four hours in Deep Haven. He slid into the lounge chair on the deck where he could watch the waves tumble in on Lake Superior. The lake's dark depths had answered the sunrise with a mirrored glow.

He clicked the call button on his phone. Steve Landry, Kellogg's police chief, greeted him.

The chief, whose lean, lanky figure belied the depth and breadth of the man himself. His wavy hair, now gray, was the only rebellious thing about the lawman. How many times had he mentored Boone over the years?

Steve was calling from his office at the police station, probably getting ready to sit in on roll call. Boone could almost taste the fresh pastries in the break room and hear the laughter from the locker room as everyone geared up for the day.

"I've barely unpacked and you're already harassing me?" Boone teased. The sun had broken the horizon, the heat of it warming Boone's cooling body. "You must be calling to tell me you've changed your mind." As good as it was to see Caleb, staying in Deep Haven, facing hours alone at the cabin, left Boone with too much silence. And silence led to thinking. And too much thinking went to places he didn't want to go—places he couldn't go, especially when he started Monday-morning quarterbacking every mistake he'd made.

"No. Just making sure you're doing well. I spoke with Rachelle and she's got you on her schedule for Wednesday."

Boone let out a groan. "I really don't think it's necessary for me to see her." He got up, opened the cabin door, stepped inside, and grabbed the towel he'd left on the living room table.

"See her once a week. Deal with your anger issues."

"I don't have any anger issues." Even schooling his voice didn't keep the hard edge out of it. He blotted the sweat off his face and neck.

"Well, you might." Landry's firm tone softened. "Rachelle needs to clear you before you come back."

"Why? She's not officially on staff or the department's payroll," Boone pressed. There had to be some way to get Landry to drop this ridiculous plan.

"My rule, Boone. I've known you too long to let you slide. Make sure your head is on right. Pursue some hobbies."

"I have a hobby. My Mustang." Boone toed off his shoes.

"You've had her restored for more than ten years. Nice as she is, maintenance is not a hobby."

Boone pinched the bridge of his nose between his fingers and tried to rub the tension off his forehead. "I don't need hobbies. I have my career."

"And you're married to it."

The words, no matter how true, still cut. Yeah, well, not everyone got lucky in love. Landry had been married more than thirty-five years. Five kids. Eight grandchildren.

He couldn't know what it was like to hit his mid-thirties with only his career status to show for it. To have his entire identity now facing destruction. Because that's really what this was about. Everything that made Boone valuable was in his job as lead detective for the Kellogg Police Department. Without it, he was...nothing.

Boone opened the refrigerator, hunger hitting him hard, and set the eggs on the counter.

"You keep working like you've been, letting all that frustration and bitterness build, you're going to burn out. And next time, you might get into worse trouble. You might not be able to rein yourself in, and then those charges might stick."

"I'm fine." Always fine. No matter what, he knew how to survive and work through the grind. "I really feel like I'd do more good being back in Kellogg." He stood at the open window and watched the breeze tease the thin boughs of the nearby birch trees, the leaves rustling and the light playing across the shimmery leaves.

He opened the window over the sink farther and pulled a frying pan from a cupboard.

"Do this. For both of us."

"Why, Steve? I still don't get it. Why am I being punished?" He'd worked hard to be the go-to guy, and now, it still felt like he would lose the ground he'd gained in Kellogg. Like, somehow, he hadn't quite moved himself into solid standing in the community. Always one step away from being cast out.

"It's more of a vacation than a punishment."

Boone let out a sharp laugh. "Call it what you want, but I know what it really is. You wanted to take me off the streets." He added a hunk of butter to the pan and turned on the stove before pulling a bowl from the dish rack, cracking two eggs into it, and scrambling them with a fork.

"You know I didn't have a choice, right?" Instead of growing defensive, the chief took the tone of the mentor he'd always been. "If I didn't put you on admin leave after the investigation, it would have looked like we didn't care. It would have hurt the department." He paused, his voice turning from mentor to father figure. "In the long run, it would have hurt you."

"I didn't cross the line, Steve." The eggs sizzled when he

dumped them into the hot pan. He began rummaging through the drawers, looking for a turner.

"I know, but…appearances. And, be honest with yourself. It was as close as close could be. You were a breath away from obliterating the line—and your career."

Boone could still see the smug look on the perp's face. Nearly a smirk when Boone had arrived to arrest him on murder charges in his condo—the one he'd paid for with stolen money. Like Margaret Vincent's brutal death was funny. How the slick marble counters and ivory carpet had stood in stark contrast to the darkness within the man's eyes.

His jaw tightened, the sick feeling coiling in his stomach.

He began opening and closing drawers on his frantic hunt for a turner to scramble and flip his eggs. Come on—the kitchen was tiny. Where would they put the cooking utensils?

It wasn't his fault the guy had resisted arrest and gotten hurt in the process. He'd tried three times to calm the guy down. Boone hated the term *police brutality*—not that it didn't happen in the world—but he'd known many officers who'd been hurt. So, he'd taken special care. But, yeah, he could admit he might have lost it when the man told him he'd put the old woman out of her misery, the way she'd begged for mercy. How her frail body had crumpled on the floor after he'd struck her. Then he'd spit in Boone's face.

He slammed another drawer shut and pulled open another one.

And then the suspect had pulled out of Boone's grip. Tried to run again.

Maybe he *had* taken him down too hard. Maybe he should have let someone else take over.

His fingers finally latched onto a metal turner and he tugged it from the drawer. He flipped his eggs, on the dark side of done. Lovely. He turned off the burner and plated his eggs.

Maybe he did need some time off.

"Boone, I've never seen you so close to losing control, and that's something you really need to get a handle on if you want a shot at being the next chief."

"Is it really about me? Or public appearances?" He sat down at the small table with his eggs and book. Took a bite.

"No. It's about you. Your future. And the fact that my best detective is worn thin."

Boone remained silent, his food turning to paste in his mouth.

"I'm worried about you. I don't want to see your career derailed. When the chief position opens up—"

"Kellogg already has a chief." Boone sat up, knocked his book to the floor.

"Well, that's the other reason I called." Landry cleared his throat. Boone imagined him leaning back, his feet up on his desk, staring at the gallery of family photos that lined his office walls. "Cynthia and I've had some long talks and we feel it's time for me to retire. I've put in my notice and the position will be advertised this week. I was hoping they'd sit on it, but they want the selection made fairly fast."

Retire. An opening for the chief slot. Maybe the validation he'd been seeking all these years. Because, yeah, he didn't have a wife or a family. He had his job. And he was good at it. At least, he thought he was.

But maybe good cops didn't miss clues and let eighty-year-old women get beaten and murdered.

"You're really going to retire?" Boone had a hard time picturing the iconic chief hanging up his badge and holster for good.

"I've done a lot here, enjoyed it even. But this job, it isn't my life. I've missed out on so much with my wife, my kids. Now Cynthia and I have all the grandkids to enjoy. I don't want my legacy to be just my public service. I want my legacy to be my family. The time I spent with them. The man I was to them."

The words carved out a piece of Boone's heart, a void not only in where his legacy would be, but the lack of any he'd inherited.

He swallowed, his mouth dry. "I'm sure they'll enjoy that."

"That, they will. You know, Kellogg isn't what it used to be."

Oh, Boone knew it too well. When elderly women were killed in their own homes...

The chief continued. "But you're good at this work, Boone. I think you'd make an excellent police chief."

And there, Chief Landry dangled the carrot, just out of reach. Stay in Deep Haven. Relax. Read the book. Chat with Rachelle. Go home better than ever and be the outgoing chief's top pick for a replacement.

Sure. He could do that. How many times had his dad mentioned he'd make a good chief some day? Far too many to count.

"Thank you, sir. I appreciate your confidence in me."

"Absolutely. You've got the book I gave you?"

Boone leaned forward and picked the book up from the floor, flicked away the dust, and stared at the blue cover. *Imperturbability: Finding the Unflappable You.*

"Is this even a real book? Or did you pull this out of a cereal box?"

"You're funny. That's a *New York Times* bestseller—I even went to a book signing. Written by the foremost expert on anger management."

"I told you I don't have an anger issue."

Steve let out a breath of disagreement and did nothing further to acknowledge Boone's protest. "That's my autographed copy. Don't lose it."

"Right. I'll take it with me wherever I go." Boone flipped to the title page to see that the book had been not only autographed but included a personal note to the chief.

"And Boone?"

"Yeah?"

"Next time we talk, make sure you're past the first chapter."

"Right. I'll be focused on this marvelous tome you've loaned me."

"Good. Get to reading. Relaxing. Taking care of your health."

"Yes, sir."

"I'm serious, Boone. Read. The. Book. You need it. By the end of these five weeks, you need to have your blood pressure below one-twenty-five over eighty-five, complete any tasks Rachelle's given you, and pass your physical—with a stress test."

"I'm fine. Really."

If dawdling around Deep Haven, jumping through hoops reading the book, and sitting on Ms. Newman's couch—or whatever she used—was what he had to do, then so be it. He'd prove to Landry he knew how to relax and do nothing.

He looked at the book and thought of the roses. He'd much rather be getting to the bottom of that mystery.

Well, maybe he'd dig into the book later. No sense ruining a perfectly good morning. He'd definitely need some strong coffee to stay awake for this assignment.

# CHAPTER 3

*B*oone tucked his book under his arm and let the fresh smell of coffee coax him through the door of the Java Cup. He'd show the chief. He knew how to relax. Read. Do absolutely nothing for five weeks.

Boone waited in line while the Monday morning crowd moved up to the counter one by one.

With the waves easy on the shore and the birds soaring on the breeze, Deep Haven really might be the place to relax.

So, relax he would.

Boone moved up to the counter and stared at the board, feeling the barista's eyes on him. He turned to her.

The blonde's eye creases deepened, her eyes squinting at him. She had the tired-but-wired look of someone used to working hard and remaining highly caffeinated. "I recognize you. You're the guy who won the People's Choice award yesterday."

Boone read her name tag and smiled. "Good morning, Kathy. Yes, that was my Mustang. I like to drive her in the summer, then tuck her away in storage."

"Nice car." She put a hand on her hip. "We always have to drive something practical in winter, don't we?"

"Yeah. My truck isn't nearly as much fun though."

"I bet." She pointed to the drink board behind her. "You should try one of our signature drinks."

"That sounds intriguing. What do you have?"

"We've got a Megan and a Vivie." She waggled her brows. "And, for Vivie's guy, you know what I'd recommend."

"I'm not—" Shoot. Kathy had turned away and went to work steaming milk to a white froth.

She smiled over her shoulder. "It's on the house."

Right. "Thanks."

"It's got chocolate with a little kick."

"Oh?" Boone wondered exactly how much caffeine he was committing to consume. The doctor had said to cut back on his five-cup habit.

Well, he should probably ease himself off of it, anyway. After all, he didn't want to shock his system.

"You grab yourself a seat and I'll bring this over."

Boone scanned the room. Several tables were already taken. Front and center sat a young couple in an animated debate over a...bridal magazine picture? A trio of old-timers who were discussing their last big catch. And then there was the man he guessed to be a lawyer type. Suit. A few gray hairs at his temples. Several deep frown lines. And a bulging briefcase that looked like it held the longest case brief in history.

Talk about needing a vacation.

He decided on a corner seat near the window. The door jangled and a few men came in dressed in jeans and matching blue T-shirts.

He popped open his book.

Kathy brought over his drink while one of the other employees stepped to the counter to take orders. "Here you go, hon." Her eyes twinkled. "I think you're *really* going to like it." She stood and watched him.

Really? She was going to wait for him to take a taste? Awkward.

He smiled, lifted the cup, and took a sip. Sweet mocha curled around his tongue. Delicious, rich, and decadent.

So yeah, a lot like Vivien, maybe.

And then fire. Burning fire. A veritable inferno in his mouth.

He sputtered and coughed. "What's—what's in this?"

She grinned. "It's chocolate with cayenne. All the rage in the big cities. I thought it was the perfect representation of our Vivie."

"Oh?" His voice cracked like a thirteen-year-old's and the room turned blurry. He blinked back the tears.

"Absolutely." She let out a sigh and then set a hand on his shoulder. Paused. "Is that too hot for you? Do you need some water?"

He caught a few glances from the men ordering at the counter. "No. No, thank you."

"Okay, well you let me know if you need anything else." She threaded her way through the tables and ducked behind the espresso machine, helping out with the line that had formed in her absence.

Right. He wouldn't need anything with the name Vivie on it, that's for sure.

Boone's body temperature had risen several degrees and his skin flushed. He swiped his hand across his brow, sniffed, and picked up his book.

He flipped open the book and started the first paragraph, trying to ignore the sense that he'd just been pepper sprayed at the academy.

One of the men from the group ordering walked over and set up camp at a nearby table. "You're the guy who was with Vivie yesterday, right?"

Boone placed a thumb between the pages to hold his place and looked up.

A large guy with a thick, brown beard and far too much humor in his eyes reached out a hand. "Casper Christiansen."

"Boone Buckam." He took the offered hand. "Just visiting. Here for a little R & R." He ignored the comment about Vivien.

Another man approached from the counter.

"Hey—you're Caleb's friend, right?"

Boone gave him a nod.

"Seb Brewster." The man set down his drink and sat across from Casper. "I heard you're going to help Caleb and me coach the team. He's been talking you up ever since we saw you with Vivie yesterday."

"Oh, that was just an…accident."

Seb raised a brow. "You should swing by and pick up a donut from my wife over at World's Best. The football team has a fundraiser every year. It's a big event—maybe you can help us sell donuts. We're always looking for another hand."

"I'll be sure to do that." Boone opened his book back up, his eyes skimming over the introductory paragraph again.

The other men brought their drinks to join the gathering at the nearby table.

"Weren't you with Vivien yesterday?" This time, a man in a deputy's uniform—one Boone recognized from Vivien's passing parade introductions—was looking at him. Cole, if he remembered correctly.

Boone swallowed. Maybe he should wear a sign.

*Vivien has a way of knowing everyone.* That, apparently, was a two-way street. Caleb had neglected to articulate on that.

The group's collective curiosity was written plainly on their faces, all eyes on him.

"You know, it just worked out that while she was admiring my car, we got stuck in the parade."

He got a few slow nods. More smirks than anything else.

"Really?" This from Casper, who took a gulp of his coffee while Boone looked at his own cup, wishing he did have some water.

"Boone?" The door clanged closed behind a man, vaguely familiar, looking at him. It took a beat for Boone to recognize billionaire playboy Adrian Vassos from Kellogg. He was the last person Boone expected to run into in Deep Haven.

He wore jeans with a blue T-shirt that matched the rest of the crew at the nearby table, his long, dark hair pulled back. Adrian nodded to the table with Casper, Cole, and Seb like he was with the Spanish Inquisition and wove his way over to Boone.

"Boone Buckam. Seriously. Small world."

Boone stood and met his handshake. "Hey, Adrian. What are you doing here?"

"I'm here for a work crew meeting. We're building a new Crisis Response Team headquarters."

So, the Vassos empire had moved from hotels to...Crisis Response Teams? Huh.

"Good to see you." Boone stepped to the side to let a customer pass. He'd always liked Adrian, despite some of his family's business tactics. Adrian never treated him as lower class.

"Do you want your usual, Adrian?" Kathy called from the now-empty front counter.

His usual? Boone looked from Kathy to Adrian. "You don't *live* here, do you?"

"That sounds perfect, Kathy," Adrian answered. He turned back to Boone. "I've been in Deep Haven since late spring. What about you—wait, was that *you* in the parade yesterday? With Vivie? I didn't know you were dating someone from Deep Haven."

Boone's shoulders slumped. "It was. No, we're not dating. I'm just here on...vacation."

Adrian lowered his voice, glanced at the couple, who sounded like they were now debating the acceptable cost of a wedding gown. "Does this have to do with that lawsuit?"

Boone frowned. "You heard about that?"

"Well, it was pretty big news."

"Landry wants me to take some time away from work. He's ready to retire."

"Oh, *that's* big news. Are you going to put in for it?"

"Yeah—if I can complete all the vacation activities he's tasked me with."

Adrian raised a brow. "Such as...?" He moved to the side to let two gray-haired women pass on their way to the exit.

Boone measured his words. "You know, read, explore the great outdoors. Lower my blood pressure and do things people do on vacation."

"Oh, there's lots to do outdoors here." Adrian nodded to the other table. "You can always come by and help us on the build. We're doing as much of the interior work as we can ourselves to save money."

"And it's for a Crisis Response Team, you said?"

"It is. It's fairly new. Team members are still being brought on board and we just purchased a helicopter."

Kathy called Adrian to the counter for his order. He wove his way through the tables, several new patrons greeting him on his way by.

Boone sat down. If he had to guess, he suspected some of Vassos's fortune may have paid for a large part of the helicopter purchase, if not all—though by the looks of it, Adrian had shaken free of some of the family constraints. He had an ease about him Boone hadn't seen before.

Adrian returned, took a drink, and Casper rose from the nearby table and headed back up to the counter.

"This region has probably needed a team like that—for Crisis Response."

"It has. You should stop by. You can't miss it—big vacant lot at the north end of town with the new construction." He looked over at the group of men drinking coffee. "I'd better head over to our table so we can get started."

The deputy's chair scraped across the floor as he slid it out of the way. Adrian pulled up a seat.

"I didn't know you knew the guy who's dating Vivie."

Boone cringed at the deputy's words.

Not. Dating. Vivie.

Adrian raised his eyes to Boone, laughed. "He's not dating Vivie."

"I'm right here." Boone shook his head. Small towns.

Five weeks. He just had to survive five weeks.

Casper came back through, veering toward Boone's table on his way back to his seat. The man smoothed his beard a moment, then offered, "You know, one of the most relaxing things to do around here is kayaking."

Adrian nodded in agreement. "That's true."

"Yeah? I might have to try that." Boone latched on to the thread of conversation that didn't revolve around the blue-eyed starlet.

"You should stop by Wild Harbor Trading Post. We have excellent instructors."

"Hmm. Maybe."

Casper took a drink of his coffee. "You should ask Vivie about it. She works there."

Oh, for Pete's— "Look, I'm not dating Vivie."

"Okay." The man held his hands up and smiled, nodded, then joined the other men at the table.

The door jangled again. Shoot.

His supposed "girlfriend" walked in. And it occurred to him that if he wasn't dating her, maybe he should be. Because she was everything he remembered.

She stood in the doorway, her perfect loose waves cascading

over her shoulders. Vivien looked behind her, as if watching something down the street. She wore a bright yellow T-shirt and tailored white shorts. As she turned back, a furrow on her brow disappeared as her blue eyes connected with his and a smile lit her face.

"Oh, it's my hero!" She walked over to his table, leaned forward, and set her palms on it. "How's it going?"

Perfect. He didn't even venture a glance at the table of men nearby where conversation had stopped like whiplash. Didn't dare try to sink behind his book to hide.

"Hi." He shoved a napkin into his book and closed it, strategically setting a second napkin over the cover when she slid into the seat across from him. He could feel all the eyes in the coffee shop turn toward them. He leaned forward and lowered his voice. "Everyone thinks we're dating."

"What? Oh, don't mind them." She raised her voice. "They're just a bunch of busybodies! I've known them forever."

A few heads turned away and the three elderly men rose to leave. "There. So, whatchya doing?" She smelled his coffee. "Oh no, Kathy did not make you a Vivie—"

"My mouth is on fire. I may need a skin graft."

"Kathy! Bring out some milk!"

Laughter from behind the coffee bar. Vivie shook her head. "Sorry. They all think it's funny." She put a hand on her hip. "I'm a peppermint mocha girl myself. What are you reading?"

She reached out to touch his book and he jerked it away. Like he might be a first grader.

She tilted her head. "Really? That's the same book you hid under the seat yesterday, isn't it? What, is it a romance? A pirate and a princess? Or a classic, like *Cinderella*? I hope it's not one of those—" Her hand flew to her lips and her eyebrows raised.

"What? No!"

She held up her hands, laughing. Aw, she was pretty, and frankly, got under his skin, in a good way. He didn't know why, but his morning was looking up. And he didn't even care anymore if the men were staring at him. Them.

She tugged a stack of paper flyers from her shoulder tote and held them out in front of him, her long lashes fluttering. "Want to help me hang these?"

"I don't know, Vivien." He made a face. "I'm not sure that's a good idea."

She placed a hand over his. Smiled. "Come on. It'll be fun. What else do you have to do today?"

His conversation with Landry replayed in his mind. "I'm not supposed to have any fun."

"That's the silliest thing I've ever heard. Aren't you on *vacation?*"

"I have to read this book my boss gave me."

She reached out again, and he tried to hold the book into place against the table. Cover it with his hand. Anything. But she snagged the book and he watched the napkin float down to the table. Her eyes moved across the cover and then she laughed, her hand covering her red-painted lips again. "*Imperturbability?* Is that even a word?"

"It is." He pressed his lips together and reached for the book, but she held on to it.

"You are already entirely too unflappable. If you ask me, that's your biggest problem. You need to let loose. Remember? Live a little." And she winked at him. "Come on..."

Boone grabbed his book when she dangled it in front of him. He looked at the expectation on her face and couldn't bring himself to say no. Because, as much as he *wasn't* dating her, he had to admit she'd shaken loose something deep inside him. Despite all the jokes, maybe a friend like Vivien really was exactly what he needed to get his life back in order. And he'd do anything to not have to sit still. Besides, he really wanted to ask about those roses he'd seen on her porch—and that was the closest thing he had to an actual case.

He looked at the book, the napkin bookmark still sitting on the first page. Well, maybe he'd do better to read later in the day anyway, when he was back at the cabin.

Away from Vivie—and the terrible burn in his chest.

Vivien watched Boone smooth the flyer onto the bulletin board inside the library entrance, punching the staples in. He'd shaved since yesterday and smelled like soap and aftershave, and she had to keep herself from leaning into it. He wore a dark blue T-shirt with his jeans and looked much more like a man in charge than a man on vacation.

She hadn't meant to rope him into helping her. No, she'd set out that morning to hang her flyers and go about business as usual. Forget the black roses. Forget Sabrina. Ensure everyone in town knew about her next play and the auditions slated for Wednesday. To let the memory of Mr. Hottie settle in her mind and not think about how much fun she'd actually had fleeing from her half sister with Boone as her partner in crime.

And then she saw Boone sitting in the coffee shop, a solitary figure in an island of conversation, and she just had to stop. She might have left him alone if it weren't for that book, however. That awful, snore of a book—no, she just couldn't leave the man like that. He needed her help maybe even more than she needed his.

So, yeah, putting him to task with the flyers seemed the right prescription for both of them. And, quite frankly, he'd been exactly the kind of help she needed. Calm to her frenzied rush. Structure to her free-for-all.

He turned, stapler in hand. "What?"

Oh, busted staring at him. Fine. "When I first met you, I thought maybe you were some sort of serial killer," she whispered.

"What?"

A few heads popped up from the reading chairs.

"Shh." She held a finger to her lips. "Why else would someone as handsome as you be single?"

He lowered his voice to a conspiratorial whisper. "I'm not sure if I'm flattered or offended. And can I just point out that you're single too? How do I know you're safe?" He stooped down to pick up a flyer that had floated to the floor.

"Touché." She gave him a sly smile. "Do I scare you?"

He smiled something cute and slightly crooked. "A little. There was that little duck-and-cover routine you pulled at the car show like you were some sort of undercover operative."

"A little *Charlie's Angels*." She chopped the air with her best karate impression.

"Whoa, there." He stilled her hands with his own. "Don't hurt anyone with those."

And with his touch, her entire body seemed to light up. Oh yes, this man was definitely dangerous.

"I assure you, I'm not trouble at all." She set her chin into her hand and looked at him, batted her lashes in her best Marilyn impression.

He frowned. "I hope not."

She wasn't sure what she'd said that caused a cloud to pass over him. He scooped up the flyers from the nearby table and stalked out of the library.

She followed him, hot on his heels. "Boone, what's wrong?"

"Nothing."

She grabbed his arm to stop him, turn him around. "Liar-liar-pants-on-fire." She pulled the flyers out of his hands. "It's my turn to help you, so..." She held out her hand with the go-ahead signal, ignoring the mid-morning traffic leaving Licks and Stuff across the street.

"It's nothing." He pressed his lips into a thin line.

"It's something." She let the silence hang between them, waiting him out.

He finally blew out a breath and his eyes flicked from the lake to Vivien. His Adam's apple bobbed.

She'd known eventually either she'd get to him or the Deep Haven air would.

"My chief called me this morning. He's retiring." He looked away, stared off into the shimmering waters of Superior where gulls begged the tourists for a meal and the breeze lifted the sails of the boats out on the water.

She narrowed her look at him. "Is that a good thing or a bad thing?"

"Good. Bad."

"Could you be more specific?"

"He's a good man. He really is. And I want to put in for the job, but he's adamant that I have to prove I'm ready for it."

"Prove it how?"

"If I want a chance at that promotion, I need to do everything he's asked me to do. This is my opportunity for the job I've been working toward my entire career."

She knew the look that passed across his face. That sense of conflict. Wanting something just out of reach. It rubbed raw the ache in her chest.

"Did you guys need anything else? More copies?" Vivien knew that tiny, mouse-like voice. She turned to see Beth Strauss pulling a cart to the book drop box, her light brown hair pulled back in a band and a tentative smile on her face.

Beth had posed the question to both of them, but her green eyes were locked on Boone, just as they had been inside the library. Interesting. Well, Vivien didn't blame her—after all, the man was gorgeous. His T-shirt fitted against his body just right. The sleeve cuffs snugged around his biceps in a slightly distracting manner and, oh, those eyes. Those eyes were lethal. The palest blue with a dark ring encircling them.

Vivien blew out a breath. "I think we're good. Thanks for letting us post this."

"Sure. I'm looking forward to auditions." Beth gave them a demure nod and turned her attention to pulling the books from the bin and dropping them into the cart. Except, Vivien noticed Beth's oh-so-interested glances back toward Boone.

"Can we stop by the football field?" Boone asked, oblivious to the eyes on him. "I told Caleb I would."

"Sure. It's near the auditorium. That's my last stop. So, how do you know Caleb?"

"We were in the Army together."

She followed him to the parking lot and let him hold the car door for her. This one was a gentleman to boot.

Boone backed the car out of the library's lot and Vivien pointed to the right for him to turn.

Vivien knew the coach had lost part of his leg in an IED explosion. The thought of Boone being in the middle of all that sent a shiver up her spine.

"When did you serve?"

His jaw tensed and he stared at the road. She pointed out the next turn and thought he might not answer at all.

"I enlisted about a year after I finished high school."

"Did you serve overseas?" She pulled open her bag and fished out her lipstick. She flipped down the visor mirror.

"Iraq."

She paused, her tube of Red Carpet mid-swipe, and recapped it. "Wow. Were you a medic too?"

He shook his head. "MP—military police."

"Are you from a military family?" She pressed her lips together and slid her lipstick tube back into her tote.

"No, I was the first. I got hurt during pre-season football practice right before my first college season. Lost my scholarship."

She saw it again—the passing gloom—as if he, too, had a past that sometimes felt like it could reach out and drag him under.

"I'm sorry to hear that."

He lifted a shoulder. "It all worked out. Any more sightings of your friend from yesterday?"

Vivien rolled her shoulders to cover the involuntary shudder the question caused. "Nope. I'm hoping she crawled back to her cave in Minneapolis." She straightened the flyers in her hand.

He glanced over at her, raised a brow, as if he might press further. Instead, he looked back to the road. "So, what was with the flowers on your porch yesterday?"

"Flowers?" She tilted her head, certain she captured the right pose. The one that conveyed she didn't know exactly what he was talking about, even though she did. "Oh, the roses. Just a prank." She waved off the question with a dismissive sweep of her hand and a laugh.

He glanced over at her and opened his mouth as if to ask another question. Closed it.

"Turn here." She steered the conversation away from the roses, and they spent the next hour making stops through town, posting the theater announcement in nearly every shop and on every bulletin board before she pointed the way to the lot adjacent to the football field.

"I think that's about all of them." Vivien folded the last flyer. "I can't think of anywhere else to put one."

Boone parked and they walked toward the field. Vivien could see a woman with curly brown hair sitting on the field in front of the stands, her camp chair angled toward the fifty-yard line and her bare toes in the shaded grass. Issy Knight, Caleb's wife. She turned as their footsteps approached.

"Hi, Viv." Issy smiled and focused on Boone. "Good to finally see you again, Boone. I keep telling Caleb we need to take another trip." She extended a hand to him. "He's happy you're going to help coach."

Boone took her offered hand. "I don't know how helpful I'll be, but I love the game."

Issy laughed and nodded toward the field. "Looks like you've been spotted."

Caleb raised his hand in greeting and waved for Boone to join him on the field.

"Do we have time?" Boone posed the question to Vivien.

"Sure."

"Want a seat in the shade with me?" Issy asked. She gestured to the extra camp chair next to her.

"Thanks." Vivien sat down, her eyes on Boone as he walked out onto the field.

"It looked like you and Boone had a good time at the car show. How long have you known him?"

"Oh, no, we just met."

Issy raised a brow.

Oh, yeah. Vivien could see the wheels turning. Issy. Former host of the *My Foolish Heart* radio show for romantic problems. "Actually, it sounds like you know him much better than I do—I mean, you know a lot more about him."

"He and Caleb were in the Army together," Issy said. "I've only met him a couple times, but he and Caleb touch base every now and again."

"That's one of the few things I know about him. Do you know why he's here? He's been a little cryptic and, I don't know... I guess I'm a little worried about him. He said he's on vacation, but he doesn't seem very thrilled about being on vacation."

Boone threw a nice spiral to Caleb.

"Yeah. He's got some health issues. He's been a detective for a long time." Issy paused. "You know, sometimes things can stay with you for a while."

Vivien knew Issy was talking about her own life. She reached out and squeezed Issy's hand.

Issy gave her a warm smile. "But God heals, doesn't he?"

Oh, Vivien longed to believe that every time she heard it. Every Sunday morning, she sat in the same pew, singing the same hymns, wondering if she could ever trust God enough to let down her guard.

She watched Boone catch a pass from Caleb. Great form, and he laughed as he dodged a tackle.

*Health issues.* Issy's words sparked every impulsive bone in Vivie's body.

Maybe she could help him not only keep his job, but also get that promotion back in Kellogg. She was the queen of makeovers, and he might not know it yet, but he was in for the full-life makeover treatment.

Boone walked over with Caleb. A tiny bead of sweat rimmed his hairline and he played with the football in his hands.

"So, you'll do it?" Caleb asked, dropping a gear bag on the ground next to Issy's chair.

Boone palmed his grip on the ball. "Sure. I can spend some time with your quarterbacks and receivers."

"Outstanding. That will give Seb and me more time to work with rest of the team." Caleb looked at his watch. "Right now, we have strength training in the weight room between eight and nine each weekday morning and we're on the field from one to four."

"Okay." Boone handed the ball back to Caleb. "I'll come tomorrow to both. I could use some time in the weight room myself." He laughed.

A few players had arrived at the field early, helmets in hand. Vivien recognized Johnny Dahlquist and Tiger Christiansen.

"And on some days, we have the special teams come in early." Caleb waved to the players who'd started doing warm-ups.

Boone turned to Vivien. "We'd better get out of here before Caleb makes me run speed drills."

Caleb laughed. "You're welcome to it."

"Oh, no thanks." He smiled at Issy. "I'll see you guys later."

"Have a great day!" Issy waved to them and they walked back to the parking lot.

Boone set his hand on the windshield frame of the car. "Did you have one last stop to make?"

"Just a quick run into the playhouse. It's around the corner."

"Well, then, let's get to it."

Maybe football was good for a man's soul because Boone looked more relaxed after his time on the field than he had reading his book at the Java Cup when she'd found him. She pointed the way to the playhouse and hopped out of the car when they arrived.

The Arrowood Auditorium sat against the trees at the southeast end of the high school, its brick exterior still fresh and unweathered by the elements.

"I need to grab a notebook I left inside. I'll be right back."

Boone nodded, sitting back in the driver's seat as if to soak in the sunshine.

"Maybe read that book while you wait." She gestured toward the book and winked at him.

"Right. The book." He lifted it from the center console and flipped it open.

She walked into the auditorium and flicked the light switch. Nothing. She toggled it again. Still nothing.

Someone must have tripped the breaker again.

Ever since the fire sprinkler incident caused by an errant football pass, the electrical system had been a little sensitive. She squinted into the darkness, getting her bearings as she headed toward the utility room at the back. She passed the curtain line and heard a scuffle and froze. Footsteps?

Probably her imagination.

She took another step. Another scuffle. Unmistakable. This time, the hairs on her neck stood up. She wasn't alone in the darkness.

Like the times she'd left the theater in NYC late. Hearing the murmur of footsteps behind her. The ones that stopped every time she did. She swallowed.

"Hello?"

*You're in danger.* Joslyn's message replayed in her mind.

No answer, and her ears pounded with the elevated pulse, the whooshing making it even more difficult to listen. She held her breath, straining to hear any sound, trying to gauge her distance to the doorway. And then the footsteps started toward her, hard and fast.

She screamed and ran, jerking through the tangle of curtains and fleeing toward the thin shard of daylight that cut under the front door sill.

Before she reached it, the door flew open and the form of a man filled the space, the light hitting his short blond hair.

Boone.

He stepped into the darkness. "Viv! What's the matter?"

"Someone is after me!" She knew she was screaming, but she couldn't stop the rush of terror. Couldn't stop the same trembling, hair-raising sensation she'd felt when she'd fled her dressing room in New York City the last time.

Talk about things sticking with people.

Boone grabbed her, put her behind him. "Anybody there?"

When no one answered, he grabbed her hand and guided her out of the playhouse, keeping himself between her and the building. She flinched when the door crashed closed.

Then he turned to her. "Are you okay?"

If she wasn't before, she was now, the way he stared down at her, his blue eyes concerned. She had the crazy urge to throw her arms around him. She might have, if he had been her boyfriend. Instead, she let herself sink against the building, her legs Jell-O.

She nodded. "Someone was there—in the dark."

"Stay here." Before he could step back inside, the door swung open and Gordy Dahlquist came barreling out.

"What in the world is going on here?" Gordy's scalp was red beneath his thinning brown hair and his paunchy form took up most of the doorway. "What's all the screaming about?"

"Who are you?" Boone leveled a look at Gordy, still keeping himself between Vivien and the stout man.

"I'm local school board member Gordy Dahlquist."

"Were you trying to hurt her?" Boone took a step toward Gordy, his fists balled and eyes tight. He'd gone from vacationer to cop before her eyes.

"It's okay." Vivie tugged on Boone's T-shirt to pull him back, but he stood cemented to the ground. "I know him."

Gordy let out a huff. "Of course I wasn't trying to hurt her. Sheesh. Who are you?" Gordy crossed his arms over his chest.

"Well, I'm not the guy stalking around in the dark!"

"I wasn't stalking anyone!" He looked Boone up and down. "And I still don't know who you are."

"Boone Buckam."

"The lights were out." Vivien looked at Gordy. "I heard footsteps in the dark, coming closer." She could see in Gordy's eyes the disbelief. She could feel the judgment of her dramatic exit.

He threw his hand toward the door. "Yeah. I'd gone to reset the breaker because the lights weren't working when I got here."

"Why are you here?" Vivien asked. She rubbed away the residual gooseflesh on her arms.

He stared at Vivien. Sighed. Tightened his lips. Finally, "I came to tell you your auditorium use agreement has been rejected. You can't practice here anymore."

"What?" She stared at him, his words like a fist in her chest. "I just hung posters up all over town announcing auditions and practices here."

"Well, I guess you'll have to do something about that."

"You can't do that—"

"Vivien, your youth *soaked* the place a few weeks ago. It cost me several thousand dollars to dry it out and repair the damage. I was—we were only letting you use it until the youth play was over. But now...no. The answer is no."

She put her hands on her hips. "This isn't really about that, is it? I think you're still mad that Peter voted for my plans for the old Westerman place." Not that it mattered anymore. The old Westerman Hotel had burned down just a couple weeks ago, along with her idea for a youth center. Still, grudges died hard in this small town.

Gordy looked from her to Boone and back. "It doesn't matter what you think. The decision was made. I came by to let you know." He turned and slid his key into the door, locking it, and walked away.

Vivien stared after him. "What am I going to do now? There aren't any other venues."

Boone reached out, gave her shoulder a gentle squeeze. "I'm sure you'll think of something."

She looked up at him. "When I do—if I do—I'll have to change every last poster we spent all morning hanging up."

"Can I help you fix the posters?"

She shook her head, biting back tears. She wouldn't give Gordy the satisfaction of knowing he'd devastated her. "No. I don't even know what I'll put on them now. Just...can you take me home?"

"Sure."

She looked back at the building. "I guess I don't need that notebook today."

They climbed back into the car, the silence filling the space as Boone drove toward her house. "Vivien, are you sure you're okay?"

Oh. "Yeah. Everything's fine." She waved him off. Smiled. "I mean, except for the fact that I have nowhere to hold auditions on Thursday, nor a place to perform the actual production." She stared out the window and watched the tourists bustling down Main Street, their hands already heavy with purchases.

"There is that. But I meant the run-in. Your scream. The way you came out of that auditorium—you were running for your life." He parked in front of her house and she ventured a glance at the porch. No black roses. Only four one-foot-wide fish eyes stared at her from the porch.

"Oh, it's nothing. I overreacted." She smiled and unlatched her seatbelt. Here he was, trying to relax, and she'd gone screaming and creating a big scene. "Hey—I do owe you a thank you." Vivien pulled her sunglasses from her eyes and tried to shake away the residual doom that hung over the afternoon. "How about lunch? It's the least I can do." She nodded toward the front door.

Boone looked at his watch then back at her, and a smile crept up his face.

He had such a nice smile.

"Sure. That sounds good."

She looked down and realized she'd snapped her sunglasses in two. Apparently, Detective Buckam wasn't the only one who needed to relax.

# CHAPTER 4

*H*e'd eat lunch with Vivien, make sure she was really okay, then go back to the cabin. He'd finish chapter one and peruse the offerings of outdoor activities.

And maybe, somehow, erase her scream, the one that still reverberated in his mind. Raw. Primal. And he hadn't missed the way her body had trembled when she'd leaned against the building to hold herself up.

The house, a petite blue bungalow with river rock at the base of each porch pillar, reminded him of some of the older neighborhoods in Kellogg. Except, of course, for the two giant fish still hanging from the porch rafters. They approached the porch steps where the fish dangled, each from a single thick cord at the center of its back, causing them to slowly rotate, their freakish faces staring at Boone.

That was creepy enough, without the memory of the black roses left on her porch and her scream that still echoed in his brain.

Admittedly, this woman was a character.

He flicked the tail of the walleye, sending it spinning faster.

"What's with the fish?" They looked to be made of papier-mâché on a wire frame, their painted scales doused with glitter.

"Hey—be careful!" She reached out a manicured hand, steadied the aquatic atrocities.

"Why? Are you afraid I'll make him seasick?"

"Funny. They're Fish Pic decorations." She gently repositioned the walleye's gaze back out across the neighborhood.

"Wow—you go all out." He leaned in to inspect the jagged teeth. "Are those teeth made out of sporks?"

"Yes, they are." She put a hand on her hip. "Good work, detective. Now, can you tell me what edition of the paper was used?"

"Right. Mad detective skills—the *Sunrise* edition."

She placed her palm on his chest with a playful nudge, the heat of it searing through his T-shirt and sending radiating waves across his entire body. "Very good. You're an expert." She blinked her long lashes, a hint of a smile teasing the corners of her lips. Her bright blue eyes met his.

He should probably run—past the gawking fish, straight down the steps—jump into his convertible, and head back to his lonely little cabin on the lakeshore. With his book. Because he was only in Deep Haven for five—scratch that—four-and-a-half more weeks.

"Are you coming?"

"Right behind you."

Sunlight cast a golden glow in the living room. Hardwood floors stretched the expanse of it and dark wood trim contrasted with the cream-colored paint. He paused at the large photograph of New York City's Central Park hung behind the frayed couch. "I'd order pizza, but I don't have my phone."

Vivien flashed him a smile. "This is Deep Haven, dear. We don't have delivery."

"No delivery?"

"Well, we did for a while, but things happened." She winked

at him. "We don't anymore."

"I see."

"Lucky for us"—she swept into the kitchen—"my roommate made a grocery run yesterday."

And there she went again, looking up at him with those big, bright eyes. Fluttering lashes. He swallowed.

"Your roommate—was that the woman who ducked behind the Chevelle with you?" Boone followed her into the kitchen, which looked like the 1950s met the 1970s. Avocado cabinet doors matched the checkerboard floor tiles. A small dining room table sat against the far wall with two chairs.

Cozy.

"Yes. That's Ree Zimmerman. We've been best friends since...forever." Vivien scrolled through screens on her phone. "Okay, here it is." She blinked at the screen. "Uh—yum. This is the one we're going to make."

"Are you sure you want to make it? We can go out..."

"Absolutely." She looked up at him. "It's healthier this way."

"If I wanted healthy, I wouldn't have picked pizza."

She laughed. A little husky and soft. "Oh, come on, you'll love it." She began scrolling on her phone. "See, cauliflower crust."

There were very few things Boone could think of that sounded worse than a cauliflower crust on his pizza. He must have made a face.

"Trust me."

Judging by her slender figure with just the right curves, Boone figured Garbo didn't indulge in the same sort of greasy, cheesy, gooey pizza of his preference. If he wanted lunch with her, it meant, ugh, cauliflower crust pizza.

It might be worth it.

She pulled mixing bowls from the cupboard and set them on the countertop.

"How can I help?"

"One sec."

She pulled out a bowl of something from the refrigerator, popped the lid off, and took a sniff.

The pungent odor of cooked cauliflower assaulted the kitchen. "We're not eating that, are we?"

She nodded. "I think it's okay."

He raised a brow at her. "Think? How often do you need to smell the food in your refrigerator to determine if it's edible?"

"Not *that* often."

"Answer under oath."

"I plead the Fifth." She turned on the oven.

"I just want to know exactly how experienced your nose is at food safety detection."

"It's *cauliflower*."

"Right. It always stinks, so I'm just wondering if it stinks more when it's bad and if you have any experience with that."

She narrowed her gaze at him. "Get the dried parsley from the cupboard next to the stove and the shredded cheese from the refrigerator. And the eggs. I told you Ree bought most of this yesterday."

"Got it." He rummaged through the refrigerator, finding some assurance that the cheese and eggs were at the front. He placed them on the countertop. "Just so we're clear, I'm not smelling any of it."

"Ha ha." She measured out the ingredients. "You just wait, Detective Buckam."

He watched her mash the cauliflower, cheese, eggs, and herbs together until she had a paste. She pulled a sheet pan from the cupboard and pressed the mixture into a flat disk and popped it into the oven.

"Now, for the toppings." She went back to the refrigerator and pulled out zucchini, bell peppers, tomatoes, garlic, and a jar of marinara sauce. She looked over her countertop garden. "Oh! I forgot the eggplant."

Eggplant? "What's all that for?"

Her mouth dropped open. "Um, hello? The pizza. You're going to love it."

"It seems really unnecessary to put all those vegetables on a pizza that already has a cauliflower crust. What about the pepperoni? The sausage?"

"You need more vegetables in your life."

"I really doubt that." He watched her grasp the knife, start slicing away on the vegetables. "Tell me about this play you want to do."

*"Then Came You."*

He stared at her. Blinked.

"Okay, Crickets, you can't seriously tell me you've never heard of it." The oven timer dinged and she pulled out the crust.

Admittedly, it smelled good. But then she slathered on the sauce and stacked on more vegetables than he'd seen at the last Farmer's Market.

"I'm sorry—I haven't." His stomach growled. Okay, maybe it wouldn't be horrible.

"It's a sweet, one-act play about a man who's pined for his childhood sweetheart for years. Everyone converges back in their hometown after college when a mutual friend dies unexpectedly."

Oh. "Sounds...charming."

She laughed. "I know, it sounds really sad—but it isn't. He realizes...well, you know the song 'Bless the Broken Road'?" She slid the pizza pan into the oven.

Boone nodded.

"It's a little like that. Like, how do the broken circumstances in our life end up leading us to greater blessings?"

He turned her words over in his mind. He hadn't grown up in a Christian home. Hadn't even become a Christian until he was in the Army. When he'd come home, he hadn't found the right church to attend. It didn't help that his former flame and high school sweetheart, PJ Sugar, attended the Kellogg Praise and Worship Center. He'd needed her out of his life...so, there went his church attendance too.

He'd been relegated to watching services from his computer.

Vivien pulled open the refrigerator door and took two Cokes from the shelf, handed him one.

"Thanks."

"All this time, the hero, Dylan Turner, was looking behind him—into his past, wishing it had played out differently—but, really, all the bad things in his life, all the setbacks, end up both shaping him into the man he is and also leading him to the love of his life."

Boone took drink. "Huh. Interesting."

She cleared her throat. "It's incredibly sweet. In the end, he has to choose whether he wants to pursue his future with a girl he's never dated before or get lured back to his high school sweetheart—who's probably going to break his heart. Again."

Boone cleared his throat, not sure he wanted to know how that one ended. "Someone has to die for this happy ending?"

"Well, the audience isn't attached to the dead guy. He's already dead when the play opens."

"That makes it so much better."

"Stop. It's really good. The part of Ashleigh is probably my favorite character ever. Being her was so..." She stopped. Blinked.

"You played the part?"

She sighed, as if chasing away memories. "I did. It was quite a shift after *Charlie's Angels*. Man, *that* was a fun show." She smiled and took a sip. "But this show is sweet and it's all about hope, the future. Letting go. I loved every moment of it."

She started singing.

*Don't let the past hold you back*
*It's time to let go—we're on the right track*
*Embrace today, you know it's true,*

*I didn't know what love was, until I found you.*

Wow. Her voice, a warm, rich alto, reached right in, disarmed him. Made him wonder why she wanted to be behind the scenes instead of on the stage.

"Beautiful."

"See, it's a fabulous show."

He hadn't meant the lyrics, specifically.

The kitchen smelled like cheese and roasted vegetables. The cheese he was okay with. The vegetables, not so much, but maybe she was right. He needed more vegetables in his life.

"Being her was so...? You never finished your sentence." He watched her, waited for her answer.

She lifted a shoulder and smiled. "Fun. All her dreams came true. She got the guy, the job, the future."

"A happy ending."

"Of course!"

Interesting. He leaned a hip against the counter. "So, do you want to talk about what happened in the playhouse earlier? Why you thought someone was chasing you?" He'd thought she'd been lying about the roses. Now he was even more certain.

The kitchen timer went off and she grabbed a potholder. "Let's see what we've got."

It smelled more like ratatouille than pizza. And she'd ignored his question.

"Vivien?"

She pulled out the baked garden and set it on the stove. "Really, it's nothing. I just—overreacted. Let's eat."

Boone checked the weight of his Coke. He figured he had enough soda to get down one slice if he was judicious with it. She lifted the pizza cutter from the drawer. "Would you grab plates from the cupboard on the other side of the sink?"

"Sure." He pulled two out and she plopped a far-too-large slice onto his. A smaller one on her own.

He'd faced dangerous criminals. He could eat vegetables. Vegetables didn't kill. Probably.

She led the way to the table for two and he sat down across from her. Stared at the bubbling cheese.

"Should, uh, should we say grace?" Maybe he was postponing the inevitable first bite, but ever since he'd become a Christian, he tried to say grace before his meals.

"Oh." She looked up at him, her head tilted and her lower lip in her teeth. "Of course." As if it wasn't altogether foreign to her but not her everyday habit.

After he finished, he stared at the slice. Waited.

Vivien took a bite. Chewed slowly. "Mmm. This is actually really good."

"You sound surprised."

She lifted her shoulder in a coy shrug. "Well, you know—first-time recipe. You never know how something new is going to turn out."

Right.

He readied his Coke and took a bite. Chewed. Drank. Swallowed.

Didn't die. In fact, it wasn't half bad.

Vivien took another bite, her eyes staring down at her plate.

"You're worried about your play." It wasn't hard to read the stony expression on her face.

She looked up at him. "I need to figure out where in the world I can hold auditions. No auditions, no play. I'll still have to find a performance location, but right now, I just need an audition spot."

Boone took another bite. He actually liked the seasonings. Huh. "What kind of creative-literary venues or shops do you have in town?"

"The library. But they don't have space." She drummed her fingernails on the table top. "There's the Art Colony, but it's usually booked for weddings, classes, or special events. The bookstore…" Vivien jumped up and grabbed a notepad and pen from the kitchen counter, hope lighting her eyes. "Footstep of Heaven Bookstore might work."

"I'd think a bookstore owner would be willing to help out."

"You're a genius."

"You thought of it, not me. Is there enough space?"

"Yeah, we'd have to move a few displays around, but it's in a converted house and Mona has a really cool reading area. I think we could totally make it work." She jotted a note on the paper. "I'll ask her tomorrow—Mona Michaels, I mean. She owns the bookstore." Vivien took another bite of her pizza. "Mmm. Seriously. This is *so* good."

He sat across from her, seeing the light in her eyes, and for the first time realized that he didn't have anywhere to go, anything weighing him down.

So, this is what relaxation felt like.

He could get used to it. He took another bite of pizza.

"I need this play." The words were quiet. Plain. They lacked all the drama and playfulness he'd come to expect from her. "I have to find a way." She looked up at him, as if realizing she'd said it out loud, a determined set to her jawline.

And he knew she needed the play just like he needed that promotion. Because the world was watching. And neither one of them wanted to face failure.

He took another drink of soda and met her gaze across the table. Her eyes were bright with hope and gratitude and determination.

"Okay, Garbo. I'm here for five weeks. I'll help you get this play off the ground." He couldn't stop himself from offering what he knew she needed. And, well, he'd be lying if he didn't admit her company over the past twenty-four hours had made his sentence in the north woods tolerable. Maybe even enjoyable.

And anything was better than sitting still.

She tilted her head, swallowed, picked at a piece of eggplant. "You don't have to do that."

"I need something to do. It'll take a lot more than reclining on my deck to read that book and helping Caleb coach to fill my days. How can I help?"

She let out a long breath, as if thinking. "Well, after I talk to Mona, we'll need to change all the posters. Next up are the auditions. You can help me run those. Just getting the scripts out. Showing people where to go. Once it's casted, of course, there will be some sets to build."

Yep. Fill up that schedule because nothing made the time pass faster than a packed agenda. "I'll do it." He smiled.

And she smiled back.

Yes, this could be exactly the relaxation he needed.

Vivien waltzed into the Footstep of Heaven bookstore the next morning with purpose. If Mona Michaels was willing to let her use the bookstore after hours for the auditions and cast meetings, then she'd be able to get all the posters corrected in time. It would also buy her a few days to locate a performance venue.

And she had Boone, who'd help her. Boone, her new friend who made her think she could, in fact, pull off this show—even without a theater. She'd find a way to show her appreciation. Give back to him the way he'd given to her. She wasn't surprised when they'd finished lunch that he'd decided to go back to the football field while she'd headed off to Wild Harbor for her shift.

The bookstore resided in a remodeled Victorian house, complete with elegant peonies blooming along the stone walkway and a front porch that beckoned readers to slow down.

Vivien hopped up the steps, frowning at her own flyer with

the playhouse still listed on it. First things first. She needed a location for auditions.

Inside the heavy wooden door, the bookstore smelled like fresh print, hours-old coffee, and Mona's famous chocolate chip cookies. The sweet treats reminded her of Boone. How painful the consumption of her garden pizza had been for him.

She had to hand it to him, though. He had some good acting chops. By the end, he'd actually pretended to like it. He'd probably eaten worse in the Army at some point. Well, clearly the man needed someone to look out for him because he wasn't very good at doing it for himself. Not if his job and his health were now on the line.

Vivien found Mona chatting with a few customers and waited her turn. It seemed they were looking for exactly the right book for a twelve-year-old girl who loved horses. And, as usual, Mona knew precisely where to direct them.

She left them to peruse her recommendations and turned to Vivien. "Good morning." Mona wore her blonde hair down and the bold print of her T-shirt said "Reading is my superpower."

"Good morning." Vivien hugged Mona. "Tell me—how's Joe's latest manuscript coming along?"

Mona beamed, her green eyes bright. "He's on his final edits. Thanks for asking."

"Of course." She gave Mona another gentle squeeze before letting go. "I was wondering if we could use the bookstore to hold auditions for the community theater show. After hours, of course. It's scheduled for tomorrow night."

"Let me check our calendar. Every so often we schedule an evening book reading."

"Thanks." Vivien followed Mona to her desk.

"Is that the one you ordered scripts for?" She began typing on her keyboard.

"It is. Did they arrive?"

"They just came in this morning." She paused, looking at her computer screen. "Okay, it looks like we can make that work. I'm actually closing early tomorrow so Joe and I can eat with Gabe at the Garden." She opened a desk drawer and fumbled through a cache of paper clips, notepads, and enough pens to fill an office supply store. Mona pressed her lips together in focus. "Oh, that's right." She closed the drawer. "You'll have to get the key from Ella Bradley's soap shop. I gave her my spare."

Vivien looked over toward the open doorway into the other business the Victorian held. The drone of a power tool starting up cut through the quiet of the bookstore. "Sounds like she's in."

Mona laughed. "Yeah. Adrian's helping her with some work, but the shop's still open."

"I don't need a hard hat?" Vivien shot a glance toward the doorway and pressed her hand against her chest in dramatic fashion.

Mona laughed. "I think you'll be fine."

"Perfect. The last thing I need today is hat hair."

"Right? That's the worst."

Vivien picked up an upside-down bookmark from the display on the counter and placed it back right side up. "I really appreciate you letting me use the bookstore. Thank you."

"Well, I'm glad I can help. Let me grab those scripts for you."

Mona returned moments later and handed off the small box of scripts.

Vivien walked over to the new shop, Essentially Ella's, which resided in the former parlor of the old house. Instead of the earthy smell of clay from the last resident—potter Liza Beaumont, now Young—the lively scents of lemon and rosemary filled the space.

It looked less like a construction zone than it sounded. Ella's boyfriend, Adrian Vassos, stood running a power drill while Ella held a shelf in place, her blonde hair up in a ponytail.

Vivien waited for a pause in the noise before interjecting, "Hello?"

The pair turned in unison and Ella smiled. "Hi. Don't mind us, just a little shopkeeping."

"This looks fantastic." Vivien admired a nearby display of organic products. "By the way, I'm in love with the shampoo I picked up last month."

Ella smiled, her blue eyes bright with appreciation. "Thank you, Vivie. What brings you by today?" She released the shelf now mounted on the wall and wiped her hands, leaving a trail of sawdust on her jeans.

"Mona said I could pick up the spare front door key from you. We're going to hold auditions here at the bookstore tomorrow."

Ella swatted the dust from her jeans. "Sure. I heard something happened with the playhouse." She walked toward the counter with the cash register. "That's really unfortunate."

Vivien frowned at the memory of Gordy's steaming, red face. "It is. My friend Boone and I have been looking for a new location."

Adrian set down his drill, his eyebrows raised. "Boone Buckam? Helping with a play?"

Vivie turned her attention to Adrian. "Yes. You know him?"

"A bit. We're both from Kellogg. I may have been stopped by him in his professional capacity a time or two."

"Oh, is that so?" Vivien gave Ella a conspiratorial wink and put a hand on her hip.

"He does like cars. I think he just wanted to check out the Porsche." He set his level on the shelf and took a step over to check the bubbles. "I'm sure I wasn't speeding."

"Right."

"Here's the key." Ella dropped it into Vivien's hand. "I'm thinking I may show up and audition too."

"That would be incredible. I'd love to have you." She turned back to Adrian. "What about you? There's a great male lead that could use a guy like you." She sized up the man, who looked rather Deep Haven-y in his jeans, flannel work shirt, and Lowa boots.

"Oh, no, not me." Adrian pulled a hair band from his pocket, gathered his long, dark hair off his face, and wrapped the band into place.

"It's not too late to change your mind. You can think about it overnight."

"No, really."

"Well, you should probably fill me in on all the need-to-know stats of Detective Buckam."

Adrian paused. "He's got a few years on me, but you know—" He gestured at the space around him. "Even Kellogg, despite being bigger than Deep Haven, still has a small-town gossip network. Boone was a regular feature."

Yes, she knew exactly. And she'd bet Mr. Vassos knew more helpful nuggets than he realized. Adrian's words confirmed her guess that Boone was likely in his mid-thirties.

She put a hand on her hip and smiled. "So, what's his story? He seems a little lost without his job." She thought of his offer to help her with the play. Obviously, he was desperate for some-thing to do. "It's like the man has never actually taken a vacation in his life. And, you know, he's not married." Which still seemed like a very curious detail, even if she had used it to her advan-tage at Fish Pic.

Adrian picked up his measuring tape and marked off incre-ments on the wall. "I know he had a high school sweetheart named PJ. Something happened their senior year and she left town."

Well, how very interesting. "Do you know what happened?"

Adrian set down the measuring tape. "Well..."

Vivien clasped her hands together. Gave her best look of earnestness. "It's okay. You can tell me. I'm just—worried about him." She looked around the empty shop and gestured toward Ella and herself. "This is just between us."

"Oh, I don't know, Vivie."

"It's for his own good."

Adrian blew out a breath. "The way I heard it, she got into trouble. They burned down a building at the country club my dad belonged to."

"They *burned down a building?*" Oh my. But there was not a single chance on earth that Mr. Law and Order would have burned down a building. "No way. That can't be right."

Adrian shrugged. "It's what I heard. My dad was pretty upset about it at the time. And Boone's dad was the director of the country club, so...you can imagine..."

"Are we talking *arson?* Did anyone go to jail?"

"Whoa. Slow down, High Speed. It was apparently accidental. She came back to town ten years later and he put a letter in the paper claiming responsibility for the fire, but that's all I know."

"So, she came back to town?" There was an unexpected little plot twist.

"Yeah. But she ended up with someone else." Adrian grabbed his water bottle and took a drink. "Poor guy. I heard she even turned down Boone's marriage proposal. PJ moved on, but it seems like the guy's been stuck."

Ouch. What kind of madness must have consumed a woman who would turn down a marriage proposal from Mr. Blue Eyes? Of course, if she was the real troublemaker—and Vivien had zero doubt that she wasn't—then she didn't belong with Boone anyway.

"You don't say." Vivien rubbed the dull ache in her chest. No wonder he was still single. He was nursing a broken heart. And yet, this PJ woman was clearly no good for him. No good at all. Had he not figured that out yet?

Vivien did the quick math, clarity striking her brighter than a spotlight. Detective Buckam was in need of a relationship rescue. A little summer romance to heal his heart and the great outdoors to heal his body. Someone without drama. Without baggage.

Definitely *not* her. Ree was right. She *had* said she was done dating. She had no room in her life for any romance or the risks that came with it. Besides, she'd learned the hard way it was never good to mix work and romance. She was done letting history repeat itself.

She flipped through her mental Rolodex of eligible women. Not just any woman would do for Boone. He had health issues to take into consideration. A sordid past with a questionable troublemaker.

And then, a brilliant epiphany. The best-made match possible. Yes.

Bethany Strauss.

Beth, who worked in the library and had likely shelved multiple books in the wrong location while they were hanging flyers because she could hardly keep her eyes off Boone. Beth, who also happened to be her coworker at Wild Harbor Trading Post, and by the way who *also* taught kayaking. Beth—petite, mousy, kind, and utterly boring. Well, unexciting. In the best of ways, of course.

Yes, yes, yes. Beth was exactly the right person for Boone.

Vivien waved the key. "Thank you both, very much. You've been incredibly helpful." She embraced Ella. "By the way, I absolutely love your pink Converse. I have a pair of leopard-print ones buried in my closet somewhere. I need to pull those out."

"Oh. Thanks." Ella laughed with surprise. "You should. Those would totally suit you."

"You guys are the best."

"Sounds like we'll see you tomorrow night," Adrian said.

"I look forward to it!"

Vivien walked out, a lightness in her steps. The birds were singing. The sun was shining.

Commence Operation Summer Love.

# CHAPTER 5

*A*pprehension curled up Boone's spine. Oh, this counseling appointment would be fun. Not only had his bookmark *not* budged in the four days he'd been in Deep Haven, but he also had to prove to Rachelle Newman that he took his health—and his career—seriously.

He was fine, thank you very much.

In fact, he'd even jumped in with Caleb and Seb to run drills at football practice Tuesday evening. Worked with the quarterback, the backups, and receivers. Okay, so he hadn't meant to lecture them, but he could tell they were seeing themselves as underdogs. They were setting themselves up for failure in their minds before they even faced their first game.

So, he'd given them a little pep talk. And maybe, just maybe, it would sink in a little. Shift their thinking.

He parked his car outside the counseling office—a one-story, mustard-yellow ranch converted to commercial space.

His phone buzzed and he pulled it from his pocket. "Hey, Dad."

"Hi. I saw Steve Landry golfing at the club last night. Thought I'd give Kellogg's next police chief a call and see how his vacation is going." He suspected his dad stood in front of the floor-to-ceiling windows of his country club office, staring out across the green. Probably wearing his usual tan trousers and polo shirt, the latter stretched tight against his girth.

No pressure there. Of course he'd call it a vacation. He wouldn't want to admit the truth of it to anyone—that his so-called son was anything less than the poster boy of perfection. Okay, so Boone had maybe called it a vacation too, to save face.

"I'm doing fine."

"I always knew you'd work your way to the top. It looks like they've already got it posted and it closes in two weeks." His voice swelled with pride.

Maybe as police chief, Boone would finally be worthy to be called the son of Roger Buckam. Being in his thirties, it shouldn't matter anymore, but…well, old hopes were hard to shake.

Caleb's words from Sunday nudged him in the cool morning air. *I've learned you have to embrace the life you have, not the one you expected you'd have—or the one others expect you to have.*

"Thanks for letting me know." He could probably use the library's computers to complete and submit his application.

"You bet. I've got to get going. Need to find maintenance to look into a gopher issue near the ninth hole. Take care."

"You too." Boone hung up and mentally added the library to his to-do list for the day.

The door chimed when he entered and he sat down on the couch in the front room. A woman with gray hair swept into a pile on top of her head came down the hallway. She wore bright white walking shoes with her gray trousers and light blue button-up like she'd just returned from a power walk.

She smiled, her brown eyes bright. There was no mistaking the family resemblance between her and the chief, though. She extended a hand. "You must be Daniel."

"Ms. Newman." He stood and shook her hand. "Please, call me Boone."

She nodded. "You can call me Rachelle. Come on back." She led him down the hall, past several other offices to the last room, flipped the With Patient sign on the door, and pulled it closed behind her.

Patient? He wasn't a *patient.*

He should turn around and walk right back out. Except, his job—his future—depended on this. And more than anything, he wanted to get back to his life that'd nearly been derailed.

So, he'd do all the things. And he'd do them well.

The space was simply appointed with two overstuffed armchairs on either side of an end table taking up half the space. The table held a large vase of fresh black-eyed Susans and Shasta daisies. A box of tissues sat juxtaposed to the bright blooms. The other half of the office was anchored by an imposing wood desk. Ms. Newman grabbed a file from its tidy surface, took a seat in the far armchair, and gestured for him to sit in the matching one.

"So, how has your morning been?"

"Good." He smiled. Convincing. "Went for an early run."

"That's great to hear." She smiled, soft and kind. "You've been in town a few days now. How has that been?"

"I think it's gone well." He shifted in his seat. "I enjoyed the car show." Hopefully Ms. Newman hadn't seen him *in* the car show.

"I was wondering if that was you with Vivien Calhoun."

Oops. No joy there. He rubbed his palms down his thighs. "A new friend."

"New friends are good." She angled a look at him. "That's a beautiful Mustang you've got. Steve had mentioned it to me."

"Thank you." Cars he could talk about all day. "As long as I baby her, she does well."

"Did you restore the car yourself?"

"I did."

"Very nice." She cleared her throat and he knew the pleasantries were over. No more car talk. Time to dig in, emotionally eviscerate him. "Let's talk about what brings you to Deep Haven. The information I have is that there was a situation involving an elderly woman."

Situation. "She was murdered." He leaned forward, clasped his hands together in front of himself. "I was arresting the suspect and he resisted." He paused. Rachelle said nothing, as if waiting for more. "I was hit with an excessive force lawsuit." He sat back in his chair. "I was cleared of any wrongdoing by an independent investigation and the civil lawsuit was withdrawn when the video evidence was made public."

"Do you feel like you made the right choices?"

"Yes. I followed my training. And the fact that the murderer would try to accuse me made me—" He stopped speaking, unable to keep the steel out of his voice. "Angry." Oh, and there he went, painting himself like a madman.

"Angry?"

"Justifiably so."

"Law enforcement is a high-stress job. Do you have techniques to decompress? To manage your anger—whether it's justified or not?"

He remained silent, stilled by a realization. She *was* treating him like a *patient*.

"Boone?"

He shifted in the chair. "It used to be working on my car."

"And since the car's been restored?"

He looked up at her. "I put my energy into work, where it should be. To be the absolute best."

She nodded, as if his answer didn't surprise her. "What is it that tells you that perfection is the only acceptable result?"

"I don't know." He rubbed his palms together. "It has its rewards. Rewards are good." People didn't die.

She gave him a slow nod. "What would happen if you let things go sometimes?"

He lifted a shoulder.

"Sometimes we use perfectionism as a means to control how we are perceived in the world. By others, by ourselves. Do you feel like you need to control your life?"

"Look, I think it's important to require excellence. There's no reason for anyone to ever do less than their best."

"And your best is one hundred percent?"

"Absolutely." He hadn't meant for it to come out like that. Hard. Angry.

"Talk to me about the difference between perfectionism and excellence."

He frowned. "Is there a difference?"

"I'd like you to consider that there could be. If there were a difference, what would it be?"

"I don't know. I think anyone who strives for excellence does so with perfection in mind."

"Can there be something unhealthy about perfectionism?"

"I'm not a perfectionist."

She sat, her soft eyes on him. He squirmed in his seat.

"When I look at your records, I see a very strong structure. High performance. That can be a really good thing."

"I think so."

"But what would happen if you failed at something? Or a case didn't go the way you plan?"

He didn't answer.

She looked at him, like an interrogator sizing up the suspect. "I want you to think about a few things. You have choices, Boone."

Except, apparently not, since he'd been banished to Deep Haven and his entire career was in limbo. He'd never really had choices. Because every day of his life, he faced expectations. Others'. His own.

"You've got some excellent qualities. You're tenacious. You persist through adversity. You're loyal and committed. You do strive for excellence in everything you do."

He nodded. "That's true."

"Do you ever use that high standard to punish yourself? Continue to beat yourself up over it?"

He didn't answer.

"Those qualities need to be harnessed for good. Not used to punish yourself by staying stuck." She repositioned in her chair. "Before our next appointment, I want you to spend some time living in the moment. Being present in the world around you."

"Okay...?"

"And don't be afraid to try new things—even if you don't think you'll be the best at it."

He may have actually flinched.

"You don't have to be the best at any of it. Now tell me, what are you enjoying most about the book Steve gave you to read?"

Boone pressed his lips together and stared at the flowers, which looked entirely too cheery, all things considered.

She let the silence gnaw at him for a few moments. "Or should I ask, how is the reading going?"

He rubbed his hand across his chest, trying to alleviate the sudden tightness. "It's going."

"Looks like the reading plan has you through chapter three by now."

Boone looked up at her. "What reading plan?"

She paused, looked back to her notes. "Hmm. I have a note here that your treatment has a plan of a chapter per day. Don't you have that?"

*Treatment?* "No." But the fact that he'd actually read and reread the first paragraph no less than twelve times should still count for something. "Are we counting words or forward progress?"

She set down her pen and clasped her hands together. "Boone, are you taking this seriously?"

He sat up in the soft chair. "Of course I am."

"You don't have to be the best, but you do need to follow the plan. Steve has in the notes here that you need to finish the book. It's one of the requirements for me to clear you."

"I've been doing other things. He told me to get a hobby. Look, some guys in the coffee shop talked about kayaking. I'll do that, okay? I've also made some friends—you said new friends are good. And I'm helping with the football team."

"That's really good to hear. Those are exactly the kinds of activities I want to see you doing. But Steve really feels this book is important for you."

"I'll get it read."

"It sounds like you've got a lot scheduled for yourself. Do you think you're getting over scheduled for a man who's supposed to be on vacation?"

So, everyone was going to call it a vacation. "No."

"How do you feel about being sent here to Deep Haven?"

"I don't think it's necessary."

"When was the last time you took time away from work?"

He stared at the gray carpet, riffled through his memories. "I went to a Blue Ox game last season."

She tilted her head. "A guys' night out at a hockey game hardly counts as a vacation."

"They were really good seats." And, well, there had been a good fight. He met Rachelle's brown eyes. Yep. He'd leave that part out. Maybe it didn't count as a vacation—but it had given him a few hours to focus on something other than work.

She looked unconvinced. "What techniques do you use for stress management?"

Considering the charges that had been leveled against him, he figured the shooting range and boxing ring wouldn't pass her test.

"Um—" He paused. Thought. "I run."

"Right. That's good. Anything else?"

He adjusted his position in the chair. Scratched his temple.

"Okay. Well, are you finding time to relax? You've told me about several activities you're doing, but they don't necessarily translate to mitigating stress in your life."

"Sure. I mean, I think so."

"Let's check your blood pressure and see how it's doing."

He tucked his T-shirt sleeve out of the way while she wrapped the monitor cuff around his bicep. He took a few deep breaths, clearing his mind to calm. And then Vivien's laughter filled his head. The way she grabbed on to life. Swept him right into the whirlwind with her. And, yeah, the way even her eyes smiled did something to both soothe and excite him. There was definitely something about his new friend that he found a little irresistible.

Like the way she glowed when she talked about theater. The lilt in her voice when she teased him. All the things he shouldn't be noticing. Because, he reminded himself, she was just a *friend*. A friend he was finding he very much enjoyed spending time with. And well, nothing said he couldn't enjoy her feminine company on his vacation.

"Boone?"

"Huh?" By her expression, he'd missed something. Rachelle tugged on the cuff to remove it.

"I said your blood pressure looks better than the last report in your record."

Well, then.

She jotted in her notes. "Whatever you're doing, keep doing it. I think as long as you stay out of trouble, you'll be okay."

He nodded. "How would I get into trouble in this small town?"

She smiled and tucked a gray lock of hair behind her ear.

"I'm glad you're finding ways to enjoy yourself. I'll see you next week."

"Thank you." He stood and walked to the door.

"And Boone?"

He paused, his hand on the knob. "Yeah?"

"Read the book."

Maybe Boone should have spent more time with Rachelle, because he may well have lost his mind when he'd agreed to help Vivien with her auditions. He knew zero—absolutely zero—about theater. His minor foray into the world of drama in middle school hardly counted, especially since he'd only done it to be near PJ.

And it had been a nightmare.

Vivien had looked so desperate though, and offering his help felt like the right thing to do at the time. It had seemed like a much better idea than sitting idle in his cabin. Instead, he was moving furniture and shelves around in the Footstep of Heaven Bookstore for their after-hours open audition.

"Could you slide those chairs out of the reading nook? We'll use that space as the stage."

She said "we'll" like he wasn't a guy on vacation, leaving before the fall weather set in. But, he was. He was leaving. Heading back to Kellogg and, if he played it all the right way, stepping into the police chief position.

So, he shouldn't have noticed when she leaned in close smelling like jasmine. And on the drive over, he shouldn't have noticed how her sable hair had glinted with copper threads in the sunshine.

He gripped the arm and back of a thick reading chair. "Sure."

This, Boone could handle. He nudged the recliner a few

inches closer to the wall before standing to survey the rest of the bookstore.

If he painted it the right way, Rachelle might consider this compliance with her directives. There weren't any foot chases or crime scenes.

Nope. He perused the titles on the nearby shelf. Just classics and new releases—every one of which looked more interesting than the book he'd been given to read.

"Do you have the box with the scripts?" Vivien buzzed around the bookstore, eager with excitement.

"I put it over there." He pointed to one of the other chairs he'd moved from the reading nook.

A few early arrivals were gathering around the coffee and tea bar where Vivien had left a platter of cookies and a bowl of fruit. Boone recognized the woman from the library along with one of the guys from the Java Cup. Casper Christiansen had come in carrying several plates of cookies that he passed off to Vivien, then took up residence against the back wall.

She'd directed Boone to a spot near the door to hand out contact sheets for each auditioner to complete. The steady stream of people whittled his paper stack down to just a few.

When the clock hit six, Vivien gave him a nod and moved to the front of the group. "We're going to keep this relaxed and low-key. I want everyone to feel comfortable." She glanced at the group of seventeen, mostly women. "Is this the first time auditioning for anyone?" Nearly half the group raised their hands and she made a few notes on her clipboard. "Okay, well, don't be shy. We're all here to support one another." She picked up a script. "I wish I had a part for each and every one of you—and I do hope that if you don't get a part in this show, you'll still consider auditioning for future opportunities."

While she spoke, Boone moved around to the far side of the room so he wouldn't block the main walkway.

"Can you tell us more about the play?" the library lady asked, her voice as diminutive as her stature.

"Sure, Beth." Vivien opened the script. "*Then Came You* is a one-act play that takes place in small-town America. It's a romantic story about overcoming the past and finding hope in the future." She flipped through her script and shared the same details with the group that she'd shared with Boone in her kitchen two days before. She finished with, "I have to tell you, this is one of my favorite plays—not quite a musical, but it does have a few songs in it."

Boone tuned out the discussion and busied himself perusing the nearby book titles.

"My lovely assistant, Boone, will help me out."

Boone dropped the book of war stories he'd snagged from the New Releases shelf and it landed with a thunk. "Wait— what?" He stooped to pick it up and looked at her.

A few giggles and deeper laughs skittered across the room.

"It's okay—you already saw that half our group here hasn't auditioned before. You're going to show them how it's done." She pumped her fist like she'd just given the cheer squad a pep talk.

"Why can't they show you how it's done by doing it?" He placed the book back on the shelf. Hadn't she just said it was supposed to be relaxed and comfortable?

She wove all her fingers together except her index fingers, which she used to point to him. "Because they need someone to show them that there's nothing to be afraid of."

Oh, there was a whole lot to be afraid of. How had he been roped into this? He caught Casper's eye across the room.

The man leaned against the wall, arms crossed, a twitch of a smile at the corners of his lips.

Adrenaline pumped through his body as he faced down Casper from fifteen feet away.

Challenge accepted. How hard could it be?

Vivien held out a script for him and waited until he walked to the front of the group and took it. Then she flipped through her own script. "Okay, let's show them a fun scene. We're not going to use one of the audition scenes I've picked because I want to see how each of you interpret them." She stopped and skimmed a page. "Okay, if you'll turn to page thirty-five, we'll start at the second line from the top." She pointed to Casper and gestured for him to turn down the room lights, leaving only the reading nook where they stood under a soft glow.

"Really?" Nothing like being put in the spotlight. Again. Something Vivien clearly had a knack for.

"It's okay. We'll just go for a few lines. This is good for them —they'll be able to see how someone comes in cold and auditions. Just follow the blocking notes already in the script. They're in all caps. It's perfect." She grabbed two folding chairs that were leaning against the wall, opened them, and plopped them down next to each other.

Perfect. Right.

"You didn't have to follow me here." Her voice sagged, regret sharpening the edge of it. She slid into one of the chairs.

What happened to the count before the ball got hiked? Uh— she'd just dove right in. No cadence. And he was about ready to fumble. Boone slid his finger down the page to the third line. "Have you—have you been...crying?" He recovered. Read the blocking.

DYLAN SITS NEXT TO HER.

"Whatever are you crying about?" He plopped down on the chair next to her.

"It doesn't matter." She wrung her hands in her shirt hem and cast her eyes downward.

"It does to me."

She turned back to him, blinked, her eyes glossy with tears.

Really—whatever was Vivien crying for?

She swallowed. Sniffed. "In two days, you'll be gone and,

well, I'll still be here." She threw out her hand toward the space around them.

Oh. Okay. Acting.

She was close. So close her jasmine scent intoxicated him. So close he could see the silver flecks in her eyes. So close, he could feel her breath against his lips.

Script. Script. He looked down to read his blocking and next lines.

DYLAN PLACES A HAND ON HER CHEEK.

No help there. He paused before finally reaching up and cupping her face in his hand, his thumb rubbing across her cheek. "Is there any reason for me to stay?"

Vivien's eyes flicked to his lips. "Me." She met his gaze, his hand still brushing the silky skin of her cheek.

He could kiss her. *Wanted* to. He might have even ignored the script and just done it, except a cough from the back of the room shook him back to his senses and he jerked away from Vivien, dropped his hand. Looked at the script. Nope. Shoot.

Vivien jumped to her feet. "Perfect." She gestured for him to stand. "Thank you, Boone. That was…excellent." She motioned for the lights and someone flipped them back on.

The crowd sat in silence until a strawberry blonde in the front row clapped and others followed suit.

What was he doing? Just over four more weeks here until he'd be heading back to Kellogg. Back to his life. And he'd never been the guy for a passing romance. Besides, he'd been acting. Hello.

The applause died down and Vivien picked up the stack of scripts, handing half to him to distribute. She winked. "Good job."

And well, maybe it was time to step out of his comfort zone. *Live a little.*

He took one side of the group, handing out scripts to everyone who asked. They had quite a crowd of auditioners, family, friends, and a few curious passersby. Besides Casper and the woman from the library, Boone recognized Ree tucked in the back taking what looked like copious notes. Hadn't Vivien said something about her being a reporter?

He could only hope his stage performance would be omitted from the news.

Vivie handed out the last of her stack of scripts and returned to the front. "So, hopefully that's eased some of your apprehension. All you do is jump up here on stage and, just like Boone, read your lines like you mean them."

Well, maybe not exactly like he did, since he kinda *had* meant them. At least, a little. Which was totally ridiculous.

She moved one of the chairs from their reading-nook stage and Boone moved the other one out of the way. "If you didn't end up with a script, we'll pass them off as the other auditioners finish. We're going to use the scene on page seventeen, which has two females and one male, and the scene on page twenty-five, which has two males and one female. I'll need you to come up in groups of three, introduce yourself, and give me a quick snapshot of your experience. Any questions?"

Heads around the room shook in response and Boone made his way to the coffee pot and cookie bar.

"Okay then, as you come up, I'll take your forms, and we'll jump right in."

Three people stood and walked to the front. The girl from the library, the strawberry blonde from the front row, and... huh. Nathan Decker, who looked to be shoved out of his seat by a twenty-something young man who resembled Nathan in no small way.

This should be fun.

"I'm Beth Strauss," the woman from the library said, projecting her voice into the small space.

Next the strawberry blonde, whose freckles made her look

younger than her likely age. She stepped up with confidence next to Beth. "I'm Courtney Wallace."

Nathan introduced himself, and Vivien set up the scene, explaining to everyone present who the characters were and giving them the scene setup before letting them jump in.

Boone nearly dropped his coffee when Beth started speaking her lines. She projected her voice across the bookstore, believable inflection in her lines.

Courtney responded likewise, moving around the small stage area like she'd done it before.

When it came to real estate agent Nathan Decker, Boone wasn't so sure. No matter how well he delivered the lines, the age difference between him and the girls translated more to fatherly advice than peer counsel.

When they'd finished, Vivien scribbled notes on the pages in her lap and looked up at the trio. "Really good job speaking from the diaphragm, Beth."

The woman smiled at Vivien's praise, a hint of pink coloring her cheeks. "Thank you," she said, her voice back to its usual library-quiet decibels.

"All of you, great job."

They nodded and took their seats while the next three hopped up there, introduced themselves, and started the scene again.

Jason Decker, apparently Nathan's son, took to the script like a seasoned professional, which left one of the women—Jennifer, maybe—a bit flustered playing opposite of the tall, curly-haired guy. The other woman, a blonde named Ella, took to the role naturally. Not quite as polished as Jason, but she definitely pulled off a convincing first read by Boone's standards.

The attendees rotated through, with several of the men filling in multiple times. A twenty-something named Adam volunteered to take several turns. He had an ease about him that diffused the nerves of several castmates.

While there was a large pool of women wanting to participate, there was a shortage of men who were auditioning. In fact, there'd only been four. The rest were either here as support or just to watch the show—and no amount of persuading from Vivien brought any of them to the stage.

Surprising, since he'd seen how convincing she could be.

When the last group left their makeshift stage area, Vivien stood in front of the crowd.

"I can't tell you all how thrilled I am to see so many of you here tonight. Willing to step up and try something new, for some of you. Willing to share the stage with your peers, coworkers, and community members. This is going to be really tough for me to cast and I hope that any of you who don't get parts will not let it dissuade you from future auditions. I can't even tell you how many times I've auditioned and *not* gotten the part. I'll be posting the cast list on the library community bulletin board by Friday evening. The first cast meeting and rehearsal schedule will be on the posting."

A hand raised in the middle of the pack. "Has a venue been located?"

"Oh, great question. We don't have our venue yet, but I hope to hold rehearsals most evenings so we'll be ready for the Labor Day weekend performances. We'll keep the cast up-to-date on the location. The show will run Thursday, Friday, and Saturday." She picked up her clipboard and jotted down notes. "Any other questions?" She looked out across the group. "No? Well, then, please eat some cookies and take a cup of coffee with you on your way out. We can't let any of these goodies go to waste."

Everyone stood, mingling, grabbing cookies. The room buzzed. Adrian wove his way in from the front door like a fish swimming upstream.

"You're late," Boone said, taking a bite of cookie. "Auditions are over."

Adrian grabbed a chocolate crinkle from the platter. "In that case, I'm right on time." He gestured toward the woman named Ella, who'd played a convincing Hannah Jones, the truth-telling best friend. "Picking up my girlfriend for our dinner date." The blonde looked up at that moment and smiled at Adrian.

Ah. That explained a lot about why Adrian was integrating himself into Deep Haven life.

Boone turned to watch Vivien work, watched her say goodbye to each of the participants with a bright glow of enthusiasm. He rolled their scene over in his mind. *Is there any reason for me to stay?* She looked up at that moment from across the crowded room and gave him a wink and a smile.

Yeah. The more he watched her, the less it felt like they'd been acting.

# CHAPTER 6

*I*f Vivien had any hope of pulling off her play, she needed a venue. Fast. Otherwise, there'd be no show and, once again, her failure could go right up in the bright lights on the marquee.

Vivien Calhoun. Wannabe actress who failed not once. Not twice. Three times.

Take a bow.

Not a chance. Not when they'd had a packed house—well, bookstore—for the auditions.

Vivien wandered along the harbor, the seagulls taunting her with their endless cries.

Maybe that hadn't been the best scene to pick for Boone. Not when it had landed their lips within inches of each other and there'd nearly been an unscripted kiss.

Except, he was leaving and she still hadn't figured out what she was doing with her life. She was not in the market for a romantic relationship. Nope. Not her. Because relationships meant vulnerability and that—that was something utterly terrifying.

She'd rather hide behind her stage persona. After all, she'd spent a large chunk of money on acting lessons, and she imagined she was more red carpet than snow-shoveled-sidewalk.

She'd woken up to another message from Joslyn—this time a voicemail. She'd made herself call Joslyn back. Forced herself to leave a message before she deleted the garbled words Joslyn had left. Yet another rant about danger and roses and she couldn't even say what else because the message had cut off.

No way. She wouldn't let Joslyn or Sabrina or anyone else leave her empty-handed again. And she certainly wouldn't add stress to Boone's life by mentioning it.

She'd taken this walk along the harbor, hoping to clear her mind. Tried to come up with a solution to her venue problem. Instead, she felt like the listless boats, rocking, tugging at their anchor lines, but not going anywhere.

She'd resisted the desire to TP Gordy's house in the early morning hours. Or let the air out of his tires so he had to hoof it around town. Even though the stout man deserved it and the extra walking would certainly do his health some good.

See? She could love her enemies. Look out for them.

Her phone buzzed in her pocket and she fished it out to check the number on the screen.

*Ravil.*

And, just like that, Joslyn's betrayal curled into her memory.

Answer? Don't answer?

What would he want?

Ravie had been special. She'd thought, maybe this time, she'd found a good one. The guy who loved her for who she was.

She walked to the end of the sidewalk, looked out across the dark gray lake that whipped up foam along the rocks, and pressed the green button—almost wanting it to be too late to answer.

"Hello?"

There was an intake of air from the caller. Then, "I—I wasn't sure you'd answer. Vivien, how are you, my dear?" Just the faintest Slavic accent. He'd worked hard to lose it completely. And it still wheedled into her, pulled her back in time to those long hours of rehearsal followed by cozy chats in front of the fire. Ice skating in Central Park.

"What do you want, Ravil?" She didn't use his nickname. Wouldn't give him that satisfaction.

"Vivie, honey, why do you ask me like that?" She could imagine him sitting in the theater office, his suit perfectly tailored. Not a lock of his dark waves out of place. Always camera-ready with his strong jawline and soft gray eyes.

She pressed steel into her voice. "I'm not your dear or honey, Ravil." Nope. Because Ravil had turned out to be just one more man who had let her down.

"What could I say to you, to get you to come back to New York? Huh? You know the stage loves you. The audience—they love you."

"I—I'm not coming back." The lure of the stage snagged her words. Caught in her throat. And she couldn't help herself... "Not now."

"So, you *do* miss it." Hope brightened his tone. "I knew you couldn't be gone for good."

She swallowed. Watched a butterfly land on the honeysuckle.

"I'm busy here. I've got commitments." At least, if she could get this play off the ground. The wind lifted her hair, tugged against her. She pulled her cardigan around herself.

"What could be more important than getting you back on the stage? I would make it worth your while. Come on, what does that little town have that you can't have in New York? There's no fame, no fortune. No fans calling your name."

Yeah. She'd been on her way to being someone. She'd had fans. The fortune? Well, not so much. But she didn't do it for the money.

Boone swept through her mind like the petals from the

nearby coneflowers, tugged by a gust of wind. The wall of strength she'd run into when she'd fled the playhouse three days before. The one-sided smile he had. Except, he was a friend. Passing through on his way back to the career he'd dedicated his life to.

And what he needed was someone like Beth. Demure. Gentle. Law-abiding.

"You have Joslyn." In more ways than one.

He paused so long she looked to see if the call had dropped. "Joslyn didn't work out. She doesn't have what you have."

Joslyn's text and voice message lurked in Vivien's mind. *Ravil fired me too.* It seemed hard to believe Ravil would really fire her. She'd stolen his attentions. Taken Vivien's role on stage. Vivien wanted to ask more—to find out what was really going on. Except, well, maybe now she knew. Joslyn was trying to keep her out of New York. And expressing any interest would just encourage Ravil.

"Please, Viv. I need you. The show needs you."

Vivien ran through the cast list in her head. "Danielle can do it."

"She doesn't have your star power."

Vivien laughed. "Oh, she does. Just ask her. She'll tell you." Danielle Berteau would tell anyone who'd listen what a superstar she was.

"Vivie, please."

She let out a breath. Because, for all the terrible ways it had ended with Ravil, he'd once been her hero. Protecting her from the dark side of the theater. The predators looking for a starry-eyed girl like herself.

"I've gotta go."

"Wait—"

"No, Ravil. I—I can't." She disconnected the call. Pressed her fingers against her temples.

"You okay?" Issy approached from the Java Cup, tugging her

sweater over her T-shirt. "I saw you on my way to the car. Looked like you could use a friend."

Vivien smiled, waved off the concern. "Oh, it's nothing."

Issy gave her a look. "That didn't look like nothing."

Right.

Vivien let out a breath. Maybe she did get tired of pretending all was well in her world. "Do you ever feel like you just can't move forward? Like you're somehow stuck replaying your past?"

Issy put a hand on her hip, raised a brow. "Really, Viv?" But her eyes were soft, without reproach.

Duh. Vivien cringed. That's why she preferred following a script when it came to all the heart-to-heart stuff. "I'm sorry— oh, Issy—I didn't mean…"

Issy reached out. "I'm giving you a hard time. It's okay." She gave Vivien's arm a soft squeeze.

Yeah, Issy would know exactly how Vivien felt—even more so. She'd spent a year trapped in her house battling agoraphobia after the car crash that had killed her mom and paralyzed her dad.

"Sometimes I feel like the past keeps dragging me back." She gestured toward the phone. "That was my old director, Ravil. He asked me to come back to New York City."

"Our past can be what we make of it. We can choose to be stuck in it, perpetual *Groundhog Day*, or we can embrace scripture. Know that God does not give us a spirit of fear, but of love."

"I don't even have a venue for the summer play. Or have a place to hold practices."

Issy took a drink of her coffee. "So, the playhouse is for sure off the table?"

"Oh, yeah. Gordy was emphatic about that."

"What about the church? You could probably use the fellowship hall or rehearse in one of the classrooms."

In the wind, the dull rumble of an engine lifted off a boat coming into harbor.

"Hmm. The church. That could work." She looked at her watch. "I need to meet Boone soon. I told him I'd show him a great spot to unwind." She glanced at Issy's coffee. "That smells good. Maybe I'll grab two to go."

Issy reached out, squeezed Vivien's hand. "You're going to do this play and it's going to be fantastic. I'll catch you later."

"Thanks."

By the time Boone pulled up outside the Java Cup, Vivien had shaken off Ravil's call, secured the church for the play, finished her coffee, and double-checked the Wild Harbor work schedule.

He had the Mustang's top down and looked relaxed in cargo pants, his crisp white T-shirt molded to his body.

She stood by the passenger door. "Can I drive?"

Boone's head jerked up like she'd just asked for his firstborn.

"Come on. I got you a coffee." She held the drink out to him. "I'll have you know, this wouldn't be the first vintage Mustang I've driven. Trust me. Not a scratch."

Boone looked at the cup. "Thanks. You didn't need to do that."

"Please? Can I drive?"

He hesitated before getting out of the car and walking over to the passenger side, pausing next to her. "Do I need to run your record first?"

"Funny. Take your coffee and get in."

"You promise you'll be careful?" He took the cup. Made sure the lid was snapped on tightly.

"Yes." She held up her right hand. "I, Vivien Calhoun, do so promise to take the utmost care—"

"Fine, fine. Just get in. Everyone is watching. And you really didn't have to get me a coffee."

Vivien smiled to the passersby who gave her oath swearing a

side-eye. "It was no trouble at all." Besides, someone had to make sure he wasn't drinking the whip-topped dessert drinks blended with ice and enough sugar to put Willy Wonka out of business. "Now, get in."

He obeyed, swung the door shut, and took a small sip of his coffee before wedging the cup between his thighs, his hand holding it securely in place.

Vivien dropped her sunglasses down over her eyes. "Buckle up, Buttercup. I have a surprise for you."

"Where are we going?" He slid his hand onto the door armrest, his fingers gripping the vinyl handle.

"Somewhere." She laughed. "I've solved my venue problem. Well, Issy solved it. We'll use the church."

"That sounds like a good plan."

She paused to look for traffic, then accelerated out of the parking lot.

"Easy, Danika. See those red octagons? They actually mean stop, which, you may not realize, means a complete and total lack of forward motion."

She shot him a wide grin. "You haven't told me how your appointment went yesterday. Sorry—I kind of had tunnel vision about the auditions."

"Ehh." He relaxed his grip on the door handle. "Moderately better than a root canal."

"Oh, that good, huh?" Vivien loved the feel of the Mustang. It wasn't modern-car smooth. No, it required finesse. And that said something about its owner.

She cranked up the radio and it wasn't long before Boone's fingers were tapping the beat on his coffee lid and he joined her on the chorus—maybe despite himself because he gave a shy smile and stopped when she glanced over.

She pulled into Honeymoon Bluff, parked the car facing the vast expanse of Lake Superior, and cut the engine. "I got a call from New York this morning."

The sun shone down, turning the lake to a rich blue. The wind reaped the pine scent from the trees.

"About?"

"I was asked to come back to the show. Ravil said Joslyn—the understudy who'd taken my role—is out."

The water sparkled in the late-morning light. "Ravil?"

"Ravil Kozlovsky. He's Russian. Brilliant actor. Great director. Terrible boyfriend."

Boone visibly winced. "Of course, a Russian," he muttered, followed by something unintelligible.

"What?"

He shook his head. "Nothing. Your ex-boyfriend called you and asked you back to New York City?"

"Yeah. Can you believe the nerve?" Vivien opened the car door and stepped out onto the gravel. Walked toward the overlook. Boone joined her, coffee cup in hand. "He's a lousy, two-timing scoundrel." And there was that familiar sting. The nausea. The choking sense of betrayal.

"You okay?"

She looked up, found Boone's eyes on her. "Yeah. I'll be fine. I just—I just have a history with men and it's not a good one. Ravil—he's no different." She crossed her arms, leaning against the railing. "He chose Joslyn Vanderburg over me. Decided she would get him what he wanted. When that didn't work out, he apparently dropped her too. Now he wants me back. Like, why would I go back to that?" She looked over at her companion, considering whether or not she should share Joslyn's cryptic messages. His features had softened over the past few days. In fact, he had a lightness about him.

Law and Order was here to relax. She stuffed Joslyn's messages right back where they belonged.

"So, you're not going back?" Boone took a sip of coffee. The wind played with his blond hair, the sleeves of his shirt.

"No. I'm not going back. I—we—have a show to put on. I

told him to use one of the others—Danielle Berteau has been an understudy for several shows. There's a girl with 'diva' written all over herself." She shifted her position against the rail. "What about you? Mr. Not-a-Serial-Killer." Her conversation with Adrian in the bookstore lingered in her mind. *I heard she even turned down Boone's marriage proposal. PJ moved on, but it seems like the guy's been stuck.*

Though, he did have those lethal blue eyes.

"Oh, not much to tell."

Right. "You must have a girl back home." She prodded, knowing he didn't.

"No. No girl." He pinched his lips together.

"That's it? That's all you've got? I've gotten more information out of sidewalk mimes than that."

He was silent a long time. Then, "There was a girl a long time ago. The first time I got the nerve to ask her out was in seventh grade. I asked her to the winter dance in the most seventh-grade-boy way. Mumbled it on the school bus."

"Lucky girl."

"She said no." He took a few steps farther down the viewpoint railing. Glanced up at a red-tailed hawk soaring overhead. She joined him and he turned back to her. "But I'm not one to give up. Even though she was way out of my league, I asked her again three years later to homecoming."

"You waited *three years* for that girl to say yes?" Oh, this was far worse than she thought.

He laughed, though. Rich and warm and tender. "I did. And she said yes."

"Well, it was about time. What happened to her?"

"We dated all through high school, despite the fact that her mom never approved. Then, I made a mistake. Let her take the blame for something stupid. I wasn't even a smoker but, somehow, I made a total mess of our senior prom night. Tried to be cool. Caught a building on fire. But PJ—that's her name—she was arrested for it."

Oh no. Clearly, she'd been wrong about his innocence.

He looked at her, a little wrecked. "I don't know that I've ever forgiven myself for it. That was the day I destroyed our relationship."

"She didn't forgive you?"

"She left town. I chased her across the entire country, hoping to beg for forgiveness. I returned home, empty-handed. Left on my football scholarship, then got injured. Went into the Army."

She nodded. "And you met Caleb."

"Yes. And then, about ten years ago, PJ came back to town. I'd waited all those years to apologize to her. Hoping we had a future. She accepted the apology, but it was too late." He shoved his hands into his pockets. "She moved on."

The rejected wedding proposal.

"I'm sorry it didn't work out."

He nodded, as if to shrug it off.

Few men loved like that. None of the men she'd dated. Not Ravil.

Definitely not her father.

That kind of love was rich and passionate and poetic. A man who waited ten years. Ten. So, yeah, either PJ was crazy to have turned down that kind of love or God had a different plan for Boone. And, if Vivien played it right, maybe Operation Summer Love would help Boone find that special someone who could love him back—or, at least, show him the possibilities.

"It sounds like you really did need a change of scenery."

He turned, his eyes settling on her. Smiled. "Yeah. The change of scenery has actually been good."

"Isn't this beautiful? I wanted to show it to you so that whenever you were feeling overwhelmed, you could sneak away to this amazing place." She nodded toward the lake. "You should also try kayaking. It's very relaxing."

"Casper mentioned that."

"There's nothing quite like the open water, being so close to it. It's like you become part of nature."

"You sound very experienced."

"I work at Wild Harbor Trading Post." She winked. "You know, the acting gig doesn't pay much and I'd be a terrible waitress."

"So, I'm adding kayaking to my agenda."

"Yes." She opened her phone and scrolled to her photo of the Wild Harbor shift schedule to double-check. "How about Friday morning? I have just the instructor for you."

"Sure."

Vivien restrained herself from throwing her hands over her head in the universal "touchdown" signal. Instead, she met his smile. "Shall we head back? You probably have football practice."

"I do." He walked past her to the driver's side. "But this time, I'm driving."

That's what he thought.

The sunshine cast crisp shadows across the field. Boone inhaled the fresh scent of mowed turf and finessed his grip on the football before giving it a short throw to Caleb. If only he could keep his brain focused on football. Not Vivien. Not the Russian ex-boyfriend who'd asked her back to New York City or the distant memories that stirred for him in the likes of PJ's Russian brother-in-law.

He'd thought twenty-four hours might have cleared his brain. Nope.

The throw flew over Caleb's head. Well, at least he'd been able to get his application for chief submitted. Now, he just had to bide his time in Deep Haven until he could get back to the real world. He took off to retrieve the ball.

Caleb held out a hand. "I got it."

Boone took the opportunity to watch the players on the field. "Keep the ball on the tips, Sam," Boone called to the backup quarterback. The boy nodded. He could tell they were trying to implement some of what he'd shown them the day before.

Caleb scooped up the ball. "Okay, I know you can throw better than that. I saw some good throws earlier in practice. You *were* telling the truth about having been the Kellogg High quarterback, right?"

"Sure, Rocket. Don't you have it all on target?" Boone laughed. "You know—it's been a few years."

Caleb scrubbed his hand over his face, only partially concealing his smile. "I don't think that's the problem."

Yeah. But there'd been something about being on the field, working with the kids at several of their practices that had bolstered Boone. Renewed his spirit.

Caleb blew the whistle. "Okay, guys, let's wrap it up." The players began gathering equipment and gear off the field.

"Thanks, Coach Buckam." Johnny Dahlquist, his blond hair darkened with sweat, walked by with Sam.

"You're welcome." Boone stood behind the players as they each took a knee.

Johnny tossed a ball to Boone and he and Sam gathered into a jumbled circle with the rest of the team.

"I saw that last pass Boone threw," Seb said to Caleb. "Are you sure this is the guy we want to help coach the team?" He grinned as he dropped a bag of footballs and cones along the sideline before stepping into position for one last huddle with the team. The hem of his well-worn World's Best Donuts T-shirt hung in tatters over his athletic shorts.

Caleb looked at his players kneeling and patted Seb's shoulder. "Tomorrow we'll split you up for the blue-and-white scrimmage game. But remember—you're all one team. The scrimmage is just for fun. Kickers, take a dinner break and then meet us back here at six."

The team gave a single clap in unison. "Okay. Go ahead and get your gear stowed. We'll see the rest of you back in the weight room tomorrow morning." Another clap.

*Stay focused.* Boone's brain had been a muddle all morning at the prospect of kayaking with Vivien. Oh, sure, he'd played it off. They were friends.

Except she left a vacancy in her absence. Wheedled her way under his skin. Brightened his day.

Like when she'd handed him the script at the auditions and asked him to read the male lead. How she'd nearly kissed him. Okay, maybe he'd almost done the kissing. The way she spoke to him—flirted with him, even—but he couldn't tell anymore. He had to face it—she was a flirt. But she *had* asked him to go kayaking. So, there was that.

And when she'd asked, his heart had reached for something his brain wasn't ready for. Because, for the first time in his adult life, he could feel what he'd been missing and it had thrummed through every part of his body, electrifying his world.

The truth was, it felt good to be invited. Wanted. Being with her always felt a little exhilarating.

Oh, what was he thinking? He wasn't sticking around. In four more weeks, he'd be back in Kellogg, vying for the police chief job.

"You want to talk about it?" Seb tossed a ball at Boone. "Whatever's on your mind?"

"Nope." Boone fumbled the ball and snagged it off the grass.

"This wouldn't have anything to do with Vivie, would it?" Caleb waggled a brow and walked out several yards for a pass.

Boone sent another high throw at him. Caleb just barely managed to jump and pull it in with one hand. Boone shook his head. "Man, I'm sorry. I don't know what's wrong with me today."

Caleb held the ball. Gave him a look. "Really? You have *no* idea? None whatsoever?"

Boone shrugged.

"I'll tell you what." He used the ball to point at Boone. "I think you're rusty."

"You know I haven't played in years."

"I don't mean football. I think your relationship game is rusty." He shot the ball to Seb.

Seb caught it. "From what I've heard around town, that might be it."

"Oh, so, what? You two are replacing Chuck Woolery?"

"Who?" Seb threw it again.

Caleb laughed. "Some old television dating show host from the eighties and nineties. I'm not even sure how you remember it." He shook his head. "I've got Issy, though. You know she used to have a radio talk show all about finding your match."

"I've dated."

"I don't mean PJ," Caleb said.

Oh, he just *had* to say her name. Boone caught the ball. Held it. "*Not* PJ. I've dated other women. And, let's not forget, I'm only here for four more weeks."

"Those lawyers and ER nurses don't count." Caleb walked up and plucked the ball out of Boone's hands. "Actually, let's go ahead and get the cones set up for the kickers."

Seb grabbed the stack of orange cones from the bag and they walked out onto the field.

"What's wrong with them? They're about the only women I meet. And, I'll have you know, there was a reporter too." Boone took several cones and began setting them up parallel to Seb's. He wasn't exactly Romeo when it came to the dating scene. The only time he perused dating profiles or clubs was for an investigation. "Unless I'm arresting them and, well, that's an automatic disqualification."

"Well, first of all, none of them have stuck around, have they?"

Okay, well, he had a point. Except... "For the record, I'm usually the one doing the breaking up."

"And why do you think that is?"

Because, if he were honest, none of them ever captured his attention. They were nice. Kind. Several were even Christian.

But they didn't spark any part of his imagination. Maybe they had too much in common. The last thing he wanted to do was sit around debating the merits of a probable cause affidavit over dinner.

No. They didn't make him laugh.

Didn't make him plunge into new things like...kayaking. Or helping with a playhouse show.

Caleb dropped the last cone and made his way back to Boone. "Seems like you're keeping yourself busy."

"I got my application turned in." Boone puffed up his chest. "You may be looking at Kellogg's next chief."

"Is that really what you want?" Caleb folded his arms across his chest. "I mean, I totally support you if it is."

Boone nodded. "Yeah. Of course."

*Embrace the life you have, not the one...others expect you to have.*

This was different. His ticket to public approval. Even though he'd told Caleb several years ago about his mother's past and her rehab after Boone got shot, he probably couldn't quite grasp what it was like to grow up in the shadow she'd cast. How many times he'd had to hide her bottles of gin and vermouth as a teen. Keep her from answering the door when her words had slushed together and her legs swayed. Knowing every time he stood next to his father, the question everyone had.

And wondering if his dad had the same question—was he really Boone's father?

Thankfully, Caleb moved on to a new subject.

"So, now that you've helped with a few practices, what do you think of the team?"

"They're young, huh?" Boone reached his right arm across his chest, pulling it with his left hand into a stretch against himself before alternating arms.

"They are." The three walked back to the sideline. Caleb picked up the ball. Stared at the field. He wore what Boone had come to know as his standard uniform. Athletic pants and a T-shirt. "What do you think, Boone?"

Boone pressed his lips together in thought, then offered, "I think you've got some talent. They just need direction and discipline. Focus."

Caleb nodded. "I agree with that. It's like they don't quite believe who they are yet. They need to quit trying to prove they're good enough and just let their natural talent shine. Know their strengths and address their weaknesses."

Boone nodded. "Are there more ways I can help?"

"Maybe just get in there at a few more practices to help the quarterbacks with some skill drills." Caleb tossed the ball back to Boone. "You've always had a knack for relating to people."

"I can do that, though I'm also committed to helping with the community theater event—" He stopped himself. Too late, judging by the silly grins of his companions.

Seb smiled. "So, the rumor you're also helping Vivien with her play is true." He rocked back on his heels. "I heard you even auditioned for it—but I didn't believe it."

"Oh, I sure catch a lot of flak for that." Boone held out a hand. "For the record, I am behind the scenes. I just helped her do a demonstration at the auditions."

"Right." Caleb and Seb exchanged a look. "Okay."

Caleb sat down on the bench and rubbed his thigh.

"Next Friday night's the big scrimmage." Seb looked at Boone.

"Got any great plays up your sleeve? An ace to pull when things are in a tight spot and you're down to the wire?" Caleb eyed Seb.

Seb smiled. "I'm not telling if I do."

Oh, that was right. Seb and Caleb squared off against each other in the blue-white scrimmage.

Caleb laughed. "Anything like Quarterback Chaos?"

"I still can't believe you used it against me during our first game."

"It was a good play. Not the kind you can use all the time—but, on those rare occasions."

Seb nodded. "Those are the best. I'll never forget the first time Coach Presley used it." He laughed.

"That's Issy's dad—he was the former coach," Caleb clarified.

Boone nodded.

"We won homecoming with it against a team we never thought we'd beat."

"Nice," Boone said.

"Everyone was screaming—the town went wild. I'll never forget Vivie—she was freaking out. She was a cheerleader." Seb started laughing. "She was running at the team, jumped on top of the pile like we'd just won the Super Bowl." He shook his head. "Oh, my word. That girl." He looked at Boone. "You picked a real firecracker. There's no one like Vivie."

Boone smiled. Well, maybe it was time to just roll with it. Admit that she had done more than pique his interest. "She *is* pretty fantastic." He looked at his watch. "And, speaking of—I need to get going. I have a kayaking lesson."

"Oh, let me guess. You're heading over to Wild Harbor?" Seb waggled his brow.

"Interesting." Caleb gave Boone a soft punch in the shoulder, eyeballed him with a self-satisfied smirk on his lips. "It just so happens that Vivien's an instructor there."

Boone wasn't the kind of guy to flush. Get embarrassed. Yet, there was annoying heat on his face. "Yeah. I know. Thanks, 'Chuck.'"

"Is this a *date?*" Caleb looked to Seb, who wore a similar smirk. "Maybe he isn't as rusty as I thought."

"Maybe not," Seb answered. "As long as he knows what he's getting himself into."

Boone laughed. "I'll see you gentlemen later—after you run that team of yours through a few drills this afternoon."

"Can't wait to hear all about it." Caleb gave him a pat on the back on his way past.

And, well, maybe those were first-date jitters he felt on the drive to Wild Harbor Trading Post. He imagined the camera-ready Vivien pursuing athletic endeavors. Somehow, out of all his outdoor activities, kayaking was the one thing he hadn't tried. He wasn't the guy who took risks unless it involved chasing suspects or leads.

Not putting his heart out there. But he'd found he couldn't help himself. He'd step out of his comfort zone for her. Even his counselor thought it was a good idea—though he was pretty sure Rachelle meant the kayaking part, not the Vivien part.

There was something about her—both beautiful and capable —that he couldn't resist.

He entered Wild Harbor and let his eyes adjust to the interior lights. Like so many North Shore outdoor shops, the merchandise was in seasonal transition. Clearance swimsuits hung near winter coats and wool gloves.

"Hey, Boone, you made it." Vivien came out from behind the counter, all smiles. She wore an off-the-shoulder blouse and a skirt.

It didn't quite look like kayaking attire.

"Hey, Viv," he said. He looked at her feet.

She wore sparkly leather sandals. Nope. It didn't take one ounce of detective skill to see she wasn't dressed for kayaking.

"Ready to kayak?" she asked and then glanced at a petite

woman, barely five feet tall, who stood in a dry suit behind a rack of brightly colored life jackets, guiding what appeared to be a family of tourists through the selection and fitting process. "I'll tell Beth you're here."

Beth? The library employee?

He caught a glimpse of her face when she looked up at him with big green eyes.

# CHAPTER 7

*N*othing soothed the heart and soul like a sweet, new romance. The adrenaline. The excitement. The sheer joy of it all.

That's exactly what Boone needed.

Vivien cast a gaze across the Wild Harbor Trading Post's newest collection of outdoor gear to where Beth was helping a family fit their children with life jackets for their vacation. Yes. Summer love—carefree, charming, and deliciously ephemeral.

Law and Order had no idea how grand a day he was about to have. The thought of it bubbled up with the same anticipation of an audition.

"It looks like she's with customers right now, so I'll wait. But you look good today."

He shoved his hands into his pockets. "Everyone keeps telling me how fantastic kayaking is. I'm not sure what to think." He wore hiking pants and a long-sleeve T-shirt. A smattering of whiskers darkened his jawline and he set those blue eyes on her. And then, the smile. The megawatt, Hollywood-worthy smile. "I'm looking forward to finding out."

She blinked. Swallowed. Beth. Beth. *Beth*. Beth was the right girl for Boone. Vivien could write that script herself—the worn-out detective finds renewal and love in the company of a sweet, quiet woman. "You're going to love it." She went back around the counter.

Boone pulled out his wallet.

"Oh, no. Today's an introductory lesson. On the house. Just sign off on the waiver form."

He tucked his wallet back into the zippered pocket of his pants and took the pen, scribbled his signature on the line of the form.

"Hey, Boone." Casper Christiansen appeared from the storeroom with a stack of shoeboxes he plopped on the countertop. "How's it going?"

"Good. I decided to buy in on all the local fun and give kayaking a go." He met Vivien's eyes across the counter. "Everyone says it's a must do."

Casper glanced at the calendar next to the cash register, looked at the lesson appointment schedule. He raised a brow at Vivien and she flashed him a smile and took the waiver from Boone.

"Looks like Vivien's getting you all set up for your lesson with—"

"I am," Vivien interjected. She held out a hand to Casper. "I've got this all under control."

Casper frowned, shot her a look.

Well, he clearly didn't understand the workings of a matchmaker. A matchmaker had to be adept. Subtle. Not scare off the prospects.

Just give the gentle suggestion, present the opportunity, and let nature take its course.

She turned to Boone. "Follow me."

She led him down the aisle to Beth as the family of five departed for the cash register with their bright yellow life vests.

She held out her hands, Vanna White–style. "Here's your instructor, Beth." Ta-da.

If only she had the confetti. The flashing lights.

Beth wrung her hands together, her feet looking stuck solid like she'd landed in spring mud. Clearly, if she was going to make la petite vixen out of Beth, the girl was going to need encouragement. A lot of it.

Vivien gave her a little nudge toward Boone. "Beth is one of our finest instructors—our current employee of the month." She placed her hands on Beth's shoulders from behind and gave them a supportive squeeze. "Not only that, but in high school, she was a champion swimmer."

Beth turned to Vivien, her words barely audible as a blush crept up her neck. "Wow. I feel like I was just offered at the annual fundraising auction." She ducked her head, but her eyes looked up at Boone.

"Oh, don't be silly! You're so quiet no one will ever know how great you are if I don't tell them."

Boone looked from Beth back to Vivien. "Uh, are you sure?"

"Absolutely! Go. You're going to have a great time."

Vivien wove her way back to the cashier's counter where Casper stood, his jaw tight.

Boone shot a look at her then back to Beth, who had finally decided to get on with it and participate in this extraordinary exercise in master matchmaking.

Except, oh, dear. Beth was on her tippy-toes trying to fit Boone with a life jacket like he was an over-sized five-year-old instead of the extremely competent, rather attractive man that he was.

"What is she doing?" Casper leaned against the wall, crossed his arms.

"Fitting him with a life jacket. Surely you are familiar with our safety policy."

"No, I mean, why is Beth taking Boone out for his lesson?"

"I think they'd be good together."

Casper's jaw dropped open. "What?"

"He needs to find someone nice to spend some time with." She shimmied her shoulders. "Summer love, darling. It's for his health." Although, perhaps she should have brought Beth a stool to stand on because she'd taken to leaping at Boone to get the life jacket snapped.

Oh, heavens.

Casper tapped his palm against his forehead. "Have you completely lost your mind?"

Vivien looked from Beth's flailing arms to Casper. "What do you mean? Beth's a really sweet girl."

"What do I mean? Vivien, are you blind? Sheesh—I know men aren't known to be the sharpest when it comes to cues, but I do have some knowledge of how relationships and attraction work." He gestured to Boone and lowered his voice. "If the man showed any more interest in you, he'd be lighting a building on fire." Casper shook his head, let out a huff of air. "He's here for you, Viv."

She stared at him, blinked at his analogy, but her voice emerged brittle. "We're just friends."

"The entire town thinks you're dating." Casper took a hiking boot from the top shoebox and began lacing it. "Everyone. Absolutely *everyone* has seen how the two of you are around each other."

"What are you talking about?"

"What do you mean *what am I talking about*, Ms. Convertible-waving-to-the-town? Going everywhere with him. And, puh-leeze—we all saw you last night at the audition together."

"Oh, that." She straightened an equipment rental flyer next to the register. "That was just acting."

"You may have been acting, but I don't think Boone's quite to your level. I don't think he was acting at all." He plopped the shoe back into the box.

She waved him off.

"Seriously, Vivie. You two practically kissed." He swept his hand across the space. "Right there, in front of everyone." He shook his head. "I thought it was a family show—I was starting to wonder."

She socked him in the bicep. "Acting." She threw the word out to him before picking up a pair of wool socks that needed to be hung. "And, *of course* it's a family show. My goodness!" She walked over to shove the socks onto the display arm and turned her attention back to Boone and Beth, spying on them between the stacks of knit sweaters and long johns.

Boone, secured in his bright-orange life vest, followed Beth to the side door, casting a look in Vivien's direction. She gave him a thumbs-up and a nod of encouragement, to which he frowned, turned, and departed out to the equipment shed.

Vivien returned to her station next to Casper. Watched out the window as Boone easily lifted Beth's kayak for her and carried it the short distance to the shore. Like a real gentleman on the silver screen. He made a second trip, grabbing the other kayak Beth had set out. He hauled it down while Beth grabbed the paddles and met him at the water's edge. She looked up at him, blinking, a smile on her lips like he was her knight in shining armor.

Oh, well, that might be a bit much. *Not quite so thick, little ingenue.*

They stood at the water's edge and Beth fumbled with the strap on her own life jacket for a few moments. It evaded her grasp, so Boone stepped up and leaned down to help her, their fingers touching. Beth looked up at him. Vivien could read the word *thanks* on her lips, followed by a smile.

And something suddenly felt horribly wrong.

Because the unfamiliar burn of jealousy singed deep in her chest and turned her mouth to pasty ash. She sucked in a breath, gripped the counter. Waited for the queasiness to pass.

She looked up to Casper's knowing nod. "Yeah. That's exactly what I thought." Compassion threaded through his words.

"Oh, stop." She plastered on a smile. "Everything is fine. Remember? I planned all this out."

She turned her attention back to the harbor, where choppy waves broke near the shore. The wind had kicked up, whipping the flags nearby.

Beth had slipped into her kayak and paddled out. Smooth and strong, even with her diminutive size. Boone, on the other hand, began struggling a short way out. For such an athletic guy, his technique resembled a brick. Stiff. Awkward. He was battling to get a good paddle position, making his strokes ineffective as waves nearly swamped him. The wind continued to pick up, the waves breaking harder on the shore.

Casper handed her a large beach towel. "You'd better take this. I think he's going to need it."

Vivien stepped outside, jogged toward the waterline. She could see Beth's lips moving but couldn't hear a word. Beth's kayak was at least sixty feet out from the shore where she skillfully worked past the waves. She maneuvered in an arc, paddling hard back toward Boone.

Vivien cupped her hands around her mouth and shouted to Boone. His kayak was parallel to the incoming waves, a hard set to his jaw as his kayak teetered with each cresting swell. If he didn't rotate it ninety degrees, he was going to—

"Turn into the wave!" she shouted. "Turn—"

Too late. He flipped right over into the icy waters of Lake Superior. His paddle went flying, the kayak now belly-up, and he vanished under the water.

"Boone!"

Vivien ran to the edge of beach. *Surface!* Maybe she should go in—

Boone surfaced with a shout. Yeah, that was cold water.

Beth paddled hard toward him, her jaw set and her eyes blinking fast.

Boone swam to his kayak and towed it to shore until he could stand and carry it out. Oh boy. Even she could feel the icy shiver.

"Are you okay?"

He said nothing. A deep furrow creased his brow, his jaw hard set. He dragged the kayak up the beach and set it on the grass next to the others.

"Towel?" She held it up to him. Tried to blot the water pouring off him. "Are you okay?"

He pushed her efforts away. "I'm fine." Then he unbuckled his life jacket and dropped it into the kayak. He squeezed the water out of his T-shirt, which now clung to him like a second skin and...wow. Muscles. She stared at him. Blinked. Cleared her throat.

Beth had paddled back and lifted her kayak back onto the shore. She came running. "I'm so sorry. It's all my fault. I should have realized you weren't right next to me."

"I'm fine. I didn't die. And it's not *your* fault," Boone growled.

Then he frowned at Vivie, rivulets of water streaming down his face and a puddle growing beneath him. "I'm done." He tugged his soggy keys from his pocket, more lake water cascading off of him.

At least it wasn't a key fob. See? Always a bright side.

Then he pulled his soggy wallet out and squeezed out the water before he stalked away from her to the parking lot.

Vivien still held the towel in her hands and ran after him. Man, he took long strides. "Boone, stop!" She raced to cut him off. "I was just trying to help."

He tossed his wallet onto the floorboard. "How are you help-ing?" He set those pale blue eyes on her, full of anger and, oh no. He looked...hurt?

"I...I thought it would be good for you?" She held out the towel again, even trying to dry off his arms, his chest.

He caught her hands with the towel, stilled them. "Thought *what* would be good for me?"

"I thought it would help if I could find you a nice girl."

He let go, leveled a look at her before opening his car door, pausing. "I thought I already had." He stripped the T-shirt off and wrung it out before tossing it on the passenger-side mat next to his wallet.

*Don't stare.* But it wasn't easy, with all that defined muscle. Like some sort of hot superhero. And by hot, she meant angry. And hot. Her eyes landed on a scar that drilled into his left shoulder like a darkened crater with rumpled flesh. A bullet wound? Because, yeah. Boone was the guy who ran straight into danger. And all those thoughts nearly tugged her right under the tide of emotions that threatened to drown her.

And, somehow, she'd hurt him.

"I'll see you around, Viv."

She frowned and blinked back tears as he slid into the seat, tugged the door shut, and drove away without another word.

Well, he'd regret not accepting the towel from her when he spent the rest of the day drying out his Mustang. Served him right for overreacting. Going all dramatic on her.

Vivien started walking back to Wild Harbor where Casper stood leaning against the door. She shoved the towel into his hands. "Don't. Say. A. Word."

# CHAPTER 8

$\mathcal{B}$oone stared at the lake from his cabin deck, his hair drying from the shower he'd taken after his lake dunk and the subsequent run he'd taken in hopes of clearing his mind. The hot water had chased away the bone-deep chill, but it had done nothing to shift his thinking. He grabbed his book and walked toward the shore, picking his way down the rocks.

*Imperturbability.*

Oh, he was definitely perturbed.

Because he really didn't know what he was doing in Deep Haven, getting mixed up in the lives of a town that would be a fading memory in four more weeks. He should be in Kellogg where he'd mastered the fine art of not making a fool of himself. Where his future sat behind a big oak desk with a nameplate that earned respect, no matter who he was.

He shouldn't care that Vivien hadn't planned to take him kayaking. Or that she'd set him up with someone else.

*I have just the instructor for you.*

He should have known it wouldn't be her. Vivie, the woman everyone knew and adored. The flirt in the room. Too beautiful and charming for her own good. He wasn't the guy who got the girl—he'd learned that with PJ, thank you.

He hadn't missed Vivien's eyes landing on his scar. The flesh where PJ's name had been tattooed until a bullet had ripped through it ten years prior. Somehow, he still felt like he was dragging around that label with him. Like he couldn't escape the shackles of the past.

*Marry me, Peej.*

He was such a fool when it came to women. He just didn't know when to let things go.

Caleb was wrong. He was more than rusty. He was completely defunct. He'd misread every part of their relationship—*friendship*. Friendship. That's all it was.

And he'd let Vivien get under his skin. Make him a little crazy. He wasn't the guy who lost his cool and just drove off.

Except, he had. So, maybe he was. Which was exactly why he'd needed a good run to clear his head. And it hadn't really helped that much.

Boone sat down on a rock and pondered the endless movement of the water, ablaze with the late afternoon light.

"Hello. Fancy meeting you here, at the water's edge."

He didn't have to look up to know who the sing-song alto voice belonged to. "Vivien."

She clambered over the rocks in leopard-print canvas shoes that had replaced her sandals. He tried not to stare at the bare skin of her shoulders or the soft dip of her collarbone. Or the way the wind tugged at her sable hair.

Unfortunately, she carried a coffee in each hand, which was never a good thing. A canvas tote bag swung from her wrist.

He stayed rooted to the rock.

"Hi. I was hoping that maybe you would help me figure out how to cast the play." She held out one of the cups to him. "I brought you a peace offering. Hopefully it will warm you up."

He nodded, uncertain what to say. Took the cup. "A run helped. And a hot shower."

She sank onto the adjacent rock and set her sunglasses back on her head, her blue eyes on him. "I'm sorry, Boone. I don't know why I thought…"

He took a sip of coffee. "Oh, sheesh, Vivien—" He pulled the cup from his lips, drew his arm across his mouth. "I've got to be honest. These coffees you get me are terrible. What is this?"

She tilted her head, a furrow between her brows. "It's a sugar-free, non-fat, decaf latte."

"I like sugar. I like fat. I like caffeine. Stop doing that."

"But, your health—" She cut herself off and turned her eyes to the lake.

"My what?"

"I was talking to Issy and she mentioned your health issues. I was trying to help you improve your health."

"I'm fine." Great. Now he had not only Rachelle and Caleb and Landry looking out for him, but Vivien and Issy too. "I don't need anyone taking care of me."

"Really? Because you're also supposed to be calm and I was trying to keep things calm for you."

"By dumping me in the harbor?"

"I may have overestimated your skills."

Ouch. "Thanks for that." He watched the sunlight on the water for a moment before turning back to her. He could do this. He took a slow breath. In. Out. "So, why Beth?"

Vivien closed her eyes, the barest hint of a smile curving her lips. "Beth is not only a library aide, she's the children's kayak instructor. It seemed like the perfect match—"

"You set me up with the children's instructor?"

"She's nice and calm and—"

"Please." He held up a hand. "I have enough people trying to help me. Who all know what's better for me than I do? You know what? I'm a big boy. I can take care of myself." He scrubbed his hand through his hair.

She set down her coffee on the ground against a rock. "You're a good guy, Boone. I've appreciated your help and I don't want you to lose your police career. You should be the next police chief in Kellogg."

"That makes two of us, but exactly what thought process led to the chain of events that landed me in the drink?"

"I wanted to help you."

"By what—setting me up with Beth?"

Vivien lifted her shoulder, the sunlight kissing the bare skin. "I guess..." She shook her head. "I figured you needed someone nice. Kind. Generous of heart." She turned, set her bright blue eyes on him. "Someone to refresh your spirit."

"Look, Beth is a nice girl. I'm sure she's all the things you say she is. But—" *She isn't you.* He couldn't bring himself to say the words. Nope, not putting his heart out there. His tongue stuck to the roof of his dry mouth. "She's not what I need."

"I thought it was a stroke of grand genius."

"Probably not so much. You should stick with acting-slash-directing."

Her shoulders sagged. "Oh, I don't have a good track record with that either."

"What are you talking about?"

She picked up her coffee cup, rotated it in her hands, and stared out over the water. Silence.

Oh no. What did he say wrong? "I'm sure you're a great matchmaker. For someone. Somehow. And, you're definitely a good actress." He swallowed, measuring his words. "Sometimes, I wonder what you're like when you're not acting."

"What does *that* mean?"

"I see glimpses of who you are. And then, I see the public persona. The perfect avatar. It's like you're afraid to let anyone in. Afraid to let down your guard."

She stared at him a long moment. Then she turned away and shook her head. "You don't understand what it's like to be..." She sighed. "Traded."

And with that word, a tear splashed down her cheek.

Oh man. He resisted the urge to wipe the drop from her cheek. "You mean in a show?"

She whisked the wetness away. Looked out at the water. "It's nothing."

"It's something." He studied her. The bow over her full lips. The curve of her cheeks now glistening with tears.

"Really—it's nothing." She played with the lid of her coffee cup. "Just those family dynamics."

"Is this about that incredibly nice half sister of yours? Have you always been so...close?"

She let out a breath and watched as a sailboat sliced across the lake.

"When I was eight, our church had a big VBS—Vacation Bible School—production. It was silly and fun and we'd been working on it all week." She paused. Took a breath. "I had a singing part—a solo. And we didn't regularly attend church, so being part of it was an even bigger deal to me." She gave a wry smile. "I got to dress up as a cowgirl. Boots, hat, scarf." She scrunched up her nose. "I was so proud of that part. I practiced all week long." She fiddled with an edge of nail polish, picking at the loose chip. "When I was done with my part, I knew I'd done well—and I felt like I belonged on that stage. Everyone loved it."

Another tear fell. She didn't bother to wipe it away. And he wasn't quite sure how to comfort his...friend.

"At the end, we were all lined up and had to go find our parents. My mom was waiting for me. And then...then I saw my dad." She paused. "I hadn't seen him for a while—he was always on business trips—I thought. I remember seeing him standing there. He was wearing a suit, and I thought maybe he'd come back just to see me perform. I was so excited to see him." She crumpled her empty coffee cup in her hands. "Only, he wasn't looking for me at all. He was with another little girl, a little younger than me. I didn't know who she was. I just froze and watched as he gave her flowers and scooped her up into his arms. The little girl was laughing and he kissed her on the cheek, and the world just dropped out from under me. Right about then, he saw me. It was terrible. He put her down and plastered on a fake smile. Told me he had no idea I would be there. That I'd done a good job with my 'little song.'" She shook her head.

Oh no.

"That was the night I found out my father had been living a double life. And I found out I had a half sister, two years younger than me. Two years. For most of my life, he'd been a fraud. Then he abandoned us. I don't even get birthday cards from him."

Sabrina. The woman she'd fled from at Fish Pic. He blew out a breath. He knew a few things about messy families. "I'm so sorry."

She nodded. Swallowed. "That night, he finally owned up to it and told my mom he wanted a divorce. They had an ugly fight. I clung to him. Begged him not to go." She closed her eyes. "I was just a little girl and he pried me off himself and told me to quit being so dramatic."

"Oh, Vivien."

"Yeah. He and his new-and-improved family moved to Saint Paul. Sabrina's living the life that was supposed to be mine. She's always hated me." She turned and looked over at him. "I've never done anything to her and yet, *she* despises *me*."

"You know it wasn't about you."

"How many hundreds of times have I heard that? I kept telling myself if I was cuter, or smarter, or sang better— anything but being me. I mean, he just left me—left us."

"I like who you are. You have nothing to prove."

"Thanks." She wiped her face. "Sorry. Here I am going on about my inner demons."

"You don't have to apologize." He stepped toward her. "But you do need to know, your father's failings don't make you a failure."

"Right."

She sounded less than convinced. "I mean it. Everything about you—the real you, goofy and sexy and flirty and fun, all of it—I like who you are." And he liked who he was when he was with her. "Does your mom still live here?"

"No. She packed up for Arizona when I left for New York City the first time. Wanted a fresh start and year-round sunshine."

"What brought you back here instead of moving to Arizona? Winter in Arizona might be tempting."

"Ree, Amelia—she's not living here right now, but she's one of my other best friends. Even though we each had big dreams, it's like Deep Haven was always at the heart of it all. I'm a north woods girl." She raised her hand, dropped it. "I'm really sorry about the kayaking."

"I feel kind of badly for leaving Beth like that."

"Oh, she's used to dealing with children."

"Funny." He laughed and she did too. Sweet and soft and sincere and... joyful.

"You should have seen yourself go bootle over bumtrinket!" She set down her crumpled coffee cup and walked to the water's edge.

"Bootle what?" He followed her, unable to stop himself.

She covered her lips with her hand, her body shaking with laughter. "Bootle over bumtrinket."

"What does that even mean?"

"The *Bootle Bum Trinket* is the name of a boat in a hilarious book. But somehow you, so completely ungracefully going under in your kayak...well, it just screamed bootle over bumtrinket." She hadn't stopped laughing.

"I think that was at least a nine-point-five for presentation and athleticism." Her infectious laughter unraveled the knots inside.

Oh, he so enjoyed this woman.

She shook her head, giggling, now wiping tears of laughter from her cheeks. "Six-point-zero. Tops." She pivoted toward him, inches away. The sun had turned the lake to fire and his heart hadn't felt so light in...forever.

He couldn't stop himself from reaching out. Taking her hand. Drawing her closer. She smelled like her usual jasmine and the wind off the lake. Equal parts sweet and exhilarating. And when she looked up at him from under her long, dark lashes, she made him a little crazy.

Especially when she curled her fingers into his T-shirt and stepped closer. It shocked him for a second, but really it was the only encouragement he needed. Clearly she was feeling it too...

"Viv." The whisper of her name left his lips and he leaned down and kissed her.

He supposed he should be sweet, exploring, gentle, but none of that emerged in his kiss. Not tentative. Not delicate. No, he kissed her like the starved man that he was, hungry for her smile, her touch.

And she was kissing him back.

She tasted like coffee and peppermint and he lost himself, just for a moment, in her response. In the soft moan that escaped her lips.

Vivien released his shirt but palmed his chest.

His chest, where she must be able to feel exactly what she was doing to his heart rate. His sad, broken, murmured heart. The one he'd come to Deep Haven to heal. So that he could go home. To *Kellogg.* In approximately four weeks...

What was he *thinking?*

He pulled away. "I'm sorry. I shouldn't have done that." He cleared his throat, setting his gaze on her tote and stepping away. "Don't you have a play to cast? We should get that done." Then, with all the strength of the cop he was, he packed away his emotions, walked past her, swiped up their discarded cups, and headed toward the cabin.

～

Without a doubt, Vivien was the absolute worst matchmaker on the planet. She still had the lingering heat from Boone's kiss to prove it. Not to mention the sweaty palms and pounding heart every time she thought about it.

Now, if she could just focus on the cast list instead of Mr. Hottie. Because the kiss had set her mind ablaze. That kiss had rocked her world. Oh, yes. The kiss that made her feel like the life of Vivien Elizabeth Calhoun might actually be the best role ever. Instead of center stage, for a second, for a very long delicious second, he made her feel like she was the center of his world and she'd wanted to hold on to it. Hold on to him.

A girl could get used to that.

Like she could let down her guard. Take off her mask. Be herself.

Thrilling and terrifying. Maybe in a good way. Like a roller coaster.

Or sky diving.

And then—what?—he'd *apologized*. Abruptly grabbed their coffee cups and practically ran for his cabin to work on the cast list.

She tried not to be offended and instead let it warm her heart a little—that the kiss had maybe surprised and shaken him as much as it had her. That underneath all the command and control might dwell a passionate soul.

Except, he was leaving. And maybe that's exactly what made the kiss safe.

Nothing like a good dose of reality to keep everything in check. Besides, she wasn't the kind of girl Boone needed. He needed someone soft and calm and steady. Not flighty and uncertain and...she wouldn't say *dramatic*. Eccentric, maybe.

"Come on in." He held the cabin door for her.

Maybe she should have run away when she'd seen him on the shore. Because moisture had still darkened his blond hair and he'd smelled all soapy and clean. He wore faded Levi's and a steel-blue T-shirt that turned his eyes the color of twilight. But it was the depth of longing—the need she'd seen in those eyes— that had taken her breath away even before he'd kissed her. The way he saw *her*. Not her façade.

Now, she realized she really had nothing to worry about because Boone had taken complete control of himself since his apology. He was all business when he gestured to the couch. "Have a seat."

She kicked off her shoes and tucked her feet up underneath herself. She tried not to let the sting of *I'm sorry* distract her. She'd kissed lots of men in the course of plays. Months of rehearsals. So this was no big deal.

At least, not until she let their argument outside Wild Harbor roll over her like heavy surf.

*I thought it would help if I could find you a nice girl.*

*I thought I already had.*

"How about a World's Best skizzle?"

Vivien snapped her head back to Boone. "Thanks, sure."

"You can't lecture me about how bad they are for me, though." He went to the tiny kitchen, returning with two skizzles on a small plate, and sat down next to her. He set the plate onto the small coffee table and leaned over the note pages she'd laid out.

Close.

She cleared her throat. "Okay, we have five roles." She tore off a piece of fried dough and popped it into her mouth, letting the sugar melt on her tongue. "I've been able to cast some of them."

"That's great."

"Jason Decker is the clear choice for Dylan. I mean, he wants to be a professional actor and is trained, so, hard to find anyone who would beat that." She scribbled a note on her paper pad. "We're really lucky to have him."

Boone looked at her list. "Female characters. You've got Ashleigh, Hannah, and Samantha."

"Right. Ashleigh is the true heroine of the story—the one he finally falls in love with. Hannah's her friend. And Samantha is the no-good-old-flame." She tapped her pen against her lips. "My top picks are Beth, Ella, Courtney, and Rebecca."

"From my incompetent, unqualified judgment, I thought Ella did really well as Hannah."

"I agree."

And Beth. She probably owed Beth the lead part after the lake incident.

"Beth surprised me." Boone sat back, poised to take a bite of his skizzle.

"Oh?"

"Yeah. I mean, she's got that tiny little voice under all normal circumstances—including potentially life-saving kayak instructions." He took a bite.

"You weren't going to die."

He cut her a look. "Do you know how cold that water is? I couldn't hear a word she was saying—like that little important direction to point my kayak *into* the wave before it hit so it didn't roll me sideways."

"But she actually can project really well on stage," Vivien agreed.

"Surprising. Shocking, even." He raised his brows. "So, you're going to cast her as the lead?"

"Okay, yes. I think Beth will be perfect. That's three of the five."

"Who's playing Dylan's ex?" Boone took a bite.

"I'm stuck between Courtney and Rebecca." She looked through her notes. "What do you think?"

He held up his hands. "I'm no expert. I'm not even an amateur."

"No, but who pulled it off better?"

"In my novice opinion, probably Courtney. She's the strawberry blonde, right?"

"Right." Courtney would have been her own pick too. "Done."

"And that leaves the role of Austin—the wise best friend—to be played by either Nathan or Adam."

She set her jaw. "I think we need to go with Adam on this one." She stared at the list. "Nathan is good, but he's too old to play the part of a peer to the rest of the cast. The characters are all in their late twenties." She tore off another piece of donut. "He'll be easy to work with, too. Nothing seems to faze him."

Boone nodded, picked up the remaining list, and looked at the names that hadn't been crossed off. "You're leaving some players on the bench."

"I hate that part of it. Knowing how disappointed they'll be."

"Unless they auditioned on a dare, in which case they'll be relieved."

He smiled at her and everything seemed okay again. Back to friends. She could do friends.

She laughed. "I can hope."

"What about music?"

"I asked Ellie Matthews to play and she agreed. She probably won't make it to all the rehearsals, but I have recorded music we can use, too."

"Sounds like everything is falling into place."

She stacked the papers back together and set her pen on top. "I'll post this on my way home. Thank you for your help."

"I didn't do much."

"You were a good sounding board." Her eyes fell on his book. *Imperturbability*. "So, future Kellogg Police Chief, tell me—how is that book you're reading?"

"Awful." He shifted his position. "I think it's worse than getting shot."

She thought of the jagged scar on his left shoulder. "Is that what the scar on your shoulder is from? From a...from a..." She couldn't force herself to say the word.

"Gunshot?"

She nodded.

"It is." He wiped some sugar from his fingertips onto a napkin.

"When?"

"About ten years ago." He made a wry face. "When PJ came back to town."

Oh. PJ. Wait—*what*? "This PJ got you shot? She didn't shoot you, did she?"

He shook his head. Laughed softly. "No. She was in trouble." He stopped, looked away. "And she was always getting *into* trouble—but this time, things were really bad. Someone was trying to kill her."

Vivien's pen clattered to the floor. "What?"

"We caught the guy. Me and Jeremy—her new boyfriend." He ran his hand over his hair. "I'm kind of making a mess of the story. The short version is I got the bad guy and the bullet wound, but I didn't get the girl—which was perfectly fine with her family because, like I told you, I'd never measured up, anyway."

The man had taken a bullet for her. A *bullet*. And she'd *still* rejected him. "I really don't understand. Why would anyone say that?"

As soon as she asked it, she regretted it. Wanted to take the words back out of the world. Erase them. Because the look on his face went from regret to something pained.

She touched his arm. "I'm sorry. I shouldn't have asked that."

Silence filled the space until the howling in her ears was finally broken by a quiet confession.

"My mom was an alcoholic and had a reputation around town." His Adam's apple bobbed. "And by reputation, I don't mean the wholesome, church-going kind."

Oh. "Boone—that's not your fault."

"Right." His voice held the rasp of emotion. "She was pregnant with me before my parents married. At my first-grade open house, I'd gone out to use the drinking fountain in the hallway and two women were standing there, their backs to me. Talking about what a fool Roger Buckam was and how that 'poor little boy' probably wasn't even his."

*Boone.* Vivien closed her eyes. "People say awful things."

"I remember going back into the classroom and seeing my dad—the man I thought was my dad. Standing alone because my mom was home sick. Sick—that's what he'd called it. She was passed out. And that's when I decided that, no matter what, I'd make him proud to call himself my dad."

"I'm sure he is proud of you."

Boone lifted his shoulder. "I just kept thinking if I could reach the next bar—the next achievement—then I'd feel deserving." He stared at the floor. "The truth is, no one knows if my dad is really my dad. Probably not even her." He shook his head. "And my dad? Maybe he heard the talk, too, because he's been there, pushing me to earn my way."

"You've never talked to them about it?"

"No. But everyone always knew. They knew who I was— what I came from. PJ's mom never approved."

"That's a terrible way to grow up."

"In tenth grade, I actually beat up a kid who said she was the town tramp."

"Kids are cruel."

He shook his head. "Oh, it wasn't the first time I'd heard it. I'd just decided it was the last time." He tore off another bite of skizzle. "She's turned her life around, though."

"Is she still drinking?"

"No. After I got shot, she sought treatment. She's stayed sober. I think my dad has had a lot to do with it. He doesn't give up."

"Sounds like someone I know."

He looked away, stared out the window at the bright streaks of sunset that lit the sky and cast an orange glow across the world.

Vivien understood. All his reasons for wanting the chief job became clear. A police chief deserved respect. Honor.

People couldn't say he was trash. "You're hard on yourself."

He nodded. "I demand a lot of myself."

"Grace isn't just for other people. Maybe you didn't get that memo."

"Grace doesn't give us a free ride."

"It's acceptance. Wherever you are."

"I don't know how to be anything else. I'm not sure if that's acceptance or just brutal reality."

She reached out, slid her hand down his arm until their palms touched, then wove their fingers together. "You don't have anything to prove, Boone."

"Says you." He leaned back against the couch. "Little Miss Proving Herself."

"Okay, yeah. Maybe."

"Vivien, there's no maybe about it. You know why I have to prove myself." He gave her hand a squeeze. "What's your story?"

Why-oh-why did she have to chase down answers about his past? Ask so many questions.

"Um, well…I told you about my dad."

"Right—but that doesn't explain walking away from a cool theater gig in New York City."

"I went off to New York City. Twice. And twice I came running back to Deep Haven."

"Why?"

"I think the first time, I was just overwhelmed by the city. The world of theater in New York City. I wasn't in Kansas anymore. I was in acting school and I froze. Just completely froze on stage. I dropped out of acting school—even though it was my big dream."

He nodded. "That's understandable. You were all alone in a new city—a huge one, at that. And the second time? Was it because of Ravil?"

She closed her eyes. Shook her head.

She let out a breath. "I told you how Joslyn and Ravil…"

He nodded.

"She was my understudy in New York and, well, something happened right before I went on stage one night and I froze. Just stood there under all the stage lights. A packed house. And I choked." Her shoulders dropped. "Joslyn got my role and my boyfriend."

"You don't want a guy like that."

She let out a sad laugh. "No."

"What happened that made you freeze?"

She lifted a shoulder. "I had this fan. Dennis Campbell. He was a bit…overzealous."

"What does that mean, exactly?" He frowned, a bit of the cop inside flashing into his eyes.

She gave him a smile she didn't feel. "He'd show up in a lot of different places I frequented. Around my neighborhood. Around the theater."

Boone straightened. "Did you contact the police?"

"Nothing he did ever ventured into the criminal. Just troublesome." She wrapped her arms around herself. "One night, I went into my dressing room and he was there. And there were roses everywhere and he was telling me how much he loved me —" She shivered, the hairs on her neck standing at the memory. "Somehow, he got between me and the door, and then, he cornered me." She could still smell the onions on his breath. Feel his cold, clammy hands on her arms.

Boone's jaw flexed. "Vivien..." And she could read the question in his eyes.

"No—nothing happened—I screamed and Ravil came in. Threw him out. But then, I had to go out on stage, and I just—I just froze."

"Why didn't you call the police?"

"Ravil said it would be bad for the show. Bad for business." She shrugged. "I believed him."

"You're more important than business."

"Well, it didn't matter. I was fired anyway. That's when Joslyn got my role." She swallowed. Blinked back the moisture in her eyes. "Ravil's mom had been extremely sick with a rare form of cancer. He needed the show to be successful to pay for her treatment."

"So, you came back to Deep Haven."

She nodded. Twisted the hem of her shirt in her fingers. "I figured I could come back here and give to the community what theater gave me growing up. If I can do that, maybe I'm not a complete failure. I want to make a difference. Not just be a pretty face."

"You are making a difference here. Look at the cast list. I've heard people talking around town about the show." He studied her. "But you still want to go back to New York City?"

"Sometimes. I think about it. I mean...it's hard to give up something you've worked your whole life for."

He nodded. "Yeah. It is."

She picked up the stack of papers and shoved it into her tote bag with her pen. "Thanks for helping me do this."

He nodded. "Anytime."

She stood and tugged her bag onto her shoulder. "I'd better go. I told Ree I'd be home by seven for our movie night. I'm super late."

"Right. Okay." He shoved his hands into his pockets and didn't make any move to kiss her.

Which was good, maybe?

At least, that's what she told herself when she walked to the car. Because he was leaving and she absolutely, definitely, certainly did not need a relationship of the romantic variety.

No. Not at all.

She slid into the driver's seat. "I'll...see you tomorrow?"

"Yes, you will." He closed her car door and walked back to his deck, where he stood like a sentinel to see her off.

Vivien's feet hardly touched the porch steps when she arrived back at her house. She pretty much floated right past the walleye and trout and let herself inside.

"Where have you been all this time?" Ree sat on the couch in the living room, wearing her pink flannel pajama pants and oversized T-shirt, a large bowl of fresh popcorn in her lap, and two sodas on the coffee table. "You got off work hours ago."

"With a friend."

Ree smirked. "A friend named Boone?"

"Yes, Ms. Nosy." Vivien plopped on the couch next to her. She grabbed the nearest soda and popped it open. Took a drink.

Ree grinned. "I'm a reporter. I can't help it. My business is other people's business."

"Right." Vivien slid off her Converse and worked her tired toes into the long shag of their area rug. "Where did you and Seth go tonight?"

"We caught the Blue Monkeys at the VFW and then stopped for ice cream."

"Very sweet." Vivien scooped popcorn from the bowl.

"Yes, he is." Ree tucked her feet up on the couch. "Speaking of sweet, when are you going to dish on Boone?"

"There's nothing to dish."

"For such a good actress, you are a terrible liar, Viv." She narrowed her eyes. "Have you kissed him?"

Vivien squirmed under Ree's gaze and shifted in her seat. Heat crept up her neck.

Ree sucked in a breath. "Vivien Calhoun kissed Boone Buckam," she declared like she was rattling off the lead for a news story.

Vivien stood and took a step toward the kitchen, but Ree snagged her sleeve and pulled her back onto the couch.

"Who-what-when-where-how?" She leaned forward and threw a handful of popcorn into her mouth.

"You left out why."

"I've got two eyes. I know the why." Ree grinned, playing with the engagement ring on her ring finger.

"Stop. It was a mistake." She covered her face with her hands. "I made a terrible mistake and set him up with Beth for a kayak lesson-slash-date."

Ree paused, a handful of popcorn halfway between the bowl and her mouth. "You did *what*?"

"It was a great idea."

Ree blinked at her. "No. I'd say it wasn't."

Vivien shook her head. "It was. She's exactly the kind of girl he needs." She looked up at Ree, whose head was tilted.

Her friend's mouth still gaped. "Really, Viv? If that's true, how did his date with *her* end up with him kissing *you*?"

Vivien's shoulders slumped. "The kayak lesson was a disaster and he got dumped in the lake."

Ree's eyes widened. She finished eating the popcorn in her hand.

"And then he left, mad."

"I'll bet." Ree grabbed her Coke and took a drink.

"You're not helping."

"Okay, go on."

"So, I went to find him and before I headed up to his cabin, I picked up a coffee to take to him. He wasn't at his cabin, but his car was there. And then I found him on the shore near his cabin and we were talking and I apologized and we kissed."

"Wow—that's some apology."

"There was more conversation, but, I don't know, he was standing there, looking at me like...like I've *never* had a man look at me. And I couldn't help it. There was this tiny little pull, like a thread between us, and I don't know...I just walked right up to him and grabbed his shirt and then suddenly he was kissing me. Really kissing me."

Ree clutched her hands to her chest while still holding her Coke. "That's *so* romantic."

"Except, then he apologized and hightailed it back to his cabin to help me cast the play." She frowned.

"Ouch." Ree set down the popcorn bowl and soda onto the coffee table before wrapping her arm around Vivien's shoulder.

"Right? Who *apologizes* for kissing someone who'd most certainly kissed him back?"

"So, you're just as responsible for this kiss as he is."

Vivien made a face. "Really, Ree?" She grabbed a handful of popcorn. "Don't we have ice cream?" She finished chewing her popcorn. "Besides, he made absolutely zero move to kiss me again." Vivien licked the butter from her fingertips. "But, it's for the best. We're friends, after all." She grabbed another handful of popcorn. "And you know what? That's all we can be. He's got an opportunity for a promotion in Kellogg and I don't even know if I'm staying in Deep Haven or going back to New York—so, really, it's a good thing." Probably.

"Just friends, huh?" Ree pulled the bowl away when Vivien reached for another handful.

"Just friends."

She put the popcorn bowl back between them. "Okay, girl who says she's not going to date anyone for a really long time but kisses the guy anyway and is upset he apologized."

"Hey—you're supposed to be on my side."

"I just can't figure out if it's your pride that's upset he apologized and didn't make another move to kiss you or your heart that's hurt over being slighted by someone you really care about."

Yeah, well, Vivien didn't even know the answer to that. "Let's just watch our movie before all the popcorn's gone. Did you decide on *Roman Holiday* or *Casablanca?*"

"I was thinking *It Happened One Night.*" She grabbed the remote. "Oh. Before I forget, there's a package on the kitchen table for you."

Vivien hopped off the couch, ready to leave all conversation about Boone behind, and walked into the kitchen to grab it. "I ordered a few props for the play. I was hoping they'd arrive before our first practice." She carried the box back to the living room and opened the drawer of the coffee table, shuffling through until she found the scissors.

Ree rose from the couch and padded over to the kitchen. "You're right. We're going to need more popcorn. What do you think?"

"That sounds good." Vivien slid the open scissor blade down the length of the box and popped open the lid. Frowned. "This isn't my order."

The box held another box. She looked at the original packaging for a return address, finding only a PO box.

"Did you forget what you ordered again?" The air popper

started whirring and Ree walked back into the room. "That's what happens when you shop online too much." She laughed.

Vivien opened the second box and looked inside.

*Breathe.* Just *breathe.*

Except, the smell made her gag. She swallowed. Tried to still her shaking hands while she fumbled to close the box.

"Viv, what is it?" Ree came to stand next to her and tugged the box flap down so she could look inside. Her hand flew to her mouth. "Oh, the smell! Are those *more* black roses?"

Vivien closed the box lid on the burned roses and the basket that held them. Out of sight, out of mind. "It's nothing." She tried to shake away the stench that stung her nostrils.

Ree grasped Vivien's wrist as she tried to shove the smaller box back into the larger one. "That's something, Viv. Don't think I'm letting you sweep this away again." She took a deep breath and pulled open the box again.

It wasn't any better on the third look. Not only burned, they smelled...putrid. Like they'd had remnants of a dead animal with them. "That's disgusting and it's creepy and you're going to call the police."

"We don't need to involve the police."

"Then call Boone. See what he says."

"I'm *not* going to involve Boone. For one thing, this isn't his jurisdiction. For another thing, the man came here to unwind. De-stress. Bug out. Under no circumstances am I going to call him about this." So, what? She'd be labeled trouble just like that girl PJ? Nope. "Not happening."

"Then you need to contact the police."

"Let's see, I was sent roses, so I'm going to the cops? I'm pretty sure that would be a first for them."

"Those aren't just any roses. They smell like death. They don't whisper sweet nothings or good tidings. Not at all." Ree sat down next to her. "You call the police or I will."

"Come on, Ree. Just let it go."

"You tried that once and it didn't work. Call or I will."

"Fine. I'll file a report. But when it shows up in the *Deep Haven Herald* police log as 'Single woman reports delivery of unwanted flowers,' I'm blaming you."

Ree handed Vivie her phone. "Here. Call the non-emergency number. It's already in my contacts."

"No. I can't."

"Then call Kyle." She took the phone back and pressed the screen several times before shoving it back into Vivien's hands.

Vivie pressed it to her ear, but even as she waited for him to answer, it added little comfort.

Boone walked through the unfinished Crisis Response Team headquarters early Saturday morning hoping to fill the restlessness he'd been fighting since he'd kissed Vivien. Since she'd poured out her story to him. Since he'd found himself looking forward to their next meetup.

And how she'd listened to him. Didn't look at him differently after she'd found out about his family.

He'd tried reading his book. Spent far more time thinking about it than actually doing it. And staring at the lake had just let his thoughts take over. Left him wrestling with himself.

He blew out a breath and shook out his shoulders. He needed to get his mind off Vivien.

Because he only had four more weeks in Deep Haven. And then, he had a job to return to. A promotion, even, if he played his cards right. And that's what he wanted.

Validation.

Because despite what Vivien said, grace was for someone else.

"Drywall or insulation?" Cole Barrett led the way through

the building in his blue T-shirt with North Woods Crisis Response Team printed across the back.

Boone skirted around two buckets of paint. "Drywall."

The headquarters building for the team had large bay doors along the first floor for vehicles and equipment. Most of the second floor held offices along with bunk rooms, locker rooms, and a kitchen.

"We'll have a helicopter pad on the roof." Cole's voice echoed in the open, two-story end of the building they had stopped in. "There will also be a storage hangar for the helicopter in the winter."

"Are you putting a climbing wall and rappelling platform in here?" Boone pointed to the bare wall where a walkway extended along the far side.

Cole leaned against the wall. "Yes, sir."

"One of the posts I trained at was set up that way—we actually had a helicopter body mounted. If you have some creative welders in your arsenal, you could do something like that. Otherwise, you could just design it with a platform and skids."

"Interesting idea. I've seen it done outdoors, but it'd be helpful to have it indoors for year-round training." Cole looked up at the two-and-a-half story bay, as if considering it. "That's a really good idea. I'll have to look into which way we could go with it."

Boone nodded and followed Cole down the hallway. See? He could do this—relax and get things done on vacation. Contribute. Not think of Vivie or the way she'd kissed him back.

Or the way his world had sort of exploded there, for a bit. He'd somehow put himself back together. Managed *not* to kiss her again.

*Focus.*

Cole made a note on his paper pad. "So, Army, huh?"

"I was. Served with Caleb Knight." And if he had to guess, Cole had served too. "You?"

"Ranger." Cole turned back down the hallway. "I never expected to land back here in Deep Haven. Not to stay. I actually had plans to become a US Deputy Marshal." He lifted a shoulder. "God had other plans. Better than I could have imagined."

That probably had something to do with the cute blonde wife with him at the parade.

Cole handed him a bucket of drywall compound. "I heard you're helping Caleb coach."

"I don't know how much coaching I'm really doing, but I sure love being back on the field. I'm having a good time working with the quarterbacks and receivers."

"It's really a great group of kids."

They continued down the hallway. "This is our kitchen-slash-break room and adjoining dining area." Cole led him through the next door where the lower half of a plumber's body was sticking out from under the sink. "Don't mind us. Just passing through."

A hand with a thumbs-up stuck out from open cabinet doors. "No problem. I'm almost done here and then you'll be good to go for your kitchen space."

Back in the hallway, Cole pointed to the far end of the hall. "Down there we have the women's barracks and locker room." He pointed in the opposite direction. "And the men's is down this way."

"Nice." Boone nodded in approval.

"So, the team is new, too, not just this building?"

"Right. The area needs a higher level, organized response team. I was tapped as the sheriff's department liaison and team coordinator. I'll remain the department liaison, but the team will be hiring its own coordinator to take over management and training."

"You're giving that up?"

"I'm finding all that administrative work is a full-time job on its own. The team is comprised of paid and volunteer positions and we cover a lot of territory."

The concept intrigued Boone. "It's surprising they haven't had a team like this before."

Cole nodded. "That's exactly what I thought. I think the right set of circumstances came together. It was time. I happened to be able to get the ball rolling."

"How many are on board?"

"We're still staffing the team," Cole said. "Our current flight nurse has a day job at the memory care facility. Not exactly ideal. And we've hired a pilot." Cole took a drink from his water bottle. "We can tap staff from EMS and the fire station when we need them. There's a lot of inter-agency coordination."

Cole led the way into another room and introduced Boone to Peter Dahlquist, the fire chief, who was working with a paramedic named Ronnie Morales. By the looks between them, they had more going on than installing insulation. Boone didn't miss the squeeze Ronnie gave Peter's bicep.

And did she just call him *Hot Stuff?*

Well, okay then.

Cole laughed and continued down the hall. "Moving on—in here we have Jensen Atwood." A man kneeled next to a cabinet where he was completing some finish work. "And, of course, you know Seb already."

He'd seen their faces at the Java Cup and a few had even stopped in to watch Vivien's auditions.

So like a small town.

They settled into the work, measuring, cutting, screwing in the drywall sheets behind the insulation team. There was something to be said about building things. Being part of a team.

Contributing.

And as the hours passed, Boone found the rhythm twining through him. See? He could keep Vivien off his mind.

It had been ages since he'd been part of a crew. Maybe Landry was right. Being a detective had been a solo endeavor for a long time. He'd put everything into it because it was his life. It was his identity. And his takeaway was a heart murmur, high blood pressure, and a lawsuit.

A door clattered shut down the hall.

"Drop your tools. Lunch has arrived." Adrian Vassos came down the hallway. "It's in the kitchen."

"Outstanding." Seb led the way and they all converged on the not-quite-kitchen.

"And, check it out." Cole turned on the kitchen faucet. "Running water."

"Nice." Jensen grabbed a stack of paper towels and spray cleaner and wiped down the countertops. "Starting to look like the real thing."

Adrian passed out sandwiches from Licks and Stuff and then tossed a bag of chips to each of them.

He turned to Boone. "I'm glad to see you've been swiftly assimilated into Deep Haven life. How's that book you've been reading?"

"I've read the first page about four hundred and seventy-six times."

Adrian raised a brow. "Ouch. That's going to hurt when you need to sit down and cram it."

"It's already painful."

Boone took a bite of his turkey and provolone, hunger hitting him hard.

"Coke?" Adrian held up a can from the cooler.

"That'd be great." Boone took the offered can and sat down on a folding chair in the would-be dining area. Plastic sheeting still covered the floor and the only table was a plywood sheet on sawhorses.

Ronnie slipped into the seat next to Peter. "These sandwiches are amazing."

"That reminds me. Megan sent me with these too." Cole pulled a Tupperware container from a duffel bag, popped off the lid, and set it on the counter. "Brownies and chocolate chip cookies."

"Oh, man. She's going to make us fat." Seb laughed. "It's a good thing I'll be running up and down the sidelines at practice."

"So true." Peter picked up a brownie and took a bite. "Worth it, though. Totally worth it. Hey, so how's the game going to go next Friday?"

"Oh, I think it's going to be a good, solid game, don't you, Boone?" Seb tore open his bag of chips.

"I agree. Those boys have really been showing up this week. Working hard."

Seb crossed his arms. "Of course, my boys will still prevail."

"Oh, I don't know. Caleb's got Tiger Christiansen on his team. He's young, but he's got spirit."

Seb nodded. "True, though I do have Johnny Dahlquist—and he's one of our only seniors."

"And my brother." Peter thrust his fist overhead.

Boone smiled at Peter. "Oh, so I know whose side you'll be cheering for. Johnny's an excellent player. I got to work with him a bit this past week." He hadn't been to a good hometown game in years. He was looking forward to the buzz of the crowd, the percussion of feet striking against the stadium seats creating a rumble as the crowd cheered.

The group fell silent, the only sounds crinkling sandwich wrappers and snapping Coke can tabs.

Adrian grabbed a folding chair from the nearby stack and popped it open to sit down with his lunch. "So, Boone, what do you make of Vivien's strange delivery?"

"What delivery?" He took another bite of his sandwich.

"The box of burned roses." He studied Boone. "Oh—you didn't know?"

Burned flowers? Again? Or— "When was this?"

"Just last night."

He swallowed. Took a drink. So, this was actually her *second* delivery. And she hadn't said a word. Hadn't reached out to him.

"No, I didn't know." And now he couldn't ignore the cop inside.

*I had this fan... One night, I went into my dressing room and he was there...roses everywhere...he got between me and the door, and then, he cornered me.*

Boone set down his sandwich, his gut knotting at the memory.

Adrian swallowed a bite then dabbed mustard off his lips with a napkin. "Huh. I figured you'd know more about it than me."

Yeah. Him too. And never mind his investigator's instincts... the seed of doubt settled in. Maybe Vivien didn't really want him to be part of her life. Maybe he'd misread her. She *had* tried to set him up with Beth.

"So, you said this was last night?"

"Yeah."

"How did you find out about it?"

"I was at the VFW talking with Kyle. His band had finished playing for the night when he got the call."

"Why didn't you say something earlier?" Boone asked.

Adrian chewed another bite of his sandwich and swallowed. "She's your girlfriend. Why didn't she tell you?"

"Contrary to popular belief, she isn't my girlfriend and we don't spend all our time together." Except, well, maybe she *could* be his girlfriend. If she actually wanted to be.

"Right." Adrian cut him a look of disbelief.

"The cast list is up. Maybe the flowers are from a sore loser," Seb offered.

"In this town?" Boone pushed aside his sandwich, his ravenous hunger suddenly gone.

"Yeah, why not?" Peter asked. "Vivien didn't seem too surprised."

Ronnie drew her brows together. "Well, you know your cousin. You never know when she's acting and when you're seeing the real deal." She pulled a rubber band off her wrist and scooped her brown hair into a high ponytail.

"Very true." Peter nodded. "She's a tough one to read."

Cole popped open a Coke. "Things still happen here. We're like any other town."

Boone shook his head. "No, you're not." But frustration cut an edge to his voice. Apparently, every guy—and woman—on the work site knew more about Vivien's scare than he did. Right. Her so-called boyfriend. And if the thundering roar in his head was any indication, his blood pressure was no longer in the safe range. He stood. "I'm sorry, I need to go."

All eyes raised to him, heads nodded.

"Sure. We'll see you at the game on Friday?" Cole stood and crumpled up his sandwich wrapper.

Seb held out a fist for a bump. "Oh, yeah. He's helping us coach—although Caleb said he's banishing him from the sidelines during the game so he gets the full hometown experience."

"Outstanding," Cole said. "Thanks for your help."

"You're welcome." Boone tapped Seb's fist, then scooped up his lunch leftovers and tossed them in the trash can. "Yeah. I'll be there."

In fact, he wasn't leaving town until he figured out who was terrorizing the girl he kinda, sorta, yes, wanted to be his girlfriend.

# CHAPTER 9

*S*unshine flooded Vivien's bedroom as she dug through piles of clothes. She'd find the ideal outfit to wear to the blue versus white scrimmage slated for next Friday or else she'd need to squeeze in a shopping trip during the week. Something that combined her indomitable team spirit with her flair for old-style Hollywood.

Because she wasn't going to let some black flowers get her down. Even if Kyle's initial report was scant on information. And, while he'd taken her seriously, she still felt like an idiot reporting an unwanted flower delivery.

Yes—clothing was the perfect prescription. She'd dress up, play the part, and pretend that nothing was amiss. And, while kissing Boone yesterday may have been a mistake, it had certainly been the most pleasant of her mistakes since...ever.

*I got the bad guy and the bullet wound, but I didn't get the girl.*

He certainly *deserved* the girl. Boone, the protector. The man who never gave up. She'd googled his name. Couldn't help herself. Lots of news story mentions as a detective in court cases, and it hurt her heart a little to think about the ugly things he had to see in the pursuit of justice for victims.

Some football highlights from high school. A middle school play.

Okay, now *she* felt like a stalker.

She turned back to her clothing pile. She'd dug out every blue anything she owned, which was actually a substantial quantity. Not that she had a shopping problem. Nope. Well, maybe she had salved her emotional wounds with a trip through the boutiques in SoHo.

She held up the fitted navy boat-neck blouse. Or maybe she should go with the blue cashmere sweater. She snagged it off the bed and looked at it in the mirror.

Yeah, maybe she did have a shopping problem. But still, the blue cashmere was probably best for the evening game. She'd just begun piling everything back into her closet, ending up with both the navy blouse and the cashmere sweater in hand, when the doorbell rang.

She opened the door to Boone, who wore jeans, a Kellogg Police T-shirt, and a hard set to his jaw that said he wasn't about to sweep her into one of those incredible kisses with those perfect lips.

"Did you have anything you wanted to tell me about?"

"Um...?" She held out the tops in her hands with a shrug. "I'm thinking I might go with the navy?" She held up the blouse and batted her eyes at him.

"Why didn't you say something to me about the flowers?"

Oh. That. She tossed the sweater and blouse onto the couch and crossed her arms, still standing in the doorway. "How did you find out?"

"I was down at the CRT headquarters this morning. Turns out, everyone in town knew about it—except me."

His tone suggested anger, if not hurt.

Oops.

"It's not a big deal. I only called Kyle because Ree said if I didn't, she would." Vivien gave him a convincing smile. "Really, it's nothing, Boone." She touched his arm. "People are just chatty. Need something to talk about."

"It doesn't sound like nothing. Not when you've had your half sister creeping around. You get black flowers delivered. Then your ex starts sending you messages and calls. That's a few too many coincidences." He frowned. "And let's not forget about the run-in with the guy at the auditorium."

"Gordy?" She waved him off. "He might be a crank. Sometimes even a jerk. But he's harmless."

"Is he? Do you really know that? And what about that crazy fan you mentioned?"

And the sunshine might as well have ducked behind one of those fluffy cumulus clouds because Caleb and Issy pulled up out front. Parked, popped the hatch on their SUV, and tugged boxes out of the back. And now, they had an audience.

Boone kept his eyes on her even as he moved aside for Issy and Caleb.

"We brought the pom-poms to sell on game day." Issy followed Caleb up the walk, each carrying a box. "I appreciate you crimping them for me."

Vivien smiled, not looking at Mr. Thundercloud. "No one wants to buy a flat pom-pom."

Boone frowned. "Terrific."

"Is there a problem?" Issy paused. Looked to Boone.

"There's no problem. Law and Order is just jealous he doesn't get a pom-pom."

Issy raised an eyebrow.

"Ms. Cheer Squad should be down talking to Kyle."

Oh. So that's how it was going to be.

He turned to her. "Really, you need to take this seriously. Don't shrug it off."

"There's nothing more to say. I already talked to the sheriff about it."

Caleb looked from Vivien to Boone. "I feel like we're interrupting something. We can—we can come back later."

"Or I can find someone else to crimp these." Issy shook her box of pom-poms.

Boone shook his head. "I just don't understand why you wouldn't say something. It frustrates me. I could help."

"It's nothing. Just stop before you stress yourself out."

Issy adjusted the box in her arms. "Are you sure you don't want us to come back?"

"It's fine," Vivie said.

"Right," Boone growled. "She says it's fine. It isn't fine. And she left me in the dark. I can't stand being left in the dark." He grabbed the porch rail with both hands. "I—I just want to hit something, I'm so frustrated."

"What?" Vivien stepped back. She hadn't realized how close Boone was to unravelling. But clearly, she should stick to theater because she was lousy at helping bring down his blood pressure. A pot of chamomile tea would have done more to calm him than she'd done.

Hopefully he didn't come unglued when he found out these weren't just run-of-the-mill burned roses. Nope. She could still feel her gut rebel against the stench.

He crossed his arms, tucking his fists out of sight. "Oh, come on. Not like that. I *don't* have an anger issue."

"Is everything okay?" Caleb looked at Boone.

"I think he's got his blood pressure up awfully high. And that isn't good for him." Vivien picked up a pom-pom and used it like a wand. "You're going to give yourself a heart attack."

"I'm not going to have a heart attack."

"Maybe we should call Rachelle," Issy offered.

"I'm fine!"

"You don't look fine." Vivien tapped her temple with her index finger. "You've got this angry vein that says you're not fine."

He shook his head again, put his hands on his hips. "Thanks for that. Just—just—thanks."

"So, we still don't know what the problem is," Issy said, her voice soft.

Boone rubbed his hand over his hair. "I'm just a little upset—"

"Angry," Vivien interrupted. "He's actually very, very angry."

"Upset." He narrowed his gaze. "Vivie here didn't tell her *boyfriend* when she got flowers from a stranger."

"Boyfriend?" This was the very same man who'd kissed her, apologized, poured out his deepest personal story to her, then carefully set her away from himself in the friend file.

"Boyfriend?" Caleb looked from Boone to Vivien.

Issy stepped onto the porch. "Flowers, huh?"

Boone nodded like the Blue Ox bobble heads they gave out on promo nights. "Oh, yeah. Not just any flowers either—weird, creepy black roses. Rotten? Burned? I'd know more, except she didn't tell me."

A furrow cut into Caleb's brow. "Okay, that is weird. Who sends black roses?"

"Yeah." Boone turned to Issy. "Would you keep something like that from your boyfriend?"

"Do I get to say something?" Vivien held up her hand. They ignored her.

"Well, no, I wouldn't keep anything from my husband," Issy said. She looked at Vivien. "Sorry."

"I'd be upset," Caleb added.

Oh, right. Ganging up on her. She faced Issy and Caleb. "Whose side are you on?"

"See?" Boone had a smug look of self-satisfaction on his face —and it was all the more irritating because he was still adorable.

Of course he'd be worried. That was the kind of guy he was.

"I'm sorry—but I really don't think it's a big deal."

The three of them cut her a look. She glanced away, the

image of the decaying flowers filling her mind. She let out a long breath before facing him. "Okay, I agree. It's weird. I should have said something." She hoisted the box from Issy and dropped it inside the house while Boone took the second box from Caleb and set it inside.

"Right. Especially if you guys are *dating*," Issy added. Spoken like a love-show radio host.

Boone smiled, held out his hand to Vivien. "Coming?"

"Where?"

"We're going to go talk to Kyle. Together."

She shook her head but smiled and took his hand and let him lead her to his car with a wave to the ever-smiling Caleb and Issy.

"See you at practice!" Caleb hollered. "Oh—hey, Kyle was down at the VFW rehearsing with his band when we picked up lunch earlier."

"Got it, thanks."

"Do you feel better now?" she asked, yanking her hand away.

He opened the car door for her. "Lots better." She got in. "Go with the cashmere."

Cashmere? *Now* he wanted to talk clothes? He closed the passenger door and walked around the car.

Got in.

"Are you going to explain why this is such a big deal to you? This doesn't have anything to do with PJ, does it?"

"No."

"Then what, Boone? What is it? Because you're kind of freaking me out."

He started the car and pulled away from the curb.

They rode in silence and Boone worked his jaw, clearly stewing on something. When they arrived at the VFW, he put the car in Park.

And didn't move.

She reached out, touched his bare arm. "Boone?"

He took a breath. Exhaled. Still didn't look at her. "There was a case I was working. Sort of a side-lined case because it seemed like nonsense to everyone. So it was put on the back burner." He rubbed his thumb on the steering wheel. "An elderly woman named Margaret Vincent had contacted the department repeatedly. She had dementia, but no family to speak of. She lived alone in a small cottage not far from the lake."

Boone reached behind her seat and grabbed his water bottle. Took a drink. "She was convinced someone was coming into her house at all different times of the day and taking her things. Making her think she was crazy."

"Except—she was, in that she had dementia," Vivien offered.

"Right. So, we humored her. I'd swing by, look around. Take her report. This went on for weeks until—" He stopped, unable to continue.

Vivien waited, wishing she knew how to help.

Boone turned. Looked at her. A little wrecked and a lot raw.

"She didn't call. Went silent. No calls to the station. I thought maybe her dementia had shifted gears finally. I stopped by to check on her and take her some strawberry jam my mom had made and...she didn't answer the door."

Vivien's gut twisted. Oh no.

"She wasn't outside. I tried the back door. It was unlocked." He swallowed. Cleared his throat. "I found her." He looked away. "She'd been beaten. Didn't have a pulse."

Vivien sucked in a breath.

"I started CPR, but it was too late."

"Anyone would need some time away after that. No wonder you came here."

He shook his head. "It wasn't just her—or the way I failed her. As I investigated the case, I collected substantial evidence against a man named Robert Smith. And when I arrived to take him into custody, he ran. And then he fought me. And I held back, Viv—I did. I didn't use any more force than I was autho-rized to use."

"I believe you." She squeezed his hand, blinked back the tears in her eyes.

"I wanted to do more. A lot more—but I'm *not* that kind of cop. I'm not that kind of man. I trust the system to take care of it. A fair trial. A fair sentence." He took another drink of water. "But he filed police brutality charges against me." Boone lifted his shoulder. "And, here I am."

Here he was. In her town. In her life. Drawn into trouble, again.

"This case isn't like that one."

He dismissed her words with a wave of his hand. "I can't take that chance."

Right. Because he was the guy who followed through. Didn't give up. Never let go.

And, even if the flowers had spooked her, the last thing she wanted was for him to worry about her.

"Okay, then," she said. "Let's go talk to Kyle."

Boone hadn't planned to claim he was Vivien's boyfriend when Caleb and Issy had shown up. Nope. He'd worked really hard to forget kissing her on the beach when she'd come to apologize.

He'd tried to push her right back into the friend territory—exactly where his brain and logic said she belonged. Unfortu-nately, his heart had disagreed, especially when he let himself remember the way she'd kissed him back.

Friend. Boyfriend. One thing was certain. He was going to make sure Kyle knew this case needed to be a top priority because he wouldn't stand by while someone put Vivien on edge. And no matter how much she tried to play it off, he'd started picking up on her tells. The way she plastered on a smile and expected everyone to move along and ignore the way she'd changed the subject.

She'd been quiet the entire drive over, her fingers playing with the hem of her shirt every time he glanced over.

"Do you see Kyle's car?"

She let out a long breath. "We really don't need to do this."

He waited.

She finally pointed to a white Tahoe in the lot.

"Maybe we can catch him on a break."

Vivien shifted in her seat. "I already talked to him last night."

"I know. Humor me." The sunlight caught the coppery strands of her hair that lifted in the breeze. He resisted the urge to reach out and snag a loose lock.

"Why are you doing this?" She pressed her lips together and he realized the rosy hue was their natural color. He'd whisked her away before she could put her lipstick on. And that made them look utterly kissable.

He cleared his throat. "Because. We need to find out who's harassing you."

"It isn't a big deal."

"Look, Vivien, I'm not sure if you're worried and hiding it or actually not worried at all. What I do know is that you'd be right to be concerned and I'm not going to just sweep it aside like that last guy did."

"But you're not really my boyfriend, Law and Order. You're heading back to Kellogg in a few weeks."

"That doesn't mean I don't care what happens to you. Someone is doing this for a reason—someone who knows what happened in New York City." He unbuckled his seat belt. "Let's go."

Vivien lagged behind him a step when they reached the front door. He turned, reached out his hand to her, and waited.

She blinked—not batting her eyes like she did sometimes. But a timid blink that looked kind of sweet on her.

SUSAN MAY WARREN & RACHEL D. RUSSELL

Her soft fingers wrapped around his hand and he led her inside.

The dark-haired waitress looked up from the counter and smiled. "Do you want to grab a seat? I'll be right with you."

"We're actually looking for Kyle Hueston."

She nodded toward the stage. "Over there."

"Thanks, Melissa," Vivien said. She pointed to a man at the side of the stage, near Boone in height, but he guessed him to be a few years younger.

They skirted around the tables to reach him. "Excuse me, Sheriff Hueston? Do you have a minute?"

Kyle looked from Boone to Vivien, then to his bandmates. "Give me a few minutes, okay?"

They nodded and Kyle led the way to a corner table. "More deliveries?" Kyle directed his question to Vivien.

"No. Just—well, Boone wanted to follow up on your investigation."

Kyle turned to Boone.

He jumped on the unspoken question. "I know you're off duty, but I wanted to find out if you have any leads."

Kyle shook his head. "No. Not yet."

"But you're working on it?"

The man sat back in his chair. "We took the report. There isn't a whole lot to go on."

The waitress arrived and placed coasters on the table before adding a glass of water to each.

"Thanks," Boone said. She nodded and walked away after the others thanked her.

"So, what suspects do you have so far? Joslyn Vanderburg? Ravil Koz—" He tugged his notepad from his back pocket. "Ravil Kozlovsky?"

Kyle looked from Boone to Vivien. He leaned forward. "Why am I getting the feeling that there's a lot more to this than what was given in the initial report?"

Vivien sat up and wrapped her arms around herself. She watched the waitress sit new customers across the restaurant, looking anywhere but at Boone.

"Vivien?" Kyle looked at her, his jaw set. "Who are these people? Why didn't you mention them last night?"

She swallowed and waited as a young couple got up and left their nearby table. "Okay, look—I don't know what to think. I mean, I sound like an idiot reporting to the police about a flower delivery and I sound like a jealous ex accusing—" She stopped, flushed.

*Oh, Vivien.* She didn't want Kyle to know her ex was a lousy, two-timing creep? The facade she maintained crumbled, just a little. And the real Vivien—the one who was beautiful and passionate and, yeah, a little lost and vulnerable—shone through. Boone moved his hand over to hers, letting his fingers settle over the warmth of hers.

"Well, you did say they were black and rotten. Smelled like a dead animal." Kyle looked up at Boone, allowing Vivien to move past her embarrassment, and Boone suddenly thought more of him, despite the gross lack of investigating that had taken place in the past twenty-four hours. Sheriff Hueston was a good guy.

Except—Kyle's words hit Boone. Hard. Dead animal? He rose from his seat. "Wait—what's this about a dead animal?"

Vivien tugged him back into his seat. "No, there wasn't a dead animal. They just...smelled. Really bad."

Kyle looked from Vivien to Boone and shook his head. "No corpse. But the evidence tech did request a respirator."

Not funny. "Did she tell you the part about this not being the first delivery?"

"No. No, she didn't." Kyle took a drink of the water and placed the glass back onto the table before giving Vivien a pointed look. "That would have been important information to share."

Vivien slid her hand from Boone's and took a drink. She

swallowed. "I didn't want to make a big deal about it. The first one didn't smell. They were just burned roses left on my porch the day of Fish Pic."

Kyle cut her a look. "We can't do a proper investigation if you don't give us all the facts."

Boone turned toward her. "Is there anyone in Deep Haven who knew about what happened in New York with that guy—Dennis Campbell?"

She shook her head. "No. I didn't even tell Ree until last night."

"What about the lady that showed up at Fish Pic?" Boone asked.

Vivien let out an audible groan.

Kyle raised a brow.

"Sabrina." Vivien took a drink and stared at her manicured nails. "Sabrina Calhoun. She's my...half sister. She lives in Minneapolis."

Kyle blinked, like this was new information to him.

"Well, Joslyn Vanderburg despises me. She even left me a weird message a few days ago."

"How do you know her?" Kyle pulled out his phone to make notes.

"She was my understudy in the show I was doing. She took over when I left."

Boone looked at Vivien. "I didn't know about her leaving you a message. When was that?"

"During the week." Vivien began playing with the damp napkin. "I tried to call her back to ask her about it, but she didn't answer. I think she was just having a meltdown or something."

"What was the message?"

She shifted in her seat. "I find it hard to believe that Joslyn would come all the way to Deep Haven to dump those roses and then ship the package."

"Maybe," Kyle said.

"Maybe not," Boone added. "You didn't answer the question. What was the message about?"

Vivien closed her eyes and took a deep breath. "She claimed that the same thing had happened to her. That I should be careful."

"Careful?" Boone pressed.

Vivien rubbed the back of her neck and looked over at Boone, her brow creased. "She said I might be in danger."

"Oh, geez, Vivie." Boone's grip tightened on his pen to the point it might snap in two if he wasn't careful.

Kyle sat back in his chair.

"She's just being dramatic," Vivien added.

Boone wrote it down in his notes. "So, you need to give us every other conceivable connection. Anyone who has anything to gain by this—be it a role, revenge, anything. It seems like your sister and the entire cast could be suspect."

"Half. She's my *half* sister," Vivien clarified. "Fine." She began listing off the different cast members, ruling each one out with her logic.

"It wouldn't be Lola Babcock. She was my roommate and we got along pretty well."

Boone rubbed his jaw as Kyle sat furiously typing notes into his phone.

Vivien continued. "Not Danielle Berteau. She'll give you twenty different requirements for her dressing room, but she's completely harmless."

Kyle looked up from his phone notes. "You mentioned someone named Dennis."

"Dennis Campbell. He's the guy who was stalking her," Boone answered.

Kyle slapped the table. "A stalker, Viv? And you didn't think *that* was important to mention when you gave the report?"

She opened her mouth. Closed it.

Boone dropped his pen. "Good grief, Vivien, what *did* you tell him last night?"

"I told him what happened. That's all Ree demanded that I do."

Boone opened his mouth. Closed it. Then read over his notes before looking back to Kyle. "So, were you able to trace back anything on the package return address?"

Kyle shook his head. "It was for a commercial mailbox business—no actual box number. When they returned our call this morning, they said they didn't have any information on who mailed it out. The tracking number linked back to a prepaid card transaction. Dead end."

"Security cameras?"

"No footage."

"You guys weren't waiting to order anything, were you?" The waitress approached from another table.

"No, sorry—not today," Kyle said.

"Oh, works for me." She laughed. "We're a bit shorthanded right now, but let me know if you change your mind." The waitress left.

Boone zeroed in on Kyle once again. "Did they remember any details about the transaction? If it was a man or woman?"

"No. The person who'd worked that shift couldn't remember anything."

"Do you have the prepaid card number?"

"Back at the office. Why?"

"I'd like to follow up on a couple things."

"No," Vivien said, looking from Kyle to Boone. "You aren't supposed to be working or stressing yourself. I didn't want you involved in this."

"I'm fine. Let me do this."

"I'm not—I won't be the reason you don't get that promotion. Really." She set her shoulders back. "It's not a big deal."

Kyle raised his brow, turned his glass on the table top, tapping his fingers against the table.

"Look, Boone, I don't know—I think Vivien is right. Let my department handle this."

"I can do some legwork for you. I know a detective from New York City from some other cases I've worked. Detective Rayburn. He owes me a favor."

"Hey, Kyle, you about ready to get going?" A guitar player tested a few chords and tuned his instrument.

"Sure. I'll be right there." He turned back to Boone. "Have you met Cole Barrett?"

Boone nodded.

"He's working the afternoon shift. If you leave a message on the non-emergency number, he can follow up and get you the information you want." He stood up. "But Vivien's right. This is our case. That being said, I don't mind you gathering some information, but I did hear through the grapevine you're putting in for the chief opening in Kellogg. That should be your focus."

Boone held out a hand to the man. "Thanks for all your help. We'll let you get back to your rehearsal."

Kyle shook his hand. "Happy to help."

In the parking lot, Boone held the car door while Vivien, still silent, climbed inside, then closed it before walking around to the driver's seat.

He gripped the steering wheel. "You don't have to pretend everything is okay when it's not."

"I don't."

"Well, actually, you do. You hadn't given Kyle any of the information he needed to investigate the case." He looked over at her. Noticed the way she blinked several times and looked away. "What I want to know is…why?"

"It doesn't matter," she said, buckling her seat belt. "You're leaving."

"I'm here now."

She met his gaze, her eyes narrowed in thought and that adorable crease between her brows. "Yes. You are. Would you like to go to church with me tomorrow?"

And he felt like he was handing her a little piece of his heart when he answered. "Yes. I would."

# CHAPTER 10

*V*ivien's life could almost look normal. She walked into church on Boone's arm the next morning. Just like she belonged there. Not as eye candy. Not for pretend.

No. For *real.* Like, maybe someday, she could have a family of her own filling a pew instead of being the add-on to someone else's family life. An outsider looking in.

Even if that's what she was.

She swallowed, let the warmth of Boone's skin against her hand settle her. Anchor her. Because as much as she loved acting, sometimes she just wanted to be herself. And maybe she'd forgotten how to be her true self until Boone came along.

How good it felt. How his eyes had held her with deep concern when they'd sat talking to Kyle. The way he'd covered her hand with his own, offering comfort.

Because in the past week, he'd shifted her entire world.

And, even if they hadn't turned up any solid leads yet, knowing he took it seriously made her feel like she wasn't such a fool after all.

*I'm here now.* When she'd looked across the car at him after sitting with Kyle, the words had settled over her like her favorite blanket.

They claimed a spot in line outside the sanctuary, where the congregation shuffled slowly past the greeters, exchanging short snips of conversation as they took their bulletins.

Boone looked rather fine in his dark-wash jeans and a pale-blue, button-up shirt.

"Are you hanging out with me at rehearsal today? It's right after church."

"Sure. My schedule is wide open."

The bulk of Casper Christiansen took up the doorway ahead of them, his wife Raina next to him and his sleeping infant, Rhett, in his arms. He turned toward them. Raised a brow. "Good morning, Boone. Vivien."

"Good morning, Casper." Boone gave a nod and then turned away when greeted by Pastor Dan on the other side.

Vivien reached her hand out and ran her fingertips down Rhett's cherubic cheek. "Don't think I can't see that smirk you're hiding behind the tufts of baby hair," she whispered to Casper. She lifted her eyes to his.

"Who, me?" He shrugged, the smile still curving his lips. "I'm not surprised you're sitting with Boone today. Not at all."

She leaned in. "Not a word, Casper. Not. A. Word."

"I mean, this makes it church-official, doesn't it?"

"Ha ha."

He nodded toward the sanctuary doors. "And you made it on time even. That's just—wow. Really impressive. Inspiring, even."

Hilarious. Just because Vivien's right-on-time had been historically just a smidge past the first hymn didn't mean she wasn't capable of a timely entrance.

"Behave, Casper." Raina winked at Vivien and gave Casper's arm a gentle nudge.

And, see? That's how it should be. A husband, a wife, their children. Together.

"Will you be joining us for the women's Bible study? We start in three weeks." Raina tugged a flyer from her Bible and handed it to Vivien.

"I'll think about it." Vivien skimmed the page, a verse written in bold across the top. *She is clothed with strength and dignity, and she laughs without fear of the future.* She tucked the flyer into her purse. For a girl who'd spent most of her life trying to control her future—or, at least, the appearance of it—Vivien could hardly imagine what living without fear of it could be like.

Boone turned back from Pastor Dan.

"I hear you've been working with the football team." Casper gave him an approving nod.

"Oh, just a bit."

So like him to shrug off any praise. Ironic for someone who so deeply seemed to long for approval. *Without fear of the future.*

The music started and Vivien led the way to her usual seat at the end of the row that held the Zimmerman family, including Ree and Seth. Vivien expected there'd be a date set before long —now that Seth's custom home building business was up and running, they'd have time to plan a wedding.

She tried to focus in on the sermon, not be drawn away by the two pews full of Christiansens. Three generations, nearly ready to spill into another row.

And the still-fresh-from-her-late-honeymoon Megan Barrett, her husband Cole, and her son Josh. Everywhere Vivien looked, families filled the pews.

Maybe that's why her flat in New York City had never felt like home. Because deep down, Vivien longed to be some-where where people knew her. Somewhere she belonged. Just like every other person who filled the church around her. Generations. And, yeah, even Ree, who'd once wanted to get out of Deep Haven, had come back home. And now, she had Seth.

Boone's woodsy, masculine scent twined around her, the

heat of his body against her as they scooched together and made room for a latecomer.

They stood for a song. Boone stared at his hymnal, as if reading a dissertation, a pensive smile on his lips. But then, when the congregation hit the fourth verse, his rich tenor vibrated deep in her soul.

"'All to Jesus I surrender, Lord, I give myself to Thee; fill me with Thy love and power, Let Thy blessing fall on me.'"

He could sing. Like, he could *sing*. And she found herself leaning into it, the lyrics echoing a tender longing in her soul. *All to Jesus I surrender.*

Surrender. As in trust. As in be vulnerable.

Not play a part anymore.

Problem was, pretend didn't break her heart. No matter what happened under the spotlight, pretend was safe. At the end of the night, she walked away from the heartache.

But maybe she also walked away from a happy ending.

After the sermon ended, she left Boone at the cookie table and made her way back into the sanctuary where the cast had assembled.

Beth stood next to Ella, Jason, Courtney, and Adam.

"We're going to meet in the classroom across the hall so we're out of the way."

They exchanged glances and fell in line, weaving through the congregation gathering in conversations and making their way into the classroom. They all stood in silence.

Apparently, a little case of stage nerves had wiggled its way into her cast.

But it was going to be okay, wherever they landed.

She had the perfect cast for the perfect play to set right all that had gone off the rails for her career.

"All right, ladies and gentlemen. Pastor Dan's wife, Ellie, will be playing piano for us. She can't join us today, though." She rubbed her hands together. "Are the rest of you ready to dive into rehearsal?"

Blinks. Glances.

"You guys have got this—we'll take it slow and you'll be just fine."

Jason looked at the others and stepped forward. "I need to talk to you."

"Sure. What's up?" Vivien sidled up next to him.

He looked away.

"Jason?" She put a hand on his shoulder. "What is it?"

He blew out a long breath and scrubbed his hand through his hair. "I already told the others. I just got a callback from my agent. I have to head to California for a part. I—I won't be around for the show."

Her lead. Her perfect lead was leaving town. To pursue his dream. Just like she'd once imagined she'd do.

She squared her shoulders. Swallowed. Smiled. "That's great! You've been wanting to get into the biz for ages—I remember you talking about that possibility last spring. When do you leave?"

"I'm actually packing up and heading out of town today. I'm so sorry."

From the corner of her eye, she could see the cast standing. Watching. Waiting to see what their director would do. She smoothed her hands over the fabric of her dress, inhaled, and slowly released the breath.

"You, sir, have nothing to be sorry about. You're going to go home, you're going to pack up, and you're going to go chase your dream." She brushed her hand down his arm, gave it a squeeze. "You're going to do great."

He didn't move. "I just—I feel badly leaving the show."

"Listen, now, you look at me." She waited until he raised his eyes to meet hers. Even though he wasn't much younger than her and they'd grown up together, Jason felt more like a little brother to her than a peer. "You deserve this opportunity. This is what you were meant to do." She gestured toward the rest of the cast. "And we certainly support you. I'm serious. You go pack up. You say goodbye to your family and hug your parents. And know"—she placed her hand over his heart—"that this is what you're meant for. We're going to be just fine here. We'll miss you, but we'll be just fine." She hoped.

He nodded. "Thanks, Vivie."

She gave his shoulder a little shake before releasing him and then giving him a big hug. "Break a leg."

"Yeah." He gave her a final squeeze. "Thank you." And he was gone.

Out of the classroom. Out of her play.

She rubbed her hands together. "All right, everyone. Let's take five while I do a little brainstorming."

"What's going to happen with the show?" Beth asked.

"We'll do the show. We'll get a replacement. The show must go on, right?" She threw her hands into the air with enthusiasm that didn't reach her soul.

"Right," Ella said, nodding in agreement.

Beth sat down at the piano and began tinkering with the melody of one of her songs. Ella slid onto the bench next to her to sing along.

Through the open classroom door, Boone stood, cookie in hand—and she found it ever-so-hot the way the little edge of white undershirt could be seen where the top button had been left undone.

He was chatting it up with Caleb and Issy.

Boone.

*He* could do it. He'd proven it when she'd handed him the script at auditions. He'd played the lead as if the part was made for him.

It was going to take every ounce of charm she had to convince him. Otherwise, there was no way the play was actually going to happen.

And another failure was not an option.

Even after the church service ended, Boone could still feel the thrumming of the hymns in his soul as he grabbed an oatmeal cookie from the fellowship hall. Sitting in the middle of a church body was far different than listening over the internet.

Maybe Caleb was right. Maybe Boone *could* find a way to embrace the life he had.

He looked at the scripture printed in the bulletin from Isaiah 43.

*Fear not, for I have redeemed you; I have called you by name, you are mine.* God knew him. Knew every way he'd tried to live up to expectations.

But redemption came from God.

Could he live a life where he was not defined by the mistakes he'd made, nor the mistakes of his parents?

The question prodded Boone. Because he'd spent his career in Kellogg trying to prove he could protect the town. And the police chief job—that would seal the deal.

So, maybe he did cling a little tightly to his achievements.

"Glad you made it." Caleb and Issy stood with fresh cups of coffee in hand.

"Thanks. I enjoyed the service."

Issy nodded toward Tiger and another boy who walked by carrying several cookies each. "Looking forward to the game Friday night."

"Me too," Boone answered.

"You've been a lot of help with the team." Caleb gave him a friendly smack on the shoulder. "We just might have to finagle a way to keep you around."

Boone laughed and then shifted. *Keep you around.* The words rose in his chest, light and buoyant. "Well, I'm glad I can help."

He hadn't had time to do things in Kellogg like coach. His job had been all-consuming.

So, yeah, maybe Landry was right. Maybe he needed to ease up. Have some hobbies.

Except, the chief job would take up more time. He'd be attending meetings. Conferences. Working with the mayor and the city council.

"I hope you got that whole situation worked out with Kyle," Issy said. "You seemed a bit edgy when we saw you yesterday."

"Yeah, we're working on it." Okay, so he'd spent his entire Saturday evening mapping out all the potential suspects instead of reading.

"Good to hear. The last thing we want around here is to stress you out." She gave him a kind smile. "Are you sitting in on rehearsals today?" Issy nodded toward the classroom the cast had disappeared into.

"I am. Even if theater's not my thing, it sure beats spinning my wheels up at the cabin."

Caleb laughed. "How's that book coming along?"

Boone clutched at his chest. "Hey—don't ruin a perfectly good Sunday morning like that."

"Right." Caleb took Issy's hand. "We'll see you later." They took a few steps away. Paused. "But, from what you said, I do suggest you get more read before you see Rachelle again on Wednesday."

"Good tip." Boone grabbed one last cookie from the table before heading to rehearsal to show his support for Vivien's endeavor. He took a seat at a table mid-way back in the classroom they'd designated for rehearsals.

He expected to find rehearsal underway, but Beth and Ella sat at the piano. Courtney stood behind them, studying her script, and Adam appeared to be deep in thought in a chair nearby.

Vivien slid into the seat next to him and if he had to venture a guess, she wanted something by the way she batted her eyes.

"Stop."

Her lips curved in a smile. She took a breath. Exhaled. Gave him another coy blink. "What?"

"Are you just going to ask or what? I can tell you want something."

"You used to do theater, didn't you?"

"No. Not really."

She tapped her fingertips together. "I know you were in a play a long time ago."

He hardly thought an eighth-grade role as Robin Hood counted. "And you found that out how?" He'd talked to Caleb about a lot of things, but not that. Far too inconsequential. He'd only auditioned because he thought PJ would be in it.

She traced her finger across his wrist, sending a tingling sensation up his arm and across his body. "You know, around."

Her fingertips felt like silk against his skin. He cleared his throat. "Adrian?"

"Nooo." She drew the word out.

"There's no one else who—hey, have you been googling me?" He shifted in the chair.

She waggled her brows. "Maybe."

"I don't even want to know what weird yearbook archive page that came from." Or whatever other parts of his past were highlighted.

"The tights were cute."

Oh boy. "You know, some parent picked up a Peter Pan costume by mistake."

She threw back her head and laughed. Like, full-on-this-is-hysterical-at-his-expense laughed.

And cried. She was laughing so hard she was crying. "I was

wondering why Robin Hood was wearing that pointy hat and shoes!"

"This. This is exactly why I don't do theater. I refuse to look like a fool like that."

She blotted the tears from her cheeks with her sweater and slid her hand into his, her face turning serious.

"I'm sorry for laughing." She obviously was trying to pull herself together. Not very well. "No, really. I'm sorry. You were just so adorable."

"Right." He looked at his watch. The book suddenly seemed like a great Sunday afternoon read.

"I need you to take a part."

He stilled. "No. No way."

"You can sing."

"I can't sing."

"I just heard you singing hymns. And you sing in the car all the time. You're a good singer."

"Oh, come on, Viv. Singing a hymn with an entire congregation is very different than being in the spotlight." He cut her a look. "You, of all people, should know that. And the car? I hardly think singing to country songs with the top down counts."

"Boone, please? I don't have anyone else. You've gotta help me. You did great reading the lines at auditions."

He raised a brow. "I'd hardly call that acting, Garbo."

"It's a bit like undercover work, isn't it?"

"No. Definitely not."

"I say it is. You take on the fake persona. Pretend to be someone else."

"That's not scripted and there's no audience. And it's for a good cause."

"It's not that different." She reached out with both hands and took his. Stared at him for a few moments. "This is for a good cause."

Wow. She had beautiful eyes. The smooth skin of her hands

warmed him. Distracted him. And maybe that was the point because then she followed up with, "I need you."

She needed him. And something about the raw scrape in her voice gave him pause. Weakened his resolve.

"You already have a full cast. I've seen the script. There aren't any other characters."

"I need you to take the part of Dylan."

He pulled his hands out of hers and stood. "What? No way."

She grabbed his shirt sleeve and held on, tugged him back down in his chair. Lowered her voice. "Please? I need you. You're already familiar with some of the lines."

"You have an actual actor cast in the part."

"No, I don't. Jason had to drop out."

"What? We just saw him."

"I know—he's been waiting for this callback for a role in California for a long time. It's his big break."

"Viv...I'm not an actor. I'm not a singer."

She looked him in the eye. Squeezed his hand. "You're the guy who shows up."

And, this time, her eyes held no guile. Just raw, honest need.

And she was right. He was always the guy who showed up. No matter how many times he shouldn't.

And before he could stop himself with the good sense of reason, he uttered the word on a heavy sigh. "Okay."

Vivien crushed him into a hug and squealed. "I knew I could count on you."

He wasn't sure how taking the lead role in the play would translate to Rachelle's list of relaxing activities. Except, well, she did tell him making friends was good.

Vivien took a pencil and scribbled Jason's name off the script, carefully writing in Boone's with her big, loopy hand-writing. She held it out to him. "It's all yours."

He took the script. "I'm going to have to read it during rehearsal."

"It's okay. I'll help you memorize it." She stood and walked up front. "Okay, everyone, please gather around."

Vivien waited as everyone stood and moved into a circle. Boone joined at the back.

"The show goes on." She winked at Ella. "In that spirit, I'd like you all to give a warm welcome to our newest cast member, Boone Buckam, who will be assuming the role of Dylan."

The circle opened up, enveloped him, and the others gave him knuckles and head nods and smiles. Even Beth gave him a kind, if shy, smile. He still couldn't believe how her tiny little voice had become fuller and deepened almost to an alto when she'd auditioned.

The weight of their expectations pressed in on him. What was he doing? How had he ever let Vivien convince him to say yes?

"Are we ready to start?" Adam stood at the front of the classroom. "I'm sorry—I'm going to have to leave in an hour."

"Okay, yes, we'll be starting from the top." She turned to Boone. "For now, just move as it feels natural. We'll go over the blocking later. This first scene takes place along a downtown street and your character is approached by the heroine, Ashleigh. You're both in town for the dreaded funeral of a high school friend. You're confused, lost, facing your own limits and mortality."

He nodded and walked to the front.

Vivien slipped into a folding chair front and center. "All right everyone, from the top of scene one."

He pretended to stand in the park—which was actually the child-sized table—and he felt like an idiot.

"Dylan!"

Oh no. Beth approached from stage left, in character. Her big green eyes landed on him, bright with surprise. She wore a dark blue T-shirt that said "Grace" across the front, paired with faded jeans. And, well, she was actually kind of cute.

"When did you get back?" She embraced him in a hug, barely needing her script.

He swallowed, read, "Last night." He glanced up at her. "I should have come by."

"Yeah. I've missed you. Have you seen the others?"

"No. Not sure what I'd say to Samantha."

"She broke off her engagement, you know."

"I heard."

"Always thought the two of you would—"

"Yeah, everyone did." Boone cleared his throat. Looked to Vivien, who gave him a rolling-hand signal to keep going.

Great.

Beth scooted up next to him. "How about we get each other through these next few days?" She reached out and took his hand, gave it a squeeze, and looked him in the eyes.

*Just acting.* "I always thought there'd be more time."

She gave a sardonic laugh. "We all did." She leaned in, pressed herself against his shoulder. "So, what do you say?"

Boone looked at the script, then to Beth. "Yeah. I could use a friend like you. It's good to see you again." He glanced back at the script, where the italicized stage directions. *They almost kiss* stood out.

Oh boy. He hadn't thought this through. He glanced at Vivien.

And by the look on Vivien's face, she hadn't actually thought this all the way through either.

The show must go on.

He leaned up to her, stared in her eyes. Not the pretty blue of Vivien's, but pretty all the same.

Beth's eyes widened.

A beat, and then she pulled away and kept going.

He had to be blushing—he could feel the heat scorching his entire body.

By the end of the first scene, he was ready to flee the county.

Seek refuge in the pages of his book. He'd had to snuggle up again to Beth as the romantic scene continued.

And they rolled straight into the second scene, which, oh, joy, had a duet.

And required holding hands.

He tugged at his collar. Someone needed to turn the heat down in the place.

Vivien's voice cut them off abruptly before the end of the scene. "Okay, everyone, rehearsal again tomorrow night at seven."

Boone bolted from the classroom. He needed a lot of work if he was going to pull this off for Vivien.

Adrian stood in the foyer, his back against the wall, like he didn't have a care in the world. "Hey, Clooney, nice job."

Boone waved his script. "You're welcome to the part."

"Oh, no, thank you." Adrian held up his hands palms out. "I'm here for Ella. Purely here as support."

"I'm a last-minute fill-in. Vivien needed me."

"You know, Boone, you just might have a type." He nodded toward classroom.

Boone looked over to where Vivien entered the foyer, flapping her arms, deep in some animated discussion with Ella and Courtney, who were doubled over. Possibly crying, their laughter sounding more like oxygen-deprived gasps. "Is that... the chicken dance?"

Adrian tilted his head, squinted. "I don't know for sure. I mean, maybe?"

Boone ran a hand through his hair. "Please let them not be laughing at me. I didn't look like that playing the part, did I?"

Adrian laughed. "Seems like your lady friends are always getting you into a bit of trouble."

"Oh, thanks for that." Boone crossed his arms. "You know, if you want to talk about getting into trouble, we can discuss the fact that your Porsche isn't an amphibious vehicle. I distinctly recall hauling it out of the lake with my truck."

Adrian pointed at him. Laughed. "Touché—though I still say that road should have some signage. I think Ella finally found the right combination of cleaners to get the smell out."

Boone glanced at Vivie, who was still laughing, and when she caught him looking, she winked.

Adrian was wrong about Vivie being trouble. Just because she'd roped him into a car show and parade the day he'd rolled into town, had gotten kicked out of the local playhouse, and then had set him up on an apparent blind date that had landed him in the icy waters of Lake Superior…

Did crazy dances in the church foyer and didn't care who was watching…

Okay, maybe he did have a type. But she made him laugh. Added enthusiasm to his day. And she also made him feel like he belonged.

If only he wasn't leaving.

## CHAPTER 11

*H*eaven shined down on Vivien because she'd pleaded her case to the school board during their Monday morning work group meeting and, even though Gordy's vote was a seemingly reluctant "yea," they'd all agreed to let her back into the Arrowood Auditorium. Which meant more clout for the community theater event. Which meant maybe she could hold on to some piece of her dream without returning to New York City.

She paced her small living room. Now, she just had to figure out how to handle the Boone-slash-Beth debacle. Or nondebacle because, well, they had real chemistry onstage. And who'd seen that coming?

Especially since Boone hadn't made any move to kiss Vivien since the whole post-lake-tumble clench. She needed a celebrity gossip scoop so she could figure out exactly what was going on behind those pale blue eyes. Maybe—*probably*—they were just friends. He *was* a bit older than her—not that age had ever mattered to her. And Beth was the same age as her, so it couldn't be that. But now, what if he was developing one of those awful show-mances? How many times did the leading man and lady fall for each other?

She'd stupidly done it herself. She let out a croak.

"What's wrong with you?" Ree sat on the couch crunching on carrot sticks, watching Vivien.

She wrinkled her nose. "What have I done?"

"Ummm?" Ree shook her head, shrugged her shoulders.

Vivien threw her hands into the air. "They almost *kissed*, Ree. Beth and Boone, right there in rehearsal."

"Isn't that in the script?" Ree took the last bite of her carrot stick and snagged another one from the plate on the coffee table. In her denim shorts paired with a tee that read "Take a hike!" in loopy script, she was the poster girl for carefree summer. Yeah, well, she had her love life all organized—as indicated by the ring she proudly wore on her left hand.

"Whose side are you on, anyway?" Vivien paused and looked in the wall mirror. She began fluffing her waves. "I knew I shouldn't have cast Beth—she's too sweet. Too adorable."

"Wait. What?" Ree dropped her carrot onto the plate, picked up the script lying next to it, and began flipping the pages. "See? Right here. The near-kiss is *in* the script. 'The couple leans in, looks into each other's eyes, and they come close to kissing.' It's just like in the auditions—you know, when we all thought you and Boone were going to start kissing in front of everyone?"

Vivien snatched the script from Ree. "We hadn't done the blocking yesterday. It was the first rehearsal. There was absolutely no reason for her to be that close to him. I told him to move naturally." She pressed her hand to her mouth. "Oh no." She turned to Ree, dropped the script. "What if that's what felt natural to him?"

"Whoa. Hold on. As I recall, you set them up just days ago." Ree twirled a carrot in her ranch dip. "There was a whole little escapade in the lake with the kayaks? The big setup and the soggy letdown?" Ree chomped through the carrot.

Vivien crossed her arms. "That was a mistake." A shiver crept up her spine. "And now, I have to figure this out." She grabbed a carrot. Crunched it.

"Figure out what? Is there something you want to tell me about Mr. Hottie?"

Vivien rolled her eyes. "You're going to haunt me with that day for all time, aren't you?"

"Well, it was the first time I hid behind a vintage car to spy on a man. I just want to know exactly what's going on with you and handsome Detective Boone Buckam. You seem very out of sorts over this rehearsal thing."

So not answering that. "How am I going to fix this?" Vivien rubbed her temples. "Just—let me think. I'm getting a headache. The show needs to go on. But not at the expense of Boone's peace of mind."

"Boone's? Or yours?" Ree waggled her brows at her.

"I can't put him under more stress." Vivien frowned before she continued pacing the floor, the creaks and groans echoing her own distress.

Ree picked up a couch pillow and chucked it at Vivien.

"Hey!" Vivien blocked the shot. "We have to figure this out."

"There's a reason they're called throw pillows. Come on, Vivie."

Of course Ree was right, but Vivien was more concerned with her current predicament. How exactly she was going to put the brakes on the Boone-Beth train she'd set into motion.

"I know!" She held up a finger. "They need costumes. Stay here."

Vivien ducked into her bedroom, dragged her desk chair over to the open closet, and climbed on top of it. She chucked the Roman robes, wise men crowns, and broken angel wings onto the floor.

They were there. Somewhere. And they'd be perfect.

"I'm not sure what this *we* thing is about." Ree called from the other room. "I don't know that I want to be a party to whatever plan you're hatching."

Vivien rummaged through the top shelf of her closet until her hands secured two rounded costume heads. *Bingo.*

She pulled the pig face over her head, tucked the opossum under her arm, and waltzed back into the living room. She had to tilt her head in order to see out the misaligned eye holes.

Ree choked on a carrot stick, coughing and sputtering. "Oh, this you need to explain." She wiped the tears from her eyes, put her face in her hands, and peered between her fingers. "What are you doing with that pig head?"

"It'll be like *Animal Farm.* You know. Allegory."

"It's a *love* story, Vivie." Ree wiped her lips and wiggled her nose between her fingers. "I think I snorted carrot up my nose."

"It can be an animal allegory love story. Petunia Pig and Prince Possum." She gave a curt nod. "Minor rewriting." She adjusted the bulbous head. "I can handle that—and, you—you're a writer. You can help."

"Um. No." Ree blew her nose. "Okay. I think I'm all right now. Thanks for your concern." She shot a side-eyed look at Vivien.

"Oh, come on. What's wrong with an ungulate and a marsupial?" The head shifted forward, blocking everything but the view of the floor.

"Where did you even get these?"

"From the vacation Bible school skit. I had the high schoolers make them during drama club. This one kind of smells like mustard, though."

"Eww." Ree snatched the pig head off of Vivien and chucked it onto the couch. "Would you just go see him? Talk to him. You're being ridiculous." She tugged the opossum head from Vivien's hands. "And leave the animal heads here."

"Can I take your car?"

"Sure—Seth's picking me up in a couple minutes. He's going

to show me his current build." She tossed the Subaru keys to Vivien. "Make sure it has enough gas."

"It would be terribly unfortunate if it broke down at his place and he had to give me a ride home." She placed the back of her hand against her forehead in her greatest damsel-in-distress pose.

"Go." Ree pointed to the door.

"Do I smell like mustard?"

Ree leaned in. Took a deep whiff. "No. You look and smell ravishing."

Vivien winked. "You're the best."

Ree was probably right. There was nothing to worry about—Boone was acting. And she was just being a drama queen. Of course he didn't have feelings for Beth.

Except, he hadn't kissed Vivien since his grand apology. Hadn't made a single move out of the friend boundary. But, maybe he was just being a gentleman by not kissing her.

When she arrived at the cabin, she pulled up the drive that wound around to the back of the cabin and parked next to a dark gray Dodge Durango with a temporary tag. She didn't recognize the vehicle.

Hmm. Maybe one of the guys got some new wheels?

She stepped from the Subaru and heard a giggle floating on the breeze. Definitely not Seb. Or Caleb. Or Kyle. Or any other man in town.

She froze. Who—?

She glanced back at Ree's car. Bail? Except curiosity got the best of her just like it had that night outside the Harry Cipriani when she'd found Ravil romancing Joslyn.

She tip-toed around the corner of the sidewalk, her heart pummeling her chest.

Nope, Boone wasn't alone.

On a blanket in the grass on the far side of his cabin sat Beth

Strauss, a little too close to him, at that. And she was laughing at something he said.

Vivien took a step back, ready to flee, but Beth looked up, their eyes connecting.

Why hadn't she brought the pig head?

"Viv." Beth smiled. "Hi."

Play. It. Cool. Smile. "Well, hello. Whatcha up to? Looks like you have a new car?"

"It's my brother's," Beth answered. "He decided it was time for an upgrade."

Boone took a drink of his Coke. "Thought we'd spend some time practicing so we don't waste your time at rehearsal."

Right. Except, they sat on a picnic blanket, the lake as their backdrop. And enjoying a lunch spread of grapes and crackers and cheese and—a baguette? A fresh baguette from the Flashy Fox Bakery? With spinach and artichoke dip?

He stood, brushing the crumbs from his lap. "Would you like to join us?"

Beth opened her mouth. Closed it. Smiled.

Vivien was no idiot. She knew a date when she saw one. She rubbed her fingertips against her collarbone. Well, wasn't that originally her whole idea? Get Boone to fall for Beth? Someone calm and sweet?

Except—no. That really was the dumbest, most idiotic scheme she'd ever entertained. And Ree was right. She only had herself to blame for the entire debacle. She couldn't just drop a man in front of Beth and then take him away. What kind of matchmaker was she?

Just call her Emma Woodhouse. Yep. Exactly that. Because while she was busy working to help her dear friend Boone, her heart had been falling for him like her very own Mr. Knightley. So full of good sense and kindness. Generously giving to others.

She caught her breath. Oh, horrid day.

"I think we've figured out the scene," Boone said, holding his script. She nodded, unable to speak.

Her Mr. Knightley was completely clueless, as evidenced by the fact that he saw nothing wrong with fraternizing with the likes of—of—starry-eyed Beth. And Vivien only had herself to blame.

"Here, let us show you." Boone hopped up off the blanket and extended a hand to Beth, who accepted it faster than a free World's Best skizzle fresh from the oven.

Vivien swallowed. Smiled. "Sure. I'd love to see it." She pinched her lips together. If only Ree hadn't convinced her to leave the costumes at the house. She put her hands on her hips. Because she'd love to shove the big, ugly, mustard-smelling pig head over Beth's petite features and coquettish smile. And, speaking of coquettish—where did *that* look come from? And was she wearing lipstick?

Vivien narrowed her gaze. "Remind me—we'll need to fit your new costumes." And, really, it wasn't like it would be the worst costume he'd ever worn. At least she wasn't putting him in tights and pointy shoes.

Although...

"Okay." Boone nodded. "Sure."

Yeah, that opossum head would suit him just fine.

Boone grabbed chairs from the deck, placing them into position on the lawn.

"You didn't have to follow me here," Beth started.

"Have you—have you been—crying?" Boone reached out a hand to Beth and sat down next to her. "Whatever are you crying about?"

"It doesn't matter." Beth looked away, her gaze toward the shimmering lake.

Boone's voice rode the summer breeze. "It does to me."

Beth didn't quite manage tears, but she was a far better actress than Vivien had imagined. And she was practically swooning over Boone.

"In two days, you'll be gone and, well, I'll still be here."

Boone reached out, his hand glancing down Beth's cheek. "Is there any reason for me to stay?"

"Oh, that's really great, guys," Vivien interrupted before the scene could finish. Before she had to see more. Her stomach turned. What had she done?

It was just too awful to watch. Because she had to admit they were perfect for each other.

Boone turned to her. "You think it's okay?"

"It's perfect." She smiled, as big as if it were opening night's closing curtain on Broadway. "I gotta go." The words came out hoarse and broken.

She climbed into Ree's car and drove away. Didn't even look back.

Boone walked down the sidewalk and watched the car disappear around the bend, the sound of its engine fading in the distance. How was it the women he cared about always left him looking at their taillights?

*You know, Boone, you just might have a type.* Adrian's words dug their way under his skin.

No. Vivien wasn't PJ.

Boone returned to the front yard and looked at Beth, whose face had drained of all color.

He scrubbed his hands over his face. "I'm sorry. I think I need to go."

She scrambled from the blanket, flushed. "Is there anything I can do?" Beth's voice, small and faint, asked. "Is she—is she mad about something?"

"No, it's okay." He stacked the food trays. "I'll talk to her. Probably just having a rough day." He carried the trays into the cabin and shoved them into the refrigerator.

Beth followed him inside, bringing the blanket she'd folded.

"Thanks. You can set that on the couch."

She dropped the folded blanket onto the arm of the couch. "I feel like I did something wrong." She wrapped her arms around her waist, her green eyes bright with moisture.

How did his afternoon go from doing a good deed with extra rehearsal time to cleaning up a mess he didn't even mean to make? "You didn't." He threw the garbage into the trash.

He hadn't thought anything of it when Beth had offered to come by to rehearse. She'd shown up with a basket full of food —and it was lunch time, so, why not? He liked artichoke dip and baguette bread and grapes. And eating outside was better than in his tiny cabin.

But maybe, the way Viven saw it... "I think I did. I'll talk to her." Because, well, the look on Vivien's face when she'd cut the scene short said everything her words didn't. The way she'd blinked, set her jaw, bolted for the car.

Beth nodded. "I should go. I'll see you at rehearsal tonight?"

"Absolutely. Thank you for coming by to help me. I'm a little stressed about getting this all done in time. Theater isn't my thing."

She nodded, her eyes not meeting his. "Any time." She snagged her purse and keys from the coffee table. "Bye."

Even though Boone walked her out, he couldn't escape the gnawing in his gut. Somehow, by trying to do the right thing, he'd upset both women.

He found his keys and got into his car.

Boone knocked on Vivien's door ten minutes later.

The door opened and Vivien stood there in yoga pants and a faded U of M Bulldogs T-shirt, a half-empty carton of ice cream in her hands.

"What do you want?" Her words garbled across the ice cream she licked off the spoon.

"Can I come in?"

She swallowed. Smiled. Slick and fake and obvious to him. "Now's not a good time." She moved to close the door.

He stuck the toe of his shoe on the sill before she could close it. "Viv, please? What's going on?"

She wouldn't look at him. Just kept spooning ice cream.

"Can we talk?"

"There's nothing to talk about."

"I think there is."

"Fine." She retreated into the house and he entered behind her, closing the door. She flopped on the couch and studied the hem of her T-shirt, poking a finger through a worn hole before grabbing her spoon for another bite.

He looked at the vat of ice cream she was polishing off. "So, this is what a Double-Chocolate Brownie Batter Hurricane day looks like?"

She licked the spoon, looked up at him. "Yep." She returned to scooping double-chocolate from the carton.

Not only was she dressed down in her stretchy pants and worn tee, but her hair hung in wild waves around her face like she'd changed in a hurry. Scrubbed her face. Her eyes had been stripped of the debutante-length lashes and she looked...incredible. Unadorned and soft and natural.

She took his breath away.

He swallowed, rubbed his hands together. "Look, Viv, I don't understand what you want. You're the one who begged me to take the lead. Got me singing these crazy songs."

"I know." She finished another spoonful and licked the spoon.

"I'm only doing it for you."

She scraped the carton, apparently after every last dribble, before pointing the spoon at him. "You're not supposed to be good at it."

Um. Okay. "What are you talking about? Why would you not

193

want me to be good at it? You want me to make a fool of myself more than I already am?"

She narrowed a glare at him. "Well, I don't want you to need to *practice*. Not outside of my rehearsals." She tossed the spoon into the empty carton and carried them to the kitchen.

"How can we be good if we don't practice?"

She came back into the living room and faced him, put her hands on her hips. "You shouldn't practice with *her*."

She stood so close, he could smell her jasmine. And a touch of citrus. Lemon? And the worn cotton of her faded shirt hugged her curves just so. The woman was going to drive him completely crazy.

"I'm pretty sure I need to practice." His voice softened, and he couldn't stop himself from reaching out to a loose lock of sable hair and letting it slide between his fingertips.

She cleared her throat. "I don't think so. In fact, from what I saw, you need to stop being so good at it."

"Why's that?"

She wrinkled her nose, looked up at him. "It looks too—too —believable. That's why."

And maybe that kiss on the shoreline wasn't an accident. Maybe she'd thought about it too. "And that's not good?" His eyes flicked to her lips and back. Her perfect, full, unpainted pink lips.

"No." Her words came out a soft whisper.

He cupped her jaw in his hand, let his fingertips graze her silky skin. "How will I memorize my lines?"

"I think I know someone who could help." Her breath fanned his neck and she licked her lips, looked up at him. Her luminous eyes held his. "You know, if you really need it." She laid her hand on his arm, the heat of it lighting a fire through him.

"Oh, yeah?"

"Yeah." She nodded, a smile on her lips.

"I'm certain I'll need practice on some parts."

"I'm sure you will." She swallowed.

And the chaos of emotions rooted him in place. "You know, Beth's a really nice girl."

Vivien narrowed her gaze at him.

"But she's not you. And, well, there's something about you I find a little unforgettable."

She shrugged one shoulder. "I'm a mess."

"Maybe I like messes."

She pressed closer to him. "I'm told I'm complicated. Dramatic. High-maintenance."

"I know the truth."

Her eyes twinkled. "What's that?"

"That's all the role you play. The one you think people expect."

She shook her head. "That's not true."

"You don't even realize it—it isn't your physical beauty everyone falls for, Viv. I mean, yes, you're a knockout. And I particularly like this look on you better than any I've seen. But you shine from the inside out. That's why people love you. It isn't what you do, what you wear, how you perform. It's your personality. Your heart." And maybe that's what he was falling a little in love with too.

Except, suddenly, tears rolled down her cheeks and splattered onto her T-shirt.

She swallowed, wiped her hands across her face. "Boone Buckam, that's the nicest thing anyone's ever said to me."

He thumbed fresh tears from her cheeks. "It wasn't supposed to make you cry."

She held out a hand. "I've had my heart broken a few too many times."

"I'm not going to break your heart. I was just trying to help you out—do a good job for you. That's all. In the play. Investigating the case." Now was probably *not* the time to tell her what he'd discovered about her half sister.

She reached out and drew her hand along his jawline, sending radiating waves of heat from her touch. Looked up at him again.

And, oh, shoot. He could get lost in those eyes.

He reached for her hand on his cheek and brushed his lips across her fingertips before weaving his fingers into her own and drawing her against himself.

Her body molded against his and he leaned down to kiss her. Captured her lips. Slow and sweet and, yes, even tender.

She answered his kiss, her lips soft and responsive.

And then she moaned and set his entire body on fire. He deepened the kiss and she returned it with the same heat.

This. This was what he needed. To just let go like a free fall into something heavenly.

Yes. She tasted exactly like a chocolate hurricane.

Nothing in his life had ever come close to the way Vivien felt in his arms. And when she twined her arms around his neck, he had to force himself to pause. Take a breath. Because more than the raw power of desire, there was the startling realization that he could fall—*really* fall—for her.

But he had a job. A life. A plan. In Kellogg.

He broke away from the kiss. "I'm—I—I should, um, go."

Vivien's eyes held his, big and bright and glassy. A smile quirked the corner of her lips.

Yeah, because he still held her tight against himself, the heat of their bodies an inferno between them. He'd made zero movement to actually leave.

Because nothing had felt so right in his life in, well, maybe ever.

*Fear not, for I have redeemed you; I have called you by name, you are mine.*

And maybe the only one holding him back from his future was himself. *Embrace the life you have.*

He swallowed, loosened his hold. "I, uh, I—"

"Shh..." She placed a finger over his lips. "Don't you dare apologize unless you're sorry."

Oh boy. He shook his head. "No. Definitely not sorry."

Her eyes moved to his lips and he kissed her again. He drank her in, held her close against himself, until they paused and she rested her cheek against his neck, burrowed in between his shoulder and his jaw.

Like she belonged there.

# CHAPTER 12

*V*ivien set down the park bench she'd wrestled from the playhouse storage room and stared at the hodgepodge of lumber, paint, and props scattered across the stage. Adam had come by with Adrian and roughed out the larger set pieces. Now, if she could just win Gordy over, there was a chance the Creative Arts Committee he chaired might be willing to select her community shows for their new grant program.

Vivien had felt undeserving of the grace Beth had shown her when she'd given her a big hug and smile at Monday night's rehearsal, assuring her all was well. Now, with two rehearsals behind the cast, Vivien felt like she had an Oscar line-up.

"I'm here!" Ree stormed through the door. "And I brought backup!" Behind her, Issy and Mona followed, dressed for a work party in T-shirts and well-worn jeans.

"Put us to work!" Mona stood facing the stage, her hands on her hips.

Vivien grinned. "You all are amazing!" She held up a bucket of paint. "Anyone ready to make a splash?"

"Oh, clever." Ree snagged up two new rollers and handed

one to Issy. "I'm too wired for detail work, so you need to give me wide open spaces to paint."

"Just don't add any glitter." Vivien pointed at Ree.

"What's wrong with a little sparkle? Megan agrees with me—a little sparkle is good."

"Sparkle, huh?" Issy pulled the plastic wrapper off her roller.

"Yes." Vivien rolled her eyes. "She's been talking to Megan about wedding plans."

"Ooh...?" Mona grinned.

Ree held up a hand. "No—don't ask. We haven't set the actual date yet."

"One of these days, you're going to have to put it on the calendar." Vivien laughed. "Here's the scoop. Gordy said he'd be coming by to take a look at what we're up to. There's a new grant available through the Creative Arts Committee. If we can win him over, it would help fund future productions."

She pointed to the paint cans. "Okay, ladies, pop open the green and brown, and you can paint the base layers on the trees Adam built for us. Oh, actually, Ree, do you want to take those lamps out back with Mona and spray-paint them gray?" Vivien pointed to a pair of neon pink lamp stands at the edge of the stage. "The paint cans are already out back."

"Certainly." Ree and Mona grabbed the lamps and disappeared.

"Okay, I'm pretty sure I can handle this." Issy poured green paint into a pan and worked her roller into it. "It's been a while since anyone has trusted me with a paint roller." She laughed. "I saw Boone down at the field."

"Oh?" Vivien grabbed a brush and popped open a small can of dark-green paint.

"Am I mistaken or does that man have a new spring in his step?" Issy began covering a large swath of tree with green and cast a glance at Vivien.

Well, if he did, he wasn't the only one. They'd spent the past two evenings together before rehearsal.

She'd asked him questions about growing up in Kellogg. His time in the Army.

The man had heart. Oh, so much heart.

And at the end of each night, they'd watched the sunset. The first night on the shoreline. The next night at his cabin. He'd even agreed to an Audrey Hepburn marathon. They'd started with *Breakfast at Tiffany's* and ended with *My Fair Lady*.

Standing on his deck with him, she'd wanted to soak it in. Hold on to it.

The sunset had turned the sky pink and orange with dark purple striations of wispy clouds. And he'd tucked her against himself when the breeze took the night from summer heat to a dusky chill.

Always a gentleman. A protector. The kind of man who showed up. Jumped in. And didn't let her down.

"Yes, he does." Issy answered her own question. "And he stayed late talking to Caleb about something." She filled her roller with more paint. "Maybe...you?"

"Oh, I'm sure it was about the blue-and-white scrimmage." Vivien began swirling darker green into the wet paint Issy had rolled onto the wood, blending in random areas to add dimension to the tree.

Issy returned to the tree and made several broad strokes. "So, are you two officially a couple now?"

A couple? Were they? Because he only had three-and-a-half weeks left in Deep Haven. And then what?

She set her brush down. "I—I don't know." She found Boone to be incredible. Amazing. Thrilling.

And that terrified her.

Issy took one look at her and put her roller back in the tray. "Oh, Viv. You look petrified." She reached out and wrapped Vivien in a hug. "Can I give you one piece of advice?"

Vivien nodded in Issy's arms.

"Don't let fear rule your heart."

"Right." Except—well, trust didn't come naturally to her.

"I know that's easier said than done, but you—"

"Wait a minute!" Ree and Mona came around the corner. "We were not advised that there was a group hug going on." Ree dropped the cans of paint into the supply bucket and ran over, wrapping her arms around the pair. "Is this what you've been up to while we've been slaving away?"

"You're entirely too cheeky. If you're not careful, I'm going to lock you out of the house." Vivien gave Ree a wink before unwrapping herself and picking up her paintbrush.

The playhouse door swung open and she looked up, hoping it might be Boone arriving from football practice.

Instead, Sabrina waltzed in.

Sabrina, in her Louboutin heels, what appeared to be a Gucci skirt, and a heavy scowl that pinched the corners of her lips.

Vivien set down her paintbrush once more. "What are you doing back here again?"

"I was told I'd find you here." Sabrina snapped out the words as she walked over to Vivien. "I just came to give you a warning. Stay out of my business."

"What are you talking about?"

"I don't know who you're paying to snoop around in my life, but I assure you, I can buy a much better attorney than you can. So, butt out. Or else." She poked a finger into Vivien's chest before turning and leaving just as fast as she'd arrived.

The door slammed shut. Vivien blinked.

They all stood in stunned silence until Ree put a hand on her shoulder. "What in the world was that about?"

"Who was that?" Mona came to stand beside her.

Issy took a step toward the door. "Umm...should I lock the door? Call Caleb? Boone? Kyle?"

"No. It's okay," Vivien answered. She turned to Mona. "She's my half sister. We're not close."

"Apparently not," Mona said. "Are you okay?"

Vivien nodded. "I'm fine. I think she's just a little hot about an investigation Boone and Kyle are working on."

She'd never really thought Sabrina would be the one sending the flowers, but now she wasn't so sure. Something had her furious enough to drive from the Cities for a mid-week meltdown.

"Your half sister?" Mona's eyes held the questions she wasn't asking.

"It's a story for another time." Vivien shook away the lingering ice Sabrina had left in her wake. "We need to get moving on these before Gordy arrives. That man is notorious for crashing a party early."

"Right," Ree said. "The lamps are drying out back. We can get going on this other set of trees."

Forty minutes later, the playhouse door opened again, this time filled by Gordy's stout frame. Vivien had wholly underestimated the amount of time it would take to get the painting done. Of course, she hadn't planned on Sabrina's interruption, or the fact that she'd had to run to get more paint from the hardware store. Twice.

And now, she felt like the entire future of Deep Haven community theater relied on the mercy of the frowning man who was pacing around the stage like a state building inspector.

*Don't let fear rule your heart.*

"We just got started on the set building, but it's coming along well." She pointed to several more half-finished pieces. "We'll be working on those the rest of the week. And, of course, you're welcome to come watch rehearsals."

"Hmm." He rubbed his jaw, looking at their sets before walking behind the curtains. "Hmm."

Vivie exchanged glances with Ree, Mona, and Issy, who now wore paint splatters from head to toe.

What did "hmm" mean?

He finally popped out from the curtains. "I hope you'll be clearing the wood stack from where it's blocking the emergency exit."

"Oh, yes, of course." Vivien nodded.

"Now."

"On it!" Ree, Mona, and Issy disappeared.

"What do you think?" Vivien tried not to pour too much hope into the question.

"Well, let's see how the show turns out." With that, he dismissed her. Walked right out the door without any indication that she might be able to secure the grant.

A man could get used to Friday nights like this. Boone grabbed a blanket from the trunk of his car while Vivien tugged a box of pom-poms out. Add to that the all clear on the echocardiogram results given by his doctor and he was feeling fairly bulletproof.

When he'd stopped by to pick up Vivien, she'd stepped out in the blue cashmere sweater. It brought out the blue in her eyes, the softness of her face. And a little bit of him stopped caring who won the game tonight.

"Do we need both boxes?" Boone pointed to the second box still in the trunk.

"Issy said just bring one for now."

"Well, in that case—I'll trade you." Boone lifted the box from her arms and handed her the blanket.

He'd been able to assist at four more football practices during the week. Rehearsals were okay—Vivien seemed happy with his role, even if he still felt a little ridiculous.

Rachelle had been encouraging at his Wednesday morning

appointment and it was hard to beat ending each day with Vivien by his side. Who would have thought he'd be game for a classic movie marathon?

He still felt like he should be helping Caleb down on the field, but Caleb had insisted he take the night off. That he needed to sit back and relax.

Relax? Maybe. He still couldn't believe Kyle had run into so many dead ends through the week. Vivien had an entire cast of suspects following her around the country. Lady Venom Half Sister. Creeper Fan. The Russian. The Prima Donna. Boyfriend Stealer. Cranky School Board Guy.

Who wasn't a suspect?

Well, he'd have warned her if he had any idea Sabrina was going to show up in Deep Haven again. It seemed someone didn't like people knowing she was overspending all her dad's money.

Surprise, surprise.

Even after the confrontation, Vivien didn't think she was the one sending the flowers. Maybe. Maybe not.

But tonight, he was going to bury all that. He had Vivien safe at his side, and he couldn't wait to see how well the teams played.

"Don't the cheerleaders need these?" He jostled the box of pom-poms as Vivien led them to the front of the parking lot.

"Oh, no. These are to sell. A fundraiser for the cheer squad." She picked one up and waved it in the air. "Go Huskies!"

Vivien led him to a table near the entry gate where a large banner read Get Your Pom On! Several young girls in blue-and-white warm-ups stood with members of the high school cheer team and Issy.

"Oh, thank you, both," Issy said.

Boone set the box down. "I definitely need to buy two." He snagged a pair of pom-poms from the box and handed cash to one of the girls.

"Good luck, ladies," Vivien said, tugging Boone toward the entry gate. "You know for a fact that I own at least ten blue-and-white pom-poms, right?"

Her smile did silly things to him. "They don't need to know that."

She turned around. Poked him in the chest with her finger. "You're a good man, Boone Buckam."

He didn't know why, but the way she looked at him, her eyes filled with appreciation and contentment, made him feel like maybe he *could* be a good man.

The low rumble of a packed stadium filled the evening air.

It seemed everyone in town had shown up for the Friday night blue-and-white football scrimmage. The stands buzzed, and the smells of grilling hot dogs and fresh popcorn permeated the air.

"I love the sound of a packed stadium." He squeezed her hand.

"We'll be here all season." Vivien looked up at him, mischief in her eyes.

They would. But he wouldn't. The thought dipped his spirits. But he was getting better. In the last week, he'd finished an entire chapter of the stupid book Landry had given him, attended another counseling session without wanting to run, and even lowered his blood pressure another three points.

Deep Haven for the win.

"Hey, Vivie." Courtney stood with a thick blanket tucked under her arm, her reddish-blonde hair stacked into a messy bun.

"Hi. Looks like you're ready for the game. How's the memorization going?"

"Excellent. I've almost got it all down." She gave Boone a smile. "I saw an online post from Jason—he's all settled into his home away from home."

An evening breeze tugged at Vivien's hair. "We'll all be saying we knew him when..." She smiled.

"No doubt."

"I meant to ask his parents how Colleen is doing."

"I saw Annalise earlier and asked. She's still in Minneapolis."

"I sure worry about her." Vivien turned to Boone. "Annalise is Jason's mom. Her daughter, Colleen, is an ER nurse at Hennepin County Medical Center."

"Wow. That's pretty hard core. They see a lot of traumas there."

Vivien nodded. "That's what I've heard. I think her parents are always trying to get her to move back home."

"I think so too," Courtney added. She waved to someone in the crowd. "Oh—I'd better go grab my spot."

"Absolutely. Enjoy the game. We'll see you at rehearsal."

Even rehearsals had gone surprisingly well—when he wasn't muddling his lines. Watching Vivien's gentle guidance and direction. Her tone softening her constructive criticism and her enthusiasm sparking energy from the cast. But his favorite treat? When Ellie Matthews joined them at rehearsal to play piano and stayed a little later to work on songs. Then, he got to hear the full, sweet resonance of Vivien's voice. Not a car-ride sing-along. Open, flawless beauty.

Boone reached down, slid his hand around Vivien's, and they walked through the ticket line with the rest of Deep Haven.

Tonight, he wanted to be part of the town with Vivien at his side.

And he let that feeling settle over him like the soft fog on his morning runs.

Vivien leaned in, her breath warm against his ear. "Normally, we wouldn't have the cheerleaders out for this, but they decided it was a good opportunity to try some new cheers and acrobatics they've been working on." They went through the line, walked through the fencing, and the field came into view.

The crowd noise rumbled. She pointed with her free hand toward the musicians warming up. "Same with the band." She squeezed his hand. "So, you get an extra special treat tonight."

Oh boy. Her words and smile heated his core. He looked down at her, caught her eyes. "Definitely a special treat."

She blinked. Smiled. And then he led her through the crowd, jostling for position as they climbed into the stands.

"Do you mind if we sit with Ree and Seth?" she asked, leaning into him so he could hear.

"Not at all."

"Thanks."

A voice called from nearby. "Hello, Vivien, Boone. Good to see you."

Boone looked up to where Cole Barrett sat with a blonde woman and a young boy in the second row.

"My wife, Megan, and"—he paused a beat—"and my son, Josh."

Megan sat snuggled up next to Cole, blonde hair loose at her shoulders and a Huskies T-shirt visible under her jacket.

"I've heard lots of good things around town about you." Megan smiled, her glance flicking from Boone to Vivien and back again, and she smiled bigger.

Adrian and Ella came down the main aisle of the bleachers, passing them. He nudged Boone's shoulder and gave a nod toward Cole's wife. "Be careful. She's a wedding planner."

Oh, dear.

Boone turned back to Megan, raising his voice over the din. "You're the one who made the goodies for the construction crew."

"Yes. Cole says I'm not allowed to keep more than a dozen cookies or brownies in the house at any given time."

Cole shot him a look with a smirk. "I've gained ten pounds since we got married this spring."

"With baking skills like those, I'm not surprised."

Cole leaned forward to let a family pass to the seats behind him. "I spoke with the design team and it looks like the structure can already accommodate the change with the helicopter mount for training if we go that route."

"Fantastic."

"Good call. I appreciate your suggestion." Cole paused. "You know, we'll be looking for someone to fill the Crisis Response Team Coordinator position. You might be a good fit."

"Thanks. I think I'll stick with drywall."

"Join us any time. We're eager to get the work done fast."

"Tomorrow?"

"Sure. Come by and we'll put you to work."

"I'll be there."

Vivien led Boone down the front aisle, her eyes searching the stands above.

"They're up there." She pointed to the spot where Ree was waving to them.

They'd managed no more than three steps up the stands when another face he'd seen around town smiled and stood. A big man with dark hair and blue eyes.

"You're the new guy helping coach?"

"A little. Just another body on the field," Boone answered.

The man held out his hand. "Darek Christiansen. My son, Tiger, said you've been really helpful."

"Boone Buckam. Thanks. He's a strong player. Great kid."

Darek gave him a slap on the back. "Enjoy the game."

Boone nodded. "Thanks."

They continued up the steps to their seats.

Vivien leaned toward him. "Everyone adores you."

"I'm just helping out." Except, her words warmed him. Because, for once, he really wasn't the cop, the detective, or the town trash. He wasn't PJ's ex or Director Buckam's maybe-son.

He was Boone. And shaking free of all the other personas and anchors that tied him to the past felt...liberating.

Especially since he could share it with Vivie.

They wove down the row to the empty seats Ree had saved.

"Have you met Ree's fiancé, Seth Turnquist?" A bear of a man with reddish-blond hair. Boone shook his hand.

"Seth moved back to town late last year. Turnquist Log Homes—he's a custom homebuilder."

"Nice. How's business going?"

"It's been really good," Seth said. He had his arm around Ree's shoulders. "There are a lot of people wanting that perfect log house."

Yeah, Boone included. He'd fallen in love with his cozy log cabin. "I always imagined one day I'd have a nice log home with a lake view."

"What are you waiting for?"

"The timing's never been right. And, let's face it—a lake-view property in Kellogg isn't exactly in the budget." Add to that the fact that he'd expected to be married long before his thirty-seventh birthday. Have a family. Share his home with the people he loved.

Seth nodded. "Yeah, Kellogg's got convenience. Supply and demand—those lakefront properties have become top-dollar sellers. I met a guy at a business meeting last week who'd been hired to remove an old ranch house and build a new custom home on Lake Minnetonka."

Boone looked to Ree. "So, the question is, who gets to store the giant walleye and trout in their room until next year's Fish Pic?"

Ree laughed. "You like those?"

Vivien unfolded the blanket. "I'm thinking they should be hung in the library. Maybe in the children's section."

Boone cut her a look. "They'll give the kids nightmares."

"Oh, stop. They will not." But her eyes twinkled as she grinned at him.

Boone looked at his watch. "Do you want a hot dog?"

"Is it a football game without one?"

"No, ma'am, I don't think it is. Pop?"

"Yes, please. Oh, and what about popcorn?"

"I think I can manage that."

She tugged on his sleeve. "Hurry back so you don't miss your team."

"Excuse me." Boone rose, made his way back to the main aisle before weaving his way to the concessions, letting her words thread their way through him. His team. It was really Caleb's team. He was just the guy who helped out.

Boone took his spot at the back of the concession line. He recognized the robust form in front of him.

Gordy turned, his eyes meeting Boone's.

"Hi," Boone offered.

"Hi."

Without his angry face on, he didn't exactly look like the kind of guy who'd go stalking Vivien. He did have a reputation to uphold. Boone didn't expect Gordy would be a savvy enough criminal to go to the extensive lengths Kyle indicated had been gone to.

Boone gestured toward the stands. "Just about everyone comes out for the big scrimmage game, don't they?"

Gordy nodded. He looked Boone up and down. "I heard you've been helping out with the team."

Boone nodded. "They're a great bunch of kids."

"We love our football around here."

"I can tell." He watched Gordy. "You know, Vivien's doing a great job with the play."

Gordy pressed his lips together. Just enough of a window for Boone to continue.

"She's really grateful to be allowed back into the playhouse. She deserves it. Everyone is excited to see the fall show."

Gordy stepped up to the counter and ordered a hot dog. "You really believe in her, huh?"

"I do. She's got a big heart for the community, for theater, for the people."

Gordy took the dog and dug out his money. "You don't give up, do you?"

"I'm not one to give up." Ever. Sometimes to his detriment.

Gordy moved away to doctor his dog with ketchup. Boone ordered two Cokes, a hot dog, and some popcorn.

Gordy grabbed a napkin and moved to leave. "You know, it wasn't solely my decision. The board had to make the call."

"Thanks. I know you hold a lot of clout."

Gordy puffed up a bit. "Well, the Arrowood Auditorium's very important to my family."

Boone gave a nod and added ketchup to the dog, then found Vivien back in the stands.

Kickoff, and the scrimmage started. The team had been divided into two groups, one blue, one white. A great chance for them to show off their skills, get some practice in, and get the town excited for the new season.

He had to admit, he'd found himself watching Vivien a little more than the game. *You picked a real firecracker. There's no one like Vivie.*

True. Throughout the game, no one in the stands cheered with her gusto. Not even close. Which made the game that much better, especially when it came down to the final seconds and the score was tied at fourteen. She'd heckled and hollered, pumping her pom-poms high in the air in between yelling coaching advice from the stands that no one could possibly hear over the crowd roar and jumping out of her seat to whistle at a good play.

As the game neared the final seconds, Caleb's team had moved close enough for a field goal attempt.

They were clear back at the thirty-yard line. Boone watched as the substitutions left the field and the tight end made his way to the edge of the field with the other players while the kicker set up for a field goal. Except, the tight end stayed in position on the field. Close to the sideline and unnoticed by the opposition.

Boone squeezed Vivien's hand. Caleb was using his play.

They had one shot to make the play work. It relied on a legal deception—a flag on the play would ruin it.

The snap. The holder stood up with the ball, scrambling out of the pocket instead of positioning it for the kick. The tight end sprinted down the sideline for the end zone, not a single defender close enough to touch him.

Boone hit his feet as the ball sailed through the air.

The tight end nabbed it just as the final buzzer cut through the roar of the crowd.

Touchdown, Blue!

Vivien shot into the air, squealing, throwing her arms around his neck. "Did you see that? The holder threw the ball!"

Boone picked her up, laughing.

"That was awesome!" Ree waved her pom-pom in the air.

Down on the field, Seb was shaking his head, patting the boys on the back as they left the field.

"I've never seen anything like that," Seth said.

Caleb finished high-fiving his players, then came to stand in front of the teams at the base of the stands. He grabbed the microphone.

He started out with a laugh. "Man, I love football."

The crowd cheered.

"You know, it takes a whole community to make this season happen. I want to thank our booster club. Also, World's Best for helping with our ever-popular donut fundraiser. Can we get a little rumble in the stands?" The crowd responded, beating their hands and feet against the stands until Caleb held up his hand and they quieted down. "I'd also like to thank my old friend Boone Buckam, who's been working with the team the past two weeks and gave us that pretty spectacular play you saw tonight."

A murmur tumbled through the crowd.

Vivien sucked in a breath. "That was *you?*" She looked up at him, her eyes shiny. "I can't believe you didn't tell me about it."

Boone smiled. Seth held out his hand for a fist bump. "Man, that was awesome. That was like an old-school Presley play."

Caleb continued. "I know we won't have him the whole season, but he's been instrumental in helping bring a solid offense and defense to the field."

*Embrace the life you have.* The words poured over Boone's soul as he watched his friend—a man who stood unapologetic and unashamed, his spirit emboldened not only by the trials he'd faced, but by his faith—speak before the town.

Caleb looked over at Seb, who shook his head and laughed. "Coach Seb says he forgives you, Boone, for giving me that play —as long as you give us a few more before you leave town."

The audience applauded and Boone raised a hand in appreciation. His eyes scanned the crowd before turning back to the enthusiastic brunette, her fingers in her mouth for an ear-piercing whistle. Their eyes met and she smiled. Big and bright and sweet. For him.

Yeah, a guy could get used to this.

Caleb's words echoed in his mind when he and Vivien wove their way toward the car. His entire life had been about expectations—to the point, he could probably admit now, he'd done the same thing to PJ. Tried to mold her into who he needed her to be.

He paused, the realization piercing his heart.

She'd rebelled against it.

Could he?

"It's too bad, you know." Vivien's words snapped him back. She looked up at him with bright eyes.

"What's that?"

"That you'll be leaving before the season is very far underway." She crunched up her nose. "You'll miss what looks to be a championship year."

"Oh, you think so?"

"I do." She poked him in the chest with the pom-pom. "You've made an imprint on this town. You've only been here two weeks and everyone already knows you. And, look—you gave them the winning play of the game."

He swallowed.

She pulled the pom-pom back and placed her palm on his chest, looked up at him. "You think you'd stay?"

"I'm here right now," he answered. He ran his thumb over the cashmere of her sweater sleeve. He wasn't ready to talk about leaving. What he wanted to do was drive Vivie over to Honeymoon Bluff and watch the sun set. Maybe work a little on that relaxation.

But yes. A guy could get used to living like this.

# CHAPTER 13

*B*oone let the sunshine warm his soul as he stood outside Wild Harbor five days later. Apparently, Vivien had decided that he needed a private kayak lesson on an inland lake.

And, with nine rehearsals behind him, he could use a break. All he wanted was to have a good time. As much as he'd enjoyed sitting with her in church again, he'd been looking forward to this opportunity to go on a real date. Zero responsibility. No cases to investigate. No lines to memorize. No book to read. No expectations.

Just be. In the moment.

Vivien had dressed down for the day, which meant she looked like an All-American girl who'd stepped out of the pages of an REI catalog. She wore pink camo cargo shorts and a zip-up hoodie over her quick-dry tank. The wilderness had never looked so stylish, yet practical.

Casper handed him the life jackets and truck keys. "You're heading to Hungry Jack Lake?"

"That's what I'm told."

Vivien snugged down the tether on the kayaks. "Yes, we are. And I'm driving."

Boone crossed his arms. "Only if you promise to actually cease all forward motion when you reach the red octagonal signs." He drew the shape for her in the air with his fingertips.

She smiled. "I stop."

Right. "You pause." He gripped the keys in his hand over the top of her open palm.

"Fine."

He dropped the keys into her hand.

"Good luck." Casper smacked him on the back then turned to Vivien. "No four-wheeling in the Evergreen truck."

"Thanks for letting us borrow it. And, really, that was only that one time."

"Twice. And don't forget—the second time, Darek and I had to come pull you out."

Vivien cut him a look and crossed her arms. "Well, the road should have been marked as closed."

Casper turned back to Boone. "Keep her between the lines."

Oh, great. "Thanks. I'll see what I can do."

They finished stowing the gear and climbed into the truck Casper had loaned them. Vivien changed the radio dial to a local station with country hits from the 1990s.

"Country, huh? I'm rubbing off on you."

"You should know by now that I don't only sing show tunes. I should have brought my new Benjamin King CD, though."

By the time they reached Hungry Jack Lake, forty minutes away, he'd determined the station was actually running on a fifteen-minute loop. Because they'd had friends in low places, he'd been a brand new man, and determined forever was as far as he'd go. Three times.

Vivien parked the truck but made no move to exit. She sat, staring out the front windshield, and took a deep breath.

Boone removed his seatbelt and turned toward her. "I ran

into a dead end on Sabrina. I can't tie her to the deliveries. Circumstantially, she's somewhat local and has a highly suspect cash flow. But I've been in contact with a detective in New York City. He's working a high-profile case right now, but when he has a free moment, he's going to look into a few questions I had on Joslyn, Danielle, and that guy." That guy. He didn't even want to say Ravil's name. "Which reminds me—did you know that Joslyn knew Danielle from a French drama school?" There went his plans for a day to relax.

She shook her head. "I thought we weren't going to talk shop." She squeezed his arm.

Oops. "Right."

"Are you ever off duty?"

Well, maybe not. He shrugged. "Okay. Right. I am today."

"Then let's go."

The sunshine and warm weather had brought other kayakers to the lake. They explored the lake for several hours before climbing onto shore and stopping at an unclaimed campsite. He pulled out the cooler with the lunches Vivien had packed and she grabbed the blanket.

She pointed to a spot beneath the birch trees. "That looks perfect." She walked over and spread the blanket on the ground.

He sat down on the blanket next to her and she popped open the cooler, handed him a sandwich.

"I hope you like turkey on wheat."

"No marshmallow-fluff bread?"

"Nope."

He said grace and then took a bite. The flavors mingled on his tongue. Turkey, provolone, lettuce, tomato...and something else. "What is this sauce?"

"It's a tarragon and avocado dressing." She took a bite of her sandwich. "How's it going with your counselor?"

"Good. I saw her this morning. My blood pressure is down. I've lost five pounds since I got here."

"Wow. Impressive."

"Thanks."

They lingered over lunch, an orchestra of bird song filling the air. Even after the food was gone, he wasn't ready to go.

He shifted his position, sitting back against the nearest tree to watch the other kayakers. She nestled herself up against him.

"So, here's a question for you...how'd you get the name 'Boone'?" She looked up at him, the blue of the sky reflected in her eyes.

"My first name is Daniel." He let his fingers slide through a lock of hair that had fallen forward on her shoulder.

"Daniel?" Her eyes swept over him, as if surmising whether or not Daniel suited him. She nodded. "So, like, Daniel Boone?"

He lifted a shoulder. "I guess. My dad started calling me Boone at a young age. It stuck."

He savored the weight of Vivien pressed up against his chest, and he wrapped his arms around her. Closed his eyes and breathed in her jasmine scent.

A man could live a lifetime like this.

"Viv...what if I could stay longer? In Deep Haven?"

"Help!" A frantic cry from the lake cut through the forest. "Help!"

Vivien bolted upright, freeing Boone to jump to his feet and run toward the voice. Vivien's footsteps kept pace right behind him.

"Help!" A woman in her mid-forties stood near the shoreline, wading out into the water toward an inverted kayak while looking back toward a young child crying on the shore. Someone was trapped under the kayak. Boone grabbed the sobbing child, a little boy, and passed him off to Vivien. "Wait here. Call 911."

He plowed into the lake, grabbed the woman by her forearm. She fought his grip, her pleas turning into frantic shrieks. The kayak was adrift and Boone couldn't see anyone in the water. "Please, my daughter. She was—she was right behind me."

She freed herself and began crashing though the water, and Boone knew they'd have two drownings if he didn't stop her.

"Let me get her." He ran after her, lunged for her shirt, and hauled her backward toward the shoreline.

"No, please." Her body heaved with sobs. "I think she had a seizure." She pulled against him, breaking free.

The wails of the child on shore tore into him. "Go to shore. Let me get her."

Vivien came up behind him carrying the child, whose panicked cries refocused the woman's attention. The child clawed for his mother.

Boone sucked in a breath and dove in. Let his hard strokes take him to the kayak.

He reached the hull and dropped under, feeling his way. The girl, a teen based on her size, was still locked into the kayak somehow.

*Come on.* He tugged at her limp body. Her life jacket was pulling against him, challenging his ability to wrestle her free.

His own body was starting to numb. Even at the end of summer, the water was barely sixty degrees and the cold robbed him of energy. *Please!*

And then he heard a splash. Saw from his peripheral vision something—someone.

Oh no.

And, no, he couldn't just have an everyday, ordinary date. Because just when he thought it couldn't get worse, Vivien dove into the water.

The mother was still screaming from the shore, her cries anguished, dire. The dark, cold water would be all their graves if he didn't get the girl free. *Please don't let her die, Lord.*

Except, as fatigue set in, Vivien popped up next to him.

"You pull her out toward you, I'll pull the kayak in the opposite direction." She disappeared under the water and he felt the body loosen from the pressure of the kayak bearing down on the flotation device. He pulled the girl free, the life jacket easily bringing her to the surface.

She wasn't breathing. He held her head above the water. Tried to give her a breath as best he could before wrapping an arm under the girl and swimming toward shore.

*Come on, Vivie.* She hadn't resurfaced and he tried to ease the grip of fear in his chest, because he couldn't wait.

Then he heard Vivien's strong strokes. She latched on to the other side of the teen's life jacket and began swimming back to shore with him.

When their toes hit the bottom, Vivien moved to the girl's feet and helped carry her to the grass.

"Oh, Tasha." The mom sobbed, clinging to her other child, trying to cover the boy's face.

Boone dropped to the ground, adrenaline fueling his cold muscles. "She's still not breathing."

Vivien pressed her fingers to the girl's carotid artery. "No pulse."

And Boone was back in Margaret Vincent's kitchen. The floor covered with blood. Frantically trying to breathe life into her.

He snapped back at the sound of Vivien unclipping the girl's life jacket. Together, they carefully removed it from her body, positioning her flat on the ground.

Boone locked out his arms and began chest compressions, counting out loud until he reached thirty and then giving her two breaths.

Vivien shook her head. No pulse.

He continued chest compressions, cycling with breaths. *Don't let her die.*

"Tasha, can you hear me? Tasha?" Vivien began rubbing the

girl's arms, moving around to her bare legs. "Do you have a blanket? A coat? Anything we can cover her with?"

The woman shook her head.

Vivien jumped to her feet, ran down the trail. She disappeared while Boone continued compressions and breaths. She returned moments later with their picnic blanket, covering as much of Tasha's body as she could without interfering with CPR. If there was a bright side, the girl wore only a tank top and shorts, leaving her in minimal wet clothing.

Tasha's mom sat on the ground, rocking her child, her lips moving, the words barely audible prayers. "Lord, you go before me and are with me. You will never leave me nor forsake me. I will not be afraid. I will not be discouraged."

The sound of it was nearly more than he could take. *Please, Lord. Don't let her die.*

"Did you get through to anyone?" His eyes connected with Vivie's.

"Yes. I spoke with Sabine Hueston in dispatch and she said they'd activate the CRT."

"They don't even have a full team."

"They have enough. They're already in the air for training. They'll be here."

Only, how long would that take? Because he wasn't sure how long they had.

Not quitting. No one—not a teenager or an elderly woman— would die on his watch. Not again.

"Do you want to switch?" Vivien reached out, placed a hand on his shoulder. "I'm trained."

"No. I've got this." He looked up at her. "For now."

She gave him a nod and after several more cycles, he let her take over for a few minutes before diving back in again. Alternating with her. Unwilling to give up. And Vivien kept talking to the girl in her calm, sing-song voice like she saved lives every day.

*Everything's going to be okay.*

He wasn't sure which gave him more relief fifteen minutes later, though. The twitch of his patient's hands or the dull thud of helicopter rotors cutting through the roar in his ears. It bolstered their efforts to continue CPR while the Bell set down in the field near the boat launch.

Then their miracle showed up. Tasha started coughing. Boone turned her to her side, let her vomit water while Vivien took her pulse, looked to Boone, and mouthed the word, "Weak."

Weak, but there. Tasha's eyes closed and Vivien kept a watchful eye on her.

"Tasha." Her mom fell to the ground nearby. "Oh, please, God. Please."

Moments later, the team approached, gear in hand. The first, a big man with dark brown hair, looked like he was going to be ill. Sweat beaded on the brows of his pasty-white face. Boone recognized the second medic as Ronnie.

He looked at the man's name tag. Rhino Johnson. "You okay?" Boone asked.

"Yeah. Sure." Rhino began assessing the patient's vitals and securing her airway. "Just not so great with flying, I guess." He looked up at Ronnie. "Low respiration rate."

He placed a bag valve mask over Tasha's mouth and nose, tilted her head, and began rescue breaths with it.

Ronnie moved with precision as she started an IV. "Be careful not to jostle her." She looked up to Boone. "How long was she under water?"

Boone turned to the mom, then to Vivien. "Four? Five minutes total?" Vivien nodded. "Her mom said she suffers seizures."

"Okay." Ronnie removed the picnic blanket, and covered Tasha in an emergency blanket. "Did you see her go under?"

"No. No one did. Her mom turned around and realized she

was under. Called for help and we heard her. It was a struggle to get her to the surface."

"Was she alone in the kayak?"

"Yes."

"No rocks or likely spinal injuries?" Ronnie moved her hands over Tasha's body.

"Correct."

"Let's move her." Ronnie looked to Rhino, who responded to her count, helping to gently set Tasha on the cot Ronnie had brought. She tucked the blanket around her.

"How long were you doing CPR?"

"About eighteen minutes total. Vivien helped."

While Rhino finished packing up the gear, Ronnie stepped aside to Tasha's mom. "We're heading to Children's Hospital in Minneapolis. They have an excellent pediatric trauma center."

The woman swallowed, muffled a sob, and nodded. "Is she—is she going to be okay?" She choked on another sob and covered her face with her hand. The child in her arms began to wail again.

Ronnie reached out, put a hand on her shoulder. "The lake is cold and that's a good thing, actually—and she had excellent care from bystanders." She gestured to Boone and Vivien. "They're both professionally trained. She's in the best care possible, okay? And we'll be taking care of her the entire flight."

The woman nodded, her barely audible thank-you acknowledged by Ronnie. "Of course."

"We're ready to move." Rhino stood next to the cot.

Ronnie gave Boone and Vivien a nod, then turned to help carry Tasha to the waiting helicopter. Within moments, they were lifting off, the heavy beat of the blades fading away.

Boone turned to Tasha's mom. "Do you have someone that can come get you? Drive you to Minneapolis...ma'am?" He didn't even know her name.

"Laurie." The woman nodded. "My sister is on her way. I

called her when the helicopter got here." She wiped the tears from her red face, now puffy from crying. "Thank you for everything you did."

"Of course." Vivien gave her a squeeze. "Why don't we wait with you?"

"She should be here any minute. She was just around the lake at the Hungry Jack Lodge." Laurie hoisted her son higher on her hip and wiped her nose.

Vivien and Boone waited with Laurie and her son, Jacob, until they had been safely tucked into her sister's Tahoe, heading for Minneapolis. They wandered back to their picnic spot, the damp picnic blanket tucked under Boone's arm, and shook the ants off the cooler before hauling it to the truck.

"You saved that girl," Vivien said.

"*We* saved that girl." Boone placed the cooler in the truck. "She may have a long road to recovery, though."

"Still. Wow." Her hands had the slightest shake, like the adrenaline was burning off.

"I thought you were a little crazy. Thought for sure you'd lost your mind when you jumped in behind me. And then, you disappeared under water. Got her free of the kayak's weight." He frowned. "You didn't listen to me, though. I told you to wait there."

She swallowed.

"You could have drowned out there."

"I didn't." She gave him a hesitant smile. "And I knew you needed me."

He nodded. "I did." *I do. I do need you.* The words caught in his throat. Because he only had two and a half more weeks in Deep Haven. And then he'd be returning to his everyday life.

Unless he really was going to stay.

He pulled towels from the truck as their adrenaline wore off, their wet clothes turning frigid. He wrapped a towel around Vivien and grabbed the second one for himself.

She stepped close to him and wove her arms around him. "I knew you wouldn't stop until you got her loose. And I also knew how cold that water was. And, I'm trained for water rescue." She smiled. "I'm not just a pretty face."

"No, you're not just a pretty face." He held her tight and felt her tremble in his arms. "Cold?"

"Yeah. I guess. And maybe...overwhelmed. I've never done anything like that before. Even though I'm trained, I've never had to actually use those skills. It feels...good."

He looked at her and felt something break free inside. The woman left him completely undone, a fact that should probably trouble a man trying to relax. Except, it didn't.

His life was totally out of control.

And it had never felt so right.

Vivien could admit that her heart and soul had latched on to the joy that came with saving a life. The message Ronnie had passed on from Tasha's mom. Healing would take time, but they were hopeful. It had made it the kind of week that caused a girl to believe that maybe, yes, maybe she could be more than the sum of her past failures. More than the broken legacy of her family.

*More than a pretty face.*

Even twenty-four hours later, the adrenaline still thrummed through her as she stepped into the climbing harness at the Crisis Response Team headquarters, the memories fresh. How one moment, she'd been sitting in Boone's arms after hours tooling around the lake. Laughing. Setting up lunch and letting the dappled sunshine warm them beneath the canopy of birch trees.

*What if I could stay longer?*

Then the cry for help had shattered the moment and Boone had jumped into action. And when she saw him go under, struggle to free the teen, there was no question. It was her role to play.

"You've never done this before?" Cole worked his hands through the harness, making sure it was tight enough before connecting the carabiner on the line that looped up through a ceiling anchor.

"Nope. Never." Vivien looked down over the two-story drop. They'd added in boulder holds and footholds on the wall. Peter Dahlquist stood there, his dark hair pulled back and the bulk of his form holding the belay line. "Peter—if you drop me, I'm going to cast you as the lead in my next musical."

"Don't even think about it. It's probably *Wicked*."

"Are there any male leads in *Wicked*?" Cole asked, looking down at Peter.

He shot a look at Vivie, his deep voice reverberating in the open bay. "No. That's exactly my point."

Vivien laughed. "I love having you as a cousin. To torture all the livelong day."

"Just remember who's holding your belay, Viv." He gave a robust laugh.

"Okay, time to get serious," Cole said. "Ready?"

This might actually be the craziest thing Vivien had ever done in her life. She nodded and Cole put a thumbs-up out over the platform. "Call down 'On belay' to Peter when you're ready."

She nodded, cleared her throat. "On belay?"

"Belay on!" Peter called, all the tease gone from his voice.

Cole turned her so her back was to the drop and faced her. "Okay, this is the hardest part. You're going to anchor your feet here"—he pointed at the ledge just behind her—"like you saw me do earlier, call down to Peter 'On rappel,' and then you're going to lean backward and let your body go parallel to the floor. I'll coach you down, but keep your knees soft and your body relaxed."

She took a long breath. Maybe joining the team as a volunteer wasn't the best idea she'd had.

"Peter's got you. He's going to let out the line, little by little to allow you to move into the horizontal position with your feet against the wall. Remember, keep your body soft, relaxed." Cole was trying to help her focus. Reassure her.

"Be brave, Vivie. You've got this," Peter's voice hollered up to her.

Yeah. She could do this. She'd helped save Tasha—who was now recovering at the hospital in Minneapolis because of her and Boone.

"Once you're out, it's easy as pie. You're just going to walk backward down the wall, keeping your core tight, arms and legs relaxed, and Peter's going to ease your line as you go."

Right. Okay. She could totally do this. Like *Charlie's Angels* kind of do this.

Except, her feet stayed in place.

"Viv?" Peter called. "I've got you."

Cole stood in front of her. "Take a few deep breaths. It's like jumping into the deep end of the pool for the first time. You'll be okay."

She nodded. Inhaled. Exhaled. Looked behind herself and stepped to the edge. "On rappel." Then she leaned back, trusted. And the flood of adrenaline swept through her body like she was stepping out onto stage.

Exhilarating.

"Keep at it, Viv—you're doing great," Cole called down from above.

"About ten more feet, Viv," Peter's voice advised from behind.

She gently pushed off the wall and then she could see the floor coming up slowly beneath her.

"Grab hold of the rope so you can rotate yourself upright while you walk your feet down the wall."

Her feet touched the floor and she threw her hands over her head. "That was awesome!"

She turned to hug Peter.

"What are you doing?" Boone stood near the doorway in a T-shirt and cargo shorts, his face drained of all color.

"I rappelled," Vivien announced while Peter stepped forward to disconnect her line.

Boone opened his mouth, as if to speak, but no words came out. Instead, he turned and walked straight back out the door.

She disconnected the line from her harness and ran out the door. "Boone?"

He stopped and turned, scrubbing his hands over his face.

"What's wrong?"

"I came to discuss the investigation—to keep you safe—and I walk in and instead of painting a wall, you're rappelling down a two-and-a-half story wall!"

"Yeah? And? We can still talk about the investigation. And paint."

"Vivien."

His voice edged—almost scolding. And maybe that was what set her hackles up.

Boone held his jaw tight and looked away. Oh—he wasn't angry. He was scared.

She placed a hand on his shoulder. "I got here early and Peter and Cole and I got to talking about the team volunteers and, well, that interests me. So they decided to teach me how to rappel."

He turned back to her, the lines on his face softening. He reached out to a lock of hair the wind had lifted and tucked it behind her ear. "I just don't like to see you hanging off a cliff. Especially without me holding onto you."

Oh. But before she could say anything else, Cole stuck his head out the door. "The painting party has begun. Are you guys joining us?"

She looked up at Boone, watched the storm pass over his face.

"Sure," he answered. "We can discuss a few things with the investigation."

"Okay. We're set up in the conference room." Cole disappeared.

"I was completely safe." She looked up at him, reached for his hand, and wove her fingers into it.

He looked at her, so much concern and care in his eyes, it poured over her.

"We should get inside." He gave her hand a squeeze. She stepped out of the climbing harness and followed him inside, shoving the harness into Peter's hands as they passed in the hallway.

Cole leaned against the wall of the conference room, pale splatters of paint on his jeans and blue T-shirt.

"Anything new on the case?" Boone asked.

"The package traced back to that prepaid card. As far as I know it was a dead end."

"What about Sabrina?" Boone pulled out his notepad from his back pocket.

Vivien shook her head. "She's ruthless, but I don't think she's quite that diabolical." She grabbed a paint can and popped the lid off. "If she's going to make me uncomfortable, she'd want a front-row seat for it."

"Like Fish Pic?" Boone made a note next to her name.

"Exactly."

Boone picked up a roller. "Ravil doesn't have a motive—he wants you back in New York City, so terrorizing you with reminders of what happened wouldn't make any sense."

"You sound very reluctant to clear his name," Vivien said.

Cole laughed at her observation and raised a brow at Boone. "She's got a point. We don't have any evidence or motive for him."

"I know. I know." Boone gave her a look. "He should have involved the police in your case. The fact that he didn't—and then fired you—well, he isn't going to win any man-of-the-year awards."

She noticed he'd avoided the boyfriend label. She picked up a roller, loaded it with paint, and began sweeping it across the wall in large W shapes.

"Well, that leaves us with Joslyn," Cole said. "She had the most to lose if you returned to the show."

"I think I'm totally awesome at this." She held up her roller. "Must be from all my years of set building."

Boone turned from Cole. "Except that's the wrong color."

"What?" Vivien looked from where Boone pointed at the creamy-white far wall back to the wall in front of her, where the dark edge of wet paint was most clearly gray. "Oh."

Cole laughed. "Sorry. That's my fault. I should have specified which can to grab." He picked up the open lid and pressed it back down on the gray. "This is for the trim."

Boone looked up from his notes. "Any more messages from Joslyn?"

Oops. "I blocked her number."

Boone looked up at her. "Oh. That would have been good to know."

"Well, no one told me not to."

Cole held out his hand for the gray-covered roller. "I can get that cleaned up. We'll need to let that paint dry before we can primer over it." He pointed to her wall, where her oversized W's looked more like an advertisement for *Wonder Woman* than anything else.

Vivien cringed. "Sorry."

"It's okay. I'm sure you can find something more fun than painting to do."

Boone tapped his notebook. "I'm going to follow up on a few things. Find out what Joslyn's been up to."

"Gordy's coming by the theater on Monday. I'm going to make sure everything is ready to go for the big reveal." She rubbed her hands together and peeled a splatter of latex paint from her fingers.

Cole set the roller down on a fold of newspaper. "Don't forget to pick up that volunteer application, Viv."

Boone's hand stilled, his pen mid-word. He looked up from his notepad, a hundred questions in his eyes.

She blinked. Smiled.

# CHAPTER 14

The blush of dawn spread across the sky, reflected in the lake. Sweat sluiced down Boone's back as he finished his run, his lungs heaving from the distance. But even five miles couldn't tame the beast inside him.

He hadn't slept well, his brain still spinning on the message his father had left the day before. He'd missed the call while at rehearsal and had been met with the excitement in his dad's voice when he played back the voicemail.

*I hear you're at the top of the list for the chief job. I'm so proud of you, son.*

Son.

Was he really ready to throw away the dream he'd been chasing for a woman? A woman who had trouble following her around? Walking into the CRT building, the last thing he'd expected to see was Vivien, dangling from the two-story-plus platform like she was playing the stunt woman in a new movie. *Volunteering?*

Maybe he wasn't doing the right thing in Deep Haven. He was going to get hurt. And everyone knew PJ had driven him to his last nerve...

He just needed to cure the turmoil that simmered inside him.

*Embrace the life you have, not...the one others expect you to have.*

PJ had once told him she liked who she was becoming. She liked the version of herself she could see in her tomorrows. And, so what if she was picking a lock when she said it? If he was honest now, it suited her to chase after...herself.

He blew out a breath. Maybe he was finally beginning to understand what she'd meant.

Yeah. No wonder she'd rebelled against him. Because now, he could see all those expectations he'd piled on PJ.

He turned toward his cabin. He liked who he was becoming too.

And he didn't want to make the same mistake with Vivien. No matter how much it terrified him.

He jogged around the corner and dodged a thin, dark-haired man on the sidewalk.

"Excuse me," the man said.

The man ducked away before Boone could respond, disappearing. All the PJ memories had him hearing Russian accents now. He shook it off as he reached his cabin.

A Chevy Silverado sat in his driveway, a layer of dust on the blue paint. Who—?

A tall, lean figure stood from the deck chair, the morning light bright against the gray hair.

Oh. Perfect. Chief Landry.

"Good. I was hoping you'd be back in time to cook me some breakfast."

"What are you doing here?" Boone slipped off his shoe and dumped the rock that had been grinding into him for the last quarter mile.

"Well, I would have called, but I wanted to see how you're doing."

"So you drove all the way up here? You could have contacted Rachelle. I'm sure she would have filled you in."

"Actually, we spent the night camping near Evergreen Lake. Got the family together for a trip before the fall weather hits." He took a deep breath. "There's a lot to be said for getting out of the city."

Boone couldn't disagree. He hadn't missed the crimes. The cases. The exhausting pursuit of justice. He smiled. "I see. While you've left them to camp grub, you decided to pop over here for, what? Eggs and bacon?"

"Oh, if you're offering." He laughed, a deep rumble. "But, no, they are all in town having breakfast at the Loon Cafe and then doing some window shopping. At least, I hope it's window shopping. We have enough stuff to take back home. Those grandkids don't travel light." He shoved his hands into the pockets of his green tactical pants. "Thought it was a good time to catch up with you." He looked Boone up and down, as if he was in formation, standing for inspection. "You look good."

"Thanks." Boone grabbed his gym towel from the rail and wiped his face. "Let me rinse off. Then we'll talk."

By the time the coffee was ready, Boone had plated pancakes and eggs for them and they sat down at the small table.

"How's the fishing been?" Steve took a drink of coffee.

Boone paused. Opened his mouth. Closed it.

Steve set down his fork, leaned forward against clasped hands. "You haven't gone fishing yet?"

"I've been kayaking. And I've been helping coach football. I've even been helping with construction on the Crisis Response headquarters building. In fact, I'll be heading over there after breakfast." Boone added another helping of eggs to his plate. Let his voice drop. "And I have the lead in the local play."

Steve's eyebrow raised. "Interesting." He took a drink of coffee. "That's good, I guess. Surprising, actually. How about the reading?" He picked the book up off the table. Flipped it open to the bookmark Rachelle had given him. On the first page of chapter two. He lifted his eyes back to Boone, waved the book in the air. "Do you want to explain this?"

"A few days ago, I helped save a teenager who nearly drowned."

He took another drink, the corners of his lips curved in a smile. "You can't avoid it, can you?"

"What?"

"The action. Diving in. You can't actually relax."

Boone set his fork down. "I've tried. I've really tried. But sitting still isn't my MO. And, you know, I can't really be blamed for some third party ending up needing to be hauled to shore. CPR. Being taken out by helicopter."

"I suppose you're right there." Steve looked out the window at the lake before turning back to Boone. "I'm not criticizing you. It probably feels that way."

Well...

"I spoke with your dad at the club." He stood and refilled his coffee cup then sat back down.

"He left me a message."

Steve took a long drink of coffee. "He's been like your campaign manager, putting your name out there for my position." He let out a deep laugh.

"I'd expect nothing less of him." Always raising the bar.

"He knows you'd be a great chief." Steve ran his hand over his two-day-old scruff. "I do too. You're sitting at the top of the pool right now, with the assumption that you're getting everything under control here." He tapped the book against the table.

"Thanks." Boone had lost his appetite.

"I did hear from Rachelle that your blood pressure's down. You keep up whatever it is you're doing here and you'll be able to return to civilization in no time." He gestured to the small cabin.

Boone stilled. "Right." He took a drink of his coffee. Because tomorrow he'd be walking into church with Vivien for the next-to-last time if he stuck to his schedule. Stuck to the expected.

Denied the man he was becoming.

"You have two weeks left on your leave." Steve cleared his plate from the table and set it in the sink with his mug. "I think it's safe to say you'll be ready to come back." He grabbed his truck keys on his way to the door. "You know, to accept your new position."

Boone swallowed, unable to answer. Because all he saw was the future he'd planned, the one with the pride of his father and the respect of his town...now pitted against the dream of something...more.

Fresh-mowed lawn and sweet gardenias filled the summer afternoon air as Vivien stepped from Ree's car and walked toward the Java Cup. Today, she'd opted for a practical wrap top and jeans paired with her leopard-print Converse low tops. Vivien was on the brink of success and all she needed was to keep everything on schedule today.

She and Boone enjoyed church together and play rehearsals. Some days, she'd find herself watching football practice. Okay, well, watching one of the coaches.

They'd fallen into a natural rhythm and when they'd walked into church the day before, it had felt like they'd been doing it for a lifetime. The comfort of his body against hers. The way they'd claimed their own spot in the sixth pew back, just off the center aisle.

They had a pew of their own. And he wasn't leaving. He wanted to stay. She'd even overheard him talking to Cole about the team on Saturday when they were at the VFW for dinner. And he'd been talking about the football season—the entire season, like he planned to still be around at the final game in October.

So, there was that.

And then she'd done the local radio show. Heard the buzz around town. It looked like *Then Came You* was going to be *the* Labor Day weekend event. A sold-out house.

She opened the door of Java Cup, inhaling the enticing aroma of ground coffee beans and fresh pastries. She glanced at her watch and stepped up to the counter where Kathy waited. "I'll take an iced Becky."

"Absolutely. Did you see the front page of yesterday's *Herald*?" Kathy laid the paper on the counter while she poured beans into the grinder.

Above the fold. She'd made it above the fold. Ree had told her about it, but she hadn't seen it yet. The picture showed Boone, Beth, and Vivien at the playhouse. Vivien had to admit that Beth made a convincing Ashleigh. And, Boone. The shot had captured him looking extra hot as Dylan Turner.

Oh, yeah. She'd noticed he'd leaned out. He'd been pretty fit to start with, but his morning runs and workouts were chiseling him to perfection. Bona fide, superstar perfection.

She remembered the practice, only four days prior. She'd been surprised when Ree had shown up with an actual photographer. It wasn't just a friend-writing-about-a-friend article. Nope. In fact, not only had the play sold out, they had a wait list. A wait list, for goodness' sake.

Her play was about to be an even bigger success than she'd ever hoped for. The thought wove its way in, warmed her heart.

She was doing it. Proving herself as more than a failure. And she could see on the faces of the cast and their families how much the play meant to them too.

"Will you save it for me?" Vivien handed the paper back to Kathy.

"Absolutely. Do you want a donut to go with that?"

"Oh, tempting, but I'd better not today. I gotta run—heading over to take a peek at the sets that were finished last night. We're getting down to the wire and Gordy said he needs to do a walk through with Peter to ensure the fire suppression system is properly charged after the summer mishap. And Emma and Kyle Hueston are going to help me set up the sound system and run through the lights."

"Lots going on." Kathy added syrup to the cup. "I heard you and that boyfriend of yours saved a girl last week." She handed the drink to Vivien.

Boyfriend. The word did funny things to Vivien's stomach. Because Boone was staying and, for the first time, Vivien could see a real future for herself. One that could include Deep Haven and theater and allowed her to discard her social facade.

Vivien lifted her drink. "Thanks for this. We'll definitely have to catch up next time."

"You bet. I'm looking forward to it."

A few minutes later, Vivien parked the car at the playhouse and scooped up the box from the passenger seat. The box of playbills, fresh from the printer, smelled like success. She balanced the box on her hip while she unlocked the door then turned at the sound of an engine pulling up behind her.

She'd know that rumble anywhere. Boone pulled up, his window down, arm resting on the edge like James Dean.

"Hey, I wasn't expecting you this early."

"Thought I'd see if we could get dinner after you're done."

She juggled the box in her hands. "Sure. Park and come on in. I'm going to go set these down."

He gave her a nod and she heard him cut the engine as the door closed. She flipped the light switch and dropped the box onto the floor.

Set pieces were strewn across the stage. Broken two-by-fours jutted out at odd angles, their raw edges splintering the light.

She covered her mouth and sucked in a breath. Oh, no. No.

The curtains had been sliced, and she stepped over broken glass where lights had fallen to the floor.

Shattered. Everything.

She jumped at the sound of the door swinging shut. She turned to where Boone stood, his mouth open, hands on his hips, as if he too, couldn't quite grasp the scene before them.

"What happened here?" He stepped up next to her and put his hand on her shoulder. "Who would do this?"

She started to speak, the sound coming out a hoarse crack. Her mind played through the scene, though, sobered by the realization that Gordy would be here any minute.

"We have to clean up before Gordy gets here." She slipped from his grasp and began pulling at the set pieces. "Before he gets here. Come on." She rubbed her temple. "What are we going to do?" She didn't even know where to start.

"Vivien—stop. What are you doing? It's a crime scene. Don't touch any of it!"

She grabbed the trash can and tried to keep her voice on the near side of hysterical. "We have to clean this up." She ran to him, grabbed him. "You have to help me. Come on! Boone, help me!"

He tried to hold her back. "Viv. You gotta let the police investigate this."

She rounded on him. "You don't understand. I can't lose this theater." Her heart pounded, her pulse filling her ears, drowning out everything else.

"Vivien—calm down."

She tore out of his grip. "You don't understand. I keep telling you—I'm going to get blamed for this. Gordy's going to *ruin* me."

"He's not. He'll understand—why would *you* ever damage the theater?"

"You weren't here. Earlier this summer, my youth show was

here. But there was an accident and they hit a sprinkler head and—"

She was hyperventilating. She leaned over, her hands on her knees.

*Calm down.*

She felt Boone's hand on her back, as if he didn't know what to do, and she could feel herself coming unglued but didn't know how to stop it.

Her breaths rushed over each other.

And then—

Gordy walked in.

The moment his eyes settled on the playhouse, the lights, the curtains, a scarlet hue started at his collar and swept up to his runaway hairline.

"What have you *done?*"

"Hey!" Boone stepped toward Gordy.

"I didn't do anything." She straightened, scrabbling hard for her voice.

Gordy poked his finger at her. "I trusted you, Vivien. I vouched for you with the school board—even after everything that happened before." He turned to Boone. "And you? I should have known not to trust an outsider."

Boone held up a hand. "Whoa, there. I think you're missing the mark here."

"No, I don't think I am. Everywhere Vivien goes, disaster is sure to follow. Isn't that right, Vivie?"

"Leave her alone. This is a criminal case, not a social lynching."

"You have no business telling me how anything should be in this town. You aren't part of it."

And that was probably the last thing Gordy should have said because Boone's eyes narrowed, his fists balled. "You think you're so high and mighty, Gordy. You think you run this town.

Well, you may have the old money. You may have the clout. But we're not the trash you treat us as."

Vivien tried to get air. Tried to speak. Nothing came out, and the room started to spin.

"How dare you—"

"How dare I what, Gordy? How dare I call it like I see it? Because, you know—who am I? I'm just Boone Buckam. Just an outsider, right?"

"Oh, I'll tell you what you are—"

Then—maybe Gordy stepped a little too close to Boone. Maybe Boone went into cop mode and forgot he was standing there as a civilian. But as Gordy's arm extended, Boone snagged it, twisted it, and had Gordy up against the wall in a second flat.

Gordy shouted, in anger and probably pain. But Boone had a fighter's grip on him.

And there went every chance she had of making peace with Gordy again and probably destroying any chance of a successful theater production.

*Oh no, Boone!* Vivien sucked in a sob. And if that wasn't bad enough, the door opened again and Kyle, still in uniform, stepped into the chaos with his wife, Emma.

# CHAPTER 15

*B*oone knew there was trouble the moment he'd heard Vivien's gasp inside the theater. He'd run in. Seen the carnage. The entire set destroyed. The lights shattered across the stage floor.

The wrecked look on her face. She'd gone into a frenzied panic and somehow, he'd left even-keeled behind when Gordy came storming in—blaming her.

So, yeah. Boone had seen red.

He should have taken a breath. Stepped back. Separated Gordy's anger from his accusations.

Instead, just like in Kellogg, everything unraveled. At least he'd stopped before he'd sent Gordy all the way to the ground.

And then the sheriff walked through the door.

Kyle took in the blast zone of wreckage before him and Boone, standing there with Gordy in a straight-arm bar, and it was all over for Boone.

"Let him go, Boone," Kyle said in a law enforcement voice.

Right. Fine. Boone released Gordy, stepped back, his hands up. "He was out of control," he said.

Gordy rounded on him. "I'm not the one out of control!"

The man shouted, his face bright red, his eyes narrowed. He pointed toward the debris. "Do you know how much money and time my family has put into this building? Do you know what it means to us?"

Boone turned to Kyle, still breathing hard. "This isn't what it looks like."

"I want to press charges." Sweat beaded on Gordy's brow, turning his receding hairline dark. "This man—" He pointed at Boone. "This man threatened and assaulted me."

"I didn't threaten you!" Boone drew in a breath. *Stop talking.*

"So, you *admit* to assaulting me." Gordy straightened his shirt and tugged his sweater back over his robust middle.

"That wasn't an assault—that was a control hold." He, too, could use his cop voice. He turned to Kyle. "And, really, the guy had it coming. He's acting like a lunatic."

"*I'm* the lunatic? I didn't throw anybody against a wall."

"You came after me!" Boone said, but honestly, it happened so fast—

He might have grabbed Gordy anyway, the way he was lashing into Vivien.

Boone looked to Vivien, who stood, her hand on her forehead, her eyes blinking. Saying *nothing.* She just stood there, letting Gordy tear into him.

Looking at him as if he'd destroyed her world.

And frankly, her expression looked so much like the one PJ Sugar had given him the night he'd let her take the blame for the country club fire, it felt like a punch, right to his heart.

He couldn't fix this. Perfect. He'd wrecked another woman's life. Maybe he was exactly what Kellogg thought about him. And the realization that maybe he really couldn't change who he was sucked the air from his lungs.

Kyle held up a hand. "Gordy, I think everyone needs to take a step back."

"No. I won't. I won't back down from this bully. I want him

arrested. Right now. And, you know what? You'll hear from my lawyer too."

Kyle blew out a long breath and nodded for Boone to step aside.

Boone followed him. "Listen—"

"I think it's best that you go."

"Fine. I'll be at the cabin if you want my statement."

Kyle gave him a grim-faced shake of his head. "No. I mean head back home to Kellogg." Kyle's jaw was tight. He lowered his voice. "I think that's really the only chance you have of getting Gordy to back down right now. He's hot about what happened and he's a powerful man. If you push him before he cools off, there's no telling what kind of destruction it will do." He looked toward Gordy, who was rubbing his arm and shoulder. "I'm going to see if I can do some damage control."

Boone rubbed his hands over his face. *Leave? Right Now?*

Kyle stepped away and then paused. Turned. "Really, I don't want to see this blow up into something that hurts your career and destroys your chance for the promotion. You belong in Kellogg."

He didn't need to say anymore. Boone could fill in the rest. *You don't belong in Deep Haven.*

And as much as Boone wanted to fight it, maybe Kyle was right.

Especially when Gordy piped up and threatened Kyle's future as a sheriff.

"Fine. I'm gone." He shot a look at Vivien, whose eyes widened.

Then, his heart banging hard against his chest, he stalked out of the theater toward his car.

"Boone! Wait!" Vivien scrambled out behind him and he could hardly stand to see the look on her face. She wiped tears from her cheeks. "What are you doing?"

"You heard Kyle. I have to go."

"Go where?" She got between him and his car and gestured toward the theater door. "We have to fix this."

"I'm leaving for Kellogg."

"Now? You can't leave *now*. The playhouse is a wreck and we only have a week to find a new location and rebuild the sets and—"

He put his hands on her shoulders, cut his voice low. Even. "No, Vivie. It's not going to happen. I have to go."

"You don't!" Her voice shook and tore a piece of his heart. Her beautiful eyes filled.

"You know Gordy's going to ruin my career. Ruin my chances for the promotion if I stay."

Her breath hitched. "I thought...I thought you weren't going to take the promotion."

And he could read it in her eyes. *I thought you were staying.*

Yeah, well, him too. The thought hit him like a punch. He'd wanted to *stay*. To build a new life here, with Vivien.

And his temper had screwed that up too. He took a breath.

"That promotion is all I've got. And I'm certainly not going to put Kyle's career at risk." He stepped away from her and dug into his pocket for his keys.

She blinked at his words, openmouthed, as if slapped. "What about the...the play?"

"The sets are destroyed, the playhouse is out of bounds again, and your male lead has to drop out. I don't think there's going to be a play. I'm sorry."

And now he really hated himself.

Tears streamed down her cheeks. "You're not going to fight for it?"

He swallowed and looked away. "What is there to fight for? Everything's gone."

His words turned his throat to acid, and he tightened his jaw. He needed to leave, now, before he did something stupid.

Like cry.

"I trusted you to help me pull this off." She was really crying now, her voice broken.

Aw. And he didn't know where the words came from, maybe the desperate attempt to pull them both back from the jagged emotional edge, but—"Come on, Vivie. Don't be so dramatic. Look at my life. It's no surprise, is it?"

Her eyes widened.

"Happy endings are fiction. Fairy tales." He pushed past her, opened his door. "I don't belong here and I should have figured that out long ago before I let myself get involved in some stupid play."

She sucked in a breath. Blinked. Her arm wrapped around her waist, the look on her face...gutted.

Oh no. "Vivien—you know I didn't mean it like that."

Except, tears freely flowed down her cheeks. He reached for her.

She shrugged off his hand, sparks in her eyes. "You just go on. Because you're right. You *should* go. You don't belong here and you most certainly don't belong with me."

He stood staring at her, at the brutal look on her face.

*You don't belong with me.*

His jaw tightened. "Nope. I guess not."

She stepped backwards onto the sidewalk while he got into the car, her breath gasping with sobs again.

He didn't look at her as she wept. Couldn't.

Not even a glance in the rearview mirror as he drove away.

Vivien tucked her head when she entered the VFW two hours later, willing the evening chatter to continue. The faces to not look in her direction. The last thing she wanted was to be in the Deep Haven spotlight. She pressed down the roil in her stomach brought on by the smells of food.

She'd grab the dinner she'd promised to pick up for Ree and then break the news.

She was leaving Deep Haven.

She'd made the decision on her drive back from Boone's cabin. His *empty* cabin. He'd left town at the speed of Superman.

Or a thief in the night, because he'd certainly stolen something from her.

Her future. Hope, even.

Signe Netterlund stood at the cash register, retying her blonde hair into a high ponytail. "Hey, Viv."

"Hi. I'm here to pick up an order for Ree Zimmerman."

"Sure." Signe nodded. "That was two burgers and fries, right? With one onion ring?"

"That's the one." She shoved her hands into her pockets.

"Let me check. We're a little shorthanded right now." She pointed at the Now Hiring sign for a cook. "It should be almost ready."

She disappeared into the back and Vivien tugged her ball cap down. Ignored the sting of the memories. The fact that the last time she'd been here had been with Boone talking to Kyle about the case.

She especially ignored the ache in her heart when she'd gone to his cabin to apologize, only to find it empty.

He'd bailed on her.

Apparently, their time together hadn't meant anything to him. Apparently, he didn't feel the raw, gaping wound in his heart the way she did in her own.

And, apparently, he really had meant the words *I don't belong in some stupid play.*

Had she roped him into things he hadn't wanted to do?

She'd been a fool to try to compete with his dream promotion. To let hope latch on to her heart.

No. Even as her heart warred for her to go after him, to call him, to beg him to come back, she wouldn't.

Couldn't.

Because that's exactly what she'd done to her dad. Cried. Clung to him. Begged him not to go.

*Don't be so dramatic.*

Boone had made his choice. She tugged a tissue from her purse and wiped her nose. Vivien didn't need him.

*Right.*

The truth scraped her raw the entire way back to her house with her bag of burgers and fries. Well, she hoped Seth was available for lunch because she'd lost her appetite.

She'd failed.

Again.

Only this time, she hadn't just let herself down, or let strangers in New York City down. No, this time, she'd let her *friends* down. Beth. Ella. Courtney. Adam. All the time Mona had put into helping promote it. The businesses who'd put up money to sponsor the show. Evergreen Resort. Wild Harbor Trading Post. Java Cup.

There was only one place she could run to in order to get away from Deep Haven.

Ree was making tea in the kitchen when Vivien came in and dropped the food bag on the counter. "What's wrong?"

"Nothing." Vivien looked away. Tried to remember some happy thought that might dam up the tears she hadn't shed.

"Viv?" Ree reached out a hand, squeezed Vivien's shoulder. "What is it?"

"He's gone. Boone left town, the theater's wrecked, and I am the biggest failure Deep Haven has ever known." She walked to the couch and slid down on it, wrapping her arms around a throw pillow she pressed to her chest.

Ree sat next to her. "Do you want some ice cream? We can skip the burgers and go straight to comfort."

"No." She never wanted to eat ice cream again. "I'm not hungry."

Ree stared at her. Blinked. "What happened?"

"The theater was completely wrecked. Like, someone totally destroyed it."

"Oh no!" Ree covered her mouth with her hand.

"Yep. And Gordy blamed me. Can you believe that?"

"What?"

"And then Boone tried to step in, which should have been nice, but then that went all kinds of sideways and he grabbed Gordy. And then Kyle showed up. And then—" She shook her head. Clenched her jaw. "It doesn't matter. Because even if some part of it could have been salvaged, Boone said awful things. *I* said awful things."

"Oh, Viv."

"I went to his cabin to apologize, but he's already gone." She waved her hand, as if she could dismiss her feelings. "He's probably still in love with his ex. Couldn't wait to hit the highway and head back to Kellogg."

"That's not fair. Boone really did want to help you."

"Hardly. He called the play stupid. A *stupid* play. Well, wow. Tell me how you really feel."

Ree took her hand. "He was hurt, angry. He didn't mean any of it."

"I thought maybe he was too. So, I went to talk to him. But he'd already left. Packed up and drove straight out of town."

"That doesn't mean—"

"Why are you siding with him?" Vivie sat up. "He's probably already got the Chief of Police plaque ordered for his desk."

Ree gave her a look. "C'mon, Viv."

"I've failed. Again. I mean—how many times will I completely screw it up?" She stood and moved to the middle of the living room. "I used to run home to Deep Haven. And now? I don't have a home anymore. This time, I've failed right here, in front of everyone who's ever known me." She blew out a breath. "Fine. I'm going back to New York. Because if I'm going to fail, at least there I can disappear into the plethora of has-beens and wannabes."

Ree got up also. "You're not a has-been or a wannabe, Viv."

But Vivie shook her head, pulled out her phone from her pocket, scrolled through her contacts, and hit Send.

"What are you doing?"

He answered on the second ring. "Hello?"

"Ravil?"

"Viv!" Ree said, reaching for the phone.

Vivien turned from her. "Is there still a role for me?"

The abrupt question had him pausing and for a second, her heart sank. Then, "Of course, sweetheart. How soon can you be here?"

She stared out the window, at the sun setting over the lake, blood red across the waves. "I'm sure I can get a flight out tomorrow if one of the girls will let me crash at their place for a few nights."

"Done. Text me your flight information and I'll pick you up at the airport."

Vivien hung up, her hand shaking only a little.

Ree was standing with her hands on her hips. "You can't be serious, Vivie. Ravil's a jerk, role or not."

"Let's be real. People only love me when I'm someone else." She moved into the bedroom and tugged out a suitcase.

Ree followed her into the room. "I think you've told yourself that story since you were a little kid."

"It's always been my experience." She threw the suitcase on her bed and flipped it open.

"You're wrong." Ree put her hand on the makeup bag Vivien had turned to grab, holding it in place.

"Well, it doesn't matter. I think Boone's still in love with the idea of his ex."

Ree released her grip on the bag. "No way."

"Yes. I really do. I think I am exactly what I tried to set him up for—a summer fling. A distraction." She tossed the makeup into her suitcase and began tugging clothes from her dresser drawers.

"You *weren't* a fling."

"Let's see—he said he doesn't belong here. He was more worried about his promotion than the play he'd committed to. Ultimately, it all came down to appearances. He didn't want to look like the bad guy. He didn't want anything to tarnish the reputation he'd worked so hard to build and earn his place in his father's life. That's the whole reason he left Kellogg a month ago. To let the dust settle." She shoved a stack of T-shirts into the suitcase.

"I don't think that's true. I think maybe that's how it started —but I think he came to want to be here. Honestly, Boone doesn't strike me as a fling kind of guy."

Vivien threw her hands into the air. "Well, a guy doesn't get over his first love. Not when he's pined for her for that many years."

Ree stilled. "Seth did," she said quietly.

And now Vivien was the jerk. "Sure. Of course, Seth did. But, Boone, he's different."

Ree stooped to pick up a pair of jeans that had fallen to the floor and gently folded them. "You're wrong about him. Just because they love deeply and profoundly doesn't mean they can never love another. It just takes the right time, the right set of circumstances." She set the jeans onto the bed.

"I shouldn't have said what I said, Ree, but I didn't mean Seth."

And, even if Boone had spoken out of anger and frustration, it didn't matter. He'd also spoken out of his heart. She'd convinced him to go along with the play. Begged him when he was so set against it. So, really, why would he think her play was anything but stupid?

She shoved the remaining pairs of pants into the suitcase and leaned her weight onto it to close the latch.

"I need to buy my ticket." She didn't even try to make her half smile convincing.

Ree remained silent and Vivien pulled up her airline app and punched in the flight details. "Look at that—I can get a flight tomorrow." She tabbed through the ticket purchase. One way to the Big Apple. Her thumb hovered only a moment over the Buy tab.

Then, "Done."

Ree shook her head. "Whatever. I'll take you to the airport."

Vivien nodded and reached out to squeeze Ree's hand. "Thanks. I need to make calls to the cast. Let them know the show is off. Apologize to the sponsors."

"I'll help."

"Thanks, but I think I need to tell them myself. It's my fault."

"It isn't your fault, Viv." Ree wiped tears from her face. "I'm gonna miss you."

"Me too." But Vivien would not cry. She found her faux smile. "Hey—don't be sad. This is what I've always wanted. I mean, how many times have you seen me off to New York City? This time, it's gonna stick."

"Yes. I know."

Vivien riffled through the clothes still hanging in the closet. "Are you okay with me leaving stuff here for now? I'll be back to pack it up as soon as we have a break in production. Probably Thanksgiving, if not sooner. I'll cover the rent I owe."

"Sure."

And that was that. She knew exactly where she was going. Because, the truth was, she'd played the game of what-if and lost. And she didn't plan on ever doing that again.

# CHAPTER 16

*T*he cold shock of his large, empty house punched Boone with reality when he slid off the couch the next morning. He hadn't even made it to the bedroom before dropping his bags on the floor and falling asleep on the couch, watching old westerns.

*You most certainly don't belong with me.*

He turned off the television and made his way to the kitchen of his small ranch, opened the blinds, the rising sun casting sharp shadows across the room. The view of the street hardly compared to the lake view he'd enjoyed for his five—scratch that—four weeks in Deep Haven. He already missed the rhythm of the town. The people.

Vivien.

Even on its remote perch, his cabin in Deep Haven hadn't felt so isolated.

Kellogg, on the other hand, had definitely lost its luster.

Worse, he'd left with a job undone. He still hadn't figured out who'd been harassing Vivien. Or now, who'd destroyed the theater.

He wouldn't sleep until he solved that case. Until he knew she would be safe.

Albeit without him.

Yeah, he should have probably stuck around Deep Haven, if only for that reason.

Vivien's laughter twined into his memories. He could see her, animated, guiding the cast through the play. Sitting down at the piano to play with Courtney and Ellie after rehearsal. Even her jumping into the lake and her determination to not quit on Tasha.

He pressed his hand against his chest. Yeah, the biggest heart problem he had was Vivien Calhoun.

If he dared to admit it, he probably loved her. Loved her smile, loved her laughter. Loved her crazy ideas and wild enthusiasm. Loved every way she latched on to life with vigor.

He shook his head. Yep, he definitely had a type.

Vivien.

Bold and courageous and so full of life. She was adventure and zeal and added a brightness to his day.

She turned a plain, ordinary day into something extraordinary.

Until he'd managed to do something to muck it up.

*Your stupid play.* Well, that performance certainly wouldn't win him the best supporting actor award. Nope. He might as well have just told her that her life dream was ridiculous.

Because that's really what he'd done. Even if he hadn't meant a word of it.

The knock at the door drew him from his thoughts.

His mom stood on the steps. She wore a puffy vest with her jeans and T-shirt, her dark blonde hair piled in a messy bun.

"Hi, honey." She rose to her tippy toes and he leaned down to hug her while she kissed his cheek. "I brought you some fresh coffee cake." She pushed past him and he closed the door. Followed her to his small kitchen.

"You didn't have to do that."

She plopped a pie tin on the countertop, the smell of cinnamon and her perfect crunchy streusel warming his kitchen. "I've missed you. It gave me a reason to stop by." She slid out of her vest. "Oh, I have your mail too." She pulled a stack of mail from her bag.

"You can set it on the counter—and you don't need a reason to stop by." He walked over to the thermostat and turned up the setting to take the cool edge off. The hardwood floors captured the chill of the morning even as the sunlight turned them to deep amber. "How did you know I was back?"

She winked. "Mrs. Thompson next door. She may have called me when she saw your car pull in."

"I was going to call." Boone poured water into the coffee pot, placed grounds into the filter, and turned the pot on.

"I figured." She pulled plates from the cupboard and grabbed two forks and a knife. "But, when I heard you'd come back early, I was a little concerned."

"I'm a grown man. You don't have to worry about me."

She paused. Studied him. "And who's been cutting your hair? It's getting long. Are you doing that on purpose?"

"Mom." He gave her a look. "It's hardly what anyone would consider long."

She shrugged her shoulder. Smiled.

She cut two slabs of coffee cake and plated them. "I'm your mom and God knows I spent enough years not acting like it. So, you have to let me be Mom." She slid a plate to him. "It's my job."

He sat down on a stool at the peninsula and took a bite of the cake, still warm from baking. "Oh, this is really good." He took a second bite, then stood and grabbed the coffee carafe.

She slid onto the stool next to where he'd been sitting. "Tell me what's been going on."

"I'm on the short list for the chief job. A decision is due any day."

She swallowed her cake and wiped her lips with a napkin. "Well, that's no surprise."

"Thanks."

"How was Deep Haven? The last time we talked, you said you were helping Caleb coach and doing something with a...play?"

And, somehow, over coffee and cake, his mom drew out the sordid details of his summer. Maybe he'd spent too much time with Rachelle because he didn't seem able to stop himself from blabbering on about Vivien. About the stalker and strange deliveries. About the play. Even about Vivien dangling from the rappel platform.

"So, here I am," he finished.

"You love her." His mom looked at him plainly.

"I don't know." He got up and collected her plate, his, and put them in the sink.

"Are you trying for plausible deniability?" She waggled her brow at him.

He grinned as he ran water on the plates. "Well, I don't think it matters *if* I do. I made the same mistake with her that I made with PJ. I didn't stand by her. When it got down to it, I wanted to protect my chief prospect." And frankly, she hadn't stood by him either, had she? But maybe he deserved that. "And I let my fear nearly box her in."

He sat down again beside her.

His mom ran her thumb back and forth along the handle of her third cup of coffee. "Boone, I've experienced God's grace poured out on me. It changed me. Freed me from my past. From who I thought I was." She placed her hand over his and squeezed, and he met her eyes. "Let God's grace do the same for you." She blinked back tears.

"You sound like Caleb."

"I always liked that guy." She smiled and took a sip. "Seriously. Don't be afraid to allow grace to transform your life. You just don't even know what's possible."

Except, he knew his dad was counting on him getting the job and, well, how could he ever let him down?

"For now, it sounds like you, Detective Buckam, have a case to solve."

"Right."

She walked to the sink and began washing their dishes.

He grabbed a towel to dry and she handed him a plate. He paused. Watched as she washed their cups.

*I have redeemed you.*

Washed away.

"Mom?"

She continued scrubbing a stain, chatting. "And, no, I'm not saying I want you to leave Kellogg or that you wouldn't make an outstanding chief. But you need to be who God tells you to be—"

"Mom." He turned off the water and stilled her hands, slipping the last cup from her fingertips and placing it on the drying mat.

"What?" She looked up at him, clarity in her blue eyes.

"Thank you."

Her head tilted, her eyes staying on his. "You're welcome." She dried her hands and wrapped him in a hug, her hand pressing his cheek against hers. "I love you, hon."

"I love you too."

She picked up her vest and walked to the door. "I need to get to Bible study. I think your dad is hoping to stop by tonight."

And, shoot. He'd much rather keep eating coffee cake with his mom.

He closed the door behind her.

*You, Detective Buckam, have a case to solve.*

Boone grabbed his duffel bag and pulled out the notes from

his last conversation with Kyle. Joslyn—yes, she still had to be the key.

He found the phone number for Detective Rayburn of the NYPD, the one who'd promised to look into Boone's questions when he had a spare minute. Well, Boone wasn't waiting around for answers any longer.

Time to make some calls.

Unfortunately, dawn didn't afford Vivien any peace. Her insides were still as wrecked and ripped apart as the playhouse. When she'd placed calls the night before to each of the cast members, she'd felt like she'd not only failed herself, but each one of them.

All the time they'd put in. For nothing. And it wouldn't even matter if Kyle solved the case. Whether or not he discovered the real culprit. Because the bridges had been burned for her.

Even worse, she'd found the women's Bible study flyer in her purse when she'd cleaned it out for the flight.

*She is clothed with strength and dignity, and she laughs without fear of the future.*

Nope. Not happening.

She'd turned away the cast's offers to help her clean up the theater. How could she let them do that?

Maybe she'd left the door unlocked. Maybe she'd invited trouble into town. Maybe it was true—maybe trouble followed her.

Whatever it was, she was the reason the place had been destroyed and she couldn't let them spend their morning cleaning on her behalf. Cole and Kyle had taken a report. Walked through the debris looking for clues only to come up empty-handed.

She just needed to clean up her mess and get out of Dodge.

Except, where would she even start?

All the large pieces Adam had built. The ones she'd painted with Issy and Ree and Mona. She lifted one of the large boards and looked at the underside.

Would-be leaves covered in orange spray paint before being pounded apart.

Her silver lamps in a thousand pieces.

Like someone had taken a sledgehammer to every set piece. She tugged her work gloves from her bag and lugged a sizeable chunk of plywood across the floor and out the back door.

An hour later, she tossed another chunk of broken set piece into the dumpster and made her way back inside. At least she was almost packed for her flight.

"Knock knock."

Vivien jumped, her fingers gripping the metal-light housing she'd pulled from the debris pile.

"Sorry. I didn't mean to startle you." Issy stood in the doorway in a pair of overalls, her curly brown hair tied back. "Hey." She took a few steps in. "I heard what happened."

"It's probably all over town by now." Vivien tossed the fixture into the trash can.

"Well, I may have overheard a few of your cast members drowning their sorrows in some cold brew down at Java Cup." She blew out a breath as she stepped over broken glass. "I stopped by your house and Ree said you were here and refusing to let anyone help." Issy picked up the box of trash bags and pulled one off the roll. "I brought gloves." She whipped the trash bag open and pulled on her gloves. "And I'm not leaving."

Vivien closed her eyes. "You aren't staging an intervention, are you? Because I have a plane to catch this afternoon."

Issy laughed. "Oh, girl, I *so* get you." She pulled the full trash bag from the can, tied it off, and slid the new bag in, snugging the edge around the can rim. "I just thought you could use a friend." She grabbed the broom and swept glass into a pile.

Vivien rubbed her hands over her eyes. "Fine." She gave her

friend a sad smile. "Thanks." Oh, she was going to miss her friends when she got back to New York.

"Sure." Issy dumped the contents of her dustpan into the can. "I think between the two of us, we can lift this big one." She pointed to one of the broken set pieces and picked up the end of it.

Vivien grabbed the other side and they carried it to the outdoor dumpster, heaving it high enough to toss in with a crash.

Issy swatted paint chips off her hands and followed Vivien back inside. "Do you really have to leave town?" She pointed to the broken park bench on the stage and picked up one end of it.

"There's nothing here for me." Vivien grabbed hold of the other end of the bench and they carried it out the back door.

Issy slapped her gloves together, blasting dust off of them before sliding them back on. "Do you remember the unsolicited advice I gave you a few weeks ago?" She followed Vivien back inside.

Vivien picked up the remaining smaller pieces, one and two at a time, and Issy grabbed the broom again.

"Don't let fear rule your heart."

"A lot of good that did me," Vivien snapped.

Issy swept the rest of the pile into the dustpan in silence and stripped off her gloves.

"I'm sorry, Issy. I shouldn't be taking it out on you." Vivien dropped two empty paint cans into the trash can. "It's just—I let myself be vulnerable. I tried to do the right thing and take a risk…and here I am. Again."

"I don't have all the answers, Vivie, but I know—I *know* God's love is perfect and I know you can trust Him."

Vivien tossed the final chunks of set into the dumpster, tugged off her gloves, and reached out to give Issy's hand a squeeze. "I thought this wasn't an intervention."

"Oh, it's not. You know when I pull off a full-fledged-

Isadora-Knight-intervention, it's a big production." She offered a pinched smile. "I bring in the cheer squad. A team huddle. My whiteboard. Definitely a whistle."

"Right."

"This is just me, as your friend." This time, Issy stepped forward and wrapped her arms around Vivien in a hug.

*Don't cry.*

Vivien closed her eyes. "It feels like my dad, all over again." Her voice cracked and she pulled away, cleared her throat.

Issy nodded. "I'm so sorry." She framed Vivien's face with her hands. "You are not alone."

Vivien pulled away. Swallowed. *Think happy thoughts, think happy thoughts.*

Her favorite theater technique to not cry when she wanted to.

And there, her heart was slammed with memories of sunset rides in the convertible. She shoved those down and pulled away. *Think different happy thoughts.*

"Well, I think that's as good as it's going to get," Vivien said, not sure if it was a statement about the status of the playhouse or of her own life. She glanced at her watch. She'd have just enough time to finish packing and get to Duluth for her flight. And head off to NYC...alone.

Issy led the way to the door and held it open for Vivien.

"You're a good friend, Issy." She turned and gave her one more hug. "Thank you for your help."

Issy nodded. "Come on. I'll drop you off." She looked at her watch. "You probably need to head out soon."

Vivien nodded, unable to speak. Well, soon enough she'd feel better—as soon as she could get her feet back onto the stage in New York.

## CHAPTER 17

*B*oone stared at the envelope in his hands, the return address from the City of Kellogg. He'd been chasing the goal for nearly fifteen years.

If he could just figure out what he really wanted. How to find a path forward from where he was. Because the words on the page formally offering him the position as police chief gave him little satisfaction.

"I expected more enthusiasm from you." His dad stood facing him, his back leaning against Boone's kitchen counter. He still wore his expensive suit pants, but he'd shrugged out of his coat and loosened his tie. His gray hair was combed precisely over the thinning spot at the back of his scalp.

Boone had managed to put him off for three days, but there was no escaping the imposing Roger Buckam when he showed up at zero-seven-hundred wanting to know exactly why Boone hadn't told him about the phone call from the city or the official selection letter he'd received on Tuesday. "Thought you'd call me as soon as you heard."

He'd asked the chief not to say anything, but apparently,

someone had talked at the country club. Boone should be grateful it took three days for the news to reach his dad.

He tossed the letter back onto the kitchen counter. "Guess I'm still in shock."

His dad opened the refrigerator and grabbed a bottle of coffee creamer. Poured a generous helping into his cup and set it on the counter. He grabbed a spoon from the drawer and stirred his coffee. "I've been talking you up for the job."

Boone took the creamer from the counter and slid it back onto the refrigerator shelf.

It should warm him that his dad was behind him. Pushing him. Boone took in a breath, recounting all the different ways this was the position of a lifetime. His career path goal finally realized. So then why did the thought of it leave a gaping open wound in his chest?

*Embrace the life you have...not the one others expect you to have.*

He swallowed, his mouth dry, and forced the words from his pasty lips. "Great. Thanks, Dad."

He probably should have used those acting chops Vivien had claimed he had. Given him a big the-show-must-go-on smile. Said it with a little more feeling. Because the man most certainly did not buy a word he'd said.

His dad paused mid-sip, his brows lowered into a deep furrow. "It's what you've always wanted."

Except, deep down, it wasn't. He looked over at Roger Buckam, the memory of his senior prom night burning through him. The smell of smoke hanging in the air. The obvious expectation visible in his father's eyes as everyone wrongly pointed the finger at PJ.

And the wrecked look on her face the moment he'd chosen to step right into those expectations and turn his back on her. The one person who'd loved him despite what was best for her.

And he couldn't—wouldn't—turn his back on the one person

who mattered this time. Because, somehow, in all the craziness of kayaks and coffees, rehearsals and would-be book reading, he'd fallen in love with Vivien and her extraordinary, contagious joy.

"No, Dad. I think it's what you've always wanted for me."

"What does that mean?" His dad put his cup down on the kitchen counter, a splash of brew slopping onto the white surface.

Too many years of pressure to do the best. To be the best. It erupted like a volcano, rivers of white-hot words pouring from his lips. "You've always pushed me to be something. Football star. Top detective. Now chief. And all my life, I have felt like I had to be those things in order to be worthy of being called Roger Buckam's son."

His dad's face blanched. "You're a talented guy. I only ever pushed you because I saw how much potential you had. Kellogg needs you as the next chief."

Boone faced off with his dad. "Kellogg does? Or you do?"

His father's voice dropped, the words edged between his lips. "Don't let yourself get sidelined again by some girl who's just going to get you into trouble."

"Oh, you mean like PJ? Vivien isn't PJ." Boone paused. Took a breath. "And I didn't do right by PJ when I was a kid, but I sure can do right by Vivien now."

"So, what? You're just going to leave town? Go back to Deep Haven and forget your life as a detective? And do what?"

His dad stepped forward, a big man. Imposing. Creases around his eyes and a permanent furrow in his brow. Deep lines of worry had etched his face.

And for the first time, Boone felt sorry for him. Sorry for the man who'd loved Boone's mom so much that he'd endured her decades of alcoholism. Who'd covered for her reputation as the town tramp. Who'd taken Boone on as his own son, even if he wasn't.

Boone offered a gentle rebuff. "I enjoy being a detective. I do. But I don't want to be chief. I don't need to be chief to prove myself." He stopped short of adding *to you.*

His dad rubbed his hands over his face and shook his head. "I just—I just don't want you to settle. You've always had promise. Potential."

"So you kept pushing me? Raising the bar? Assuring at every turn that I knew I wasn't enough?"

His dad opened his mouth. Closed it. Then lifted the letter from the counter. "Are you really going to walk away from this opportunity?"

He'd have laughed if it weren't for the desperate look on Roger's face. The man couldn't even see what he was doing. "Yeah, Dad. I am." Because, if it wasn't too late, he finally knew where he belonged. And this time, he wouldn't—couldn't—lose the girl again. Not if he could help it.

His dad nodded and walked to the door. Paused, his hand on knob. "If I was ever the one who made you doubt your worth, I...I didn't mean to."

It was the closest thing to an apology that Boone had ever heard from the man. The door closed, leaving Boone in the silence.

Thirty minutes later, Boone knocked on the chief's office door. The man looked up, his eyebrows raised and green eyes alert.

"Well, if it isn't my favorite north woodsman." He stood and bent his lean frame over the desk, taking Boone's hand to shake.

"Do you have a minute?"

"Of course." Steve gestured to the chair across from his desk and sat back down. "You aren't worried you won't pass the fitness test, are you?"

"No. I'm pretty sure I could smoke most of the department." Boone tried to lighten his mood.

Landry laughed. "You look like it." He picked up his cup of coffee and took a drink. "I was worried when you came back early, but Rachelle assures me that, with the exception of the book, you've exceeded all the benchmarks—your blood pressure is down, you've found activities to participate in. And, I heard the city has extended you the much-anticipated offer."

Boone tugged the letter from the city out of his pocket and laid it down on the desk and sat down. "I need you to know I'm turning down the offer. I wanted you to hear it from me."

The smile disappeared from the man's face, weathered by several decades on the job. "Why would you do that?"

Boone pushed away the whispers from his past. The ones that told him to earn his way. To be who he was expected to be. "One of the things you told me is that I need to be a man who's more than my job, and you were right. But the truth is, if I stay in Kellogg, that's all I'll ever be."

Landry studied him. "I see." He picked up a baseball from his desk top and turned it in his hands, looking at the autographs of the Little League players he'd coached. "I see," he repeated.

Boone ran his hand through his hair. Why did doing the right thing mean seeing hurt and disappointment in the eyes of the people he cared about? "I'm sorry."

Landry's brows raised and he set the ball back down on its wood platform. "Here I thought I was training you up to pass the torch."

"I know. I've had a great career here—I don't regret it." He shifted his right arm, the once-familiar brush of his Glock in its shoulder holster now causing a peculiar chafe.

"So, this is what I get for putting you on leave?"

Boone cringed. "Maybe. I finally realized that who I am isn't dictated by where I came from or what I do."

Steve stared at him. Blinked. "Well, good."

"What?"

"Good." He stood and walked to the front of the desk, leaned against it. "It's about time."

"Sir?"

"Don't get me wrong—you'd make an excellent chief. But I started thinking on my way home from camping. No, you hadn't read the book. And you had more things going on in your life than you ever have before. But..." He rubbed his fingers on his temples. "You looked satisfied."

Yeah. Maybe that was it. The feeling of fullness that came with knowing he had nothing to prove. Boone nodded.

"Go on—get out of here."

Boone headed for his office. The clerk looked up, making her blonde ponytail bob. "Hey, Detective. Did that investigator from NYPD get ahold of you?"

Boone shook his head. "Detective Rayburn? I spoke with him a few days ago. He was going to look into a few things for me."

"Check your messages," she answered.

"Thanks."

He wove his way through the cubicles to his office and picked up his phone, punched in his message code.

The detective's voice, with his New York accent, came over the line. "Hey, it's Detective Rayburn. I followed up on those questions you had. Looks like you were right. Joslyn Vanderburg has a criminal record—mostly petty stuff. But I also looked into that stalker you named, Dennis Campbell. I'm emailing you the details. You're going to want to see it."

Boone logged onto his computer and waited for Rayburn's email to download. He clicked on it and began opening the attachments. A picture of a man. Dennis Campbell. He opened another one.

No way.

Time-stamped security footage of Joslyn meeting with Dennis outside a coffee shop. Before Vivien left New York City. He scrolled through more. In fact, they went clear back to before the first incident that Vivien had told him about.

He clicked back to Rayburn's email, and the truth bit into him. *Joslyn had set Vivien up.*

And, he'd bet she was responsible for all the flower deliveries too.

Another email from Detective Rayburn popped up. Boone opened it.

*Not done yet, but I was able to link one of the flower deliveries to Joslyn Vanderburg, as well. She used a prepaid credit card, but that card had also been used to purchase a plane ticket to Duluth at the end of July. Guess whose name was on the ticket?*

Gotcha.

*I'll send you anything else that comes through. For now, we're going to keep building the case. I advise letting Vivien Calhoun know. I think Vanderburg is more about harassment and thinks she can fly under the radar, but you never know what'll set somebody off.*

The thought put a knot in Boone's gut. He picked up the phone, paused, swallowed hard. After a moment's more hesitation, he dialed Vivien.

Ringing, ringing. No answer.

Okay. So she didn't want to talk to him. He got it, but this was important.

Boone tried again. Same result.

Breathing out his frustration, he punched in Caleb's phone number.

Caleb picked up on the first ring. "Hey. Missing us already?"

"Yeah. I actually am. I'm heading back—I can explain more later. But do you know how I can reach Vivien? She's not answering her cell. I need to talk to her."

Silence.

"Caleb?"

"Issy said she left town the day after you did."

It didn't even matter that his doctor had given him the all-clear because Caleb's words sent Boone's heart into a manic pace. "Where'd she go?"

"New York City. Ree told Issy that Ravil was picking her up at the airport. He was putting her back on stage."

The exact worst place for her.

Boone grabbed his notes and shoved them into his go bag. He had a show to catch.

~

Vivien stepped from the taxi and hustled down the sidewalk to the theater. The Friday buzz of New York City vibrated in her bones, jarring her after three months in Deep Haven. She'd expected three days back in the city would be enough to reacclimate her, but she still didn't feel settled.

Maybe today she'd get through rehearsal without a glance back at Deep Haven. Without longing for the soothing sounds of Lake Superior or the wind rustling through the birch trees.

She looked up at the theater marquee, where a staff member held the letter-changing pole, adding the "h" to Calhoun underneath the show title *Beauty and the Beast.*

Her name was being put back onto the marquee. It should fill her with that sense of excitement. The rush. The fulfillment. She waited for it to hit her. Waited for the glow of pride. The validation.

Nothing.

If anything, her heart sank.

She entered through the back door of the theater, her Converse making a dull thud against the concrete hallway. Fifteen cast members had gathered in the green room, discussing published reviews and auditions.

She'd caught a few curious glances her first day back. The up-and-down eye sweeps casting judgment over her.

A few heads nodded in acknowledgment. Some genuine smiles from the cast members she'd been closest to.

Ravil had been more than accommodating, arranging for her

room and treating her like his VIP. So she had to share the cramped apartment with three other girls from the show. At least that made rent more affordable. And it wasn't too long of a taxi ride to the theater.

"Anything you need, Vivien. I want to keep you happy," Ravil had said, but there was an edge to his voice. He looked tired and he'd lost weight. She'd asked about his mother, but he'd raised a hand, his eyes turning glossy. Off limits. Instead, he'd turned the conversation to ticket sales and critic invites to her opening night. "You're going to turn this show around, Vivie." His smile didn't reach his eyes. Then, he'd abruptly turned away. "I need to go make some calls."

Still, the void had lingered through each of the three rehearsals. The sense of family she'd longed for was gone— almost as if it had never existed. And the uncomfortable awkwardness that hounded her every time she had to pretend she was falling in love on stage had become palpable.

"Bonjour! So good to have you back!" Her new understudy, Danielle, had leaned forward and thrown her willowy arms around Vivien before kissing her on each cheek like she was still in France.

Vivien had plastered on a smile, her guard settling into place. "Thanks." Danielle had never liked her and, based on the raised brows of the other cast members in the room at the overt display of false adoration, nothing much had changed.

It probably hadn't helped that Vivien had stolen her chance at the limelight. Ravil had promptly moved Danielle from the lead role back to understudy. No business like show business.

Now, Vivien made her way through the gathering cast for today's rehearsal.

"We're starting in fifteen minutes." The stage manager wove through the cast. She paused in front of Vivien. "After rehearsal, you'll need to try on all your costumes." She looked Vivien up and down like she was a slab of meat in the butcher shop window, her mouth down-turned in a deep frown. "They might need to be let out."

Vivien tugged her sweater around her body and sucked in her stomach. She'd spent a lot of years starving herself for the stage. So, yeah, she'd decided when she left town the last time she was done brutalizing her body to fit a mold. She liked onion rings, hot dogs, burgers, and ice cream.

She set her shoulders back. She wouldn't think about those things because they just took her back to Deep Haven. To Java Cup. To Footstep of Heaven Bookstore. To football.

She blew out a breath.

To Boone.

"Sure," Vivien said and pressed past the crowd to her dressing room. She opened the door and escaped into the quiet space. For all the heat of the stage lights, her dressing room was always impossibly cold in the old theater. She shivered, her eyes tracing the long crack in the paint that nearly traveled the entire wall. Several chunks of plaster were missing from the ceiling and three bulbs in the dressing room mirror had burned out.

*God, what am I doing here?*

She sank down onto the chair in front of her makeup mirror, dug through her purse for her lipstick. Her fingers scraped across a folded piece of paper. She tugged it out and unfolded it.

The women's Bible study flyer.

*She is clothed with strength and dignity, and she laughs without fear of the future.*

She let the verse take root in her soul. Maybe Ree and Issy were right. Maybe she had let fear rule her life instead of living honestly in her faith. Trusting God. She'd been afraid to love—okay, not love. She didn't *love* Boone. Yet. But, she'd been afraid to let someone in. She'd paraded around with the safe choices—like leading men for her life. No real commitment.

Until Boone. And, oh, she'd pushed him away, her own accusation sounding juvenile in her head. *You don't belong here and you most certainly don't belong with me.* Yeah, she'd been dramatic at the playhouse. And, while he hadn't handled it exactly like the smooth officer he could be, she had probably been looking for a way to confirm her doubts.

She pulled out her new cell phone and punched in Ree's number.

"Hello?" Ree answered, her voice tentative.

"It's me," Vivien answered.

"Viv! Where are you calling from? I don't recognize the number."

"I lost my phone somewhere between JFK and the apartment and picked up a prepaid one."

"Oh no! How are you doing? I miss you."

The sound of Ree's voice split the loneliness deeper.

"I miss you, too." Vivien paused, closed her eyes. "I would have called sooner, but I didn't know what to say. Ree, I'm not entirely sure what I'm doing here." Footsteps padded by outside her door as cast members began to assemble for rehearsal.

"I know *I'm* not sure why you're there. I told you that." The words held gentle rebuke.

"I have to do this. Right?" Vivien didn't try to conceal the doubt in her voice.

"Only you can answer that." Ree's soft tone reached across the miles.

Vivien leaned forward, resting her head against her hands and closing her eyes. "I just…I don't know."

They let the silence fill the space between them until Ree asked, "What about Joslyn?"

"Haven't seen her. I heard no one's seen her since the week she was fired. She stormed through, hollered about her check being less than it was supposed to be, then disappeared."

"Well, that's probably a good thing, right?"

"I suppose." In truth, Vivien wasn't sure that anything about New York felt like a good thing.

"Hey, um...you should know Boone called me."

The sound of his name constricted the vise around her lungs.

"He did? What did he want?" Not that she should care. Except, she did.

"I don't know. He couldn't leave a message because my voice mail was full. I saw his number on my caller ID."

"He probably wants to make sure Gordy isn't blasting him in the *Herald*." Except, why should *he* care? He wasn't coming back to Deep Haven.

She'd taken care of that.

Vivien could hear a door knock over the phone.

"Oh, nuts—I gotta run. I'm sorry. Seth is here to pick me up."

Vivien took a deep breath. "It's okay. I have rehearsal."

"Call me back later?" Ree asked.

"Sure. You guys have fun."

"Break a leg."

Vivien disconnected the call and checked her watch. Two minutes. She wove her way to the stage where the first-scene actors had assembled, warming up with vocal scales and facial gymnastics.

They would all put on their costumes, their makeup, and they'd pretend. She'd pretend.

Only she'd had the one man who'd seen through all the glitz to the real her.

The deep, husky laughter. The pale blue eyes. Ice cream and car rides. Dunks in the lake. Cauliflower vegetable pizza. A pew in the church.

A surprisingly ordinary and utterly incredible life full of...joy.

Joy. The kind that thrilled the soul. The kind that comforted the heart and grounded her. The kind that, yes, made being

Vivien Elizabeth Calhoun not only who she was, but who she wanted to be.

"Let's start with the library scene," Ravil said.

Vivien nodded to him and moved to her starting mark. She turned to face Jeremiah Douglas, the male lead. He stood on the stage in his skinny jeans and hoodie. Not exactly beast-like.

Definitely not Boone-like either.

Several other cast members moved into position and Ravil gave them a nod to begin.

The words came easily, scene after scene. They always did. But, even when the music started and she nailed every note, every step of choreography, it left only a hollow echo in her soul. Not even the climax of the story could warm her heart.

Because the sense of belonging she'd been seeking didn't come from the outside world. It didn't come from praise and good reviews. It didn't come from applause or the exacting direction of a show.

*She laughs without fear of the future.*

It came from her heavenly Father.

Oh, why had she ever thought she should leave Deep Haven again?

"Okay, that's good." Ravil held up his hand for them to stop and paced back and forth before walking up to Vivien and placing a hand on each of her shoulders, like claws, holding her in place. Creases tugged at the corners of his lips, aging him beyond his years. "Great job today. You're perfect."

"Thanks." Vivien gave him one of her stage-worthy plastic smiles until he loosened his grip and she backed away.

"Ravil?" Danielle appeared in the wing. "There's someone waiting for you in the office."

"Oh. Sure." He rubbed his hands together. "Good work, everyone. Get some lunch." He disappeared behind the curtains, along with the rest of the cast.

Vivien stood alone on the stage, wishing more than anything

that she was sitting in the Java Cup with Ree and Issy, talking football and engagements and work—all the completely wonderful and ordinary pieces of life.

The stage lights went dark and Vivien could finally see into the expanse of the dim theater. A lone figure stood up from the red velvet seats, backlit by the exit lamps near the doors to the theater lobby.

Oh boy. She sucked in a breath.

She'd know those broad shoulders anywhere. He stood there, looking every bit the hero as the first day they met.

Boone. Boone was in New York City. In the theater. Watching her rehearsal.

Somehow, she made it to the edge of the stage, slid down to the main floor, and met him in the dim light of the auditorium.

"What are you—what are you doing here?" Her words came out in a breathy rasp.

He wore jeans and that super-soft blue T-shirt that turned his eyes a devastating shade. He stood so close she could smell him. His intoxicating, masculine scent.

Her throat went dry.

His eyes met hers, his voice rough with emotion. "I'm sorry for the things I said."

She nodded. Swallowed. "I'm—I'm sorry too."

"I never meant them." He reached his hand out to hers and she wove her fingers into the warmth.

She nodded. "I didn't either."

No excuses. No justification.

She swiped a tear from her eye. "But, seriously, what are you doing here?" She laughed. It came out like a nervous giggle.

He nodded toward the stage. "There's a show I had to come see. I'm a really big fan of the star."

"Are you now?"

"The biggest."

"Just so we're clear—I'm Beauty, not the Beast."

He laughed, the rich deep tones warming her core.

"Beauty, huh?" He raised a brow.

She nodded.

"Yes, you are." He lifted his hand and let his fingers play with the waves in her hair. "It's interesting. Ironic, even."

She looked up at him, her body electrified by his nearness. "How's that?"

"Oh, I don't know—a show all about looking past the exterior. Seeing the heart."

"Maybe there is a little Beast in me." She lowered her voice. "But you do see my heart, don't you? You know the real me."

"I meant how you see me." He gave her hand a gentle squeeze. "Viv, you made me see myself differently too. Made me see that I could live a different life—one I wanted, not one I had to live. And when I got back to Kellogg, I realized I didn't want that life if it wasn't with you. And if being in *your* life means moving to New York City, then, well, that's what I'll do. I'm not afraid to start at the bottom of the roster at NYPD."

"What?" He could not be serious. She raised her hand toward the stage. "But—here?"

"I'm not leaving you, Vivie. Not now. Not ever, if you'll let me stick around."

"Then you'll have to follow me back to Deep Haven because I don't want this anymore."

Vivien led him to the stairs at the side of the stage and onto the main stage floor. "All this?" She raised her hands toward the sets surrounding them. "It leaves me as empty as those seats out there. I don't belong here. Maybe I never did. Maybe that's exactly why I kept running back to Deep Haven."

He reached for her. Wrapped her in a warm embrace that set her heart pounding. She buried her face against him, inhaling him.

She'd missed this. Missed every part of him. She twined her arms around his neck.

He met her eyes. And smiled. And then he leaned down and kissed her. Sweet, tender, satisfied.

Like this time, the guy got the girl.

Boone held her face in his hands, rubbing his thumbs across her cheeks before releasing her. He wove his hand around hers. "As much as I would love to continue this—I do have some concerns about your case." And just like that, he was in detective mode.

All the warm fuzzies melted. "My case?"

"The deliveries." He looked past her toward the stage wings and lowered his voice. "Is Joslyn here?"

"No. I was told she cleared out her stuff and picked up her last check at the beginning of August." She tightened her grip on his hand. "Boone—what's going on? You're kind of freaking me out." She pulled away and raised her hands. "I feel like I'm gonna have to bust out my *Charlie's Angels* moves again."

He wrapped his hands around hers. "Easy, 'Kelly.' From what I've seen, those are lethal weapons." The tease faded from his eyes and he released the hold with his second hand. "We believe she's responsible for the burned flowers you've been receiving. And the destruction at the theater."

Vivien's brows raised. "Joslyn? I mean, I didn't trust her, but...wow. You found proof?"

"Yeah. And, your fan-slash-stalker that caused you to freeze on stage? Looks like she hired him too."

Vivien sucked in a breath. "Why? To get me out of the show?"

"I think so. She knew what had happened at acting school when you left New York the first time. I guess she thought she'd take advantage to further her own career. And it worked. We found a plane ticket purchased by her the weekend your flowers showed up."

"But why would she come to Deep Haven? Why would she try to spook me there?"

"She knew Ravil was ready to ask you back. Probably felt that if she kept the stalker fresh in your mind—"

"But she sent me a text to warn me."

"To throw you toward the idea that you're still being stalked. And, if she warned you, then you wouldn't suspect her. She never called you back, right?"

"Well, I did block her number. But I wouldn't have returned. At least, if it hadn't been..." She placed a palm on her chest, the memory of their fight vivid. "I'm so sorry."

He squeezed the hand he still held. "Me too. We're not sure why she destroyed the playhouse. I have a NYPD detective who's been helping me with the case."

"You don't think she'd do anything—now that I'm here, do you?"

"It's possible. They're looking for her now." He looked down at her with so much concern it nearly unraveled her. "I—I'm worried about your safety."

She nodded and lifted her free hand toward the stage sets. "I have to figure out how I'm going to get out of here—out of this show."

Boone nodded, his eyes focused on hers. "Do you have an understudy?"

"Yes." Danielle would be thrilled to be back in the spotlight.

"And she can take over?"

"Yes, but I told Ravil—"

"Have you signed a contract?"

"No, I just showed up a few days ago and started rehearsing —" She froze, his words about NYPD finally clicking. "Wait, what are you actually doing here? Why aren't you in Kellogg, in the chief position?"

A lopsided smile slid up Boone's face. "I turned it down."

"You wanted that job."

He gave a wry smile. "No. Everyone else wanted me to have the job." He lifted the hand he held and placed his other hand over the top, cupped hers in between his own. "But I wanted other things."

She blinked at him. "Just like that, you turned it down?"

"Yeah. Just like that." He nodded, released her hand.

She let his words twine through her soul. "So, Detective Buckam, are you applying with the Deep Haven sheriff's department?"

Again, a lopsided smile. "Actually, I'm turning in my badge." He traced his fingertips over her knuckles.

"Really?"

He looked at her, clarity and resolution in his eyes. "Over the past month, I've been working on this little building project for the Crisis Response Team. It seems they like my drywall skills and might want to keep me around. If you want to live in Deep Haven, then I'll be applying for a position with the Crisis Response Team there."

Boone. Living in Deep Haven. "That would be amazing." Understatement of the year. And she didn't even care if she had a silly grin on her face.

"And, you know, the team does need volunteers."

"Really? You'd...be okay with it?" Her fingers brushed across the fabric of his shirt, his heart beneath her palm.

"Vivien, you need to be you. That's who I've fallen in love with."

Love. She looked up at him, the words easy on her lips despite the many times she'd tried to deny it to herself. So obvious. "I love you too."

He held her against himself, his voice soft against her ear. "And if I don't get the job, I'm sure something else will come along. I'm pretty good with cars. And maybe Casper will need someone at Wild Harbor to hand out towels to unsuspecting tourists."

She giggled. "Funny."

He drew her closer, his strong arms anchoring her. "Should

we head home? Let the NYPD find Joslyn while you're safe with me in Deep Haven?"

Safe with him...at home, in Deep Haven. Yes.

She spent twenty minutes searching for Ravil and calling his phone before resigning herself to writing him a note. She tucked it into the doorjamb of his office.

"No luck?" Danielle leaned against the corridor wall. "I think he went to meet someone."

"Oh, hey. Um—I need to leave. I wanted to tell him in person."

"Leave...?"

"The show. I won't be able to do the show." Vivien looked at Boone and then turned back to Danielle. "I know you've been playing the part and—and I think the role belongs to you now."

Something lit in her hazel-green eyes. "Oui."

Vivien turned and led Boone to her dressing room.

"So that's Danielle?"

"Yes. She's been playing Belle since Joslyn left."

Boone pressed his lips together. "Hmm." And he looked every bit the bodyguard as she gathered up her belongings and said goodbye to the few remaining cast members.

She—no, *they* were going home.

# CHAPTER 18

This was probably the opposite of relaxing.

Because Boone could nearly taste his heartbeat as he stood in the right wing of the Arrowood Auditorium for opening night. The cast had jumped back into rehearsals and had somehow even convinced Gordy to let them back into the playhouse. He suspected the man was hoping to save face after acknowledging Vivie was innocent, especially when the rest of the school board was prepared to sanction him.

Yeah. Boone *almost* felt sorry for him.

The cast and volunteers had worked late into the evenings to finish the new sets with raw materials donated from Turnquist Lumber, and the curtains had been repaired by a skilled seamstress.

Like Vivie said—the show must go on.

Still, even after four final rehearsals, Boone couldn't help but think that stepping out on stage—and *singing*, no less—was still an abysmally bad idea.

But he'd do it. For Vivien. And because it felt good to be back in Deep Haven. It hadn't taken Vivien long to pack up her suitcase. She hadn't actually unpacked much of anything. She'd shoved her shoes and T-shirts back in, left her short-term roommate, Lola, a goodbye note, and they'd hailed a cab.

"I think I'm getting cold feet," he said to Vivien as she snuck up to him.

"Don't look at the audience."

He dropped the curtain and Vivien held out the leather jacket. Boone slid one arm into it, then the other.

He shouldn't have been surprised the way everyone had come together to fix the sets at the playhouse. He'd even seen Gordy's stout body pacing around backstage as the expertly repaired curtains were installed.

"Don't you look like Dylan Turner." Vivien straightened his collar.

"This is a bad idea."

She pressed both her hands against his chest. "You can do this."

"No, this is a *really* bad idea."

"If anyone can pull this off, it's you." Then she rose on her tiptoes and kissed him.

And, well, when she put it like that, it was hard not to believe it.

"The show must go on. Get out there. I'll see you afterward." She kissed his cheek. "Ten minutes to curtain everyone," she said in a hushed voice and took off for the backstage crossover to the left wing.

Ten minutes to get himself together.

His phone vibrated in his pocket. Oops. He'd probably better leave that offstage.

Detective Rayburn. He swiped the screen. "What's up, Detective?"

"Hey, Boone. You were right. I went back through the area security footage and store records where the prepaid credit card was purchased. We found footage of Danielle Berteau with Dennis Campbell *before* he'd met with Joslyn Vanderburg. We tracked Joslyn down in Los Angeles. Turns out she's been there since late July."

"No kidding." Boone rubbed his hand over his jaw.

"Yeah. We checked with the airlines and her ticket to Duluth was never used. And she was scammed into meeting with Dennis. She showed the local detective text messages she'd received from someone who'd spoofed a talent agent's phone number. The so-called agent turned out to be Dennis Campbell —which is why she was meeting him at the coffee shop. She'd never seen him face-to-face before."

"And Berteau?"

"Turns out, she hired Campbell and set up Joslyn to get her out of the show too. We were able to arrest her at the theater. Campbell's in custody too. We found evidence that will tie them to the flower deliveries. Order receipts and phone records."

"Outstanding." He shot a look toward the stage, to where Beth was supposed to be standing in the wings. Should he be worried that she was late?

"Unfortunately, you were right about something else too."

His tone turned Boone's blood cold. "What?"

"You had me dig around on Ravil Kozlovsky. He's in debt —*deep* in debt—to a man with established ties to the mafia. Your hunch was spot-on. Berteau and Campbell were responsible for the flowers, but not the vandalism in the Deep Haven playhouse. We think Ravil Kozlovsky did that. We found a plane ticket from a week ago, right about the time of the vandalism."

Boone's heart pounded in his chest. "What?" He'd thought it was a long shot when he'd left Rayburn the message asking him to dig around in Ravil's finances and recent travel. He'd nearly chalked it up to a bit of reprisal—it wasn't like he could think the best of the man.

A chill gripped his heart. His Saturday morning run almost two weeks ago. The stranger he'd nearly plowed over. "Why?"

"Not only does he have his mother's health care bills, but he's also got a bit of a gambling habit."

"Loans?"

"Something like that. He gambled before his mom's diagnosis. Got himself into debt. Then tried to win it back to pay for her treatment. The show receipts look like he started skimming off the theater."

"He was stealing from the show to pay off his debts." And he needed his big star, Vivien, back on the stage. How better to get her to agree to return than to destroy everything she had in Deep Haven?

"Yeah. And for treatment costs. Looks like it all started to catch up with him and when he dropped Vivien from the show, the revenue tanked—revenue he's been skimming. Not only is he going to lose the theater, he's got people who are probably looking to kill him. These aren't people who play nice or practice loan forgiveness."

No doubt. Boone felt a little sick—and it had nothing to do with opening night.

"When a few cast members were questioned at the theater, they said he became a little unhinged when she left, again. That he'd been aggressive this week. In a panic."

"He's afraid."

"He picked the wrong people to get into debt with."

"You think he's coming for her?"

"He's in the wind. Could already be there."

"She's with me tonight. I'll keep her close."

"He's dangerous, Boone. Has a rap sheet in his former country. Be careful." The detective hung up.

Adrian stepped into the room, dressed all in black. "You've got five minutes before curtain."

"Want to trade? I'll be the stage manager and you can play this part?"

"No way. I still can't even believe Ella convinced me to do *this*."

Boone moved into his starting position. He could just see through the curtains a packed house. He shouldn't have looked.

"Places!" Adrian stage-whispered.

Boone blew out a breath and walked out onto the dark stage. He found his mark. *Here goes nothing.*

The lights came up.

"Dylan!"

For a moment, the voice, the form rattled him.

Not Beth. Beautiful Vivien, his Vivien, walked onstage in the role of Ashleigh.

Huh. She was perfect for the part, of course, every inch the starlet in her white and blue floral swing dress and cardigan sweater. The cinched waist of the dress accentuated her slender figure and a navy pillbox hat was pinned into her sable hair.

And, somehow, it was fitting to get to stand here, even playing a role set in the past, and choose a new path. A new future.

Choose to fall in love again.

She walked right up and threw her arms around him.

"When did you get back?" Vivien's bright blue eyes looked up at him.

He swallowed. *Line!* "Last night. I—I should have come by."

Vivien-as-Ashleigh released him. "Yeah. I've missed you. Have you seen the others?"

"No. Not sure what I'd say to Samantha." He looked down at her and caught the gleam in her eyes. Oh, she sure was beautiful.

"She broke off her engagement, you know." Vivien stepped away, faced the audience.

"I heard."

She turned, keeping her body open to the front of the stage, and held his gaze. "Always thought the two of you would—"

"Yeah, everyone did." But Dylan would have been a fool to marry Samantha. Engaged or not.

Vivien closed the gap between them. "How about we get each other through these next few days?" She took his hand, her gaze meeting his.

He nodded. "I always thought there'd be more time."

"We all did." She leaned in, pressed herself against his shoulder. "So, what do you say?"

What did he say? His mind went totally blank. All the lines he'd memorized. Gone.

So he spoke from the heart. "I think it's time I stopped letting my past dictate my future. Stopped living based on expectations and public opinion."

Except, maybe he didn't miss the mark too far, because right on cue, tears fell down Vivien's face. And she wasn't acting.

Somehow, he managed to get his head together. Managed to draw on every bit of rehearsal and muscle memory he had. And when they reached the final scene and Dylan and Ashleigh admitted they loved each other, Boone let his fingers trail down Vivien's cheek and he drew her to himself.

She looked up at him from under her dark lashes, a smile curving the corners of her lips.

He kissed her, soft and sweet.

The lights went down on the show, the stage turning to darkness while the packed house applauded and the curtains closed.

And he took advantage of the darkness and let the kiss linger a moment longer. Let Vivien's arms curve around him and let her mold her body against his.

She pulled away, a soft giggle filling the darkness between them. "We have to get off the stage." Her fingers wrapped around his and she tugged him off stage just before the lights came up and the curtains opened.

The audience continued to applaud. The cast stepped out in order, starting with Ella.

He leaned in. "I blew a few lines."

She clapped her hands together as Ella bowed. "No. It was perfect."

"What happened to Beth?"

"She sent me a message that she had laryngitis." Vivien winked. "I'm not entirely sure I bought it."

The rest of the cast made their stage entries. The applause filled the room.

He smiled, probably a silly, schoolboy grin. "I think your show's a hit." He held out his hand and led her out onstage. They took their bow and then the full cast joined them, along with Adrian. The cast pointed in unison toward Ellie at the piano, who raised a hand and waved to the applause, though blinded by the spotlight. They then gestured to Kyle in the sound booth and his wife, Emma, operating the light board next to him.

Boone looked to his left. To his right. Out into the audience. All the faces who'd become part of his everyday world. Friends. Peers. And he had a place, right in the middle of them all.

She leaned toward him, her lips brushing his ear, and whispered, "I think *you're* a hit."

The lights went down and they exited the stage before the house lights came up again.

Adrian held out his hand for a fist bump. "I didn't know you had it in you. That was impressive."

"Thanks. I have an excellent acting coach."

"I'm going to grab a couple guys to set up the chairs and tables for the after-party."

Oh, yeah. Boone had forgotten about that part. The audience lingered in the auditorium while the cast worked their way through, greeting the attendees in turn.

He turned to Vivien. "I need to talk to you."

"Sure."

"Vivie?" Megan Barrett ducked around the curtain, holding a stack of plastic tubs in her arms. "Sorry to interrupt—great job, by the way—loved it!" She held up her sweet treats. "I have cookies and bars. Do you know where I could find some platters to put them on?"

"Yeah. Follow me to the green room. I brought a few from the church kitchen." She turned to leave.

"Hey." Boone grabbed her arm. "They arrested Dennis Campbell and Danielle."

Vivien blinked. "Danielle? What about Joslyn?"

"I'll explain later. But first, I really need to talk to you about Ravil. He's—"

"Viv!" someone yelled. "You coming?"

"Yes!" Vivien called. She turned back to Boone, a deep V creasing her brows. Then she visibly straightened and shook her head as if brushing off his news. Focusing on the tasks at hand. "I want to hear everything, but after the party, okay? I won't be long and I won't go far." She held up her right hand. "I promise."

"I'll come with you."

A crash from the lobby caused them all to jump.

"That sounded suspiciously like a table falling." Vivien opened the door and glanced into the lobby. Megan's son, Josh, was helping Adrian with a table. "Would you help them? We need to get those set up and the food out within the next five minutes or everyone will leave."

He hesitated. "Sure."

Megan hefted her tubs against herself and Vivien took the top two off the stack.

"I'll be back in a few minutes." Vivien gave Boone a wink. "You look worried. Don't worry—the hard part is over."

And she walked away. He turned and jogged over to help relieve Josh from table duty.

"Thanks," Adrian said.

"Sure. Is this the last one?"

"We've got one more serving table and two round tables to set up."

Kyle and Cole pulled the legs out on their table and locked them into place before setting it up against the one Boone and Adrian had finished working on. "Let's grab a few of the rounds." Adrian nodded to the folded tables against the far wall.

Boone looked for Vivien. They were surrounded by people they knew, he reminded himself. What could possibly happen here?

There was something about that opening night post-party. The electricity. The sense of accomplishment.

And, even if Vivien was in the back room plating finger sandwiches from the Flashy Fox Bakery and sliders from the VFW, nothing could dampen her spirits. Not even whether she secured the Creative Arts Committee grant or not.

Boone had come for her. He loved her. They just had to make it through the party until they could have some time alone together. Make plans for the future.

The one she intended on having right here in Deep Haven with her very own leading man.

Megan placed an empty tub on the worktable. "This tray is full. I'm going to run these out to the lobby." She hoisted a platter of baked goodies.

"Perfect."

Ella filled the doorway as soon as Megan disappeared. "Can I help you with those?"

"Would you take these trays out?"

"Sure. Are you joining us?"

"I'll be there in a minute," Vivien said. "I want to take the trash out before it's filled up again with paper plates from the party. I'll bring it out to the lobby."

"Oh, good call." Ella lifted the trays, handed one to Adrian when he popped into the doorway. "Off we go."

Vivien hoisted the trash bag from the bin and tied off the top before slipping out the back door and carrying it toward the dumpster behind the auditorium.

The stars twinkled across the velvet night sky and she stopped to take it in.

*Who needs Broadway when you have a marquee like that?*

Not her. She hefted the bag high and dropped it into the dumpster. Done.

She rubbed her hands together. Back to the party and her leading man.

"You're better than that."

She gasped.

The voice, close, set the hairs on her neck on end. She turned.

Ravil.

"What are you doing here?"

"I think you know." He stood in the darkness, the streetlight casting deep shadows over his stony features. It had the effect of sharpening his cheekbones to severe and hardening the angles of his face.

She put on a smile, hoping it concealed the way his approach caused her heart rate to spike. "You caught the show?" She stepped away from the dumpster and he stepped sideways, into her path.

A sudden breeze blew the putrid smell of the dumpster toward her, turning her stomach.

"I did." He narrowed his eyes. "We had a deal, Vivien."

A deal? "I'm sorry, Ravil. I know you were counting on me, but it's over. So what *are* you doing here?" She slid her hand into her pocket. Felt for her phone.

Her fingers only found a folded tissue and a stick of gum. Shoot. She'd left her new phone in the green room. "Don't you have a show—"

He reached for her, snatched her wrist. "You've ignored all my calls. Left me to come chasing after you." He yanked her against him, ran his finger down her jawline, causing her to shudder. "You've cost me so much, Vivie."

"You're hurting me!" She jerked away from his touch, trying to step away. But he clamped down on her wrist.

"You have to come back with me." He pulled her toward the parking lot.

What—? "What is wrong with you? No!" She dug in. Tried to sink her weight down against him. But he weighed at least seventy-five pounds more than she did and she couldn't get enough leverage. Still, she slowed him.

"Don't fight me." He took a fistful of hair, pulled it tight, and leaned in close, his eyes dark with something sinister. "I don't have a choice here, Vivien. You have to come."

"For what? You seriously think you can make me return to the stage?"

"I don't have a choice."

And the way he said it slid something cold down her spine. He wasn't in his right mind.

"No. I have a life here. I belong *here*."

Her shoes scraped across the pavement. He twisted her hair with a harsh tug until she cried out.

"Help!"

His fist cracked against her skull and the metallic taste of blood filled her mouth.

He tightened his grip, throwing her against the wall, his fingers sinking into the soft flesh at the base of her throat.

"Ravil—" she whispered.

"Don't fight me." His gaze turned lethal, his grasp digging

deeper into her flesh. Closing off her airway. "You did this to me!" His stale breath reeked of alcohol.

Did what? Except, there was nothing rational left in Ravil's face. His bloodshot eyes were wide, unfocused. His usually well-groomed waves stood in all different directions and several days of growth covered his face. Feral...

Okay, maybe it was time to shift gears. Use some of her theatrics. *God, please, buy me some time.*

She relaxed enough that he loosened his grip on her hair. "I care about you, Ravie. And I care about your mom. How are her treatments going?"

He swallowed, shook his head. "Stop talking."

"That's expensive, isn't it?"

"Stop talking!" He turned back to her, slamming his fist into the building, exploding right beside her ear.

She flinched.

"But if you tell me about it, maybe I can understand...maybe I can help you."

He grabbed her around the back of the neck, dragging her toward the parking lot, muttering to himself.

She stumbled backward against a trash can along the sidewalk. He caught her, his eyes narrowed like she had fallen on purpose. For a moment, she thought he might hit her again.

"Let's try to work something out," she said softly.

He stared at her. Her heart hurt for him, just a little, as she seized the opportunity to reach behind her and wrap her fingers around the metal handle of the can lid. Because she felt bad for him.

And this was definitely going to hurt.

With one swift jerk, she swung the can lid, clocking Ravil like a real Charlie's Angel.

Ravil let out a foul word and grabbed his head with one hand while reaching to regain his grip on her.

She ran, tripped, screamed.

Ravil shouted, called her a name, closed in on her.

"Hey!" Yelling. Footsteps.

She scrambled to her feet in front of Ravil. "Help!"

And just as Ravil stretched out his hand to snag her, a body flew through the air. Tackled him onto the grass edging the parking lot like an MVP linebacker.

Boone, of course.

Ravil threw punches at Boone, landing one square on his jaw and temple while swearing.

Kyle ran toward the scuffle in the lawn where Boone had trapped one of Ravil's wrists, was rolling him over into an arm bar. But Ravil had gotten in a couple good licks, bloodying Boone's nose and slicing a gash above his right eye.

Kyle joined in the fray and the two of them were able to pin Ravil to the dewy grass.

"Cuffs?" Boone looked at Kyle. Blood dripped from his forehead and swelling started to morph the right side of his face.

Kyle held out his empty hands. "I'm off duty. I don't have cuffs."

"I have cuffs." Cole stepped forward. Kyle gave him a funny look and Cole shrugged. "Hey—you never know."

Boone wiped the blood from his brow. "This man assaulted Vivie and tried to kidnap her."

Ravil had something to say about that and about Vivien— and maybe they should make sure the children were inside because it was definitely not G-rated.

Cole locked the cuffs.

Kyle gave Boone a nod. "You good?"

"Yeah. I'm good."

Ravil tried to pull away from Cole. "Don't even think about it or we'll add to your charges."

"What charges?" The words spat from Ravil's lips.

Boone leveled a look at him. "We'll start with Minnesota Criminal Codes 609.25, 609.224, 609.748, and 609.595."

Kyle tilted his head. "Wow, that's impressive."

Yeah, that was her guy. Very impressive.

She turned into Boone's open arms and sank against him, letting the strength of his embrace cradle her against his chest. Safe.

"Are you okay?" Emotion thickened his voice.

She nodded, blinking away the flash of all that might have been. All the ugly possibilities. "You?" She tried to shake away the adrenaline flooding her veins. "He came at you like a wild animal."

"I'm fine. I just need you to be okay." He brushed his fingertips down her face and pressed a kiss to her forehead.

Oh, Boone. "You do know you're bleeding, right?"

"I'm fine," he answered again, giving her a crooked smile before releasing her.

A patrol car pulled up, the red and blue lights casting a glow across the parking lot, and Ravil was read his Miranda rights and placed inside.

Vivien finally let out a long breath when the car drove away and Megan approached them, first aid kit in hand.

"You really know how to put on a show," Cole said to Vivien, sliding his hand around his wife's.

Vivien wanted to laugh, but she still shook. "You know me. I go for the dramatic." She looked at Boone. His eye was swelling shut and he had gauze from Megan pressed against the cut on his forehead. But he did give her a crooked, if bloody, smile.

Kyle came to stand next to them. "You showed a lot of restraint." He drew his hand across his jawline in thought. "I'm not sure I would have stood by and taken hits like that."

Boone planted his feet. "I knew he wasn't getting away."

Vivien wove her arm around Boone's. "I think this tough-guy leading man and I are heading to the hospital to get some stitches."

"Me? Stitches?" He pulled the gauze away to check the bleeding, a rivulet dripping down his cheek.

Cole raised his brows. "Oh, yeah. You need stitches."

Megan looked away and Kyle grimaced.

Vivien pressed his hand and gauze back against his brow. "You'd better leave that for now."

"I'll send a deputy to meet you there," Kyle said. "We'll need to get statements and photographs of both of you."

"Come on. I'll drive." Vivien held out her hand for the car keys and Boone tugged them from his pocket. "Just don't bleed on the upholstery."

# EPILOGUE

The twist of fall—the oranges, yellows, and reds, with a wisp of wood smoke to chase the early chill away—poured over Boone when he stepped from his travel trailer. It hadn't taken Nathan Decker long to find him the perfect piece of ground to build on, one sold by a family from the Cities eager to offload the land in an estate liquidation.

Just outside of town. Lake view. Quiet. Already cleared for the home site.

When he'd stopped to pack up his own house in Kellogg, even his dad had shown up to help. Maybe it had been regret deepening the creases around his eyes. And, regardless of DNA, Boone still longed to connect to the only man he'd ever known as his father.

His mom had asked him incessant questions about the property he was buying outside of Deep Haven. Five acres of birch, pine, and spruce. Plenty of room to park his new travel trailer—his home until Seth could finish his build.

He'd had two days on the job in his new position with the Crisis Management Team. He'd expected to feel a sense of loss when he turned in his badge before leaving Kellogg two weeks prior. Instead, he felt ready.

Redeemed. Not by the work of his own hands.

Like the autumn air was signifying the end of something old, the readiness for something new.

He picked up *Imperturbability* from his camp chair near the door, yesterday's mail still sitting beneath it. He thumbed through the mailers, his fingers stopping on a crisp white envelope with his dad's handwriting. He tore it open and unfolded the letter, snagging the enclosed photograph before it fell to the ground.

*Your mom found this while cleaning the back closet. I think it answers the question you didn't ask.*

Boone looked at the photo of his parents leaning against a new 1984 Oldsmobile, the faintest curve of his mother's abdomen. The color was faded but, no, there was no doubt. He was looking at an image of himself. He blinked. Swallowed.

He looked exactly like his dad. *His dad.*

He turned back to the letter.

*Don't say it. I'm older, wiser, and wider now—but, back in the day, that was me. Pretty good-looking guy.*

Boone shook his head. Laughed and swiped a stupid tear from his eye.

*You've never had anything to prove to anyone. Certainly not to me. I'm sorry.*

Ree's car pulled up and Vivien stepped out of the passenger side. She wore jeans and hiking boots and the only thing on her face was a big smile. Oh, she still wore her fancy lashes some days and he enjoyed seeing her all dressed up too. But all on her own, she was a knockout.

She carried two to-go cups in her hands and used her hip to swing the car door shut behind her.

Ree waved before driving away.

"Are you ready to commit to buying your own car?"

She laughed. Her soft, pretty laugh. "Actually, Ree and I were just talking about that. Wanna do some shopping with me?"

"Definitely."

She stood facing him, the morning light casting a glow over her hair.

"I brought you something." She lifted a cup.

"Tell me it isn't coffee."

"It is." She raised a brow, her smile spreading into a grin.

"We've talked about this before." He reached out and tucked a loose lock of hair behind her ear.

She held the cup out to him, batted her big blue eyes at him. "Trust me."

He took the cup. "This isn't a healthified version, is it?"

"Nope."

"It's not a Vivien, is it? Because, I'll take the real thing over the drink. Any day. And, I'm not sure I have enough water in my trailer tank for that."

"Trust me."

He took a sip. Chocolate. Caramel. Sweet.

She giggled. "It's a Megan."

"That's a relief."

"I think one of me is enough."

He laughed. "I think you're right." Boone snagged her hand, pulled her close. "And that's just perfect." He tucked his head against the soft curve of her neck, inhaled her jasmine scent before releasing her.

He took her cup and set it down on the truck bed with his own. Then he reached for her hand and led her across the cleared site. It sat just above Highway 61 with the open waters of Lake Superior stretched out to the horizon. An invitation to all things possible.

"What do you think?"

"I think the place needs some work."

He laughed. "Yeah. I think it does. When Nathan said he

knew of just the right property, I couldn't pass it up."

She walked out across the home site, the wind lifting her hair from her shoulders. "So, you're finally going to build that house of yours with a lake view."

"I am. Seth is coming by to show me the final design after a few changes I requested. He plans to break ground tomorrow. Said he wanted to fast-track what they could before the weather puts everything on hold."

"Wow. Amazing."

His gaze settled on her. "Yes, amazing."

She turned, an uncharacteristically shy smile curving up one side of her face as she walked back to him, wrapped her arms around him, and kissed him.

Oh, her kisses. She tasted like caramel and fresh air and everything he'd longed for his entire adult life. He drank in the delight of it, as only she could quench his thirst. And when he deepened his kiss, she clung to him, like she felt it too.

The electricity between them lit a fire. He ran his fingers through her hair, holding her in his embrace. Because with Vivien, he was completely undone.

He slowed their kisses, catching his breath. She leaned away, a slow smile on her lips.

"*You* are amazing," he said, his lips against her ear.

She giggled. "Thank you. I find you rather incredible too."

He tugged his car keys from his pocket. "Want to take her for one last spin before she heads into storage for winter?"

Vivien walked over to the red convertible. "I'm going to miss her."

Boone laughed. "She'll be back out in spring."

"Oh, I forgot! I have something else for you." She dug through her bag, held up a copy of the *Deep Haven Herald*.

*Curtains for former Broadway director when Deep Haven hero tackles him post-show*

"Nice, huh? Ree saved you an extra copy to frame."

He ran his hand across his cheek. The yellowing had faded and the stitches had finally been removed. "I gotta say, I'm not sad to see that show close."

"Me either." She toed the ground with her boot. "I actually called Joslyn in LA."

"You did?"

"Yeah." She folded the newspaper back up. "I wanted to close that door. Let her know I forgive her and thank her for trying to warn me." She let out a deep sigh and looked out at the lake for a moment before turning back to him. "It felt good to come to peace with it—with her."

"So, you're like BFFs now?"

She laughed, a cute kind of snort. "Let's not get carried away." She swatted him with the paper and nodded toward the car. "I think it's a Funfetti Cake Batter ice cream kind of day. What do you say?"

"Something to celebrate?"

She grabbed her coffee from the truck. "I think so. You drive."

He raised a brow, surprised she didn't want to get behind the wheel. "Okay. Top up or down?"

"Down. Definitely down."

She winked and slid into the passenger seat and he started the engine. He never got tired of that rumble. They pulled out onto Highway 61 for town.

Vivien stretched her arms over her head and let out a robust "Woohoo!" The breeze tugged the laughter from her lips and the leaves rained down on them like confetti.

And, as the wind lifted Vivien's hair and she turned up country music star Benjamin King on the stereo, Boone looked to the open road, ready for whatever God wanted to put in front of him.

# CONNECT WITH SUNRISE

Thank you so much for reading *Then Came You*. We hope you enjoyed the story. If you did, would you be willing to do us a favor and leave a review? It doesn't have to be long—just a few words to help other readers know what they're getting. (But no spoilers! We don't want to wreck the fun!) Thank you again for reading!

We'd love to hear from you—not only about this story, but about any characters or stories you'd like to read in the future. Contact us at www.sunrisepublishing.com/contact.

We also have a monthly update that contains sneak peeks, reviews, upcoming releases, and fun stuff for our reader friends.

As a treat for signing up, we'll send you a free novella written by Susan May Warren that kicks off the new Deep Haven Collection! Sign up at www.sunrisepublishing.com/free-prequel.

# OTHER DEEP HAVEN NOVELS

**Deep Haven Collection**

Only You

Still the One

Can't Buy Me Love

Crazy for You

Then Came You

Hangin' by a Moment

Right Here Waiting

**Deep Haven Series**

Happily Ever After

Tying the Knot

The Perfect Match

My Foolish Heart

Hook, Line, & Sinker

You Don't Know Me

The Shadow of Your Smile

**Christiansen Family Series**

Evergreen

Take a Chance on Me

It Had to Be You

When I Fall in Love

Always on My Mind

The Wonder of You

You're the One That I Want

For other books by Susan May Warren, visit her website at
http://www.susanmaywarren.com.

USA TODAY BESTSELLING AND RITA AWARD-WINNING AUTHOR

# SUSAN MAY WARREN

PRESENTS

## ANDREA CHRISTENSON

*Hangin' by a Moment*

A
DEEP HAVEN
NOVEL

Turn the page for a sneak peek of the next Deep Haven novel,
*Hangin' By a Moment* …

# SNEAK PEEK

## HANGIN' BY A MOMENT

It was a little thing. Stupid really.

Colleen Decker had already made it through six hours of her ER shift at Hennepin County Medical Center in Minneapolis without any problems. Sure, there had been that kid who kicked her, but she wouldn't blame him—it hurt to have gravel cleaned out of a road rash from a bicycle incident. And then there'd been the psych patient who thought he was Genghis Kahn and ran around the ER shouting about taking over the world before finally being subdued by a few of her larger nurse colleagues. And don't even ask about the woman who came in with stage 4 lung cancer. These patients didn't faze her. All in a day's work at HCMC.

No, it had to be something small. Embarrassing.

A flash of a frat boy's bicep tattoo, a crash of an instrument tray falling to the ground, and suddenly Colleen had jumped for the nearest space she could cram herself into.

Clearly, she hadn't licked the past. In fact, it had found her in this 12x12 foot storage closet. She curled herself into a smaller ball under the shelf full of cleaning products and rubbed her hands up and down her arms, the scrubs she wore making a swish with each pass.

"Get a grip." She spoke into the silence. A dim beam of light shone under the door, illuminating a stack of sheets, folded hospital tight. She closed her eyes. Concentrated on her breathing. "You have to go back out there."

Without warning, the door flew open. Colleen shot up. Julie Brage filled the open space, the light from the outer hallway shining around her.

"I've been looking everywhere for you." Julie crossed the few steps, crouched down, put her hands on Colleen's knees and looked into her eyes. "It's okay to be freaked out."

"I'm not freaked out." Maybe if she repeated the mantra often enough she would believe it. She reached up and adjusted her strawberry-blonde ponytail, pulling the elastic tighter around her hair.

Julie sighed. "Colleen, you have been missing from your unit for fifteen minutes, are sitting in the supply closet next to a wet mop, and you jumped a foot in the air when I came in. That says *freaked out.*"

"I just didn't expect anyone to find me here. That's all. I needed a minute to myself."

Julie speared her with a look.

Okay. Maybe more like fifteen minutes.

"I'm sorry. I know we're busy. I'll come right out and get back to work." As a nurse on the night shift, Colleen knew the importance of each team member. They couldn't afford for her to be absent. She stood to her feet. Brushed herself off. Took a deep breath.

"You'll do nothing of the kind." Julie stood as well, crossed her arms. "Are you in here because of Genghis Kahn? He's been moved to the psych unit."

"No."

"Colleen, I know you said you were fine after the incident

last night but you've been jumpy your whole shift, and then you left the unit without telling anyone you were taking a break."

"I'm sorry. It won't happen again." She took a step forward… or tried to anyway. Julie refused to budge.

"This isn't about following procedure. I'm concerned about you." Julie gentled her tone, uncrossed her arms.

"You don't need to be. I've had a short break, and now I'm fine."

"Look. Anyone would be having a hard time adjusting after that trauma."

*Don't get too close.* The police officer's voice from the night before snaked through her mind. *This guy is a lot more dangerous than he looks. Don't let the good looks and charm fool you.*

"The whole thing is my fault anyway." Like a drum beat the words pulsed—*my fault, my fault.* If she'd followed procedure, it wouldn't have happened. She touched the Band-Aid on her neck.

"Are you kidding me? How is it your fault that a criminal held you at knifepoint?" Julie tossed her head, her light brown curls brushing her shoulders.

The events of her shift well before dawn Sunday morning washed in again. She saw herself leaning over the patient to give him a drink of water. Saw the doctor spilling the instrument pan.

"I should have listened to the officer. I got too close to the patient."

"How would you have known that he would find that scalpel and cut himself loose from the bindings holding him to the bed? You trusted your instincts to help someone who was hurting."

*Please, just a sip of water.* The criminal's voice in her head this time. *Help me out here. I can't do it myself. My cup's right over there.*

"Yeah, and my instincts were wrong." Just like always. "I should have stayed on my side of the room and just let the officer and the doctor handle it." She closed her eyes and took a deep breath, the air in the closet pungent with bleach and orange-scented cleaner. When she opened her eyes, Julie was looking straight at her.

"Colleen, there is no way you could've known that things would go down that way."

True, she hadn't known that the gunshot victim in her ER room would take advantage of a Code Blue in the room next door. She also hadn't foreseen that he would be fast enough to pull her to his chest and hold the scalpel to her neck in a desperate attempt to escape. "I guess you're right."

"Of course, I am." Julie put her hands on her hips and grinned at Colleen. "I'm always right. Listen, I came to find you because Nicole came in early and asked me to track you down. I think she's going to recommend you take a few days off."

"Thanks for the heads-up. I don't really think I need any time off." As long as no more criminals came in for treatment or pans of instruments crashed to the floor or any tattooed men reminded her of events from years before...

Yeah. She'd be fine.

She relaxed her arms. Rolled her shoulders. "I'll go find Nicole right now." Colleen brushed past Julie and walked out of the closet.

Taking a left, she walked to the central hub of the ER. At the corner of the main desk stood Nicole Miller, the ER nurse supervisor.

"Ah, Colleen. There you are." The heavyset woman in navy scrubs turned toward her. "It seems I missed all the excitement last night."

Colleen tugged at the hem of her scrub top. "Oh, you know, just another routine day in the HCMC ER. It wouldn't feel right if there wasn't some excitement." She tried for a jaunty smile.

"I've read the report of the incident. Could you come into my office for a few minutes? There are some items I want to go over with you."

Colleen glanced at her watch, 5:30 a.m. Nicole really was in early. Usually she didn't grace their floor until after 7 a.m. on Mondays. She followed the older nurse into the semi-private space adjacent to the busy ER. Nicole left the door open, then sat down behind her desk and gestured for Colleen to have a seat.

"As I said, I read the report from last night." Nicole picked up a sheet of paper from the desk. "Was this your first time assisting in a room with a prisoner?"

Located near downtown Minneapolis, Minnesota, the Hennepin County Medical Center regularly treated gunshot victims. They also saw many patients who came in under armed guard. The night before hadn't been anything unusual.

No. The problem had been with Colleen.

"I've been in multiple situations where there was a police presence in the room. Including violent criminals." She rubbed her damp palms across her scrubs.

"And are you aware of our protocol for those situations?"

Oh, she knew the protocol all right. Don't touch the patient. Wait for the police officer to give permission before approaching the gurney. Do what the doctor asks you to do, and *only* what the doctor asks you to do. "Yes, I know it."

Nicole jotted a few things on the paper she held. "Was there any particular reason you felt you could ignore it last night?"

"I don't know. He seemed so harmless." Even to her the excuse sounded lame. She fought the urge to touch the Band-Aid on her neck. The one covering the small cut the scalpel had left behind.

"You thought the man, this Joseph Terranova, who came in strapped to a gurney, under armed guard, with a gunshot wound seemed harmless?" Putting down the document, Nicole sat back in her chair. Waited.

Colleen thought about arguing that he had a kind face and

really nice clothes. And wow, that sounded stupid even as she thought it. "Um. I don't know what to say."

"No, Colleen, *I* don't know what to say. Your actions endangered the whole ER. I'm just glad that officer was able to act quickly enough that no one was hurt."

A replay of the night before flew into Colleen's mind. The man's arm around her, scalpel at her throat. A glimpse of a tattoo where his shirtsleeve was rolled up. The police officer's hands outstretched in a "calm down" motion. The movie picked up speed and she saw another officer appear in the door, Taser in hand. She felt again the stiffening of the body behind her as the darts at the end of the wires hit their target.

Her breath sped up. She blinked several times and the images faded.

Nicole folded her hands. Laid them on the desk. Her gaze gentled. "I think you should take some time off."

"Are you firing me?"

"No. Not at all. I'm just wondering if it isn't a good idea for you to take a short leave of absence."

"I'm fine." If she kept saying it, maybe it would stick.

"That's not what the rest of the team is telling me. I heard you've been jumpy all night. You've been forgetting things. Making simple mistakes. There's no shame in taking time off. Working the ER, especially one like ours, is stressful. It can get to you after a while. Even if something like last night hadn't happened." Nicole unlaced her hands and shuffled a few papers on her desk. "I see that you are already taking a day off later this week."

"Yes, I'm going home for my grandma's anniversary party. She remarried eight years ago, and my parents are throwing them a party." Maybe now would be a good time to stop rambling. Nicole didn't care about her family history.

"Okay. Why don't you take the rest of the week off and all of next week as well. I really think it will do you some good."

The thought of home, of her mother's arms, and the memory of the smell of something delicious in her grandmother's oven flooded her. She bet the late September leaves were beautiful right now. Going home to Deep Haven for a while suddenly didn't seem such a terrible idea.

"You're right. Some time off wouldn't hurt. But I'll only go for a week. I'll be back before you have time to miss me."

"Fine, take a week. Call me next Monday and we'll see about you taking more time than that. I think you should at least consider taking a month or more."

Colleen caught her supervisor looking steadily at her. In her eye, a look of...pity? There was no reason for Nicole to pity her. She was all right. She would go home, eat some of her grandmother's pie, and be back in a week.

She was just fine. She'd prove it.

# ACKNOWLEDGMENTS

The process of writing this novel has been an act of faith. I can't tell you how many times I thought the task might be impossible —and, it was. Except for God. He sustained me and carried me through every part of this novel's writing. I'm grateful to my Lord and Savior, Jesus Christ, who used this story to minister to me in so many ways.

Thank you to my husband, Brian, whose steadfast encouragement helped me endure the long—and, let's face it—grueling —process of writing *Then Came You*. Thank you for the grace and love you give me every day. For understanding what stories mean to me. You always help me with my guy-speak, let me think I'm funny (I *am* funny, right?), and head off to the grocery store countless times so we have actual food for dinner. I'm blessed to have you as my partner and best friend.

My boys...you inspire me and make me smile every day. Thank you for your words of encouragement and your infinite confidence in me. Thank you for the many times you waited patiently while I "finished my thought" on my manuscript and frantically kept typing for a Mom-minute (aka a really, really long time). Thank you for making me laugh and reminding me that sometimes you need to have a chocolate-brownie-thunder ice cream day.

My mom, thank you for your enthusiasm and prayers. For the many times you checked in to see how my writing was going. For sharing my stories with pretty much everyone you know and everyone you don't know. (Well, that is if you've ever actually *met* a stranger, which I totally doubt.) For your hilarious bookstore schemes to get my novels on the shelf (that you were forbidden to actually execute) and for your impromptu check-in calls and brainstorming thoughts.

Susan May Warren, who operates at ninety miles per hour and still has time to stop and encourage, pray, and troubleshoot those niggling scene goals with me. We joke about our experience being the BUD/S of writing, but, well, the only easy day *was* yesterday, so there's that. I'm grateful no boat crews or drown-proofing were actually involved in the writing process of this novel, nor was any life in jeopardy. But I did always know that I had a specialized, highly trained team watching my back and if I needed an exfil, you were always there. Thank you for the incredible gift of Boone Buckam. It has been my honor to write his story and let the world see him grow past his scars and all that has held him captive in his life. And Vivien? Of course, she, too, was one of your creations and I loved pairing her with Boone! Thank you for pushing me to go deeper and stretch myself beyond my comfort zone. I'm so grateful for our partnership and friendship.

Lindsay Harrel, master planner. We're off writing and changing things up and there you are—steady and sure. We're glad you never made us do push-ups when we veered off the mission. Thank you for your mad organizational skills, your ability to know the course and keep all of us on track. Thank you for your grace and flexibility. For believing I could do this. I'm so grateful to work with you.

Andrea Christenson and Michelle Sass Aleckson...how

many times did we wonder what we'd gotten ourselves into? By the grace of God, we have done more than we ever imagined, and what a privilege it is to walk through this experience with each of you. The humor through hardship, our web calls, and knowing you totally understood every utterance of joy and despair that left my lips. I always knew I could count on you to bounce ideas around and help me see a fresh solution to my literary dilemma. I'm so proud of the work we've done together. Thank you for your cheers, friendship, and prayers. Just. Keep. Swimming.

Barbara Curtis, you are an absolute gem. Your editing skills take my stories to a whole new level. Thank you for the incredible care you give each manuscript. Your attention to detail, the questions you pose, and the nuggets of encouragement you drop into all the red "ink." You are a treasure and you help the story shine. I'm so grateful to have you as editor and friend.

Rel Mollet, you are a total rock star. What else can I say? From social media graphics to proofreading to online events. Behind the scenes, you do an incredible amount of work and it's a privilege to know you and work with you.

Ryan Zollinger, firefighter and EMT. Thank you for letting me pick your brain for insights into the emergency medical field to get the details right. I'm sure it isn't every day you're grilled about near-drownings and the exhaustive efforts to save a life. Because of you, my scene says more than "they did some stuff." You helped me bring layers and depth to my rescue scene. I'm incredibly grateful to you and Debra for giving me your time and proofreading the scene for me. Any mistakes left are purely my own.

Tari Faris, you prove that one can never be too young to be a wise sage. Thank you for reminding me that God always has the answers I seek. Thank you for sharing your experience with me, lending your ear to my confused ramblings, and directing my eyes ever back to the One who gave me this opportunity.

Thank you to proofreaders Lisa Gumpton and Bobbi Whitlock. Your attention to detail and fresh eyes have been critical to closing the gaps and ensuring my readers don't get story-whiplash. I'm grateful to have proofreaders with such keen knowledge of Deep Haven.

Cover artist Jenny Zemanek—once again, you've created a beautiful addition to this series and captured the perfect glimpse of the story for the cover. Thank you for sharing your incredible artistic talents and creating such eye-catching designs.

My Book Therapy huddles—aka my prayer warriors. Barbara, Deanna, Gracie, Heidi, Jenni, Kristi, Mandy, Nancy, Suzy, and Tari. From lost sleep to injuries to complete and utter burnout, you bolstered me with your prayers, encouragement, and enthusiasm. Thank you for being part of my writing family.

For the ladies of the CCM, thank you for letting me share my passion for fiction and all things "books" with you. For being my sounding board, prayer partners, and cheerleaders. Though thousands of miles separate us, you are never more than a call, text, or message away.

Thank you for my local writing critique group—April, Danika, Julie, Kendy, Kelly, Linda, Melinda, Melody, Nora, and Sandra. It's been such a tough year to connect and yet your steadfast support has been instrumental to my journey. Thank you for letting me be part of the stories you tell and for helping me grow as a writer.

A special shout-out to the Sunrise Publishing Support Crew. Thank you for your open-armed, avid-reader enthusiasm for these novels. Your encouragement and collective excitement are contagious. You warm my heart with your posts, reviews, and personal messages.

And, of course, I'd like to thank the Academy. That is, the Novel Academy members who join me each Thursday night for our peptalks. The camaraderie and support from the group is a highlight of each week. I never know where the chat topics will go and it's brought me laughter and tears. Novel Academy is an amazing family that I'm grateful to be part of.

Readers, you have been a blessing to me. Thank you for welcoming my stories onto your shelves and sharing them with others.

Breathing life into a novel is a team effort and I'm grateful to each and every person who has walked this road with me. Whether you are named or not, know my heart is filled with gratitude for your support.

# ABOUT THE AUTHORS

 USA Today bestselling, RITA, Christy and Carol award winning novelist **Susan May Warren** is the author of over 80 novels with nearly 2 million books sold, most of them contemporary romance with a touch of suspense. One of her strongest selling series has been the Deep Haven series, a collection of books set in Northern Minnesota, off the shore of Lake Superior. Visit her at www.susanmaywarren.com.

 **Rachel D. Russell** is a member of Oregon Christian Writers, My Book Therapy's Novel Academy, and is a regular contributor to the Learn How to Write a Novel blog. When Rachel's not cheering on one of her two teens at sporting events, she's often interrogating her husband on his own military and law enforcement experience to craft believable heroes in uniform. The rest of her time is spent cantering her horse down the Oregon trails and redirecting her three keyboard-hogging cats. Visit her at www.racheldrussell.com.

CPSIA information can be obtained
at www.ICGtesting.com
Printed in the USA
BVHW081103020721
611053BV00007B/462

9 781953 783080